Missing Letters

Meg Miller Rydzewski

XNARD PRESS

Missing Letters

Copyright © 2013 by Meg Miller Rydzewski
Cover art by Johnpaul Colman Rydzewski
Xnard Press

This is a work of fiction. The names, characters, places, and events are either products of the author's imagination or are used fictitiously, and any resemblance to actual persons, living or deceased, business establishments, events, locales is entirely coincidental.

ISBN: 978-0-9889741-2-8 (hardback)

ISBN: 978-0-9889741-0-4 (paperback)

ISBN: 978-0-9889741-1-1 (ePub)

www.MegMillerRydzewski.com

This book is dedicated to my wonderful family. I love you.

Table of Contents

Prologue

Nantucket Yacht Club - August, 1972

Bread's *The Guitar Man* drifted up from the deck below.

Mick stood on the top forward deck of *The Elena*, a stunning, 165-foot yacht owned by his father, the industrialist Frederick McWallace Blithe. His forearms rested on the rail, one jeans-clad leg propped up. The warm wind whipped at his white button-down. Clouds raced across the narrow wedge of moon. The glow from the Brant Point Lighthouse twinkled atop the inky black of the harbor. He breathed deeply and scrubbed a weary hand through his thick, brown hair.

Former classmates at Harvard would have been surprised to see him in such an environment. They knew he came from money, but he didn't flaunt it. Though tall and handsome, he didn't act like he knew it. He was a nice, hard working young man who took his schoolwork seriously, loved his family, and loved his girlfriend. If one could have found fault in him, it would have been that he was too serious.

Faint laughter drifted from other yachts moored in the harbor, clashing with Mick's mood. The twenty-one year old recent college graduate was at a crossroads, and he hated it. It was only a matter of days before he'd need to have a very uncomfortable talk with his father, the outcome of which would shape his entire future.

The world was in turmoil. He didn't know a single person his age who supported the war in Vietnam, but his father had told him that it was his responsibility as an American to answer the call to duty. Though fearful, he'd agreed with the man and he'd stepped forward when his number came up in the lottery. It was the price one paid for freedom. But when his physical exam revealed a slight heart murmur, he was given a 4F deferment and sent home.

Mick's mother, Elena, had practically collapsed in relief -- and then promptly began worrying about the heart murmur. His eyes met his father's once in a while as they watched coverage of the war. It was clear that the man understood the guilt Mick felt at not being able to do his part, and he was sympathetic.

So, Mick found his own battle to fight.

His summer internships during college were spent in Washington, DC, his hometown. In the summer of 1969, he was assigned to help with the National Environmental Policy Act. This led to his involvement in planning the first-ever Earth Day. In the summer of 1970, he'd helped with the Clean Air Act deliberations. By the time he had graduated from Harvard in 1972, he'd been accepted to Georgetown Law. This pleased his father, who wanted him closer to home so he could learn the family business.

If Mick had had any intention of joining Blithe Industries, he'd have chosen corporate law. But Mick quietly planned to study environmental law. He wanted to protect the environment from corporations that chose profits over the health of the planet. Sadly, this group included the family business.

Over the past few years, he and his father had been at odds about the environmentally damaging nature of some of Blithe Industries' businesses. Weapons, chemicals, tobacco, paper processing – Blithe was involved with some of the worst offenders – but his father scoffed at any suggestion he should exit them. Blithe Tobacco had been in business since 1796. Blithe Rifle Company had been established in 1820. As far as his father was concerned, exiting those segments would be tantamount to ripping the company from its roots. He wasn't about to do that simply because they offended his son's ideals.

Unbeknownst to Mick, while his father was unwilling to make major changes to the complexion of the corporation, he actually did see his son's points and had begun diversifying the portfolio. He did it quietly and hoped to surprise him when he joined the company. Fritz, as he was known to most people, thought highly of his firstborn and namesake, and looked forward to one day passing the reins to him.

Mick reached down and stretched his quadriceps. He'd indulged his enthusiasm for waterskiing every day on this trip and was sore from it. An involuntary chuckle bubbled from him. Vivian, his girlfriend, just didn't have the knack for it. On a weekend trip to New Hampshire the previous spring, she'd endured countless unsuccessful trips across Lake Winnipesaukee. She joked that the only thing she learned was how to be dragged through the water at twenty-five miles per hour —and have water go places it shouldn't. She'd never managed to stand up, but she was a good sport about it.

Vivian Mallory was the first girl Mick had ever truly loved. He had met her in a pre-law course the previous fall, when they'd been assigned as partners on a case study. She was quirky, whip smart, and always ready for a debate. Sylphlike, she had brown eyes that sparkled when she laughed, and soft, curly brown hair that begged to be touched. Unlike other girls he'd met, his interest grew after he'd been intimate with her.

As the semester progressed, passion, respect and admiration turned to love, and he was thrilled to discover that it was mutual. She shared his ideals and inspired him. They began to talk about the future. Mick knew his family wanted him to return to Washington after graduation, so he encouraged her to join him in applying to Georgetown Law, which she did. Happily, they were both accepted.

At spring break, he brought her home to Blithe House to meet the family. While it was true she came from modest means, she was beautiful, smart and Catholic – a winning combination, he thought. He had hoped the family would embrace her, and initially it seemed they had. But over crème brûlée one night, Vivian had effectively accused Fritz of profiteering on the back of mother earth. In return, Fritz had asked in a deceptively calm voice what her parents thought about her hippy sensibilities. Later, both had regretted the force of their words, but not the meaning. It was clear that they had reached an impasse.

It took Mick three weeks to convince Vivian not to break up with him. By August, they were stronger than ever, but she declined the New England cruise. He couldn't blame her, but he missed her badly. Hopefully, she was having a good time at her family's home in the Outer Banks of North Carolina.

They'd had to rebuild part of the home in July due to damage from Hurricane Agnes, so August was reserved for rest and relaxation. She'd sent him a snap shot of her sitting on a dune at Jockey's Ridge, the ocean behind her, the sun and wind in her hair. She was tanned, happy and beautiful, and he missed her. On the back of the photo, she'd written their initials inside a red heart.

Mick loved his father. Fritz was a hard worker, a good Catholic, and when he wasn't traveling, he was an attentive father. He was dedicated to his employees, took his responsibility toward them very seriously, and was a good leader. But the man was proud and stubborn. He seemed immune to Mick's arguments and had ironclad expectations that he would join the business. Subterfuge was Mick's only option.

His younger brother, Thomas, encouraged the debate about the environment. Mick couldn't really see why his brother cared -- sad to say, Thomas didn't seem the caring sort. It was more likely an effort to distract Fritz from whatever Thomas was up to. In the last year and a half, Thomas had transformed. Whereas for most of his life he'd manipulated situations in order to be the center of his father's attention, he'd recently become practically allergic to it.

Thomas was slightly taller than Mick. At twenty years old, he was charismatic and brilliant, his body effortlessly sculpted to perfection. Whereas Mick took after Fritz with his lean build, dark hair, pale blue eyes and fair skin, Thomas resembled Elena, his mother, whose own father had been a 6-foot 4-inch Greek diplomat. His black hair, dark eyes, muscled build and olive skin made women swoon.

The previous fall, young Thomas had shocked the family by eloping with an eighteen-year-old freshman scholarship student at Radcliffe. He'd only known the beautiful and quiet Cassandra for three weeks. After the marriage, he had made his young wife drop out of Radcliffe and tend house for him in Cambridge.

Vivian had been shocked when Mick told her about Cassandra giving up school. She'd said she couldn't imagine any man demanding the same of her. Whenever the four of them got together near campus, she looked at Thomas and Cassandra as if they were insane. Over time, it became clear that there was no love lost between Thomas and Vivian, and she disdained the deferential Cassandra, whom Vivian felt was not doing her part to advance the feminist movement. Mick wished Vivian could do more to get along with his family, but also appreciated her resolve on what they both saw as essential issues.

Their mother had been alarmed at the speed of it all. She'd confided in Mick that it didn't seem at all like the sort of thing her immature, playboy son would do. But Cassandra appeared to be a nice, intelligent girl who was completely in love with Thomas. She was certainly an extraordinary beauty.

Mick suspected the marriage might be part of efforts to dodge the draft, though the few times he's been with them, they did seem really absorbed with one another. Plus, the student deferment Thomas had sought seemed fairly secure. Still, he shook his head while thinking about him. They were as different as two brothers could be.

Elena hoped her younger son would settle down, and it seemed he had. The newlyweds had dropped off the family radar. They had, in fact, missed every family event until this trip. At the last minute, Fritz had realized he couldn't make it. Surprisingly, Thomas and Cassandra had appeared instead.

The music floating up from the lower deck abruptly stopped. He straightened up and stretched. It had been a fun day – water skiing, sunbathing at the Yacht club, browsing around in town, then enjoying dinner on the yacht. A relaxing vacation before the inevitable return to reality. He knew how happy family vacations made his mother, and it had certainly shown that day on her lovely face.

   ***

Thomas Blithe watched his beautiful young wife put a record on the turntable. The ocean breeze ruffled his hair and shifted the black silk shirt that he wore unbuttoned against his bare, muscled chest. He smiled with the pleasure of it and looked around at the white upholstery of the deck furniture, the smoked glass doors, the wrap-around bar, the plunge pool on the aft deck, below. He took a sip of Macallan whiskey. The yacht was pure enjoyment.

Cassandra turned toward him as *Nights in White Satin* began to play. Thomas' dark eyes flashed and he nodded his head to her. She closed cornflower blue eyes and began to dance, her

5

waist-length, glossy blond hair slipping back and forth over her shoulders as she swayed. White cut-offs accentuated her long, tanned legs. The breeze plastered her long-sleeved batik-print peasant top against her lovely form, making clear the fact that she was not wearing a bra. Cassandra was nineteen years old, slim, an unparalleled natural beauty. She was irresistible to any man who met her, and she was his. He'd made sure of it.

The two of them made a good-looking couple, he knew it. He saw the looks women gave him, knew he was attractive, and he capitalized on that as often as he could, even after he was married. Always on his own terms, and those were very strict. He was always in control -- especially with Cassandra. Yes, he'd chosen well. Her eyes opened and he held out his hand to her. A shadow passed across her face as her delicate bare feet carried her to him, her eyes cast toward the floor. Anyone watching would think she was shy, but he knew better.

His long fingers slid under the hem of her shirt, then downward, where he stroked the marks below her bikini line. "Mine." He murmured.

"Yes, Thomas," she whispered back to him, and shivered.

Mick walked around the corner onto the deck and Thomas dropped his hands. Lost in thought, the older brother padded over to the bar and removed a beer from the refrigerator, then made himself comfortable in one of the white captain's chairs. The bottle hissed when he opened it. "So, what are you two up to?"

Cassandra quietly said, "I... was just turning in. Goodnight Mick."

"'Night, Cassandra."

She gave Mick a small smile and returned her eyes to the floor. "Goodnight Thomas."

Thomas grabbed her hand as she walked past him, and pulled her into his lap. He kissed her deeply and tugged gently on her long hair. "Be down soon." He gave her a dark look and pushed her up, then watched her disappear down the companionway to the lower deck, her fingers pressed against her lips.

Mick wondered at their dynamic. The air practically crackled around them. He'd never seen a man look at a woman the way Thomas looked at Cassandra. It wasn't like

6

that with Vivian. He found Vivian beautiful and responsive, but he laughed with Vivian, exchanged ideas. There was affection between them, as much as there was passion. They were partners. With his brother and sister-in-law, that did not appear to be the case. "She looks like she's lost weight. Is she okay?"

"Perfectly well. Why, do you ask?" Thomas' eyes narrowed. He shifted in his chair to face Mick, his brow arched.

"She's just... changed a lot since last fall."

"Yes, she has. She's even more beautiful," Thomas replied a shade icily.

"Of course, Thomas. She's a lovely girl," Mick said. He decided not to ask why Cassandra seemed so much more reserved than when he first met her last fall. An uncomfortable silence passed between them. "So, have you thought about what you'll do after Harvard?"

Thomas smiled and picked up his drink. "Well, unlike you I don't have my future mapped out with Blithe Industries," he responded curtly.

Mick was tempted to tell him about his plans to study environmental law, but didn't. "Thomas, you just need to sit down with Dad and tell him your ideas."

But Mick knew Thomas was right. Fritz didn't see Thomas at Blithe. Thomas and Fritz had a contentious relationship. His father didn't seem to appreciate Thomas' tendency to dominate every conversation, insinuate himself into every situation. But he'd changed over the past year, so maybe Fritz would reconsider...

"Don't worry about me, big brother. I'll figure it out." He stretched his long legs out, crossed them at the ankle and looked up at the moon.

"With your grades, I should say you will. You were top in your class again this year, weren't you?"

Thomas inclined his head and took a big sip of the expensive whiskey.

"You could do anything you want. What do you think would make you happy?"

Thomas held out his hand, palm up. "World domination, of course," and he squeezed his palm tight, as if crushing something within his grasp. He laughed.

"Of course. Makes sense," Mick laughed.

They shared a comfortable silence and sipped their drinks.

Thomas smiled and shifted gears. "So, what is your pugnacious girlfriend up to this week? Taking a ride on that Greenpeace ship?"

"Nothing quite so exciting. She's in Nags Head with her family. They're dealing with the aftermath of Hurricane Agnes. Did a lot of damage down there."

"So they own the place? I thought they just rented each summer."

"Nope, they own it. Her family is from North Carolina – Greenville and Nags Head. They love it down there. Wish I'd been able to go. Maybe next summer."

"Sounds like you're serious about this girl. Have you broken the news to Fritz? He's likely to have a conniption at the prospect of an activist daughter-in-law."

Mick frowned into his beer. "Based on what happened at spring break, I think you may be right. We... don't discuss Vivian. But he did have me promise not to elope like you did. Said Mom would have a fit. So. Thanks for that."

Thomas laughed out loud, something he rarely did. "Anything I can do to help."

"Incidentally, why did you do it? Elope, I mean. You could have had a big party. You used to love a good party."

"I didn't answer Mom and Dad when they asked me. What makes you think I'll answer *you*?" He frowned.

"Why wouldn't you? It seems like an innocent enough question. And given I'm facing an uphill battle with respect to Vivian, I figure you might as well throw me a bone."

"Very well," he sighed. "Cassandra hasn't any family money. A big wedding wasn't possible in the traditional sense."

"You mean traditional in that the bride's family usually pays for the wedding."

"Precisely. And since she couldn't pay for it, this was the only option that would preserve her dignity. I don't have that kind of money readily at my disposal -- I'm on the family dole until I'm twenty-one."

"Why couldn't you tell Mom and Dad that? They wouldn't have cared."

"It's not really about Mom and Dad, is it?" He shook his

head. "They would have insinuated themselves into every aspect of it. I just wanted to marry her. The 'how' was Cassie's decision."

That showed an amazing amount of sensitivity, thought Mick. More than he'd expected Thomas had. "I see." He nodded. "You mentioned Cassandra is an only child. What are her parents like?"

"It's just her mom now. She's in California. We haven't met, but I've spoken with her on the phone."

"Wow. Married a year and you haven't met? What's she like?"

"A bit... rough around the edges. They aren't close."

Going by Thomas's look, he seemed to want to keep it that way.

Thomas took another sip and looked out at the water. They sat in silence for a few minutes.

"Ok, well, I think I'll turn in." He took his beer and stood.

His brother looked up at him and smiled. "Scuba tomorrow? Captain says we can swing by and drop anchor near the Port Hunter wreck on our way back to Newport. It's just off Falmouth."

"Sure, sounds like fun. What do you know about it?"

"It's a freighter that collided with a tug and sank in 1918. Bow's at about 20 feet. Rudder at about 85 feet. I've heard it's largely intact. Should be a great way to close the summer. 8 a.m.?

"Yup. See you at breakfast."

As his older brother walked away, Thomas returned his gaze to the ocean.

***

Mick descended to the lower deck and made his way along the outer passageway. He passed Thomas' cabin along the way and involuntarily glanced toward the light shining through the window.

Just inside, he glimpsed Cassandra changing into her nightgown. Her back was toward him as she lifted her shirt, and there were bruises on her back – lots of them. Mick stepped back in horror, then turned and looked out at the twinkling lights along the dock, eyes wide, mouth open.

Time stopped for a moment and he could almost hear his heart beat. He knew now what was going on with them. He should have suspected something like this. After all, it wasn't the first time Thomas had done something like it. But it had been so long, Mick had thought that was all behind them...

He recalled the few times he'd caught Thomas victimizing younger kids. Parties, summer camp – it happened when he could get younger kids alone, kids who didn't know him. And he'd... do things to them. He somehow knew what to say to them to keep them quiet, too. By the time he was eight years old, Mick had learned to shadow his brother to keep him out of trouble.

When Thomas was nine years old, he'd caught Mick following him. After that, the younger boy had become harder to track, frequently completely eluding his older brother. He was very smart. Calculating. Mick had known that about Thomas at a very early age, and it scared him.

And it wasn't just kids Thomas victimized. They'd also had a few pets as children. The animals would get hurt but no one ever saw it happen. Their mother had just thought it was bad luck. After a while, she had given up on having pets. Mick remembered being relieved -- he'd always suspected Thomas was responsible but he'd had no evidence. He'd suggested as much to his mother once, but she'd just rolled her eyes and said Thomas was a rough boy, not a bad one. Mick had realized after a while that acknowledging Thomas' mean streak would be impossible for his mother.

Now he realized with horror that Thomas had effectively secured himself a ready target -- by marrying one.

Impulsively, he turned and tapped on the door. Cassandra opened it, clutching her robe closed. Her eyes were large on her face and she darted a glance down the passageway, as if she were afraid someone would see Mick there. "Yes?" She asked.

"Cassandra, I need to speak with you. May I come in?"

She looked nervously at the passageway. "I, um, alright." Reluctantly, she let him in.

He closed the door and turned to her. "I have to know something." Mick felt sick in his stomach as he asked, "is Thomas hurting you?"

Cassandra swallowed hard and answered quickly. "No, no, of course not," she said.

"Cassandra, please, let's talk."

She glanced at the door. "No. Mick, that's not a good idea. Please, just go away," she urged.

"I'm not going away. Tell me what happened to your back."

"My back?" She glanced at her window and realized she had neglected to close the curtains. She squeezed her eyes shut for a moment.

"Mick, it's nothing. I just slipped and fell in the apartment." She pulled her robe tightly around herself.

"Cassandra, I'm no doctor but I've taken my share of hits playing sports. Some of those bruises are older than others. What I saw wasn't the result of a single event."

"Mick, you don't understand. Everything is fine," she protested nervously.

***

The bedside alarm went off at seven-thirty. Mick reached out and switched it off. He sat up and looked out the porthole. The sky was gray. He yawned, rolled out of bed and pulled on his swim trunks and a t-shirt. He brushed his teeth but skipped combing his hair – no point if he was going diving.

Since Mick didn't have any appetite for breakfast, he grabbed a cup of coffee from the dining room and took it to the sport deck on the fantail. He figured he'd organize his equipment before the dive and think about what to say to Thomas.

When he reached the deck, he saw that Thomas was already there completing the dive check. He wore a full-length dive suit but had left the top of it hanging at his waist while he worked. His back muscles rippled and a gold chain around his neck winked as he hoisted an air tank onto the rack behind the dive bench.

He looked up and smiled. "Ah, there you are. Not hungry this morning, big brother?"

"I thought I'd eat when we're done." Still unsure of how he wanted to approach the topic of Cassandra, Mick decided to shelve the discussion until they were back aboard. He'd think about it during the dive. He pulled off his shirt and put one leg, then the other, into his dive suit. He hopped while he pulled it up. "Where's the deck hand?"

"I'm a master scuba diver, Mick. I don't need someone else to prepare the tanks. Besides, it's peaceful this early in the morning, don't you think? Nice to be alone with one's thoughts." He flashed his brother a bright smile. "It's gonna be wicked pissa," he joked in a Boston accent as he finished with the last of the equipment. He straightened up and pulled on the sleeves of his wetsuit.

Mick gave him a weak smile and looked out at the water as he shoved an arm into a sleeve of the wetsuit. "Captain says it's going to storm in a few hours."

"I heard that, too. Visibility won't be as good this morning since it's so choppy, but since we're starting the return trip to Newport at 10 o'clock, there's no time like the present."

The hatch opened and Elena stepped out on the deck. She was a slim, fit, dark-haired beauty who looked ten years younger than she was. She wore a gold print sarong over an elegant coffee-colored maillot with gold accents. Mick thought she looked lovely and happy. "There you are, boys. Mick, your father is on the ship-to-shore. He says he needs to speak with you now. And you know that actually means now." She chuckled.

"Any idea what it's about?" He asked.

"He said something about the classes you registered for at Georgetown Law. You'd better scoot."

"He's got spies there, too, Mom?" Mick put his hands on his hips and looked heavenward. "Oh dear God."

Thomas gave him a humorless look. "Not going to help."

"Not spies, darling. He isn't a stalker. He received a summary of your pre-registration in the mail. He just wants to talk about your course selection."

Mick sighed and affectionately put his hand on her shoulder as he trudged off, calling over his shoulder, "sorry, Thomas. Looks like I'll have to skip this one."

"Yeah. I got that." Thomas sat down and looked out at the water.

Elena looked at her son sympathetically. "I know you're disappointed, Thomas. Can I be your buddy for this dive?" Her son had a tendency to sulk when his plans were disrupted, and no one enjoyed that. *Such a baby*, she thought. *Yet he's married.* It was hard to believe. "It's been a while for me, but I think I still remember how it's done." She laughed.

Thomas' brow furrowed a moment, then he slapped his knees and stood up. "Why not?" And he gave her a smile.

"Cassie's dive suit should fit you. It's over here."

"Just stay close to me down there, okay?"

"You don't have a thing to worry about, Mom. I'm an expert." He motioned as if straightening his bow tie and laughed. *He really is irresistible*, Elena mused with a smile.

***

The conversation did not go well with his father. He'd had to confess that he had no plan to work at Blithe Industries, that he had a different plan for himself.

His father was livid. Mick knew this because the man was quiet. Too quiet. Mick's discomfort with his father's silence always caused him to say too much, which didn't help matters any. His father had mastered what Mick and his Catholic school friends referred to as 'the confessional treatment,' in which a priest remains silent for so long that, in distinct discomfort, the confessor blathers on to fill the silence, often revealing far more than he had originally intended. His father was gifted, that way.

"We'll discuss this when you return to Washington," he said, and the call disconnected. *Oh boy. A 24-hour reprieve.*

Mick then placed a lengthy call to Vivian. She was supportive and sympathetic, and she encouraged him to stand his ground and reassured him that everything would work out. She reminded him what fun it would be once school started in DC. By the end of the call, he felt much better. He headed to the dining room.

***

Cassandra yawned, stretched contentedly and watched reflections from the water dance along the overhead. She was alone in bed, though her husband's pillow still held his scent and the imprint of his head. She listened to the seagulls and inhaled the fragrance of the ocean as it wafted in through the porthole across the room.

In the en suite bathroom, she turned on the shower to let the water warm up. Cassandra pulled her peach satin negligee over her head, gathered her long tresses above her neck and turned around to examine herself in the three-way mirror. Her back was a road map of pain. There were other spots elsewhere on her body, too. She sighed deeply, turned and stepped into the shower, wincing at the sting of the spray.

The bruises were a tradeoff she could live with. As she

shampooed her hair, she worried about what Mick had seen and hoped he'd kept his mouth shut. Thomas was a bit more into the role play than she was. So much so, in fact, that she wondered if he was role playing at all. It was true, her life with Thomas was far from perfect, but he was rich and incredibly handsome. Or, at least, he'd be rich very soon. It would all be worth it in the end.

***

Mick finished the morning paper, put down his coffee cup and checked his watch. It was ten after nine -- time to have that talk with Thomas. A steward came in to check the buffet.

"Good morning. Do you know where my brother is?" Mick asked the man.

"Sir, I believe he went scuba diving."

"He was going to go with me, but I had to take a long call. He wouldn't have gone alone."

"No, sir. Your mother accompanied him."

"My mother?" His brow was furrowed as he shoved his chair back and walked out of the dining room. He descended to Thomas' cabin and knocked, but there was no response. Out on the deck, he saw Cassandra reading a novel on a chaise longue beside the plunge pool. "Cassandra, where is Thomas?"

She looked up at him with surprise and confusion, at a momentary loss for words. "I haven't seen him since he got up to dive with you this morning. Why?"

He waved her question away. "Have you seen my mother?"

"No."

Mick's frown deepened and he turned abruptly to head down to the dive deck. The two tanks that Thomas had prepped and set out were missing.

He rushed to the intercom. "Captain, my brother and mother have not returned from their dive. It's been just over an hour."

The implication was clear. The tanks on the yacht held only 72 cubic feet of air when filled to 3,000 psi at 72 degrees F. For a leisurely warm-water dive to an average depth of about 40 feet, a tank would last about forty-five minutes. Maybe longer for his mother since she was so petite. But the water here was colder than average and a good part of the wreck was deeper than 40 feet. Plus, there was a current. All of these factors meant air would be consumed more quickly. They should have been back by now.

"I understand, sir. I'll notify the Coast Guard. Where were they going?"

Mick explained about the wreck and the captain told him he'd relay the information to the search and rescue team. He grabbed a pair of binoculars and dashed up the companionway to the top deck. Cassandra saw him sprint by.

"What's going on, Mick?" She stood up and followed him.

He spoke as he scanned the water. "Mom and Thomas went diving. They should have been back by now."

Her jaw dropped. "How long have they been gone?"

"Over an hour." The color drained from Cassandra's face.

Mick knew that as a fellow diver, Cassandra understood the worry.

"I'll check this side!" She ran to the other side of the boat and began scanning the water, too. The water was getting choppier, which was making it harder to see what might be floating out there above the wreck. "I don't see anything! Do you?"

"Not yet. Keep looking! There's another pair of binoculars in the side compartment of that club chair over there."

The captain came on the p.a. system and called for all hands on deck. He gave instructions to the crew to scan the water.

Given *The Elena*'s proximity to Falmouth, a Coast Guard vessel arrived within minutes. En route, officers had requested and received information regarding the two divers. They had their descriptions, including the equipment they wore. They knew their experience level, their assumed dive plan, and their estimated time of departure. As divers plunged into the water, a helicopter appeared and began sweeping the area for signs of Thomas and Elena.

The ship-to-shore was occupied constantly until the Coast Guard arrived. At that point, Mick was able to get a call through to his father to let him know what had happened. "What's your closest harbor?"

"Woods Hole," Mick said after conferring with the captain.

"I'm on my way," his father said before he slammed the phone down.

Mick and Cassandra left their position on the top deck and moved to the bridge deck so they could hear what the Coast Guard was saying over the radio. They knew at this point that their only hope was that the two divers had surfaced and been swept away by the current. The wreck was, after all, over fifty years old. There were no pockets of air left down there.

By nine forty-five, the storm had started to roll in and the swells were increasing in size. The captain of the Coast Guard vessel instructed the captain of *The Elena* to move to calmer water, so he pulled into Woods Hole. It was wrenching for Mick to leave the scene – his throat was clenched tightly with fear and unshed tears -- but the captain was adamant. The Coast Guard was doing all that could be done, and the safety of the passengers and crew on the yacht were a priority.

At ten-thirty, the Coast Guard suspended the search due to bad weather. They sent a bulletin out to all vessels in the area to be on the watch for the two divers. Mick sat down and put his head in his hands.

***

Fritz arrived later that day in heavy seas. Due to the weather, he'd been unable to fly any closer than Boston, where he had a car take him to Falmouth. He spent the five hours in transit reflecting on his life, his marriage, his son. He was physically and emotionally exhausted when he boarded *The Elena* at Woods Hole.

Mick rushed to the fantail when he heard a launch approach. Through the driving rain, he saw a deck hand help his father onto the yacht mid-swell. He dashed across the deck and into the lower salon. He pulled off his rain parka and embraced his son. "Mick, have they found them?"

His son closed his eyes and gave his father a last squeeze before he stepped back. "They had to call off the search pretty early on, Dad. They'll try again once the storm blows through. The only hope is that Mom and Thomas surfaced and drifted."

They both knew the likelihood of survival was close to nil at this point, but neither said it.

His father nodded, concern etched in his face. He scrubbed his hands through his hair. When he opened his eyes, they were filled with all of the fear and despair he'd felt over the hours, and he wept. "Oh God, Elena... Thomas..."

Mick had never seen his father cry, and the sight pierced

his heart. He wrapped his arms around the older man and they wept together, shaking with the force of their emotion. If ever Mick had wondered how deeply his powerful father cared about his family, those questions were dispelled in that moment.

    ***

The storm had died down by evening, but it was too dark to resume the search. The Coast Guard would be back at it at sunrise.

Mick, his father and Cassandra sat at the dining table and pushed food around on their plates. There were no words any of them could offer to comfort one another, so they remained silent. After dinner was cleared away, the three moved to the salon to continue their vigil.

At midnight, his father told Cassandra to get some rest. He promised to tell her if there was any news. She reluctantly headed below. While thoughts of Elena and Thomas occupied their minds, they settled into an unspoken agreement not to reminisce. Reminiscence would allow for the possibility that they didn't survive, and neither of them wanted the other to think of that.

At first light, the two were jolted out of their thoughts when the yacht pulled up anchor and began moving out of the harbor. They refreshed themselves and were all on deck when the Coast Guard vessel arrived to resume the search. A deck hand distributed mugs of hot coffee. Divers plunged in and disappeared into gray water.

Just before noon, they heard the faint chatter of the radio from the wheelhouse. The captain appeared at the hatch and gave Fritz a sad look. "They've found Mrs. Blithe," he said and swallowed. "On Tuckernuck Island. She... didn't make it. They're bringing her to Falmouth."

His father just stared at the man as if he didn't understand. Mick put a hand on his shoulder, "Dad," he said. He guided him to a bench and sat him down.

He lowered his head and his shoulders sagged. "Elena," he whispered and shut his eyes tightly. "My beautiful Elena."

Mick choked back tears and turned to the captain, "Any word on Thomas?"

The captain was just about to speak when the radio began to chatter again. They stepped into the wheelhouse and listened to the captain of the Coast Guard vessel speak to one of his officers on a speed boat near the wreck. The two men moved to the rail and listened while they watched. The divers had a body and they were handing it into the speedboat. Mick looked at Fritz, who looked up at him with wide eyes.

Fritz began shaking his head. "No, no, my son too…"

Cassandra, who had been standing on the deck below, saw Thomas as he came out of the water. "Thomas! Thomas!" She shrieked and collapsed on the deck in tears. A deck hand tried to comfort her but she screamed and shoved him away.

Mick scrambled down the companionway to reach her and wrapped her in his arms as she wept.

***

Falmouth's Chief of Police, Mark Moynahan, finished speaking with the Coast Guard captain and turned to Fritz, who was standing with another man. "Mr. Blithe, can we speak privately?"

"Of course." Fritz led him into the salon and gestured to a club chair.

The Chief took a seat across from Fritz. "Sir, I am very sorry for your loss. And I'm sorry to have to discuss it at this time, so soon after you identified your wife and son, but I do have a few questions, given the circumstances."

"Circumstances?" Fritz looked confused.

"There's no easy way to say this, Mr. Blithe. Your wife's airline was cut. And, when we found your son tangled in the wreck, his diving knife was missing from his leg sheath. We can't find it. The storm really kicked up the ocean floor."

"What in the world are you implying, Chief?" He shook with barely concealed fury.

"Mr. Blithe, I'm not implying anything. I'm merely trying to get to the bottom of some facts. Your wife's line was cleanly cut, not ripped or pulled from its socket, as it might have been if she had become snagged." He paused and exhaled. "Sir. Can you think of any reason why your son might have wanted to harm your wife?"

"Are you out of your mind? Thomas was a bright, handsome, outgoing boy. He was newly married, top of his class at Harvard. He had no quarrel with his mother. They'd enjoyed a very pleasant week aboard the yacht. I spoke with Elena just last night. All was well. Elena absolutely doted on both of our boys." Fritz shook his head angrily. "Chief Moynahan, this is a tragedy, not a crime scene!"

"Has your wife's behavior changed recently?"

"No. She is as cheerful and caring as ever."

"Was your son happy?"

"Yes, he seemed to be. He was very busy this year, between school and his new wife, so we didn't see as much of him as we'd have liked, but when we did see him, he appeared to be content. In fact, he seems to have matured quite a bit this year."

He frowned and nodded his head. "I'll be in touch, sir."

"I'd like to take my wife and son home," he said quietly.

"Yes, sir. They are already en route to the Medical Examiner's office in Boston. The M.E. expects to conclude the examination tomorrow, at which time they should be released."

"Thank you."

"Sir." The Chief nodded and left.

***

With twenty years on the job, Chief Mark Moynahan had seen it all. He and his team had investigated all manner of crimes. So, that morning, as he did a cursory examination of the bodies brought up from the Sound, he was unsurprised to suspect something awful: that a son had viciously killed his mother. Maybe he was jaded. Maybe he was ruined for life. He shrugged off the labels. Humans could be twisted. He knew that well.

He'd had a busy day. One claim of battery, one petty theft, and a violation of a restraining order had had him in and out of the station while he tried to finish paperwork.

Moynahan trudged up the steps and into the Falmouth Police Station. He looked up. "I'd be so pleased to discover there's some fresh coffee."

The patrol officer on rotation at the desk discreetly put away a copy of the *Christmas Elves All Year!* catalogue. "Yes, sir, just made." He glanced around to make sure he hadn't been observed.

The Chief poured a cup before retreating to his office. He took a sip and closed his eyes as he felt the warmth reach his belly. Just as he sat down, the phone rang.

"Moynahan," he answered.

"O'Boyle," said the Boston M.E.

"What have you got, Steve?"

"First, the facts. You make of them what you will. If you want my opinion, I'll give it." The thick Boston accent was very familiar.

"Okay, shoot."

"Son had scratch marks on his face. His mask was off when they found him, right?"

"Right."

"Well, the mother has skin cells under her nails, consistent with scratching someone. We've collected them. Something happened down there. I'll leave it up to you to speculate what."

"Got it, Steve. Anything else?"

"Nope. Both died of drowning. Just a matter of why."

"Right. Thanks. Bodies ready for release?"

"Yup." The line disconnected.

The Chief hung up and looked heavenward before reaching for the phone once more. He checked the card in his pocket and dialed.

"Yes?"

"Mr. Blithe, the M.E. is done with his work."

"Thank you for letting me know."

"We'll keep you informed."

"You do that, but I'm telling you now that it was just a terrible accident. My son would not hurt his mother."

"I'll let you know the result of the investigation."

"Thank you."

Moynahan put down the phone and stretched. *God, what a day.* He got up and made his way through to the office Detective Jim Ryan shared with a colleague. He wanted to get their take on the situation. Blithe certainly painted a perfect picture of familial bliss, but the evidence wrinkled it.

The Chief leaned against the doorway and shared the M.E.'s findings.

"Alright. Well, that information doesn't change my opinion at this point. Frankly, it could go either way." Ryan said.

"Let's have it."

"Scenario one. Son decides to off his mother. He cuts her line. She struggles, scratches at his face, knocks the mask off, he panics, gets entangled, drowns."

"Likelihood?"

"Based on what we know now? Minimal. We've interviewed everyone on the yacht and no one knew of any strain in the relationship between the two victims – not his wife, not his brother, not his father, none of the crew. More investigation could raise the number."

"Next?"

"Scenario two. She gets hung up on the wreck first, struggles, he tries to extricate her and can't, so he cuts her free, causing her to panic. After all, water's pouring into her mouth. She fights him in fear, he gets hung up in the process, they both drown."

"So?"

"We've looked at it from all angles. It's a toss up. It's not unheard of for rescuers to die in process of rescue."

"Right. So, not enough to point the finger."

"No, not enough, and that's the consensus of the other detectives I pulled into this," the detective confirmed.

"Cause of death is accidental drowning?"

"Looks like that's the best we'll get. We haven't identified any motive for homicide, so I can't justify pushing for more. Anyway, perp is dead, if that's what he really is."

And if the son did it, it won't do his family much good to know it, he thought with a sigh. "All right. Write it up."

***

Vivian left the Outer Banks for Greenville as soon as Mick called with the news about Elena and Thomas. She quickly packed and headed to Washington, DC.

When she opened the door of her new apartment at Alban Towers, Mick rushed into her arms. They undressed quickly and sank to the floor. She understood the urgency – he needed the closeness, the comfort, and it had been weeks since they'd last seen each other. Afterward, she'd held him while he talked about what happened. She wiped tears from her eyes, determined to stay strong for him. He'd told her again how much he loved her. They made love more slowly the second time.

Unpacking her things with her the next day helped him get through the hours. Since she'd returned earlier than planned, they had the place to themselves -- her roommate would not arrive for another week. They spent every possible moment alone with each other.

A few days later, Vivian attended the joint funeral held for Elena and Thomas. He'd asked her to meet him at Blithe House, so they could travel together. At the church, as she stood by Mick's side and gripped his hand tightly. She peeked at Fritz and felt his pain. As much as she disagreed with him on so many things, she felt terrible that he'd lost his wife and son. After the burial, they'd gone back to Blithe House for a reception, but Mick was too distraught to stay long. Instead, they went for a silent walk in Dumbarton Oaks.

The following two weeks were a blur of activity for Vivian. Her friend from Radcliffe – now her roommate -- arrived for her job on the Hill, and together they explored the neighborhoods, getting acclimated. She registered for classes and attended orientation. While she had expected to see Mick, she knew he'd be busy with family matters. Previously, they had discussed which classes they would take, so she knew she'd see him once school began.

On Labor Day, Mick met Vivian for dinner. They sat across from each other at the Zebra Room on Wisconsin Avenue, a noisy, slightly seedy place that made good pizza. The place was packed, the tables filled. They'd picked the spot because it was close to Vivian's apartment and was popular among students. He'd waited until their pizza was delivered before breaking the news.

"You're doing what? Mick, we were going to do law school *together!*" Vivian was incredulous.

Mick looked into her eyes, a pleading expression on his face, "Please try to understand. After everything that's happened, I need to help my Dad with this. It means so much to him, and he's alone now."

"I understand that. What's happened to him – to you – it's devastating! But you're changing the entire course of your life, changing your entire game plan! Changing what was going to be *our* game plan. What happened to fighting the environmental fight? Joining your father at Blithe is simply unconscionable! What about law school?"

"Vivian, I've just realized that family comes first. Life is short. Sometimes far too short. I'll go to law school later if it makes sense."

"If it makes sense? Nothing you're saying makes sense! I thought we were going to be family to each other. What about that?"

He took her hands in his. "We can be, Vivie. I'm just not going to do what we planned I'd do."

Vivian's eyes filled with tears. She shook her head, anguish on her face. "I fell in love with an entirely different man. Someone who shared my priorities in life."

"Don't look at me like that. I am still the same man. I'll just focus on making a difference at Blithe. I'll work on my Dad over time, try to get him to see what we see. Improve the world that way."

"You know that's not going to happen, Mick. He's a stubborn man, far more stubborn than you are. The reverse will happen, and you'll end up just like him. I mean, look at you right now. He's gotten his way with the first major step you wanted to take!"

Mick bristled and the expression melted from his face. "My father is a good man. If I end up like him, I'll consider it a life well spent."

"I understand family loyalty, Mick. I really do. But do you hear yourself? You've done a 180! You've completely abandoned what we were going to do together, as a team. What about some loyalty to me? To the cause?" She blinked away angry tears. "I'm sorry, Mick. This just won't work for me. I've got to do what I feel is right for the world. And I can't do that while the man at my side is doing the exact opposite, as if I approve of it. I would be a hypocrite." Her mouth twisted in disgust at the thought.

Mick tipped his head back like he'd been slapped. "I see. So that's it."

Her eyes grew large and she blew out a breath. "I guess so, Mick. I'm just so disappointed…" She looked down at the table and added quietly, "in *you*."

His chair scraped back. He dropped money on the table for the bill, picked up his jacket and pushed out into the evening, taking great gulps of air. Traffic roared by on Wisconsin Avenue. Blindly, he headed toward Massachusetts Avenue. His chest burned with the effort to contain his emotions. By the time he'd reached National Cathedral, he realized he couldn't head home yet. His father would want to talk some more. They'd done a lot of talking in the past few weeks. It had become something they both enjoyed.

But he needed time to think, to process, so he crossed over and walked across the grounds of the Cathedral to the Bishop's Garden. The sound of his footsteps along the pathways pierced the quiet of the garden. At a stone bench, he stopped and sat, bathed in moonlight.

Mick couldn't believe what had just happened. How could someone he loved so much throw him away so easily? He'd thought they would marry, have a life together, children, grow old together. He'd known she was passionate about her cause, but hadn't realized she would choose it above all else. He didn't know how he could trust his judgment again. He'd been so wrong about her.

In the span of two weeks, he'd lost his mother, his brother and the woman he'd hoped to marry. The tears fell easily in the darkness. The direction of his life had changed dramatically – yes, he had done a 180, as Vivian had said. And looking back on it, he was similarly surprised at how quickly it had happened.

But it felt right. Supporting his father – his last remaining family member – was the right thing to do. His father was a good man, the best he'd ever known. How could she not understand that? Though it hurt to think about it, he was glad he'd discovered Vivian's priorities before marrying her.

A girl giggled nearby, piercing his thoughts. Mick heard a boy's voice, too. Teenagers necking in Bishop's Garden. He wiped his face and pulled himself together. Nodding his head with fresh resolve, Mick got to his feet and headed down the hill. He'd cut through St Albans campus to Garfield, then cut through St Sophia's parking lot. Blithe House was just over a half mile down Massachusetts Avenue from there.

***

Nestor Carson came from the Great Smoky Mountains in East Tennessee, the sort of place where folks regularly ate fried squirrel or rabbit for breakfast -- that they killed themselves. He'd been raised with a healthy distrust of government. Two tours in 'Nam spent hacking his way through jungle, people and animals only served to heighten that distrust. Any government that'd make its boys do that --

become that -- didn't deserve trust.

When he got home after losing an arm below the elbow, there was no ticker tape parade. No one seemed to support Americans being there at all, and he figured he'd wasted his time. As soon as he could, he left the stinking VA hospital. He was grateful he still had legs. A lot of the other soldiers had come home without them.

Lacking sufficient focus, drive or money to get home to Tennessee, Nestor had set up camp right there in the National's Capitol, and lived like his papa had taught him -- one with the land, under nobody's thumb. It suited him fine. From his well-camouflaged location in Rock Creek Park near Mass Ave, he could prowl the garbage cans of Embassy Row to stock his larder. And nobody could hear him scream when the nightmares came.

He'd met the man a few times while making his rounds. He'd decided to call him Casper, because his hair was so blond it was almost white. Casper wore camo, like vets tended to do, but he didn't look like any vet he'd seen before. He was too tidy. His hair, his nails, his shoes. Nestor noticed these things because it was the little details that helped him stay alive. He could sometimes see the devil in details, and it scared the crap out of him. That's why he carried the machete under his flak jacket. He'd only had to use it a few times, and he'd felt better after. The nightmares had gone away for a while.

Casper was older, maybe mid-forties. Older vets didn't wear camo, so he figured the man had an agenda. But Casper was the only one who seemed to see Nestor -- most folks just looked right through him, as if he wasn't there. So, when the man talked, Nestor listened. When the man asked questions, he answered. When the man wanted to go for a walk, Nestor walked with him.

In mid-September, Casper pointed to a mansion along Embassy Row. He told Nestor about the draft dodger living there. Said the boy's daddy paid someone to get a deferment for that spoiled boy, and the boy was a no good. Said the boy liked hitting women – that he'd seen him do it with his own eyes. Nestor didn't have many scruples, but he had his own sense of justice. And one thing he couldn't abide was anyone hitting a woman. Well, except that for that commie in Củ Chi. But most of the time, Nestor figured the devil was in men who hit women. Maybe he'd have to do something about it, and he said as much. Casper just nodded.

A week later, as Nestor went about his usual rounds just after dark, he looked up at the big house on Massachusetts Avenue. A cheap car pulled up the semicircle drive to the door and a woman stepped out. She was a pretty redhead, in a trashy kind of way. After pushing the doorbell, she pulled out a compact and checked her lipstick, rubbed her teeth. When a uniformed maid opened the door, the woman said something to her, then turned and stepped back to lean against her car. The maid closed the door. A few minutes later, the door opened and out stepped a handsome young man dressed in a tuxedo. He looked confused and said something to the woman, who approached him. They exchanged heated words, then she stepped back and stumbled. He moved to grab her arm and she wrenched away, giving a yelp. Nestor sprang forth from the shadows.

The man known as Casper watched the scene unfold from a car idling in a driveway across the street. A smile played about his lips. As Nestor charged forward, the woman dashed to her car and peeled out into light and fast traffic. The disturbed man grabbed Mick by the throat. 'Devil!'' Nestor roared. He pushed the young man down on the ground, pulled the machete from his waistband and slammed it down on the boy. Seemingly dissatisfied with the result, Nestor continued to hack away while cars pulled over and drivers shouted for him to stop.

Casper pulled away from the curb and disappeared into traffic.

Chapter 1

Arlington, Virginia - September, 2010

Curled up in the passenger seat of a single engine plane, Faith Warrior turned to the pilot. "Okay, Paul, I'm feeling a little queasy now. Just keep it steady."

"I KNOW, Mom." Paul, an undersized four-year-old, frowned. His dark eyes were large beneath his soft, brown bangs. His round, babyish cheeks were pale and smooth. He looked out the window at the scene below. Full of skyscrapers, the city was square-shaped and well defined. It stood out from the surrounding area. The little boy banked left, hard, a determined look on his small face.

"Ugh, my stomach. My head," Faith rubbed her temples. "We've seen enough, now. Let's head back."

Grumbling quietly to himself about bossy-pants mommies, Paul belligerently steered the plane lower.

"Paul, we're going down too quickly, and you're headed in the wrong direction. We need to turn around to get home."

The little boy abruptly slowed the descent and sharply turned. The combination of actions caused the airplane to stall.

"Oh my God! Oh my God!" Faith became hysterical. Paul didn't know how to restart the engine mid-flight. Neither did his mother. Heart pounding, Faith looked into her little boy's wide eyes and saw his terror. His chin wobbled and he began to cry. There was nothing Faith could do to keep the plane aloft. They were going to crash and die! Her baby would die!

The only thing she thought was that she must find a way to comfort her little boy. She gathered Paul in her arms and hugged him tightly, telling him how much she loved him. As she rocked him back and forth, she grabbed the yoke and tried to keep the airplane gliding forward, but she knew that her efforts to save them were futile. The only sound they heard was the wind whistling past. Faith joined her son as he cried, telling him again how much she loved him. Telling him they would always be together. He would never be alone...

***

Heart pounding, tears streaming down her face, Faith sat up in bed in disbelief that it was just a dream. It had seemed terrifyingly real. She glanced at the clock. Five fifty-eight – two minutes until the alarm would go off.

She took a few big gulps of air and closed her eyes as she exhaled. When she had calmed down, she'd decided there was no sense in trying to go back to sleep. There were lunches to make, breakfasts to cook. Faith pulled on her soft, white robe, turned off the alarm before it rang and went downstairs to find some coffee. She pulled her long, thick brown hair into a ponytail.

Her husband, Chris, was at his desk peering into his laptop's screen, a steaming mug of coffee in his hand. His brown, wavy hair fell across his forehead and his preppy tortoise shell glasses reflected the glow of the computer. He looked up at her as she approached and gave her a warm smile. She loved his brilliant smile, especially the way it always reached his sexy brown eyes.

"I just had the worst nightmare of my life." Faith poured a cup of coffee and settled into the armchair next to the desk. "Want to hear about it?"

"Sure," her husband said, sitting back and looking at her.

Faith told him the story. "Paul is good at a lot of things, so it's easy to assume he knows more than he does. Maybe this is what my brain was telling me."

"Either that or you should always check to see how tall your pilot is before boarding a plane," Chris joked. "Sorry." He patted her hand. "Hon, it's no surprise you had an anxiety dream. Today's a big day. But I know you'll do great."

Faith smiled and sipped her coffee, thinking about it. He was probably right. But maybe the horrible dream was also connected to the dramatic change that had recently occurred in her life, change that affected her children. Just four weeks before, they had moved across the country to northern Virginia. Their kids were in a new school. Chris had started a new job. And, after five years at home raising children, Faith was planning to go back to work. All of the change was unsettling.

She'd worked in finance for years before starting a family, but she didn't want to go back to the same role. The hours were crazy and if she wasn't at work, she was on the computer or thinking about work. She recalled there was barely enough time in the day to see her husband before bed, much less take care of children.

"My interview is at nine-fifteen." The prospect of trying something totally new was exciting to her, but a little nerve-wracking, too. Faith was exploring the possibility of becoming a fundraiser for her undergraduate alma mater. It would be a highly social job but very flexible. Her success would be measured on funds raised and number of contacts made with prospective contributors.

"Yup. How do you feel?"

"I'm going to have to tell them I only want part time work. I'm nervous about their reaction." After much thought, Faith had realized that while so many dual-income homes run well, she didn't want to outsource her kids after school. She wanted to have her cake and eat it, too: to work while the kids were in school and be with them in the afternoons. And she wanted work she could feel passionate about.

"Well, it's going to be fine with them or it's not. Either way, things will work out the way they should. Don't feel guilty. Working part time is not a cop out. It's what will make you and the kids happiest." He went back to his computer screen. "These mommy wars are ridiculous."

Faith smiled as she stood up. "I know, thanks honey. I just wish I'd realized the part-time thing earlier," she murmured to herself as she sipped the strong brew.

This is going to suck. No one interviews for a full time job and then tells the employer, "oh, by the way, I can only work 8:30-2:30." No one. Well, what's the worst that could happen? They could say no and I'll keep looking.

An hour and a half later, lunches made, kids dressed, teeth brushed, Faith dropped her children at school.

"Mom, I hate this raincoat."

She bent down, put an understanding hand on her Kindergartener's shoulder and looked into his eyes. "I know, Graham, it's a little too small and it isn't red. I ordered a new one, the same as this one but a size larger and in red. It should arrive soon. Have a good day, sweetie. I'll see you at three." She kissed his forehead.

Graham waited in line with the other kindergarteners to enter the building. He looked like such a big boy in his school uniform with the necktie.

Faith clutched Paul's hand to walk to his Pre-K classroom. He was so cute in his light blue raincoat, with his round baby belly. His backpack, containing his mid-morning snack, lunch, and naptime 'stuffie', looked massive on his back. Though four years old, Paul still looked babyish. Faith liked to think that God, knowing Paul would be her last, was letting her have a baby for a little longer.

As she helped him hang his coat and unpack his backpack, Faith thought about how warm and cuddly he had been when she had picked him up out of his bed and carried him down to breakfast an hour earlier. She gave him a hug and a kiss on his plump cheek, and reminded him that she'd pick him up at 3pm. "Okay, Mom!" He sat down to do some coloring. His teacher gave her a reassuring smile and Faith ducked out.

"Mom, wait!" Faith turned to see Paul running down the hallway toward her. He threw himself into her arms. "I forgot to give you a kiss!" He gave her a big smacking kiss, then turned and ran back to his teacher. She smiled and shook her head, wondering if all parents think their kids are so cute.

Faith dodged raindrops on the way to her car. She had to quickly get home, shower and dress for her interview. If only she could stop her heart from racing.

An hour later, as she drove up the ramp from the GW Parkway onto Key Bridge, the lovely view of Georgetown appeared before her. Faith would never tire of seeing the brick buildings, church spires and cobblestone roads. Turning right onto M Street, she was reminded how terrible the traffic is there. Another wrinkle to the whole back-to-work thing, she thought. *How in the world will I get to and from work fast enough to have enough time to work?* Telecommuting would be appealing.

Her iPhone rang as she drove down Pennsylvania Avenue. "Hello, dahling," she said when she clicked on the speaker.

"Are you wearing it?" Faith's best friend, Anne O'Malley, asked suspiciously.

"You know I'm not."

"Come on, the red suit looks so good on you. It's your power suit."

"It's too bright for today. I told you I wasn't going to wear it."

"If I didn't love you so much, I'd break up with you. You know that's the magic suit."

Faith made the buzzing sound for 'time out'. "Anything else, master?"

"No, Le Stink. Just good luck."

"Thanks," Faith said with a smile.

"Ok, my sista from another mista."

"Anne, you know you can't pull that off."

"Oh, I can pull it off, alright."

"Dude, I don't know any thirty-seven year old woman who can pull that off."

"Says the thirty-seven year old woman who still regularly uses the word 'dude'."

"Oh, sa-nap! Call ya latah." Faith smiled as she disconnected to peals of laughter.

Arriving at her destination, Faith checked her look in the shiny chrome of the elevator door. She'd blown out her long brown hair and it fell in soft waves below her shoulders. Her suit was a crisp navy blue with black grosgrain accents. The pencil skirt and fitted jacket complimented her slim figure. A strand of pearls at her throat set off a white satin shell beneath the jacket.

She wore diamond and pearl earrings and the elegant, stainless steel watch her husband had given her for their first anniversary. On her left hand, her platinum engagement ring and wedding band sparkled. On her right she wore the distinctive, ornately engraved signet ring her mother had let her take from her jewelry box when she was five years old, playing dress up. Though it was clearly a man's ring, it reminded her of her childhood and she never took it off.

The look was completed with elegant, black cap toe sling backs and a large black leather handbag that was big enough to hold a folder with her résumé and notes. Faith felt she looked the part of a successful fundraiser. Now if she could just get them to take her part-time. "Oh frickety-frick," she muttered, shaking her head in distaste at the task ahead.

The elevator chimed its arrival. Faith took a deep breath, crossed her fingers and walked purposefully inside. She turned to push the button for her floor and saw it was already lit, then glanced at the man standing against the back of the elevator. Elderly, he was dressed impeccably, and he had clear, blue eyes. His thick, white hair was perfectly groomed.

"I see you're visiting the Office of Advancement, too," he said with a smile, in a slightly wobbly voice.

"Yes, I am," she responded and returned the smile. *Good God, why are my palms so sweaty*, she thought. *Five years ago, I sat across the table from CEOs of major corporations and peppered them with questions, without any fear at all! Pull yourself together, Faith.*

The elevator door slid open. Faith let the old man go first, then stepped ahead of him to open the office door for him.

"Thank you, my dear." The man walked toward the receptionist, who stood up and smiled at him in recognition, then ushered him down a hallway. She returned a minute later.

"I'm sorry about the wait. Who are you here to see?"

"Good morning. I am here to see Mr. Holland."

"And your name is?"

"Faith Mallory Warrior." Her name always caused a double take.

As the receptionist called Mr. Holland's line, Faith sat down in a comfortable armchair. Moments later, a young man in shirtsleeves approached.

"Mrs. Warrior? I am Ian Murphy, Mr. Holland's assistant. Please come this way." Faith followed him down hallways that had street signs. Each sign had the name of a university landmark – a building or a street. *Neat way of helping people find their way through the labyrinth of cubicles and offices*, Faith thought.

"Can I get you coffee? Or water?"

"Water would be great, thanks." Faith looked around Mr. Holland's office. There were pictures of dogs everywhere – prints, sketches, photos. The office also had a spectacular view of the city. Ian brought the water and left.

"Faith. Thanks for meeting me again," Bruce Holland breezed toward her and extended his hand, then closed the door. He was as stylishly dressed as he had been when she'd met him for lunch a few weeks before. She heard a dog barking and Holland quickly reached into his pocket and pulled out a cell phone, silencing it.

"Please, take a seat." As Faith settled into a low couch, Mr. Holland sat across from her. "At our last meeting, I realize that I did almost all of the talking before we ran out of time. I'm sorry to say I'm pressed for time again, so let me just cut to the chase. We're very interested in you, given your background. We've decided that the most expedient way to evaluate you is to throw you into the water, so to speak."

Faith looked expectantly at Mr. Holland, waiting for him to continue.

"We're going to see how well you do. We've got a prospective donor in the conference room just next door. We'd like you to go in there and solicit funds. If you're successful, you've got the job."

Faith's mouth went dry. He wasn't kidding about throwing her into it. "Okay... do you have a standard set of points that you make when doing this, any best practices to share before I go in there?"

"No." He smiled slightly. "Well, we do, of course, but not for you today. Okay, good luck. Oh, and you've got only 20 minutes." With that, he stood up, gave her a big smile and extended his arm for her to follow him into the hallway.

A little dazed but heart pumping madly, Faith took a sip of water, then stood and followed him. "It's down there on the left," he said, and vanished. She stood there a moment and listened. It was very quiet. She only heard the faint sound of a copier humming. *Well, it's not like I haven't walked through interview fire before...*

As she ventured down the hallway, a young woman popped her head over a cubicle wall and peered at her through coke-bottle eyeglasses, then disappeared again without a word.

Trading floor language came to mind. Faith fired off a string of expletives in her head as a way of psyching herself up, then cleared her throat, smoothed her jacket, and walked to the conference room door. Faith opened the door and stepped inside.

"Well, hello again, young lady." The old man from the elevator stood up from his chair by the window, a warm smile on his face.

Faith smiled back at him, stepped forward and grasped his

wrinkled, outstretched hand. "Faith Mallory Warrior."

The man tipped his head to the side, as if he hadn't heard correctly. Then took a closer look. "Why yes," he said softly, "you do appear to be." *There's that reaction again. My married name really does make me feel stronger.* He quickly composed himself and said, "Frederick McWallace Blithe. Call me Fritz."

"I assume you know why you are here."

He chuckled. "Yes, I'm getting old and people want my money. I suppose there are worse places to put it than in a good university."

"I'm wondering why you came in here, rather than have someone come and meet you at your home or office. I'm sure someone would have been glad to make the trip." Faith's brow furrowed. It seemed wildly inappropriate to ask a donor to come in to the school's office to hear a pitch.

He shrugged. "I'm an old man. I don't get out much anymore. This was an excuse to go somewhere for a while. I actually offered to come in."

Faith nodded and smiled kindly. "Mr.... Fritz, I'm a bit new here, and I don't entirely know where to begin, but maybe it would help for you to hear my story. This school put me on a good path, something it does for so many of its students."

"I assure you, I would very much like to hear about you."

Faith smiled at him, looked around the room and then stood and walked to the sideboard where refreshments lay. There was a decanter of coffee, a decanter of hot water, ceramic cups and saucers stacked up, and a wooden box holding a variety of teas. "Would you like something to drink?"

"Yes," the man replied, "plain tea, please." Faith selected a packet of Earl Gray, filled a cup with hot water and dropped the tea bag into it, then placed it gently on a saucer. She took a small bottle of water for herself and then brought both drinks to the table, where she sat across from the old man.

As she placed the cup and saucer in front of him, his eyes appeared riveted to her signet ring.

"It might surprise you to learn how many of this school's students did extremely well in high school and then foundered in their first semester of college. A lot of bright kids get into good schools because they're bright – not because they know how to study or have any discipline. The first term at a school like this is an eye opener for many. It certainly was for me. I got here and found that almost every other student had been at the top of their class, too. I had to step up my game."

"You... lacked discipline?" He asked distractedly. His bushy eyebrows drew together.

"It's a long story, but yes. My mother did the best she could, but she was single parent with a very busy law practice, teaching and so on. I was largely left to my own devices. I didn't get into trouble, but I lacked supervision. My mother saw my high school grades and standardized test scores, which were excellent, and she didn't inquire about my study habits. So, I got here and I had to work twice as hard as anyone else to do well since I was learning skills along the way that I should have acquired in high school.

"But while I was there, I learned much more than just how to do work. I learned a work ethic, I learned how to think, and I left school with a clear, well-considered sense of right and wrong." Faith's enthusiasm was palpable. "This university did that for me, with its strong liberal arts core, the required study of Philosophy and Ethics, and the moral themes the school emphasized throughout my four years there."

The old man sat back and regarded Faith, then took a deep breath. He looked to be bracing himself. "What is your mother's name?" It sounded like a statement rather than a question, and it jarred her, given that it was completely off topic.

"Vivian Mallory."

"Environmental law?"

Faith nodded with a puzzled expression. "Yes, she specializes in environmental policy. How did you know that?"

Fritz put his hand up, as if to wave her away. "And your father?"

"I never met my father. He died before I was born," she said uncomfortably.

Faith glanced down, surreptitiously looking at her watch. *I'm running out of time.*

She looked up at him. "Getting back to the school...The university solidified the good tenets my mother taught me. But the point I'd like to emphasize is that the university invests in the future. Its graduates go on to be upstanding, highly productive, forward-thinking members of society; people who don't take shortcuts in life.

"Contributing to the school's scholarship fund will help more students graduate without the encumbrance of student loans. This will allow them to take more chances with their careers, to have the potential to make a big difference in the world, free from the worry of meeting that monthly debt hurdle. It will also allow more graduates to not put off many of life's important steps, such as marriage and family. Too many people these days defer that fundamental living due to financial burdens, and I believe it takes a toll on society. A contribution now will pave the way for change in the future."

"And what happened to you after university?" *Again with the personal questions?*

"I moved to New York City, worked for a year as an analyst for an investment bank -- much to my mother's disappointment," she chuckled, "then returned to school to earn an MBA. After that, I became an equity analyst for an investment management firm. I left that world five years ago when my husband and I had our first child."

He looked completely spellbound, his eyes searching her face. "Tell me about your children."

Faith wondered what this information could possibly have to do with a contribution but he seemed friendly and very interested, so she continued. "I have two smart, wonderful boys, ages four and five."

"And your husband? What is he like?"

She paused, growing uneasy about the line of questioning. "He's a smart, funny man. He's Chief Technology Officer for a consulting company."

The door swung open and Bruce Holland appeared. "Mr. Blithe, how are you?"

He paused a moment, gathering himself. "I am as well as an old man with aches and pains can be, Mr. Holland. And how are you this morning?"

"Doing well, sir. So, you have met one of our graduates, Faith Warrior. Has she made a good case for a contribution?"

"Yes, she most certainly has."

"So, what say you?" He asked congenially.

"As it turns out, I am not the person you need to ask."

Both Faith and Bruce looked at one another with confusion, then back at Mr. Blithe. "I'm sorry, to whom should we speak?" Bruce asked.

"You should speak to her." And he pointed at Faith. "My granddaughter."

Faith's mouth dropped open and she turned her head slightly, looking at him cautiously out of the corners of her eyes. "Excuse me?"

Mr. Blithe smiled warmly and said, "I should have known it when I first saw you in the elevator. Your eyes are just like Mick's. Your hair is just like my wife's... but the ring made me take a closer look." He gestured to the signet ring. "I couldn't find that signet ring among my son's possessions. He must have given it to your mother. I thought mine was the only one left." He held up his right hand and showed her his matching ring.

Faith's eyes grew large as she looked at his ring. She looked down at hers. "It belonged to my father? My mother never told me." She looked up at Fritz. "I've worn it for decades. My father... his name was Mick?"

"Unofficially. His full name was Frederick McWallace Blithe, Jr. Mick was his nickname."

Bruce Holland, looking utterly uncomfortable, quietly excused himself and the door softly clicked closed behind him.

He looked at her in wonder and then laughed. "You obviously don't get your height from your mother."

Faith was flabbergasted and nodded slowly. "My mother is very tiny." She shook her head as if to clear it. "Wait, how is this all possible? And how are you so sure? What happened to my father? Why have I never met you before?"

He blew out his breath. "Your father was killed in a mugging. Well, not exactly that. He was killed by a deranged Vietnam veteran back in 1972."

"I was born in 1973."

He nodded. "Your mother, Vivian, was a very bright woman, as I remember. Very opinionated."

"Yes, absolutely. Wait a minute. So, you met my mother but you didn't know about me?"

"She was my son's girlfriend when he was at Harvard, and during the summer following his graduation. She did not tell me about you. Mick, your father, died before you were born."

"Why didn't she tell you about me?"

"That I cannot answer. But I can say that she and I did not

see eye to eye on a few things."

"What things?"

"Well, the nature of some of my businesses."

"What is your business? What did she dislike about it?"

"Firearms, originally. Perhaps you've heard of Blithe Rifles. The company goes back several hundred years. It's one of the oldest in our portfolio. But we've branched out into different businesses in different industries, not all of which have been very good for Mother Earth. Now the company with all of its different parts is known as Blithe Industries."

Faith sat down. She knew Blithe Industries. It was one of the largest privately owned companies in America. She'd had to know it because a few of the publicly traded companies she'd researched as an equity analyst competed with some of its business units. She recalled speculation that it would IPO at some point so that the founder could cash out.

He noticed her shock but continued. "It's run by a board of advisors, now. They consult me on things but it tends to run itself now. So, I live a quiet life." He closed his eyes a moment. "Too quiet."

Faith tried to pull herself together. "Do I have... other family, too?"

Fritz frowned. "No, sadly you don't. Your grandmother and uncle also died that year." He put out his hands, "1972 was a very bad year. But not as bad as I thought an hour ago, because now I know it brought you." He smiled, tears in his eyes.

Her grandfather stood, walked around the table and sat down next to her. He took her hand. "Faith, your presence here today was a gift from God. I can't express how happy I am to have met you."

***

Faith's cell phone rang as she drove home an hour later. When she saw who it was, she pulled over and answered. "I got your text," Chris said. "How was the interview?"

Faith's voice shook. "You're not going to believe this. I met my grandfather today."

"What? Since when do you have a grandfather?"

"Right. Right? Crazy! Insane!" Faith gesticulated wildly. "At the interview, they made me do a pitch to a prospective donor. When I told the man my name, he said I was his granddaughter! I never did know my father's name – just that he was an environmental activist named Mick who had died before I was born."

"Well, who is this guy?" Chris asked.

"You'll never believe it. He's Fritz - Frederick McWallace Blithe. As in Blithe Industries."

Chris snorted with laughter. "Okay, okay, you got me. Who is he really?"

"I'm being absolutely serious. He's Fritz Blithe."

"Good God," Chris whispered loudly. "This is incredible. So what did he say?"

"He said he wants to be in my life. He wants to meet you and the kids. He wants his family back. I invited him over for dinner tonight."

"Oh boy. I can just imagine the call you had with your mother. What did she say?"

"I haven't called her yet. I just don't know what to say. Frankly, I feel like keeping this to myself for a little while."

"Okay. Well, Paul rarely gets through a meal without yelling or throwing food at his brother."

"Well, we're his family. Fritz will just have to get used to it. Listen, be home early. I need help. He's arriving at six."

"Okay. I can be there by five-thirty. Oh, wait – did you get the job?"

Faith laughed. "I didn't even stop to ask. I was completely shell shocked. Fritz – Granddad – walked me to my car and I just left. Wait," she said almost to herself, "no, there's no way I can call him Granddad. That just feels too strange." She came back into focus, "Sorry, anyway, I'll call tomorrow and see if Bruce will even talk to me."

"Oh, I think he'll talk to you!" Chris laughed and hung up.
***

Faith put the finishing touches on the salad and adjusted the flatware on the table.

"Where is he? He's twenty minutes late. The kids are starving." Chris looked at the kids as they hit each other over the head with Nerf swords and shouted at each other.

"I know. We'll just have to go ahead and feed them. Not that they'll eat this masterpiece." She gesticulated toward the oven. Faith sighed. "I can't wait to fast forward twenty years, when one of them is in the army, or dating some unworthy girl who can't cook and he'll say, 'oh, gosh, mom, I can't believe I ever complained about your cooking.'"

Chris chuckled. "You won't need to wait that long. Just wait until they're in high school and ravenously hungry all of the time. They'll eat anything you serve them."

Faith gave him a dejected look. "And they still won't appreciate it, right?" Chris gave her a sympathetic look.

"We're all unappreciative animals until we're grownups, honey."

Faith wiggled her eyebrows, "I don't know about that. You're still a bit of an animal."

Chris growled and grabbed her around the waist. "Truer words were never spoken. But I am an appreciative animal." As was usually the case between the couple, what started as a light kiss quickly deepened. His hands slid up her back and tangled in her hair.

Breathlessly, Faith leaned back and gave him a sultry smile. "I really hope you'll hold that thought for later."

Chris growled and gently bit her ear, then let her go.

Faith smiled as she tidied her hair. "Okay, let me feed the boys, but you and I should wait to eat for a little longer." She looked out the front window, where the light from the street lamp revealed an empty sidewalk. "I wonder what could be keeping him." She paused a moment. "Today feels like a dream. Was today a dream?"

He tucked a lock of hair behind her ear. "It certainly was a crazy day. How do you feel about suddenly having a grandfather in your life?"

As she moved to the kitchen to pull together the kids' meal, she considered her response. "I'm not sure. Happy, surprised, a little alarmed, shocked… I mean, I love my mom and her family, but I always felt like a part of me was missing because I didn't know the other side. I don't look like my mother. She's tiny with brown eyes. Fritz says I look just like Mick did – tall, blue eyes, pale skin. I can't wait to see a photo of him. He also said my hair comes from my grandmother."

Vivian came from a large family in North Carolina. Faith had three uncles, two aunts and what seemed like an army of cousins. Family reunions were a zoo. Her maternal grandparents were both deceased, but she had fond memories of them. They'd been immigrants from Ireland who had bootstrapped themselves from nothing. Her grandfather had been a teacher in Greenville, North Carolina. In an entrepreneurial effort to capitalize on his free summers, the couple had opened an Irish pub and seafood restaurant in Nags Head. For several decades, the family had moved back and forth between Greenville and Nags Head. When it had come time for her grandfather to retire from teaching, the family had moved to Nags Head full time.

While her grandparents had provided a comfortable life for their brood, there hadn't been much money for higher education. The children had needed to earn scholarships and help one another. For example, her Aunt Susan had moved in and helped care for Faith while her mother finished law school and launched her career. That was the way her mother's family was – they all helped each other to reach goals. Vivian had later helped her younger siblings through school. When all was said and done, every one of the kids had graduated from college, and four of them had advanced degrees. They were a vocal, hard working, highly principled group, and Faith was proud to call them family. She looked forward to telling Fritz about them.

She took another look out the window before collecting the children's dinner plates, and sighed at the still-empty sidewalk. "Boys! Dinner!"

***

Once the kids were in bed, the kitchen put to rights, and laundry pushed through, Faith sat down to her laptop. Her curiosity about her father, Mick, was overwhelming. Unfortunately, there was little to find. She read that he'd been murdered on the front stoop of his family home. It was reported to be a random crime by a homeless vet. But given it happened in 1972, internet access to details was limited.

An hour later, she concluded she'd need to do a library search to get more information. And call her mother, which she wasn't yet ready to do.

With a sigh, she stretched and headed to bed.

Missing Letters

Chapter 2

The incessant beeping of the bedside alarm roused Faith and she gave it a good slap before dragging herself to a sitting position. "I am *so* tired," she groaned.

Chris put his pillow over his head and mumbled in a monotone, "Time to make the lunches... time to make the lunches..." Faith swatted him with her pillow and pulled on her robe.

She made her way downstairs, turning on a few lights as she went to create the illusion of daytime, and put the coffee on to brew. Light was beginning to slant through the plantation shutters in the kitchen and she could hear birds chirping. Faith sadly pondered the events of the previous evening. Her grandfather had never shown up, never called. He hadn't given her his number, so she couldn't ask why. The emotional roller coaster that was the last twenty-four hours had left her utterly exhausted. Coffee, she thought, and lots of it.

As she turned off the house alarm and opened the front door, a cool breeze kissed her face. It was one of those early September days in Arlington, Virginia, when one got a distinct sense of autumn approaching -- a snap in the air. Faith inhaled deeply, enjoying the fragrance. She loved autumn.

"What the..." Faith rolled her eyes as she spotted the newspaper lodged in the front hedge again. "Mother fudgecake! How hard is it to aim for the stairs? Seriously! I absolutely suck at baseball and my aim isn't that bad." Faith muttered to herself. "He has *got* to be doing this on purpose!" She pulled the paper from the new hole in the neatly shaped boxwoods and tried to fluff up the greenery to hide the hole. Unsuccessful at that, she loudly cursed the newspaperman.

That's when she realized her neighbor had heard the whole thing as he climbed into his car. He laughed and waved.

"Oh hey, ha ha! Good morning!" A flush of embarrassment accompanied her cheerful wave.

The rubber band snapped against her fingers as she pulled it from the paper, prompting a smothered expletive. A quick scan of the front page showed nothing major had occurred overnight. Turning to the business section, she froze as she read the headline. The color drained from her face and her mouth dropped open. "Oh my God. Oh my God! Chris!"

She tore up the front stairs and into the house. Chris hurried down from the second floor, "What? What is it?" Wordlessly, eyes huge, she passed the paper to her husband. Chris rubbed his eyes, and then read aloud, "Billionaire Frederick Blithe Dead at 85."

Faith sat down on the couch and stared blindly ahead, tears pricking her eyes. "How can this be? I only just found him!"

Chris sat down next to her and gathered her in his arms as she began to cry. "I'm so sorry, honey."

After a few minutes, he picked up the paper again and continued to read the article. "It says he was found in his office in the Blithe Building yesterday evening by a patrolling security guard. It appears he had a heart attack." Chris looked at his wife, then down at the article. "An autopsy is planned."
***

Faith pulled into the driveway after dropping the kids at school. Her eyes were puffy behind dark sunglasses, but she'd pulled herself together. She knew she should call her mother, but was still angry at her for keeping her in the dark all of those years. That call could wait.

She put on another pot of coffee and sat down to her laptop to search for more news about her grandfather's death. Nothing new popped up. She decided to read more about Frederick Blithe's life. About her family. Research was a calming activity for Faith.

Wikipedia had a vast write-up that included details of Blithe's personal life, businesses and charitable activities. She learned that he had actually had two sons, Thomas and Mick. Thomas had died in his early twenties, consistent with what Fritz had told her. No grandchildren were mentioned. No siblings were mentioned. She checked the company's website and found the list of the Board of Directors and the executive team. She didn't see any other Blithes on the roster. That's not to say one of them couldn't be a cousin or something, but she didn't have that genealogical information. Based on what she knew, Fritz really did seem to have been alone in the world. *How sad.*

She read the rumors about his plans for the conglomerate. In interviews over the years, he'd publicly mulled the idea of selling each business individually as a way of maximizing the total conglomerate's worth. He'd debated the theory of the "conglomerate discount," which suggests that the market value of a diversified company is typically lower than the sum of the parts due to less market understanding of the stock, among other things. As an operating entity, Blithe had found the conglomerate arrangement to be useful since it lowered the company's overall risk. Lower risk meant lower borrowing cost, which contributed to the success of many capital projects. But the stock market doesn't always reward diversification in one stock since investors can diversify risk themselves by investing in different stocks of their own choosing. Most recent speculation was that Blithe had finally decided to go forward with an IPO.

The doorbell rang at around 1pm. A distinguished, well-dressed man in his late-sixties regarded her bedraggled appearance. He was marathon-runner lean, his gray hair clipped very short. Dark brown eyes peered at her. "Mrs. Warrior?"

"Yes?"

"My name is George Hopewell. I am – was – Frederick Blithe's personal attorney. May I speak with you a moment?"

"Yes, of course", Faith said in surprise. She tried to tidy her hair and stepped back, ushering him in. Mr. Hopewell walked into her living room and turned to her. "I gather that you've heard the news about Mr. Blithe."

"Yes," she said, eyes wide, "I saw it in the morning paper. I just can't believe it."

"I am very sorry for your loss. May I sit?" As Faith nodded, Mr. Hopewell sat down and motioned for her to sit as well. "So, you are Frederick Blithe's granddaughter."

Faith nodded. "That's what he told me yesterday. I had no

idea."

"Mr. Blithe came straight to my offices after he left you yesterday. Mrs. Warrior, he appeared ten years younger than he had earlier in the day. He was completely transformed. It was astonishing. You really should know that."

A lump formed in Faith's throat and she stared at her clasped hands. "Thank you for telling me that. It means a lot to me."

"And there's more," he continued.

Faith looked up at him.

"He changed his Living Trust on the spot. You, Mrs. Warrior, are his heir."

Faith's mouth dropped open. "I'm what?"

"His heir. What was his is now yours, with the exception of some minor bequests and estate taxes, et cetera."

Faith was speechless. She just stared at the lawyer, her body frozen.

"Mrs. Warrior, are you alright? May I get you a glass of water?" He looked toward the kitchen, as if unsure of whether to just get up and rummage through her cabinets for a glass.

"I'm just... I'm overwhelmed. Yesterday I found out I had a grandfather. I found out who my father was. And my grandfather is already gone. I just... I don't know what to make of it all. And now you tell me he's made me his heir? Still more I can't fathom." Tears pooled in her eyes. "I was really looking forward to knowing him. To having him in my life."

Mr. Hopewell swallowed in discomfort. "I... can understand your feelings. It is an overwhelming time."

"I'm sorry, Mr. Hopewell. I'm just a bit of a mess today. I'm sure you thought you were delivering good news. And you have to know I'm really touched that he did that, but I didn't even think about it. I was just really hoping to have him in my family."

He paused. "He could have used family, too. He's kept himself quite busy over the years but I know he's had lonely times. I said he looked ten years younger yesterday, and I believe it was hope that did that for him. He had hope in his voice, eyes, posture... I've known him for decades and never saw him like that. You did that for him."

She nodded and swallowed the lump in her throat. "I'm angry. I'm sad and angry."

"I understand, and please believe me when I tell you how very sad I am for your loss."

Faith wiped tears from her cheeks. "Thank you, Mr. Hopewell."

He took a cleansing breath. "So. You needn't do anything immediately. Things have been running smoothly for the past several years as Mr. Blithe gradually stepped away from the business. However, there are some critical decisions to make as soon as you are legally able. The Living Trust allows the estate to bypass probate, so everything can be settled relatively quickly. Therefore, sometime soon, I'd like to explain the decisions you'll need to make."

Faith looked at him and slowly shook her head, trying to comprehend it all. "Decisions?"

The doorbell rang again. She rose and went to answer it. "Faith Warrior?" Two large men in dark suits stood before her. One wore an ill-fitting suit with a brown and mustard colored tie that clashed with his good looks. The other seemed too tidy to be real. 'Not a hair out of place' seemed an insufficient description.

"Yes, I am Faith Warrior."

The man with the bad tie held out his badge. "I'm Detective John Harris with the Metropolitan Police Department. This is Special Agent Brian Maxwell with the FBI. May we come in?"

Faith felt like surprises were popping out of every corner. "Yes, of course," she said, and stepped back to let them pass.

As the men entered the living room, Mr. Hopewell rose from the couch and extended a hand to the FBI agent. "George Hopewell."

"Sir," acknowledged the detective. He turned his attention back to Faith. "Mrs. Warrior, may we speak with you in private?"

"What is this in reference to?" Faith asked.

"We are here about your grandfather, Frederick Blithe." The Special Agent regarded her.

"I see. Well, Mr. Hopewell was his personal attorney, and he undoubtedly knew him better than I did, so I think he can hear whatever you have to say."

"Very well," Special Agent Maxwell said. "Based on your use of the past tense, I gather you know what happened to your grandfather?"

"Yes, I read it in the newspaper this morning. I just can't believe it." She shook her head slowly and gazed blindly out the window. "I only just met him."

Maxwell raised an eyebrow. "According to Mr. Blithe's personal assistant, you are his only family. You only just met him?" Both men stared at her.

"My mother was pregnant with me when my father died. She never told his family about me. We met each other for the first time yesterday. It was a surprise to both of us."

Maxwell turned to Hopewell. "Sir, may I ask why you are here today?"

"I am Mr. Blithe's personal attorney and the Successor Trustee of his Living Trust. I came here this morning to inform Mrs. Warrior of her status."

"Which is?" continued Maxwell.

"Mrs. Warrior is Frederick Blithe's primary heir, as of yesterday."

Harris spoke up. "And she learned of his existence just yesterday. The day he died," he deadpanned.

Maxwell added, "I see we have more to discuss."

Faith immediately understood what he meant. Her grandfather had rushed to change his will and this cast her in a new light. Perhaps she was now a suspect in something. Was he murdered? She was afraid to ask.

Mr. Hopewell spoke earnestly. "I can assure you that Mrs. Warrior was as surprised to learn of her inheritance as you were. I only just informed her. She could not have known before I arrived. I spent several hours with Mr. Blithe yesterday afternoon making the modifications to the Trust, which was then witnessed by myself and my assistant."

Special Agent Maxwell looked interested. "How did Mr. Blithe conclude that she is his granddaughter?"

"Her age, her physical appearance, the identity of her mother, and the signet ring she wears," Hopewell responded.

"Will you do a DNA test?" Maxwell asked.

The attorney was taken aback, "Mr. Blithe did not see the need. He was quite sure."

"I am happy to take a DNA test. I'd like to know for sure that we're related. It's important to me." Faith interjected, then frowned and added, almost to herself, "of course, that might be mildly insulting to my mother...."

"Mr. Hopewell, who had previously been designated as Mr. Blithe's primary beneficiary?"

"Through his Living Trust, Mr. Blithe had identified a few recipients of relatively small sums, but the lion's share was to go to his private foundation."

"Who was to run the foundation?" Maxwell asked.

"A Board of Directors – a group of people hand selected by Mr. Blithe. These people would handle charitable disbursements per his requests, choose other worthy charities, and liquidate his assets or invest them to match the contributions. Yesterday, Mr. Blithe completely removed the foundation from the equation. Mrs. Warrior will control everything."

"Mr. Hopewell," Maxwell turned to Detective Harris, "we will need to see copies of the old and the new Living Trust documents. Can you get them to us?"

"Of course. In fact, I have the drafts on my laptop if you'd like to see them right away. To get the signed copies, we'd have to return to my office."

Maxwell quickly turned to Faith. "Ma'am, may we see the documents?"

Faith knew this was just a courtesy but appreciated it nonetheless. "Of course," she quickly responded.

"Thank you. May we use your printer?"

As Faith showed them to her desk, Hopewell pulled out his laptop and tapped it awake. He slowly walked behind as he navigated to the documents on his hard drive.

She connected the printer cable to the laptop and the printer started humming. Faith sat down in a daze.

"Mrs. Warrior," Detective Harris spoke up, "we will have more questions for you. Can you come to the station?"

"Yes, of course," she responded. Then did a double take at the clock, "but it's almost two o'clock and I'll have to go and get my boys from school at three."

"Ma'am, is there someone you can call to get your children?"

Nodding, Faith picked up the phone. She called her husband and briefly explained the situation. He agreed to immediately leave work to get the children.

The men were deep in discussion, looking at the

documents and arranging for the signed copies to be retrieved. She excused herself to change her clothes. Upstairs, Faith washed her face, mechanically applied some makeup and brushed out her hair. When she had changed, she took a deep breath and rejoined the men downstairs.

    ***

Maxwell, Harris and Faith sat around a table in an interview room at the station. She'd been asked a variety of questions about her background. "Do I need a lawyer?" Faith looked anxiously from Special Agent Maxwell to Detective Harris. "Am I some sort of suspect in this?"

"Mrs. Warrior, we have no reason to suspect your involvement in this based on what we now know. But we are very early in this process. As I mentioned earlier, the more help you can give us, the faster this will be resolved. You were one of the last people to see your grandfather, so there may be something you know that will help the investigation," the Detective responded.

"Why is the FBI involved?" She asked.

Maxwell spoke up. "Your grandfather was a man of influence. Other people of influence want to know what happened to him. While Mr. Blithe may have died of natural causes, we won't know until an autopsy is completed. That should be in the next day or so. But if further tests are required to arrive at a cause of death, results could take weeks. In the meantime, the FBI is assisting the Metropolitan Police in their investigation."

"Which people of influence?" Faith was curious.

"My superior officer is privy to that information – I am not. Let's just say that your grandfather had friends in high places." Maxwell looked down at the papers in front of him. "You said you only discovered you'd inherited his estate when Mr. Hopewell told you this afternoon. Do you have any idea why Mr. Blithe would rush to change his will?"

Faith shook her head slowly. "No, I don't. I know he was very happy to have discovered me. He made that clear to me. Mr. Hopewell told me that was his impression, too. But I don't understand the urgency about changing his will. Do you know if he was ill?"

"We won't have a full report on that until after the autopsy," the detective answered.

"Very well, Mrs. Warrior. That's all I have for the moment." Maxwell handed her his card. "Please call me if you think of anything else."

Detective Harris stood up, "I'll ask one of the officers to take you home."

"Thank you." She stood up from the table. "Will you keep me informed?"

"Of course," the detective assured her.

***

A very polite police officer held the door for her and as she stepped out of Metropolitan Police Headquarters onto Indiana Avenue. She inhaled the fresh breeze and saw a sleek, black limousine at the curb in front of the building. The passenger and driver doors opened simultaneously. Mr. Hopewell stepped out and a uniformed driver came around to the sidewalk. "Mrs. Warrior? Your car is here."

"My car?"

"Yes, ma'am. Roberts will be happy to take you anywhere you wish." The uniformed driver nodded to her and stood by the door.

Faith turned to the officer, "I guess I won't need that ride, Officer."

"No, ma'am, I guess you won't." He smiled and touched the brim of his hat. "Have a nice day."

"Thank you," Faith murmured as she stepped towards the limousine.

"Mrs. Warrior," continued Hopewell, "there are things we should discuss."

"Of course. But I do need to get home to make dinner. Can we talk on the way to my house?"

"That would be fine."

They settled into the back of the limousine. Faith looked around at the elegant interior. Smooth, soft leather seats in a buttery tan color. Burled wood detailing. A compact bar equipped with a coffee maker and tiny refrigerator. A compact, built-in console with a flat screen TV, laptop, fax and flip-out desk.

Faith had been in limousines before, years ago in conjunction with her work. But this was unlike anything she'd seen before. It was an exceptionally elegant mobile office.

Hopewell interpreted her reaction. "Mr. Blithe did not like

to waste time. He had this car specially designed to meet his needs." He paused. "Mrs. Warrior, I have told you I was Mr. Blithe's personal attorney. What you might not appreciate is that this means I worked solely for him. I handled all of his personal legal affairs, or coordinated with outside counsel when the matters were outside of my purview. For instance, I brought in outside counsel on some of his more complicated personal investments. Corporate matters are handled by the corporate legal department."

Faith nodded. The limousine pulled away from the curb and began snaking its way through the early evening traffic.

He continued, "I worked harmoniously with Mr. Blithe for thirty years. If you wish, I will continue on in this same capacity for you."

She saw the concern in his eyes. "Mr. Hopewell, this is all happening very quickly. Yesterday morning, I didn't even know I had a grandfather. Today, I found out he's dead and that I'm the heiress to a fortune, with unimaginable complexities. I *definitely* want your help. Let me assure you of that. I would be grateful if you would continue doing what you're doing for the time being and we will sort our way through this together. We can talk about the status of this arrangement again in a few months, to make sure we're both happy. Is that agreeable to you?"

"Yes, ma'am. Quite agreeable." He reached into his briefcase for a folder.

"Mrs. Warrior, I'm sorry to have to discuss this with you now, but arrangements need to be made for Mr. Blithe's funeral. If I get your approval on a few of them, then your grandfather's personal assistant and I can begin working on them tomorrow morning." Mr. Hopewell handed her a slim file. "Here is a copy of his wishes. It's very thorough."

Faith opened the file and looked at the papers. Her grandfather really had been very thorough. He had specified where he wanted the service, the music, the readings, the flowers, the casket, and the details of his burial site. He'd also included a list of all of the guests. Her grandfather did, indeed, move among influential people.

After a few moments, the lawyer said, "if you wish, I can make these plans on your behalf."

"Of course, Mr. Hopewell, please do. And may I say how

thankful I am to you for handling it."

"It's no trouble. Mrs. Abernathy, Mr. Blithe's personal assistant, will help me. The police have said that their investigation will not hold up plans for a service. Once the autopsy is completed tomorrow, his body will be released to the funeral home. Mrs. Abernathy has tentatively scheduled the vigil for Friday evening and the funeral Mass for Saturday afternoon. Is that acceptable to you?"

Faith was silent for a moment as a fresh wave of grief swept over her. "Yes, that's fine," she said in a small voice.

Hopewell paused, as if unsure whether to go on. "Incidentally, you should meet Mrs. Abernathy. She's worked for Mr. Blithe for at least fifteen years. A most reliable woman. I believe she and the rest of his house staff are wondering what will become of them."

Faith saw the concern in his eyes. Obviously, the staff was distraught. "Let's not do anything for now. Can you let them know that I'd like to meet with them after the funeral? Well, not that day, of course."

"Of course," responded Mr. Hopewell. "Mrs. Abernathy can also provide you with anything else you need. Here is her number, along with the numbers for the rest of the staff, myself included." He handed her a sheet of paper with ten names and their phone numbers.

"Thank you." She took the sheet and tucked it into her purse.

"Regarding Blithe Industries... I'll delve into the details of the estate later, but you might wish to know that the parent company maintains a strict program of reinvesting the lion's share of its earnings, married with strict capital discipline. I'll elaborate on that further another time, but each investment had to clear ROI hurdles."

Faith failed to understand why this needed to be discussed right now, at the same time as the funeral arrangements. It seemed inappropriate.

Glancing at her expression, he added, "you'll understand in a moment why this is important to discuss right now. Now then, the company's remaining earnings are paid out in the form of dividends. Blithe pays its shareholders an annual, variable dividend that is dependent upon corporate performance. There's a relatively simple algorithm involved.

Much the same way employees earn their bonuses. It also occasionally pays extra dividends if it has more cash on hand than it can profitably put to work. Again, this was consistent with Mr. Blithe's discipline."

The attorney paused and looked at her over the top of his glasses. "What I'm getting to, in my circuitous manner, is this: last year, your grandfather's 80% share of Blithe Industries' dividends amounted to approximately $320 million dollars. If the company were publicly traded, his stake might conservatively be estimated to be worth $18 billion dollars. This estimate is based on comparable companies' multiples and assumes a conglomerate discount."

Faith blanched and had to take a deep breath.

"Mrs. Warrior," he looked pointedly at her. "You must have known that your grandfather was one of the wealthiest individuals in America. But I suspected you didn't know the full extent. And this is something you need to know right away, before the press gets wind of the fact that you are his heir."

"No, I didn't know," Faith answered quietly, slowly shaking her head. "I know the names of many of the wealthiest people in America. They are in the news all of the time. But my grandfather must have lived very quietly. His name flies under the radar, you know? Even when he told me his name when I was in that meeting, I didn't realize who he was until he explained." She rubbed the back of her neck. "Through my work, I used to know the names of the people with large stakes in publicly traded companies. But the owners of the privately held companies tend to be less well known."

"Mr. Blithe did live very quietly. He lived quietly, moved among influential people quietly, invested quietly and he donated quietly. Over the years, he has given much of his annual income away to various charities. His feeling was that one man simply doesn't need that much money."

"I can see that. Good grief, what does one do with all of that?"

"That is a conversation for another time. Ah, we have arrived." Mr. Hopewell turned to Faith. "Mrs. Warrior, I imagine you have quite a bit to discuss with your family. Why don't I come back in the morning and we can talk further then? You should be briefed on the corporation and his other investments, properties, etc."

"Yes, that sounds like a good idea. Say 10am?"

"Very good." The lawyer remained in the limousine and began packing his papers away.

Roberts opened the door and took her hand to help her from the car. "Will there be anything else, ma'am?"

"Oh, no, and – I'm sorry, I didn't properly greet you. Hello Mr. Roberts. That's all for me tonight." She quickly added, "-- but Mr. Hopewell will need to get home."

"Yes, ma'am." said the driver. He gently shut the car door, and walked around to the driver's side.

Faith turned to the house and saw her children sandwiched in between the blinds and the windows, their faces excitedly pressed against the glass. They looked so adorable and so amazed to see her get out of such a grand vehicle. She couldn't wait to get into the house and sweep them up.

"Mommy!" Her boys ran to greet her. She knelt down to hug them. Her smaller son grabbed her face and said, "Time to rub noses!" They brushed noses in an Eskimo kiss, both of them grinning at each other.

"Mom, you'll never guess what happened at school today!" Her older son started speaking a mile a minute. "And what's the deal with that huge car outside? Who was in that? Why were you in it? Was it cool?"

"Okay, okay, boys. Give Mom some room. She just got home." Chris sauntered up and ruffled the boys' hair. "Why don't you go play Wii while Mom and I get dinner on the table?"

The kids agreed and ran off into the other room, arguing good naturedly about which game they'd play.

Chris put his arms around her and kissed her tenderly. "Hard day?"

"Hard. Bizarre. Sad. I'm much better now, though," she smiled and gave him a squeeze.

"Just relax while I get dinner ready. You need a break." He walked into the kitchen. Faith followed.

"There were a lot of calls this afternoon for you, by the way," Chris commented. "Reporters. I guess the word is out that you're Blithe's granddaughter. And your mother called."

Faith grimaced.

Chris took a package of pork chops from the refrigerator,

tore it open and arranged the chops on a cast iron grill pan.

She looked at him. "Um, Chris, there's something you need to know."

"What's that?" He asked as he washed his hands.

"I'm not sure how to say this, so I'll just come right out with it."

Chris added olive oil, salt, pepper and garlic powder to the chops. "Okay…" Chris looked at her with a worried expression, and then put the pork chops in the oven.

"My grandfather left me everything."

"Yeah…" For a moment, Chris just looked at her. Then his eyes grew large. "Oh crap. You mean he left you everything."

"Right. Oh crap." Faith stared at him.

"It never occurred to me that a man you knew for two hours would do that."

"I know – I had the same reaction. Apparently, after meeting me, he immediately went to his lawyer's office and changed his will, I mean, his Living Trust."

"How much are we talking here?"

"His stake in Blithe Industries is worth billions. And he was taking home hundreds of millions in dividends each year."

"Each year. I need to sit down." Chris walked to the kitchen table and slowly lowered himself into a chair.

"Things are going to change." Faith looked at him. "And I'm guessing they're going to change very soon. For now, the only people who know I've inherited are my grandfather's lawyer, his personal assistant, his driver, the police and the FBI. But that's got to change very soon. People are going to want to know who's in charge."

"I'm guessing you're in charge." Chris said seriously.

"Yes, I'm in charge, or I will be soon. I'll be in charge of that major corporation. Good God. I'll be in charge." Faith slowly lowered herself into the chair next to Chris's, staring blindly ahead.

"Okay. Breathe, Faith. Wait, I need to breathe, too." The two sat in silence for a few minutes.

"Security, Faith. We have to be much more concerned about security."

"Security." Faith looked at him.

"For the kids, Faith. I don't want to sound paranoid, but…." Faith's eyes grew large at that.

"You're right. Good grief. I've just lost my grandfather. Now we've got to worry about the kids."

"We've got an alarm on this house, so for now I think we're okay. But if people start showing up on the doorstep... We also need to talk to the school to make sure the kids aren't vulnerable in any way."

She looked at him. "I need to find out where my grandfather lived. Maybe that's an option if we feel unsafe here."

Chris nodded. "You mentioned your grandfather's lawyer. Can he help?"

"Yes, he's my primary resource. I spent some time with him this afternoon, and he's coming back here tomorrow at 10am."

"Okay," Chris responded, "I want to be here for that meeting."

"Good. I want you to be here."

He sniffed the air. "Pork chops need to be turned. Let me get the rest of the meal together."

"Mom!" She heard Graham yell from the other room. "Paul won't pop my bubble. Tell him to pop my bubble so I don't die!"

"Paul!" Faith yelled back, "Pop Graham's bubble or I'm turning off the Wii!"

***

Faith and Chris were both exhausted.

Chris climbed into bed. "What a day. You okay?"

Faith looked at him. "Honestly, I'm not sure which way to turn right now. My grandfather is dead and I've just started to think about the obligation he had to the tens of thousands of employees he had."

"Faith, he had a plan in place until yesterday. Just because you're now at the wheel doesn't mean you have to drive the bus. You can still divest, do what he was planning to do."

"But is that what he would have wanted me to do? I mean, if all he wanted to do is leave me some money, he could have just added me to the list of beneficiaries and still launched the foundation with the remainder. I don't know what I'm supposed to do." She looked at him. "The only thing I know is that I can't do this without you."

"I'm here, honey. But what can I do?"

"I did some reading today about the company. One of the four segments is media and tech driven. Your space. Plus, without a doubt, the entire organization yields synergies by leveraging centralized functions. That includes technology, on every level, in every function. I'm sure they've got talent in place, but I don't know those people. I know *you*. I trust *you*."

Chris turned off the bedside light and drew Faith into his arms. "It sounds like you've already made up your mind to get involved with the corporation."

"No, I'm just trying to wrap my head around all of this."

Chris took a deep breath and exhaled. "You are not in this alone. We'll figure it out. Just give it some time." She hugged him closer and kissed him, then rested her head on his chest and let her eyelids close. Chris watched his wife drift off to sleep and wondered at the sight of her. He hugged her closer and went to sleep.

Chapter 3

By eight in the morning, the kids were at school and Faith was at home in front of her laptop. The steam from her mug of coffee curled upward into a shaft of sunlight that crossed her desk. The doorbell rang. Chris stood up and looked at Faith. "I'll get it," he said.

A petite, attractive woman with a chin-length bob of curly brown hair stood on the porch in a tailored chocolate-brown suit, her face devoid of any makeup – she didn't need it. Her gold jewelry was simple, the white poplin shirt she wore beneath the jacket was crisp. The overall look was organized, capable and serious.

"Vivian, how are you?" He said as he stepped back and let his mother-in-law in.

"I'm fine, thanks, Chris. How is,..." She stopped when she caught sight of Faith at her desk. "Oh Faith, honey, I've been so worried." She moved forward, as if to embrace her, then thought better and stopped. "I tried calling so many times. Why didn't you return my call?"

Faith stood up and looked at her mother. "It took some time for the urge to scream at you to dissipate. It's still lurking, though, so just be careful what you say."

"I get it. Do you want to hear my side of it?"

"Sure, I'd love it. Though I would have loved it more about thirty years ago."

Chris ducked into the kitchen, leaving them alone.

Vivian sighed loudly and sat in the nearest chair, seemingly not trusting her legs. But as soon as she sat, she popped back up again and began to pace. Vivian always paced when she spoke about difficult subjects.

"Mick was the love of my life. We met at Harvard, in a

pre-law class. Cliffies were able to take some classes there. It became serious rather quickly – we had similar interests, similar goals and, well, great chemistry. We planned to go to Georgetown Law together, but the summer before school started, his brother and mother died in a diving accident. Mick decided his place was with his father. He scrapped his plans for school to work for Blithe Industries – one of the very companies we'd both wanted to fight against, given the nature of some of its businesses. Hearing him tell me this, well, it was like an out of body experience. I was shocked. And then I was furious. I felt he'd failed me, and I told him so. He'd ruined everything, our whole life plan. I broke up with him.

"A few weeks later, I realized that I'd been too rigid, that nothing was worth losing him. I loved him so much – couldn't imagine life without him. I tried calling but he didn't respond. I'm sure he was angry with me, too. So I sent him a letter. Too late, I guess. A day or two later, I saw on the news that he'd been murdered. A week later, I found out I was pregnant.

"I went to the funeral and I gave Fritz my condolences. He was devastated, a mess. He'd lost his whole family in the span of two months. I'd planned to tell him about the baby – about you – but he was so angry with me for hurting Mick. He said some awful things. So I kept silent.

"It wasn't until years later that it occurred to me that he only said those things out of grief. That he probably would have embraced the knowledge of you. But I felt it was too late, and I was ashamed to confess the truth to you, so I didn't do anything."

"All of these years, I could have had a relationship with him. He said that meeting me was a gift from God. I missed out on a grandfather who thought that way about me – it just breaks my heart."

Her mother swallowed hard. "Faith," she said quietly, "I'm so sorry. I really messed up. And I know that any apology I could make would be completely inadequate. Completely. You have every right to be angry with me. But I hope one day you'll forgive me."

Faith was silent for a few moments. "Mom, I'm really upset about this. Thank you for talking to me about it, but you'll need to give me some time to wrap my head around it."

"Okay, I understand. I love you, Faith. You know that,

don't you?"

"Yes, I know it, Mom. And I love you too. I'm just really angry with you."

"I know. Okay, well, call me if you want to talk about anything, or if you need any help. I'll always be here. I'll show myself out." She gave her a sad smile as she left, closing the front door softly behind herself.

***

At ten o'clock, Chris, Faith and George Hopewell sat around their dining room table.

"Mrs. Warrior, your grandfather's largest investment is his roughly 80% stake in Blithe Industries. The other 20% is held by employees in the form of restricted stock – part of the corporation's compensation package. Blithe Industries is a diversified conglomerate comprised of sixteen subsidiary companies across four business segments. What began as Blithe Rifle Company over 200 years ago evolved considerably over time, particularly during Frederick Blithe's tenure as CEO. The company now purposely blends cyclical and non-cyclical exposures to produce more reliable annual results. Mr. Blithe loved to plan, and steady results allow for that."

Hopewell handed Faith and Chris a spreadsheet with lots of segment detail and continued. "As you see on this page, Blithe Industries is broken down into four main segments." Faith squinted. *Good grief*, she thought, *someone must have won a bet about how much information could be crammed onto one page.* She chuckled at the memory of an old co-worker giving her a magnifying glass as a Secret Santa gift because of her own packed spreadsheets.

"Did you have a question about something?" Mr. Hopewell asked.

"No, no," Faith quickly answered, stifling her smile.

"*Blithe Defense* includes Blithe Rifle Company, two military weapons companies, and a fire and security business. *Blithe Materials* includes four companies in the paper and chemicals industries. *Blithe Media and Technology* includes online media programming, chip design, advertising, electronic gaming and syndicated radio. *Blithe Essentials* includes basic household products, personal care products, food processing and tobacco."

Faith commented, "Though one might not really call

tobacco an essential."

"Ask that of anyone who's ever tried to quit smoking," he said seriously.

He went on. "Many of the brands Blithe Industries owns are household names." He went on to list a few, all of which were well known to Faith, and probably every other American.

"Now," he continued, "onto the issue of inheritance. My assistant and I will work together over the coming few weeks to coordinate the transfer of assets to your name, Mrs. Warrior. None of this can happen until the cause of Mr. Blithe's death is determined, of course. Simultaneously, we will work with your grandfather's accountants on the tax issues associated with your inheritance."

Even the mention of the possibility of murder made Faith feel ill.

The lawyer looked pointedly at Faith, "I would imagine that word of your inheritance will get out once we begin to process your inheritance. You might think a bit about how you'd like to handle the resulting attention."

Chris spoke up, "Mr. Hopewell, that is actually my primary reason for being here right now. I'd like to discuss with you the issue of security. We've already had to disconnect our house phone because of the relentless calls from reporters. We're concerned that once word gets out about Faith inheriting, we'll have to worry more about our kids' safety."

The lawyer nodded. "Mr. Blithe occasionally received uninvited visitors at his residence. He had household staff to deal with that. For now, I will ask the security detail to shift focus to your home here. Longer term, however, you might consider Mr. Blithe's home in Washington as an option for you. It's quite secure -- and quite lovely, I might add."

"Where is his home?" Faith asked.

"It is on Massachusetts Avenue, mid-way between Wisconsin Avenue and DuPont Circle."

Chris looked at Faith and then again at the lawyer. "He lived on Embassy Row?"

"Yes," the lawyer responded, "it is sometimes referred to as Embassy Row. He lived next door to the British Embassy."

"I thought the Vice President of the United States lived next door to the British Embassy." Chris said.

"You are correct. The Vice President lives on the west side

of that embassy, on the grounds of the US Naval Observatory. Mr. Blithe lived on the east side, further down the hill."

"I see." Chris said and looked at Faith, a small smile on his face. "He lived on the east side of the embassy."

Mr. Hopewell looked expectantly at the couple. "Do you have any other concerns?"

Faith hoped Chris wouldn't say anything about Grey Poupon. He looked like he might. She looked at her husband with a straight face but laughter was in her eyes. *Goofball.*

***

Faith placed the sandwich in front of Mr. Hopewell. "Truly, you need to eat. We've been talking for two hours and it's lunchtime." When he looked as if he'd decline, she added, "I was making sandwiches for the two of us anyway. What's one more?" He looked exceedingly uncomfortable at her gesture. Chris winked at him from the end of the table.

"I, er, thank you." He unfolded his napkin and placed it in his lap. Faith sat down with her plate and said grace. As she began speaking, Mr. Hopewell's eyes widened.

Once she'd finished praying, she said to him, "I can see you're uncomfortable with all of this. I certainly don't mean for you to be. Working with me is likely to be far different than it was with my grandfather."

"Yes, ma'am, I imagine it will be."

"I am not a formal person and I'm very direct. I would like you to feel comfortable enough to speak your mind."

Hopewell looked relieved and he smiled at her. "Thank you, ma'am. I'm sure we'll rub along just fine."

"I don't want you to rub my wife, Hopewell." Chris looked at him over his sandwich. Faith glared at her husband.

The lawyer cleared his throat, obviously uncomfortable. "It's a British saying, sir, it means we'll cope well."

"You're not British, Mr. Hopewell."

"No, sir, I'm not." Chris smiled at the lawyer.

"Ah, yes." The lawyer closed his eyes and smiled. "You're joking." The lawyer looked relieved.

Chris gave the lawyer a big smile and chuckled.

Faith glared again at Chris. *Goofball!* She mouthed.

***

Chris left to get the kids from school and take them to the park while Faith continued to work with the lawyer.

Mr. Hopewell had given her a rundown of her grandfather's favorite philanthropic causes, handing her a spreadsheet that itemized disbursements over the prior five years. Interestingly, his largest personal donations were to environmental funds. Perhaps it was his small way of reaching out to his son.

They then returned to the topic of her grandfather's assets, starting with Blithe Industries.

"As I previously mentioned, your grandfather stepped away from the operations of the business a few years ago. He has in place a very capable management team. Things appear to be humming along. That said, now that you are the majority owner, it is your prerogative to step in at the helm." He paused to look at Faith and then continued. "It's just something to think about, and there's no rush. Just know that your grandfather used to really enjoy it, and given your background, I believe you would be a quick study."

"It's something to think about," Faith replied. She really did love equity research, learning about companies, examining their operations and assessing opportunities. Working at an operating company would be different, but she could feel her interest piquing.

He continued, "whether or not you are involved with operations, you should know something very fundamental about the company. Mr. Blithe always maintained strict capital discipline. Each investment the corporation makes, no matter how large or small -- from the expansion of manufacturing facilities, to the growth of distribution fleet, to the purchase of another subsidiary -- must pass very stringent profitability hurdles. Mr. Blithe always measured his company's profitability on the basis of cash, rather than earnings. As we've all seen in the corporate headlines, earnings tend to be easier to manipulate than cash."

Faith smiled. Her grandfather ran his company using the same principles she had espoused coming out of business school. It warmed her heart.

"Now," Hopewell continued, "before I delve into the individuals who run Blithe Industries, let me touch on your grandfather's other assets."

Faith jotted a few quick notes, then drew a line in her notebook and looked up at Mr. Hopewell. Seeing this, Mr.

Hopewell's affection for her swelled. She was obviously a very diligent person. She wanted to get this right.

"Your grandfather loved technology. It's where he made all of his personal investments." This struck Faith. She had not expected an octogenarian to know or care much about the latest technology.

"I can tell you are surprised by this. But your grandfather started the Media and Technology segment himself. This was his major contribution to the company." *Of course the investments had occurred during his tenure,* she thought. *Such opportunities hadn't existed in prior generations.*

"Dozens of years ago, your grandfather began investing in technology in earnest. At first, he threw seed money at a variety of ventures. Some of them failed, but some of them became huge successes. He personally met years ago with many of the biggest names of today. Once he had a feel for the direction of things, he invested bigger sums. He also invested in people. If he met someone who truly impressed him, he was inclined to follow his gut instinct. Of course, these speculative investments were only made in his personal portfolio – never by the corporation. His gut instinct contributed greatly to his wealth."

Mr. Hopewell handed her another spreadsheet. Here, he'd itemized the investments her grandfather had made over time. Dates, amounts invested, current values. Some of the current market valuations were beyond imagination. Her grandfather had had a good eye. *Oh my,* she thought. *Chris will have a field day with this!*

"Depicted on this page are current market valuations of existing, live investments. Well, as of yesterday's close. The valuations on the next page are best guesses of still-private investments. These valuations were based on the multiples enjoyed by publicly traded comparable companies."

"I see." *Good God!* Faith examined the list of several billion dollars of investments in the biggest names in technology. Looking at the dates, her grandfather had obviously gotten in at the very beginning of many of these companies. He was clearly a visionary.

She quickly scanned the latest investments and had no idea what the companies did. *Is this where the future is taking us?* She had an urgent need to speak with her techie husband. He would be fascinated – and would hopefully know what to make of it all.

"Now, I'll shift gears if I may. Your grandfather has a number of properties." He handed Faith a spreadsheet. "Primarily, they are homes. He did not enjoy hotels, so he maintained residences in a few key cities. To date, everything he owns is fully staffed and maintained, including the security. Here is a list of properties and other details." He handed her a list. *San Francisco, New York, London, Paris, Capri... good grief!* "Should you want to visit any of them, or go anywhere for that matter, you need only contact Mrs. Abernathy. There is a private jet. Again, Mrs. Abernathy can make any travel arrangements. She can also arrange for favorite foods, etc., to be onboard and at your destination when you arrive."

Faith looked up at him in exasperation and dragged a hand through her hair. "Homes around the globe. A private jet."

"Mrs. Warrior," Hopewell said, "you needn't worry. I will inform you of everything over the next few days. If there is anything you want to change, discontinue, etc., from what Mr. Blithe did, Mrs. Abernathy and I will be happy to handle it for you until you better understand who to talk to in the organization. A few weeks from now, you will not feel so adrift. I will make sure of it."

"Ok, thank you," Faith replied quietly, regarding the list.

"Let's move on to a brief discussion of the executives who run the parent company and the Board of Directors who have been handling operations in recent years." Hopewell looked at Faith. "Once word gets out of your inheritance, they will want to speak with you rather urgently."

"Yes, I can imagine," Faith said. "When will they know?"

"I will inform them after transfer of the assets is complete. However, they may find out before then. I cannot predict this."

Dear God, oh God, oh God, what am I supposed to do! Faith's thoughts were in turmoil. *This is just too much!*

Mr. Hopewell stopped a moment and looked at her. He leaned toward her.

Speaking quietly, he said, "Mrs. Warrior. As intimidating as this all sounds right now, none of these people are smarter than you are. I have watched you, I have researched you, and I have seen your grad school transcripts. You are a force to be reckoned with, whatever you might think."

"I've been away from the work force for five years, Mr. Hopewell."

"Irrelevant. You'll feel caught up in no time."

She inhaled deeply a few times and focused on the trees moving outside of her window. She looked at Hopewell and smiled. "Thank you." Faith flexed her fists a few times.

"Wait," she looked up at him. "My grad school transcripts?" Faith turned and frowned at him.

"When your grandfather had me change his will, he also asked his security team to research you. I happened to receive a copy of that report. Had he seen it, he would have been very proud. I am sure of it."

Faith swallowed hard, feeling like a small child starved of praise.

"He remarked to me when he changed his will that he felt meeting you was a message from God. That you should take your rightful place. You were cut from the same cloth. He was angry about not knowing you sooner and he wanted to correct this error as quickly as possible. That was why he acted with such urgency."

"The police asked me about that and I didn't know. Now I do." Faith took a ragged breath and exhaled. "Thank you." She smiled sadly at him.

He smiled back at her reassuringly. "Now then, back to Blithe Industries." Hopewell took a sip of water. "The company is overseen by a Board of Directors. Each subsidiary company had its own small group of executives that reports up to the parent company's executives. Functions such as Human Resources, Taxation, Corporate Finance, and even, to some extent, Sourcing, are largely centralized, which helps the conglomerate save money through economies of scale."

It sounded like a streamlined operation. The company produced a fairly steady rate of organic growth and also made some tuck-in acquisitions to gain market share and create additional synergies.

In equity research parlance, this was what some might call a "grinder" company. One that could reliably produce moderate growth, some margin expansion and steady cash flow each year. If it were a publicly traded stock, Blithe Industries wouldn't sell at a huge multiple of earnings, but it would attract investors who wanted to reduce portfolio risk, and it might be of particular interest to Value investors.

The doorbell rang. Faith got up to answer it. As she approached the door, a flashbulb went off outside of the window next to the door. Faith turned and saw someone peering in.

"Mrs. Warrior, don't open the door." Mr. Hopewell took her arm and led her into the kitchen, pulling down the shades as he went. He pulled out his cell phone and hit a number on the speed dial.

"Mrs. Abernathy," he said. "Please send a security detail to Mrs. Warrior's house immediately." He listened for a few minutes then said, "I understand. Yes, thank you. Please do that." The lawyer looked at Faith, "Mrs. Abernathy informed me that news of your inheritance has hit the newswires. This explains the photographer. Given this response to the news, I feel you can no longer remain here. Please pack whatever essentials you and your family will need for the night. The accommodations are quite good, so there's no need to bring anything but your essentials. A security detail is on its way to escort you. Mrs. Abernathy will send people here tomorrow to collect whatever else you want. Please call your husband and ask him to take the children directly to your grandfather's home."

"But the investigation isn't complete. How could we stay in his house?" Faith looked frantic. How could she utilize her grandfather's home when she seemed to be under suspicion of murdering him?

Hopewell took her hand and turned her to look at him. "Listen to me. I am confident that you didn't murder your grandfather. It's only a matter of time before that is confirmed. I also know that he would have wanted to help you in any way he could. He would never have wanted you to suffer because of his death. *Never.* Now, let's go to Blithe House."

Faith's head was spinning. She grabbed her cell phone and called her husband. "Chris! The news is out." She peeked through the blinds and saw three news trucks outside the house. "Reporters are camped out on the sidewalk in front of the house. We need to move to my grandfather's house. You know where it is. I'll meet you there with our things. Mr. Hopewell called a security detail to get me out. Ok, see you soon."

Heart pounding, Faith took the stairs two at a time, pulled luggage down from the closet and methodically packed a bag for each of them. She packed an additional bag with toys for the kids, their pillows and some bedtime books. Within twenty minutes, it was all in a pile by the front door.

Mr. Hopewell's cell phone rang. "They're here, just outside the door. We'll let two guards in to carry the bags. Roberts will escort you to the car. I'll lock up behind you. Ready?"

Faith pulled on a jacket, smoothed her hair and grabbed her purse. "Ready."

As soon as the door opened, a flurry of camera flashes blinded Faith. A strong hand took her elbow and guided her through the crowd. "Mrs. Warrior! What does it feel like to suddenly be a billionaire?" "Was your grandfather murdered?!" "Mrs. Warrior, look this way please!" The reporters shouted questions at her. Faith kept her head down and quickly made her way to the limousine. Roberts handed her into the back and the door clicked shut. She looked out through the darkened windows and saw the crowd, which now included her neighbors, too. They were all talking animatedly to one another and pointing at the limousine and her house.

The door opened again and Mr. Hopewell slid in. The trunk thumped shut and the limousine inched forward through the crowd.

"Good grief!" Faith exclaimed.

"Indeed," the lawyer said. "Your grandfather didn't get this sort of attention. I suppose you are quite a curiosity."

The limousine drove down Lee Highway and turned left onto Spout Run. As it inevitably accelerated into the shadows of the trees that arched overhead, Faith ached to hold her children and her husband. With so much change in the last three days, she longed to hang on to them. She peeked at Georgetown across the river as they swept down onto the George Washington Parkway.

"Mr. Hopewell, you've been incredibly helpful and kind," Faith said as they climbed the ramp up to Key Bridge.

He smiled and looked over at her. "Well, it is my job to become indispensable to you."

"You're good at it." She smiled back at him.

***

Missing Letters

The glided up Massachusetts Avenue and slowed to turn left into the driveway of an elegant, sandstone townhouse. Blithe House. The building was similar to many of Washington, DC's historic landmarks, inspired by the classical architecture of ancient Greece and Rome. It had four stories. There was a semicircle driveway in front of the main entrance and a connected driveway that led to a solid wood gate flanking the right side of the building. As the limousine turned toward the gate, it automatically opened.

"Your grandfather was raised here in this home." Faith turned to the lawyer with surprise on her face. "Your father and uncle were, too. Because of that, Fritz could never bring himself to sell it, even though it was far too big for him."

The driveway beyond the gate curved behind the building. There, a smooth stone courtyard led to a six-car garage along what seemed to be the back of the property. Four cars were parked in uncovered spaces to the right of the garage. The garage had rooms above -- she could see lights on in most of the windows. The second floor of the garage was connected to the left rear corner of the second floor of the main house by what looked like a suspended, enclosed hallway. The hallway was of modern design with lots of glass and steel. Though it resembled a glassed-in bridge, it somehow complimented the rest of the architecture. Because of the glass, it didn't obstruct light to the courtyard.

The lawyer pointed to the hallway she was looking at. "Residential staff offices are above the garage, accessible from the main house by that corridor. They are also accessible from the door you see in the garage."

A tall, sandstone wall surrounded the courtyard. Faith then glimpsed a garden beyond the garages, which was also walled. She could hear a fountain splashing. Utter privacy. The size of the property was far greater than it seemed from the street – or even from the driveway.

Roberts opened Faith's door. As she stepped out, a back door opened on the main house and a plump, pleasant-looking woman walked purposefully toward her, her hand outstretched. She looked to be in her early sixties.

"Mrs. Warrior. I'd like to welcome you to Blithe House. I am very glad to meet you. My name is Mrs. Abernathy. I am – was – your grandfather's personal assistant. I am so sorry for your loss."

Though the woman was smiling, her eyes were quite sad. "I'm very sorry for *your* loss, too, Mrs. Abernathy." Faith gave the woman's hand an extra squeeze.

The older woman's smile wobbled a bit as she visibly acknowledged how hard the last few days had been. "Thank you. Well, let me get you settled in. I'll show you the way." She walked into the house ahead of Faith.

"Your husband and children arrived about half an hour ago. They are upstairs. I took the liberty of arranging dinner for the children, which they are eating now. Children's fare, but quite healthy. Our cook utilizes only organic ingredients, much of which are grown in the greenhouse behind the garage." *Greenhouse?* "I've also asked the cook to prepare dinner for you and your husband, to be served a bit later. I imagine you'd like to get the children sorted out, first." Faith was taken aback by the woman's thoughtfulness.

"Thank you so much. Yes, I'd love to see my children now."

"Of course. Come this way." The assistant led Faith down a hallway through the center of the house to a door that opened into an atrium foyer. The first floor was elevated from the street, providing a measure of privacy to the front rooms.

Faith felt like she was in a museum. She admired the glossy marble floors inlaid with neoclassical designs and edged with brass piping. A sweeping marble staircase with an ornate bronze railing led to the second floor.

A large formal sitting room was on one side of the foyer. The walls were painted a midnight blue, which heightened the crispness of glossy white moldings and wainscoting. The furnishings were classic and elegant. Crystal and porcelain lamps sat atop warm, mahogany tables. Silver picture frames held black and white photos. A pair of elegant slipper chairs was clustered with a sleek, navy blue velvet couch. A rich oriental rug in red, blue and cream drew it all together.

There was a large portrait of an elegantly dressed couple hanging above the fireplace. The woman was young and darkly beautiful, and sat gracefully while the man stood beside her chair, his hand gently but possessively gripping her shoulder. She was dressed in a long, emerald green evening gown. The man wore a tuxedo and looked very much as she imagined her grandfather would as a younger man. He was clearly at least ten years older than the beautiful woman. Mrs. Abernathy saw her staring at the painting. "Your grandparents," she confirmed with a nod.

In the curve of the grand staircase, a marble topped table displayed a large, ornate silver vase cascading with yellow frangipani and dotted with tiny pink roses. The staircase was carpeted with a red oriental runner held in place by bronze bars. A large, pale blue glass chandelier gave an unexpected delight of color when she looked up into the atrium to begin her ascent to the second floor. Old oil paintings hung in regular intervals everywhere in the atrium, many of them portraits of people dressed in clothing from different points over the last few hundred years. "More family," Mrs. Abernathy noted with a sweep of her arm toward the gallery.

At the top of the stairs, Faith stepped into a large, square gallery. Again, paintings were everywhere. The floors were hardwood but were largely covered by oriental rugs. Glossy white doors led off in different directions. Mrs. Abernathy headed to the first door on the right and opened it, revealing a grand dining room, which was unoccupied. Dishes from dinner had not yet been removed, so it was clear that her children had dined there. There was food beneath one seat, a telltale sign that Paul had sat there.

Faith turned her head toward the sound of children's squeals from across the gallery. She headed in that direction, opening the door directly across the dining room. Inside, she found her children racing around in a huge room. "Kids!!" she called. "Mommy!!" her children raced to her and threw themselves into her arms. She hugged them tightly. Her husband sauntered toward her, a ball in his hand and a smile on his face. She loved his unflappable demeanor. He looked so relaxed, despite everything that had happened. It calmed her to see him.

Her husband kissed her cheek. "Look honey, there's a ballroom." He smirked at her and tossed the ball in the air and caught it.

"Mom! You are never going to guess what's upstairs!" Words spilled so quickly from Graham's mouth that whole sentences sounded like one long word. She laughed and knelt down so she was eye level with him while he talked. He was so cute in his school uniform, with only one side of his shirt tucked in, a sweaty boy at the end of a day. He explained that there was a room on the floor below that had every gaming system imaginable, and that they'd played there before dinner. "It's incredible!" She hugged him.

Mrs. Abernathy stood behind Faith and smiled. "Mr. Blithe enjoyed technology. You will find evidence of his fascination almost everywhere in the house."

Faith looked around at a massive, empty room that spanned the entire depth of the house. Rather than white molding, here the molding was ornate gilt. The flooring was a highly polished inlaid oak. Though still neoclassical in design, its mood was more Italian. The walls were painted a creamy color. Pale yellow silk curtains hung beside tall windows along three sides. Crystal chandeliers hung from gold medallions on the ceiling. Gilt framed mirrors strategically hung here and there so guests might check their look. "Do I see some cherubs up there?" Faith whispered to her husband, pointing toward an alcove at one end.

"Yup. Some nice chubby guys." He grinned again at her. "Graham wants his Stomp Rockets for target practice." Faith stifled a laugh then almost fell over when Paul launched himself at her legs. She picked up the laughing boy and smooched his plump cheeks. He burrowed his face into her neck. Faith breathed in the fragrance of his hair and closed her eyes. There was nothing more relaxing than holding one of her children.

"Mom," Graham said quietly as he stood beside her, "Dad says we're here because there's something wrong with our house. What's wrong with our house?"

"I'll explain things once Mrs. Abernathy here is done showing us around, okay Big Guy? Everything's okay." She smiled at him and ruffled his hair.

"Okay, Mom." He took her hand.

"Mr. and Mrs. Warrior, I'd be happy to show you to your rooms now, if you'd like to unwind. Your bags have already been delivered upstairs. I'll show you more of the house along the way."

"Thank you, that would be great."

Mrs. Abernathy led them back to the gallery, then through a door at the rear. This revealed a stacked staircase that appeared to span all four stories, unlike the grand staircase in the front of the house. They ascended and went through a door positioned identically to the one on the floor below. Here, the gallery was much smaller, leaving more room for the living spaces.

"Guest suites are to the left." She gestured to a door on the left side of the corridor. Family suites are to the right, through this main door," Mrs. Abernathy said as she walked toward a set of double doors on the right. Faith oriented herself. *Okay, family rooms are above the ballroom. Guest rooms are above the dining room.*

The double doors revealed two hallways. One led directly from the open doors to the side of the house, with a window at the end. The view was incredible. She looked over the treetops at downtown Washington. The other turned right and had two doors. "There are four suites here in the family wing, each with its own full bathroom and sitting area. She gestured to the corridor on the right. The master bedroom is at the end of this corridor. It also has a sitting room." She turned to Faith, "your grandfather's things are in there, where he left them. Nothing has been disturbed. I thought you might want to… well, perhaps you'll want to look through them before deciding what to do. If you want anything boxed up, let me know and I will have the staff handle it."

Faith looked at the door, longing to go inside and learn more about her grandfather. *His room.* Mrs. Abernathy continued, "I've put you in the two rooms off of the first hallway. They overlook Mass Ave. There is a connecting door, in case your boys need you during the night."

"Thank you, Mrs. Abernathy. That is really helpful." Faith turned to the first bedroom and opened the door. It had two queen-sized beds with puffy, white duvets and white sheeting. The décor was in neutral colors. She noted the blackout liners behind the curtains with appreciation. It was like a guest room at the Four Seasons. The bathroom was finished in a tan marble and had a large tub and walk in shower. Fluffy towels were stacked up. Flowers were in a vase by the sink.

The boys jumped on the beds and argued about who would sleep where, then squealed when they saw a TV in the small sitting area. Faith walked to the window and looked down at Massachusetts Avenue below. The sky had darkened and lights twinkled below.

Chris walked through the adjoining door and flopped on one of the beds, then clicked on a TV.

Mrs. Abernathy cleared her voice from the boys' doorway. "Dinner will be served in the dining room on the second floor at 8pm. If there will be nothing else, I'll leave for the evening."

"Of course!" Faith suddenly remembered she was there. She walked to the older woman and shook her hand. "Thank you for everything. So much."

"Mrs. Warrior, I'll be in my office at 9am tomorrow morning. I assume you'll want to discuss many things. If you take the staircase to the first floor, you will see a hallway just in front of you that will lead to the elevated walkway. That leads to the offices in the rear building. Oh, and after cook leaves this evening, please do not open any exterior doors or any windows on the first floor. The security system will be activated. I'll explain how the whole thing functions tomorrow. You will meet Mrs. Lucie, one of the housekeepers, in the morning."

"Thank you." Mrs. Abernathy nodded, smiled and left.

Faith turned and exhaled. "Okay, boys, time for bathie!" They scampered into the bathroom as Faith turned on the water. After they climbed in and were chattering away, Faith dug through a bag to find some bath toys. She laid out their PJs and a few books, located their toothbrushes, toothpaste, dental floss, cotton swabs and hairbrush, and laid out the small medicine kit she always carried when they traveled. *Always be prepared* was her motto.

She returned to the tub, soaped them up then chatted with them as they played. She explained that she'd learned that she had a grandfather, but that he'd died before they could meet him. This was his house and he had wanted them to come for a visit. The seemed to accept it.

After a nice, warm bath, she dried her boys with the soft, fluffy towels, brushed their hair and teeth, flossed their teeth, inspected their ears, then got them dressed and ready for stories. Chris walked in, snuggled down with the boys and began reading. Meanwhile, Faith went through to their room, which was the mirror opposite of the boys' room, and unpacked their things.

Story time over, the boys took one last trip to their bathroom, and then she tucked them in, placing sippy cups of water on their nightstands. Ten minutes later, prayers and songs were finished and she kissed them goodnight. 7:45pm. She had time to tidy up a bit before heading down to dinner.

"My head is spinning." Chris looked at her over his glasses as he lay on the bed.

"I know, right?" Faith stopped brushing her hair and looked at herself in the mirror. "What in the world is going on?"

Chris got up, wrapped his arms around her from behind and kissed her ear. "It's going to be okay."

She turned in his arms and laid her head on his shoulder. "It will be, as long as you're with me." She tipped her head up and kissed him. "I'm just worried about the kids. Heaping even more change on top of what they've already experienced. Not to mention the increased danger."

He gave her a squeeze. "Don't worry about the kids. They're resilient. And we'll be extra careful from now on."

"Right. Okay." She sighed. "Oh, I can't even think straight right now. I'm hungry. And I would really like a big glass of wine."

"Me too. Given the events of the day, I think we can make an exception to the drinking rule." Chris and Faith had a longstanding agreement to reserve alcohol for the weekends.

On their way to the dining room, they investigated the guest suite. The guest rooms were clustered around a common area with a full wet bar and TV sitting area. A lovely, fresh flower arrangement in a crystal vase sat on a gleaming table.

While the plush, off-white carpeting was consistent throughout the suite, the bedrooms were decorated in a far more interesting manner than the children's rooms had been before they moved their furniture in. Rather than beiges, each guest room had a distinct style and color.

One was decorated with navy blue fabric wallpaper and matching floor-to-ceiling drapes. The headboard on the king-sized bed was upholstered in a stark white. The bed linens were a crisp white trimmed with navy blue. Blue and white Chinese porcelain vases had been turned into lamps with elegant white shades. The Chippendale furniture was a rich cherry.

Another bedroom had a distinctly yellow theme. In this
room, the walls were covered in a pale yellow-on-white toile.
The fabric was repeated in the drapes and throw pillows. The
lamps in this room were more contemporary – their bases
were simple, large blocks of transparent Lucite. These sat upon
mahogany nightstands that matched the king-sized sleigh bed.
The desk was Lucite, paired with a comfortable, white-
slipcovered armchair. Two overstuffed, white-slipcovered
chairs flanked a mahogany coffee table.

The last guest room's walls were painted a matte, Kelly
green. The drapes and bedspread were a crisp white to match
the ceiling and woodwork. The sofa was upholstered in a Kelly
green and white lattice pattern that matched the pillows on the
bed and the cushions on two white faux bamboo armchairs.
Retro touches appeared in the form of the white, oval-shaped
glass chandelier and side lamps. The furniture was all a modern
white lacquer with stainless steel accents.

Each bedroom had its own full bath, decorated in
matching style. The bathrooms were stocked with elegant
shampoos and conditioners, body lotions and bath soaps. Big,
fluffy towels were stacked on built-in shelves. Spa-style robes
hung from hooks next to the showers.

"Incredible," Faith whispered.

***

"Your grandfather enjoyed good food," Chef Massey
explained as he plated their dinner. He was a very lean man,
tall, with salt and pepper hair. The cook was a formally trained
chef who had a special interest in organic gardening. When he
was not cooking, he was tending the garden behind the garage.
It had indoor and outdoor raised beds, enabling growth year
round.

The chef laid out spinach salad with warm goat cheese in
shitake vinaigrette, and an entree of spicy tilapia crusted with
pecan-panko crumbs, accompanied by sautéed carrots and
baby potatoes. He poured them glasses of a Chilean
Chardonnay.

"Mr. Blithe enjoyed eating from his own backyard. You
might call him a locavore. All of the vegetables you are eating
tonight came from his garden. He did not eat red meat very
often, instead preferring a good piece of fish or poultry. He
also enjoyed my vegetarian dishes."

"But you know how to cook red meat?" Chris poked at his fish. Faith smiled, "Chef, I've been trying for years to get my husband to eat more vegetarian food, but he's a die-hard meat eater." Faith laughed at her wording and looked at her husband.

"Yeah, yeah, I know. Die. Hard arteries. Got it." He took a spoonful of his fish and tasted it. His eyes widened. He took another bite. "Say, this isn't half bad!"

The chef turned to Faith. "Enjoy your meal. Please ring the bell when you are ready for dessert, or if you need anything." He pointed out a button beneath the edge of the dining table then left through a door at the back of the room.

Chris lifted his glass of wine. Faith lifted hers. He looked at her seriously. "To Fritz Blithe. May he rest in peace."

"May he rest in peace," she murmured solemnly and took a sip.

***

The man who was known to Nestor Carson as Casper sat in a wingback chair in his study. The glow from a single lamp far across the room barely touched him. He took a long sip of whiskey and stared at the ice glistening in his glass.

He'd watched the woman, Faith Warrior, arrive at Fritz's house. Well, her car anyway. He shook his head with fatigue. Blithe House had only been empty a few days. He sighed. More to do.

Chapter 4

Faith sat up and looked at the clock. Six a.m. She was disoriented when she looked around the room then suddenly realized where she was. It all came back to her. She lay back down and stared at the ceiling. *Ok*, she thought, *it's Friday. The kids need to get to school.* She got out of bed and went into the bathroom.

She took a quick shower, then dressed in a pair of jeans, a t-shirt and a sweater and slipped into loafers. Cell phone in hand, she tiptoed into her sons' room to get their empty lunch bags and went downstairs to figure out what to do. She needed to make lunches and breakfast, then get the kids up and ready.

Frick. I do not even know where the kitchen is.

She decided to follow the chef. Faith went to the dining room and opened the door the chef had used. It led to a service stairwell. If her sense of direction and space was right, this stairwell was directly behind the rear stairwell she'd used to get downstairs. In fact, there was a doorway that led in that direction. She opened it and there it was – the other stairwell. *Ok, so there are at least three stairways in this house...* Next to the stairwell was an elevator. She took the staircase down to the basement level.

Since the first floor was elevated off of the street, there were high windows in the basement. Rather than some dark, creepy space, this basement was bright, airy and fully modern. She took a door that led in the direction of the dining room above, and found herself in a large closet that held household cleaning supplies, including a housekeeping cart outfitted with a vacuum, extra paper goods, racks of cleaners and cleaning rags, bags for linens and space to stack garbage bags.

The next door led into the kitchen. White subway tiles

served as the backdrop all the way around the room, up to the high windows. The walls were painted white. The countertops were a white marble lightly veined with black. The floor was some sort of travertine. Three stainless steel-topped islands were positioned in the middle. There was a prep sink in the middle island. All of the equipment looked to be of commercial quality.

On the far wall were the stove, ovens and another prep sink. On the right wall, there were refrigerated cases, like one would find at a grocery store. A stainless steel door labeled 'Freezer' followed these. Racks on the left wall, beneath the windows, held pots, pans and storage supplies. On the wall on the backside of the building was a cleaning station with two commercial dishwashers. Rolling carts held plates, cups, glasses, flatware and table linens. There were also several closets that on further inspection held vases, serving platters and bowls, additional glasses, flatware and dishes.

Faith heard a door close and some footsteps. A door swung open at the end of the room and a woman appeared in an apron. She looked to be about Faith's age, with dark hair and a gentle face.

"Oh, hello!" she said as she caught sight of Faith. She rushed forward. "My name is Renee Lucie. I'm the housekeeper. I thought you might get up early, given you've got kids. Mr. Blithe got up early, too." She rambled a bit. Faith took her hand and shook it.

"Faith Warrior." Faith smiled. "Mrs. Lucie? Ms. Lucie?"

"Mrs." She smiled.

"I'm sorry to be abrupt, but my children need to get to school, so I was hoping I could make their lunches, get breakfast on the table, that sort of thing. Can you show me where the coffee maker is? And if there is any bread, meat, cheese, that sort of thing?"

Mrs. Lucie's mouth dropped open. "Oh, ma'am, you don't need to worry about anything like that." She smiled. "Mrs. Abernathy told me to expect you this morning. I work the early shift. I arrive at five forty-five in the morning. I take care of breakfast, groceries, flowers, shopping and other household support, then I leave at two p.m." She added, "I like to be home when my children finish school. Another woman takes over from two p.m. to ten o'clock. Her name is Mrs. Loper.

She handles any afternoon requests. She can also help with your children after school. She has grown children, so is very experienced. She's also very nice."

"You have children? What ages?" Faith asked.

"Eight and eleven. Both boys, like yours." She smiled. "Breakfast is ready in the lower dining room whenever you want it. That's just through there." She pointed to the swinging door. "I made your boys' lunches. Since I don't have their lunch boxes, I used some cooler bags we had here in the kitchen." She motioned to the counter, where two insulated lunch sacks sat.

"I hope they like spaghetti and meatballs. I prepared it this morning. It's in the insulated jars next to the bags. In the bags they'll find apple slices – I put some lemon juice on them so they won't brown – a bit of chocolate pudding and some carrot sticks. There's an ice pack in each bag. In case they don't get milk at school, I included thermoses of organic milk. Mr. Blithe always liked to eat organic food."

Faith was shocked. "Thank you so much, yes, I'm sure they'll love that."

"I will be happy to prepare their lunches going forward. Just let me know their preferences, at your convenience, so I can pack what they're sure to like," Mrs. Lucie added earnestly. She took the lunch bags from Faith's hand and put them on the counter. "Come through here, ma'am. Let me give you some coffee." She headed through the swinging door.

There, Faith found a lovely, informal dining room. The sideboard had three chafing dishes set up; two insulated carafes, one labeled coffee and one labeled tea, and milk and half and half appeared to be in two other insulated jugs. She saw small cereal boxes, a pitcher of syrup, a bowl of mixed berries, a plate of bagels, a cluster of bananas, and a plate of cream cheese and butter sitting atop a dish of ice. A toaster sat beside the bagels. Faith smelled eggs, bacon and pancakes. "The same goes for the breakfast, ma'am. If there is anything you would prefer or anything you dislike, please let me know. I prepared a number of things this morning, not knowing what you'd like."

"Thank you, it all looks wonderful." Faith inhaled the aroma.

Two flat panel TVs were flashing on the wall. One was

tuned to CNBC, on mute. The other was tuned to Morning
Joe. Mrs. Lucie motioned for her to sit, then put a steaming
cup of coffee in front of her. "Would you like milk or half and
half?" she asked.

"Milk, please. Thank you."

"Can I get you a plate of food?" The housekeeper looked
hopeful.

"Oh, please don't trouble yourself. I'll do it." Faith looked
at the clock. Six forty-five. She needed to account for the
additional commuting time. The boys needed to get up. She
pulled her cell phone out of her pocket and called Chris,
upstairs.

"Hello?" Chris's groggy voice greeted her.

"Honey, breakfast is ready. Would you get the boys
dressed, teeth brushed and bring them to the dining room in
the basement? And quickly, please."

"Okay." There was silence.

"Chris. I know you're still lying down. Don't go back to
sleep. Get up." More silence. "Seriously, dude! Up! Up!"

"Okay! Okay! Be there in a minute."

Ten minutes later, Chris and the boys entered the dining
room through a door to a central hallway. Obviously, he'd just
taken last night's stairway directly down. *Why didn't I do that?*

"Mom, pancakes!" Paul smelled correctly, dropped his
backpack and ran to the table. Mrs. Lucie came out from the
kitchen. Introductions were made and the housekeeper happily
set about making plates for them.

As the boys tucked into their breakfast, she motioned to
the sideboard. "Mr. and Mrs. Warrior, the papers have
arrived."

Chris looked at Faith and smirked. No more going outside
in his PJs in the early morning! He got up and took a paper,
then sat down and sipped his coffee while he scanned the
headlines.

Mrs. Lucie popped back into the room. "Ma'am, what
time should the boys be at school?"

"They have to be there by seven-fifty or so, no later than
eight a.m.," Faith replied.

"Very good. Roberts is waiting outside, whenever you are
ready." The housekeeper located the boys' backpacks and
placed a lunch bag in each. Faith looked at the clock. Seven-

oh-nine a.m. They needed to leave by seven-thirty, Faith guessed, in order to get back over the bridge to Arlington.

Oh Frick, homework! Faith ran to Graham's backpack and pulled out his folder. She quickly scanned his assignments. "Graham!" she barked. "We've got to get the homework done – we forgot last night." She looked at the clock. *Ok, we can do this.*

Graham grumbled but came around the table and sat down. She slapped the first assignment down in front of him, then a pencil, and told him what he needed to do. "Quickly!" she urged. He moved faster.

"Yup. Here we go." Chris calmly passed a section of the paper to Faith, then picked up the next paper. Right there, at the top of the business section, was a photo of her walking toward the limousine yesterday. She looked like a deer in headlights. The title of the article was, 'Blithe Heir Revealed.'

"You said it. Here we go." Faith read the article while she urged Graham through his homework.

She finished the article and recapped it to Chris as she packed up Graham's backpack:

"So," she sighed. "They know that I'm his granddaughter and they know he changed his will right before he died. Wish I'd thought to disable my LinkedIn account, because now they all know my entire CV."

She glanced at Chris. "The neighbors mentioned I'm a nice person, so at least I've got that going for me. Man, it's just a matter of time before everyone I ever worked with or went to school with starts talking to the press. Frick, and people I dated, too." Here eyes grew large, "Oh, no, what about the shenanigans in high school? Or, oh no...." She dropped her voice. "The shenanigans in college."

"Calm down, Faith. You've lived a good life, been a good person. Everyone has youthful indiscretions. It's nothing to be embarrassed about. You're still friends with your high school group. They're not going to talk badly about you."

Faith looked at the clock. Seven twenty-eight a.m. "Kids, time to go! Mrs. Lucie, where is the bathroom on this floor?"

She popped her head into the room from the kitchen. "Just go out the door Mr. Warrior came through and head toward the rear of the house. There is a bathroom on the left. 'Bye kids! Have a good day!" She smiled and waved.

Faith dropped a kiss on her husband's mouth. "Are you going in to work?"

"I'll go in for a little bit just to clear my desk. I want to be here this afternoon to see what unfolds." Faith nodded and smiled, then kissed him again.

"Bye Mrs. Lucie!" they chorused and followed Faith to the bathroom. Paul yelled, "Thanks for the pancakes! Mommy only makes them on the weekends!" Faith chuckled. Once finished there, they trooped upstairs and out into the courtyard where Roberts stood by the limousine.

"Yay! We get to ride in the big car!" The kids started hopping up and down.

Faith frowned. "Um, Roberts, I think we'll take our minivan."

"Aw, come on, Mom!" Graham said. Both boys' heads drooped.

Roberts nodded and gestured toward the garage. "Yes, ma'am. Come this way." He clicked a button and one of the garage doors opened. Inside, Faith could see the entire length of the garage. There were six bays. She saw a silver Range Rover, a bright red Smart car, and a navy blue Jaguar coupe. Faith's humble minivan was on the end. The last parking space was outfitted as a mechanic's station. *Roberts must do maintenance, too.*

"Ooh! Mom! I want the little red one!" Paul pulled on her wrist. "Come on, Mom!"

Graham piped up, "No, Mom, I still want the limo!"

"Boys, we're taking the minivan." She opened the rear door and helped the boys into their car seats. Once secured, she looked up to see Roberts in the driver's seat. *Okay, whatever.* Faith got into the forward passenger seat. "Do you know where the school is?"

"Yes, ma'am," he replied, and backed out of the garage. The front gate swung open and they turned right onto Massachusetts Avenue.

"I don't understand why we can't take one of those cool cars. We always ride in this stupid car." Graham scowled at Faith.

"Mister, we don't use the word stupid. And our car is just fine. We'd attract too much attention showing up in a limousine for car pool." Faith looked out the window at the

84

trees along Rock Creek Drive.

"I want to go to the zoo!" Paul recognized the road they usually took to the National Zoo. He'd rather go anywhere than go to school.

"We can go to the zoo tomorrow. It's Saturday. AND," she emphasized, "Now we live even closer to the zoo. So it'll be super easy." She smiled at her boys in the back seat.

"Paul," Graham announced, "we are NOT going to the monkey house this time. It smells disgusting." Paul frowned.
***

As they pulled into the long car pool drop off line, Faith looked at Roberts. "Any chance you could remove the chauffeur hat?" Roberts took of the hat and placed it in his lap.

"Can I wear it?" Paul asked. Roberts passed it back and Paul happily put it on.

"Just follow the cars through the parking lot – there's a specific route they take before they arrive at the drop-off location. Ok, turn in here and stop in front of that teacher." She pointed to a woman standing next to a red traffic cone.

The teacher opened the car door. "Good morning, boys!" She glanced at Faith. "Good morning Mrs. Warrior!" She looked pleased to see her, then perplexed when she saw the hatless, though still uniformed, driver. *Obviously, she hasn't read the business page.*

"Hi, Mrs. Swanson!" Faith smiled. "I love you, boys! See you at 3!" She grabbed the hat off of Paul's head. The boys both kissed her on the cheek before jumping out and scampering up to the group of kids waiting to be brought inside. She could see Graham gesticulating wildly as he talked to his friends. Paul teetered along with his big backpack. *He is so cute*, she thought.

The minivan doors slid shut. Roberts pulled out and began the drive back to Washington, D.C. "Ma'am, the security detail would like to speak with the principal about the school's security procedures. It's highly likely that she won't talk to them unless you are present. Could you call the school and set this up for this afternoon before we pick up the children?"

Faith was glad he brought it up. She herself had been a touch worried. "Absolutely. Good idea," she responded. She pulled out her cell phone and hit speed dial. The school secretary picked up.

"Hi Ms. Monahan. This is Faith Warrior, Graham and Paul's mom. I was wondering if the principal is available for a quick question?"

"Hi Mrs. Warrior. Just one minute." She put Faith on hold. Two seconds later, the principal picked up.

"I've been expecting your call, Mrs. Warrior." The principal, Mrs. Wilson, was a no-nonsense woman in her sixties.

"So you've read the business section," Faith stated.

"Actually, I heard it on CNBC this morning. I'm very sorry to hear about your grandfather," she said sympathetically.

"Thank you, Mrs. Wilson. So you understand why I'm calling. This inheritance has made me more concerned about security. Would you mind if I came in this afternoon to speak with you about it?"

"Not at all. Why don't you come to my office fifteen minutes before dismissal?"

"That would be great, thank you. Um," Faith wasn't sure how to say it. "I will have a few gentlemen with me. Security people. I hope it's alright for them to ask questions, too."

"Security people. That's not a problem." Mrs. Wilson seemed unperturbed.

"Thank you, Mrs. Wilson. See you this afternoon."

Faith put her cell phone away and looked out the car window. *This is crazy. This is just crazy. Bodyguards. Mansions. Jets. Having to leave our house. And here I thought moving from Texas and going back to work represented a lot of change! It's just too much.*

"Ma'am," Roberts spoke up. "The detail was very fond of Mr. Blithe. We are sorry for your loss."

"We? Roberts, are you a bodyguard?"

"Yes, ma'am. I am both driver and bodyguard. There are three others on the detail."

She finally noticed the bulge in his jacket beneath his left arm. "Why so many?"

"We stagger shifts so you always have at least one guard on duty, 24 hours a day." He explained, "There's a security room above the garage. The entire house is visually monitored." Roberts noted her look of alarm and added, "not the living quarters, ma'am. Just the hallways, exits and all

86

angles of the exterior of the property." She relaxed.

"What is your background?"

"I was US Army Special Forces, ma'am. All of us on the detail were. We've all been with Mr. Blithe for about ten years."

Faith exhaled. *I have got a Green Beret driving me around. Unreal.*

She frowned as she looked at the passing scenery. "Roberts, what do you know about what happened to my grandfather? The police didn't tell me much. They just said it appears he had a heart attack. But they seem to suspect something more. I'm guessing that as part of the security detail you might be able to tell me something."

He leveled his gaze at the road, "Mr. Blithe drove himself that evening. A guard followed in a separate vehicle, as is the protocol in such situations. They waited in the garage of Blithe Building while Mr. Blithe went to his office. Security in the building was usually excellent, and the building is the corporation's territory. Whenever we brought Mr. Blithe to the building, we waited outside."

"Why did he go there that evening?" Faith asked. "From what I've heard, he rarely went there anymore."

"I don't know, ma'am." He shook his head and thought for a moment. "I only know that he seemed very animated when he returned from meeting you that afternoon. If you'll pardon my commenting on it, he looked really happy. He took the stairs from the garage to the office, which was unusual for him. Usually, he entered the house first. In fact, he took the stairs two at a time, which is unusual for any man his age. I learned later that he went to speak with Mr. Hopewell. Mrs. Abernathy told me he was in Mr. Hopewell's office for well over two hours. Then, he went to the house for an early dinner. After that, he left for Blithe Building."

"And he was found when?" Faith frowned.

"He arrived at Blithe Building at around 5:30pm. He was found dead at around 6pm by an employee who saw his light on and went to say hello."

"Do you think it could have been murder?"

"I don't know, ma'am. He was a very wealthy man. Maybe someone stood to benefit from his death." He paused then looked uncomfortable, suddenly realizing how his words might be interpreted. "I'm not referring to you, ma'am." He continued, "but your grandfather was in his eighties and he's had his health issues."

"Really? Was he in poor health?" Faith looked at him.

"Nothing major, but I understand he was taking various medications. We drove him to his doctor appointments, and he's had appointments more frequently in the last few years."

Faith looked at the Watergate as they took the ramp down from Whitehurst Freeway. "Do you know of anyone in particular who might have argued with him recently, or had an axe to grind?"

"No, ma'am. He was a nice man who lived quietly these past few years."

***

When Faith returned to the house she went to the kitchen to find another cup of coffee. While there, Mrs. Lucie filled her in on how the household functioned.

She explained how to reach any of the household staff on the house phone. There were buttons for Housekeeping, Chef, Assistant, Legal and Security. If Faith needed anything for the house, including any personal items, if she noticed anything that needed attention of any kind, if she wanted any particular food for breakfast, lunch or snacks, if any of her family became ill, or if she needed help with her children, she should call Housekeeping. Mrs. Lucie or Mrs. Loper would pick up all of those calls. Effectively, Mrs. Lucie and Mrs. Loper were like house mothers, freeing Faith up to do – *what?*

If Faith had any special requests for dinner she should call Chef. She assured Faith that chef would be happy to make two meals, one for the kids and one for Faith and her husband, but Faith rejected that idea. "We try to eat as a family. So let's see how it goes with just one dinner." Mrs. Lucie appeared to approve of that.

Each Monday, the chef always provided her grandfather with a menu for the week. Mr. Blithe would mark it up and hand it back. Mrs. Lucie would have chef do that for her, too, starting on Monday.

The housekeeper peppered Faith with questions about her family's likes and dislikes. The house would be stocked with all of their favorite things. Faith was asked her preferences on laundry care. She was also told that if there were repairs to be made, sundries to be bought or any questions, comments or concerns about the house, Mrs. Lucie and Mrs. Loper would coordinate it all from now on. They would also coordinate menus with the chef, direct all landscape and other maintenance, and oversee all cleaning. The chef would do the grocery shopping.

Mrs. Lucie also informed Faith that two ladies, Mrs. Clarke and Mrs. McComb, cleaned the house each day. From 11am to 2pm, these ladies buffed and polished every surface, made every bed, cleaned every bathroom, changed every dead light bulb, and did all of the laundry. Faith let it sink in for a moment that she might never again have to clean a toilet. *I think I could live with that.*

She glanced at the clock. It was 8:55am. Time to find Mrs. Abernathy's office.

Faith thanked Mrs. Lucie for the coffee and climbed the stairs to the first floor. She walked straight ahead to the rear left corner of the building. Looking left, toward the front of the house, she saw a door. Curious, she opened it.

There she found the tech/game room the boys had mentioned. They were not joking. The room had an entire wall dedicated to gaming systems. Stationed before the huge, flat panel screen were two long, comfortable couches, a long, slim coffee table and a few modern looking recliners. On one side of the TV, a packed shelving system held all of the gaming systems' accessories. The other held a gaming library so large it rivaled a retail store.

Another wall was dedicated to tech gadgets. Shelves held a large variety of e-readers, tablet computers, super thin laptops, digital cameras, smart phones and many other gadgets Faith had never seen before. Mrs. Abernathy was serious about her grandfather's interest in the latest technological advances.

Shaking her head in wonder, Faith closed the door and turned to the hallway that suspended over the courtyard. It was a beautiful day. The sun shined through the glass hallway. Faith could see the trees outside moving in the breeze.

The hallway led to a stairwell, probably to the garage. But to the right just before the stairwell was a small, tastefully appointed reception area. Two club chairs flanked an elegant coffee table. A handsome built-in wet bar had a small refrigerator and shelves beneath a counter that held a sleek, fully automatic espresso and cappuccino maker. The shelves above were stocked with fresh fruit, biscotti, different teas and sugars. The shelves below had cups, plates, flatware and napkins.

Faith stepped closer and saw the beautiful simplicity of the buttons on the coffee machine. *What's one more cup of coffee? I've only had three so far....* She looked left and right, took an elegant, bowl-like cup and placed it beneath the spout. She pressed 'Medium Cappuccino with Frothed Milk' and waited. Within one minute, she held a steaming, perfect cup of cappuccino. She sipped it and closed her eyes. *Delicious!*

"Oh, hello Mrs. Warrior." Faith jumped and almost sloshed her coffee on herself. Mrs. Abernathy stepped out of her office to meet Faith. She smiled as she saw Faith with her cup. "It's pretty amazing, isn't it?"

"It's insanely good. And no clean up, which somehow makes it taste even better." Faith smiled conspiratorially.

"Would you like to come in?" Mrs. Abernathy beckoned her to follow.

Mrs. Abernathy sat behind her desk and Faith sat in a club chair opposite her. "We've got quite a lot to discuss. However, you've had to deal with quite a lot in the last few days, so perhaps we should just talk about the more pressing things today."

"That would be good, thank you, Mrs. Abernathy. The first thing we might want to talk about is your future," Faith replied.

Mrs. Abernathy looked at her lap. "Yes, ma'am. The thought had crossed my mind that you'd want to bring in someone of your own."

"Let me assure you that I don't currently have a personal assistant. I'm a stay at home mom who only just started to explore the idea of returning to work." Faith smiled. "Mrs. Abernathy, I would be quite grateful if you would continue on as you are. I'm sure my grandfather thought quite well of you, given you've worked for him for so long."

The assistant's eyes clouded a bit. "Your grandfather was a very nice man. We worked well together. I would be happy to continue on as your assistant."

"Good, then that's settled." Faith smiled warmly. "Now,

what are the most pressing issues?"

For the next two hours, they discussed her grandfather's funeral arrangements, what to do with Faith's home in Arlington, and the phone messages Faith had already received. Many people had sent their condolences, including some major political figures and many people Faith had never heard of. This reminded Faith that she hadn't checked her email lately. There were probably tons of emails from her friends.

As they wrapped up, Mrs. Abernathy said, "Mrs. Warrior, there will be a special Board meeting on Monday." *One week after my grandfather's death – it feels a little inappropriate for it to be so soon.* "Would you like to attend?"

Her heart pounded a bit. *Ok, here it is.* "Yes, I suppose I should. And I'll bring my husband, too. Can you find out what the agenda is?"

"Yes, ma'am. And I will let the CEO's assistant know you and Mr. Warrior will be there."

Faith stood up and stretched. "I'll let you get back to things." As she walked to the office door she asked, "Where is my grandfather's home office?"

"It's just down that corridor." The woman pointed left. She motioned with her arm. "It's my office, then your grandfather's office, then Mr. Hopewell's office, then our assistant's office, then the security office." She looked back down at her papers. Clearly, the woman had a lot to do.

Faith wandered down the hallway and opened the first door. It was cheerful and surprisingly small. The desk was a heavy wood and looked antique. The leather wingback chair behind it looked very well used. Framed photos were artfully arranged on the walls, documenting a full life.

Directly in front of her, on her grandfather's desk, she found a framed photo of two young men standing with her grandfather and her grandmother. *Mick and Thomas!* Both of the young men were tall and handsome, but one looked like her grandfather and one had her grandmother's coloring. *Which was which?*

Her eyes darted around to make sure she was unobserved. She turned the frame over and unlatched the backing. There, penciled on the back of the photo, were the names positioned just as the people were in the photo, and the date. Her father was the one who looked like Fritz. She put the frame back together again and ran her fingertips over her father's face. She realized that she could see her father in her children's faces, and a lump formed in her throat. She put it down and looked at the other photos, smiling through her tears.

On one wall there was a built-in shelving unit that held photo albums, a collection of books and memorabilia. *I need to go through those albums.* She turned her attention to the windows behind her grandfather's chair. Faith stepped toward them and looked at the picture frames that were lined up on the windowsill. They were candid family photos. Fritz, Mick, Thomas, Elena – they all looked happy and beautiful.

She sat down in her grandfather's chair and let the air escape from her lungs. She imagined her grandfather sitting here in this chair, looking at the photos. She shook her head to keep herself from crying and stood up. That's when she looked out the window at the sight below.

The backyard was enclosed with a tall stone wall. A cute green wooden door that very much reminded her of the story *The Secret Garden* was embedded in the back wall, presumably leading to the alley behind. There was a beautiful glassed-in green house and a hoop house directly below her. To her left was another glassed building that appeared to have curtains or shades suspended along the top. It was connected to the rear left of the house. To the right was a decent-sized grassy area with a handsome shade tree and a bench below. As she watched, workmen were assembling a luxurious playhouse. She dashed out of the office and back to Mrs. Abernathy's desk.

"Why is a playhouse being constructed out back?"

The assistant looked up. "Oh, I'm sorry I neglected to mention it. Before Mr. Blithe went in to meet with Mr. Hopewell that last day, he asked me to arrange for one. He asked for the nicest one I could find that would safely fit the space. There's a prescribed fall zone that must be maintained, or it would have been larger. I hope you like it." She paused, as if unsure of whether to say more, "Mrs. Warrior, your grandfather was really looking forward to knowing your children. He made a few more requests that day. The house is about to be fully stocked with a very large amount of toys and a library of children's books. And in case you didn't see it, there's a zip line going up in the garden. He wanted to make it a children's paradise. He wanted it all to be a surprise."

Faith's throat became tight and she nodded. As she turned away her eyes filled with tears. She made it to the suspended hallway before she sagged against the wall, slid down and cried her eyes out.

***

The house was extremely quiet. Faith sat in her room and wrote a list of things that she needed to do. It included going through her grandfather's things -- both in his bedroom suite and his home office -- getting additional details from Mr. Hopewell about the foundation, and getting bios of all of the top executives at Blithe Industries. She picked up the house phone and called her assistant and attorney and placed her requests. Until she went through her grandfather's office, she felt more comfortable working upstairs in the sitting room, so she asked that they leave the documents on the table just inside the family suite.

Then, she opened her laptop to check her email. She wasn't surprised that she hadn't received any cell phone calls. All of her friends used email, text messaging and Facebook to communicate.

She logged on to Facebook and saw that the format had changed. Again. She grumbled as she tried to navigate around. *Frick. It's like going to a grocery store you've been to a hundred times, only allotting ten minutes since you know where everything is. But you get there and find they've moved everything. A sign may as well read 'feel free to leave your complaints in our complaint box' above a picture of a toilet.*

She had twelve direct messages from friends. Some were expressions of condolence. Some were expressions of surprise about the news. Her best friend, an old high school classmate named Anne O'Malley, had sent a message saying she imagined Faith felt heart broken, and that if she needed a shoulder to cry on, to call her. Anne knew her well enough to know that no matter how much time she'd spent with her grandfather, his loss would be enormous. Faith sent brief messages back to all of them and logged off. She had some very good friends. Especially Anne.

Her email box was jammed with a combination of spam, messages from reporters asking for interviews, and messages from strangers asking for money. She found it all very disturbing. She added 'change email address' and 'tighten online security' to her to-do list and logged off. She decided she'd ask Mrs. Abernathy how her grandfather handled his online security, email address, communication, etc.

Faith's stomach grumbled and she looked at the clock. 12:15pm. She took her cell phone and made her way to the lower dining room. There she found a lovely luncheon set out on the sideboard. She helped herself and sat down. A few minutes later, the doorbell rang.

She looked around, unsure of whether to dash up and answer it or let Mrs. Lucie do it. A moment later, the housekeeper entered the room. "The police are here, Mrs. Warrior." She looked concerned. "They'd like to speak with you."

"Thanks, Mrs. Lucie." Faith took a last bite, then went upstairs and through to the foyer, swallowing as she went.

Detective Harris and Special Agent Maxwell stood in the formal living room.

"Good afternoon, gentlemen." Faith approached and shook their hands. "Please, sit down."

After they sat, Detective Harris spoke up. "Mrs. Warrior, we wanted to personally convey to you the autopsy results."

Faith sat down. "How did my grandfather die?"

"Your grandfather died of natural causes. The medical examiner said your grandfather had advanced coronary heart disease. His heart showed signs of scarring, suggesting he's been grappling with this for years. His death could have happened at any time," Harris said.

"I see. Thank you for telling me."

Maxwell spoke. "We're very sorry for your loss, ma'am."

Faith nodded. The two men stood and walked to the door, then quietly left.

What Faith knew of coronary heart disease was limited, but she had heard of people dropping dead from it when hearing startling news. *Did I cause my grandfather's death? Roberts had said he was so happy that he was taking stairs two at a time! Oh dear God.* Faith sat and cried.

    ***

News traveled quickly, helped along by the press release the police issued to announce that the investigation was over.

Roberts came for Faith at 2pm to leave for the school. Another guard on the detail held her door as she soberly climbed into the minivan, a man named Sawyer. He climbed into the back rear seat and the minivan pulled out of the gates.

Traffic was bumper-to-bumper on the ramp up to Whitehurst Freeway. Faith was lost in thought when Roberts slammed on the brakes to avoid hitting the car in front of them, which had abruptly stopped and put on its turn signal. Great. Another lost tourist. She looked at the license plate. New Hampshire. The 'Live Free or Die' state. The bumper was littered with stickers lambasting the Democratic Party.

Live Free or Die. The backbone of the country. She thought back to 9/11. She had been living and working in Manhattan during that terrifying time. Thankfully, none of her friends had perished that day, but she had friends who had seen things no one should ever see. The event had had a colossal, lasting impact on her, despite having been in midtown when it happened.

She vividly remembered taking a bus to work the next day. She hadn't even bothered to try taking the subway. Even if it wasn't closed, she didn't want to go down there. The silence on the bus had been deafening. People had actually looked into each other's eyes, which *no one* does in New York City since it's typically taken as a sign of aggression. At one point, the driver had barked at a passenger and Faith had dissolved into tears, exiting the bus five blocks early.

The minivan turned into the school's parking lot and Faith led the men to the main entrance, where the principal's office was.

Ms. Monahan, the school secretary, greeted her. "I'm so sorry for your loss," she said as she left her desk to walk to the principal's door. The word was out at school.

"Thanks," Faith gave her a sad smile.

"Mrs. Warrior?" Mrs. Wilson was a very slim, well-dressed woman in her sixties with penetrating eyes that completely offset her smile. Faith mused that these seemed to be a classic school principal attributes. She gestured for Faith and the two men to sit in front of her desk.

"Thank you for giving us the time, Mrs. Wilson. As you know, I've discovered I'm Frederick Blithe's granddaughter. That fact, in and of itself, would be enough for me to worry more about my children's safety. But what you might not know yet is that I'm also his sole heir. This raises my anxiety level appreciably."

"I can understand how you feel, Mrs. Warrior, and I thank you for sharing the information with me. Heightened security risk of any single child in this school means heightened risk for all of them."

"Let me introduce two of the gentlemen on my grandfather's longstanding security detail, Mr. Roberts and Mr. Sawyer."

Mrs. Wilson nodded to the men. "What questions do you have?" For the next fifteen minutes, the men asked questions about entrances and exits to the school, fire drill procedure, how guests enter the school and how that access is controlled and how volunteers at the school are screened.

"Now I've got a question for you," she directed her gaze at the bodyguards. "Are you VIRTUS trained and certified?" Faith nodded her agreement that this was an important question to ask. She'd just completed her training the prior week.

"Ma'am? What is VIRTUS?"

"It's the background check and training process mandated by the Archdiocese to ensure the safety of any children you might come into contact with here at school," Faith said. "She's right. You need to go through it."

"Ma'am, we've gone through exhaustive FBI background checks. Your grandfather would not have hired us otherwise." Sawyer said plainly.

"While that is all well and good, it is not VIRTUS," the principal replied. She handed two thick packets to Faith. "Have them fill these out and schedule their training."

"Will do," Faith assured her. "Oh, but there are four on the detail. I'll need two more." She handed the four packets to Roberts who accepted them with a nod.

"We'll submit them tomorrow," he said.

Reassured that the boys were as safe as was practicable in any school, the three of them stepped outside and waited in the courtyard for dismissal.

A few of the other mothers Faith knew approached and offered condolences. Looking around at the congenial way the parents interacted and the smiling faces of the children as they exited the building, Faith was reminded of her first impression of the school. *This place feels good.*

It had been a surprisingly easy decision to choose this

Catholic school over public school, despite the public school system's outstanding reputation. It came down to practicality. If Faith went back to work, it would be far easier to have both boys in the same building. It was an added bonus that Faith wouldn't have to do CCD since the boys would get their religious education during school hours.

Another mom approached, baby in her arms and kindergartener in hand. "Faith, I'm so sorry about your grandfather. Please let me know if I can help in any way. Meals, or a play date, grocery shopping, whatever."

Faith was touched by the gesture and thanked her, then watched her walk away. The woman had been a corporate lawyer for a Fortune 500 company.

She looked around at the other mothers who were chatting happily with other mothers, relieving their children of their backpacks, setting up play dates. Accountant. Equity analyst. Lobbyist. Advertising executive. Publicist. All of these women had left the work force to focus on their children. She knew from talking to them that many of them, like her, wanted to get back to work but still wanted to be there after school. All of them were frustrated by the fact that high level jobs are rarely part time.

"Mommy!" Paul ran up and jumped into her arms. "Rub noses!" They rubbed noses while Roberts took Paul's backpack. Sawyer saw Graham approach and took his coat and backpack while Graham hugged Faith's waist.

Faith gave both boys big smacking kisses on their cheeks, took their hands and led them to the minivan in the parking lot. "Did you have a good day?" And so began the after-school data dump. *I wouldn't miss this for the world.*

***

Chris was home when they arrived. Or so they heard from the chef, who was bringing groceries into the house. "He's gone to the solarium."

Faith assumed the chef meant the greenhouse. Since she had wanted to see it and also check out the status of the jungle gym, she brought the boys around to the back of the garage.

The boys whooped with joy when they saw the play set being constructed in the rear garden. This was no ordinary swing set. It was a work of art.

A tree house had been constructed high up in the shade

tree. A rope ladder led up to it. Faith spotted a bucket on a pulley rope attached to one side – a nice old-school touch. A clatter bridge led from the tree house to a medieval-looking two-story structure that had a lookout tower on top and an enclosed fort below. A knotted climbing rope hung down one side. A spiral slide led off the back.

The lookout tower led to a rigid, arched bridge that, in turn, led to a similar lookout tower on the other side. This second tower was still under construction but Faith saw an enormous climbing wall and a zip line leading to a heavily padded pole about 30 feet away from the tower. A sandbox was housed in the base of the tower. Below the bridge were the swings.

The boys ran to the first tower and opened a small door at the bottom. Inside, they found a staircase leading to the lookout tower. A switch on the wall turned on lights in the tiny room, where they saw a little table and chairs. "A club house!" Graham yelled.

Roberts nodded to Faith to let her know he had the kids under his watchful eye.

Faith wandered to the greenhouse and looked for her husband. There she found orderly raised beds and a literal bounty of fruits and vegetables. At one end was a long potting table with supplies stocked on shelves below.

The raised beds outside of the greenhouse were also growing well. She spotted some pumpkins peeking from beneath large leaves. But she did not see her husband.

She looked beyond the greenhouse to the other glassed structure in the left rear corner of the property and she stood stock-still.

Her husband was running on a treadmill in a small, state of the art gym. She saw a punching bag, various multi-function weight machines, a shiny set of hand weights and a set of free weights with a bench, an elliptical machine, a stepper and a stretching area.

Next to the stretching area was a rack stocked with foam rollers, exercise bands and balls. Chris was watching a television monitor. A fan lazily swept back and forth in the corner.

A nearby table held a lovely flower arrangement, some glasses and a pitcher of iced water with lemon slices floating on top.

Sunlight glistened off of the water in a lap pool that stretched the length of one side of the long building. Nearby, a stack of fluffy white towels sat on a wooden bench. She also spotted a whirlpool and three doors. The first was a wooden door with a small glass window that she surmised was a sauna. Two more doors stood open. One was a full bathroom. The other contained a massage table, a hair dressers station and a manicurist's table.

No freaking way. This house is an oasis! She rubbed her eyes as if to clear the mirage. *Nope, this is for real.*

Faith opened the glass door and stepped inside the room. She was met by a blast of Foo Fighters. Chris looked at her as he pounded away on the treadmill and grinned. "Honey, there's a gym," he said between gasps.

He turned the treadmill off and walked over to her, giving her a kiss. "How was your day?"

"Ok, I guess. The police came by. They said my grandfather died of natural causes. The Medical Examiner confirmed it."

"That was fast. Well, I'm really glad that's been resolved. I know it really disturbed you that there was even a question of whether someone killed him."

She heard little feet gallop up behind her. "Mom! A swimming pool inside the house!" The boys shoved past her and ran to the pool. They ripped off their shoes and socks and dipped their feet in. "It's warm, Mom!" Graham shouted and, with a yelp, promptly fell in. He came up coughing and laughing. "Hey Mom, I can stand up!" The lap pool appeared to be about four feet deep, so Graham could stand on the tips of his toes and keep his face out of the water.

"Me too, me too!" Paul shouted, and jumped in fully clothed.

They all started laughing. Both boys swam like fish, but although Faith didn't need to, she kicked off her shoes and jumped in fully clothed along with them, soon followed by Chris.

Roberts, standing in the doorway, tried not to smile but couldn't help himself. He ducked out and returned to the security room.

Forty minutes later, the four of them tiptoed up the stairs, past the entrance to the office suite and across the suspended hallway to the main house. They had shed their wet clothes and wrapped themselves in towels. Faith carried their clothes in a separate towel.

Please don't let anyone see us, please don't let anyone see us...

"Mrs. Warrior, may I take those for you?" A middle-aged African American woman stood in their path, trying not to smile. "I'm Mrs. Loper," she added.

"Oh, uh, ha!" The others scurried up the stairs and out of sight. "Yes, thank you, Mrs. Loper. And, uh, how do you do?" She extended a damp hand and the other woman took it, smiling more deeply.

"Fine, thank you, ma'am. I wanted to let you know that your children's snack is ready. Shall I bring it up to your rooms?"

"That would be lovely, thank you. My older son needs to do his homework now, and a snack would be great."

Mrs. Loper nodded, "I've brought their backpacks upstairs. Perhaps later you can tell me more about Graham's school uniform, so I'll know what clothes to lay out for the children each evening for the next day."

Faith was dumbfounded, once again. "I've got a schedule I can show you. In fact, a Google calendar you can subscribe to. Wow, that would be incredible. Thank you."

"You're very welcome, ma'am, and we actually do use Google calendars in this household. We all have Gmail accounts." She added, "Dinner will be ready in the formal dining room at 6pm."

"Oh, there's no need for formality. Why don't we just have it in the downstairs dining room."

"I'll tell the chef," Mrs. Loper replied, turning towards the stairs with the wet clothes, a smile still on her face.

Faith looked down and saw a puddle of water on the slate floor at her feet. She tried to take an edge of her towel to dry it, lost her balance and fell on the floor. As she pulled her towel back on, she looked up and remembered the video cameras. *Frickety frick.*

***

Dinner was over and the kids were asleep. Faith and Chris stretched out on a bed in their room and looked at the papers.

"So your grandfather and your father disagreed on

environmental issues, yet your grandfather planned to leave it all to environmental causes?" Chris scratched his head.

"Strange, isn't it? Maybe it was his way of making amends."

They looked at the list of prospective recipients that her grandfather had worked up in conjunction with his foundation's board. The list of organizations touched on every major environmental hot topic -- clean air, clean water, clean energy, organic foods, and environmental education. He had earmarked funds for private companies, universities and foundations that focused on environmental issues. Faith had never heard of many of the companies.

"It seems a shame that all of these will lose out on funding because of you." Her husband spoke what was on her mind.

She nodded slowly. "Maybe that doesn't entirely have to happen." She turned to him. "When I think about my grandfather and my father, I think of two men who were very passionate about different things. From what I understand, my grandfather was passionate about his company – about carrying on a legacy and about taking care of his employees. He took the responsibility very seriously, and he took pride in it.

"My father was passionate about saving the environment – despite the decision he made to join Fritz at Blithe Industries. What if I find a way to blend these – find a way to bring the two of them together, as a way of honoring both of them? That would be a worthwhile endeavor, don't you think?"

Chris looked deeply into her eyes and took her hand. "I love you, you know?"

Faith smiled, "I know. I love you, too."

Chris' eyes darkened as he stroked his fingers down her cheek. He pulled Faith into his arms and kissed her deeply. The papers were shoved on to the floor.

Missing Letters

Chapter 5

Faith's alarm sounded at 6 a.m., as usual. She slapped it around twice, knowing she wouldn't have to make breakfast, then got up and showered. As she was leaving the bathroom, she heard a soft tap at her door. She made sure her bathrobe was secure, then opened the door.

Mrs. Lucie held a tray with a carafe of coffee, two cups, the Wall Street Journal and the Washington Post. "I thought you might like a cup before you come down," she said.

"You are a goddess, Mrs. Lucie," Faith smiled at her. The housekeeper looked embarrassed and pleased at the same time. She turned and left.

Faith sat down on the couch and clicked on the TV to Morning Joe. She loved hearing the political commentary each morning, especially because she was once again in DC, the heart of politics. She didn't think of herself as a political person, but she had strong views on certain things and enjoyed hearing good-natured, clever debate.

She prepared a cup of coffee and brought it to her husband, rubbing his back. "Time to get up, sleepy head. I have coffee!"

One eye immediately opened and he rolled over to reach for it. "Agrghblch," he said sleepily.

"My sentiments exactly," she smiled. Faith picked up a paper and did a sweep. She scanned the front-page headlines, and then flipped through, section-by-section, scanning headlines. She'd go back later to read whatever articles caught her eye. This had been her approach when she was working, so she could prioritize her time. She thought it was funny how she found herself slipping back into the old habits.

"I've got a lot to do today, mainly going through my

grandfather's office and personal rooms. I need to figure things out. What are you up to today?"

Her husband sat down next to her, cup in hand, and ran a hand through his hair. "I've got a few meetings, but my afternoon is open. Did you say you wanted me to look at a list of your grandfather's tech investments? I could start doing that this afternoon."

"That would be great. I have no idea what most of those companies do."

"I also need to call my parents and fill them in on all of this." He waved his arm around at the house.

"Living here will certainly make hosting Thanksgiving a bit more comfortable, don't you think?" She gave him a big smile, thinking of their blended family all together.

"Ha! With my three brothers, all of their wives and kids, my parents, your mom and whichever of your family comes to town – yes, I'd say so." He smiled and sipped his coffee.

"So we're staying?" She asked him.

"Yes, we're staying."

"The wake is tonight. I'm thinking of asking my mom to babysit while we go."

"You're ready to forgive her?"

Faith frowned. "Not yet. But I will. And the kids haven't seen her in a while."

"It's really good of you to think of her in the middle of all of this."

"It's hard NOT to think of her in the middle of all of this." She glanced at the clock. "Time to get the boys up."

Faith crept into the boys' room and began to sing. Softly at first, then louder, to the 'Good Morning!' tune from the movie, *Singing in the Rain*:

"Good morning, good morning!
It's time to start out the day,
Good morning, good morning, to you!
It's time for little babies to get out of bed,
They'll have their diapers changed and then they will be fed!
Good morning, good morning!
It's time to start out the day,
Good morning, good morning, to you!"

Faith sang the same song every morning when she woke

up the boys. She'd made it up when Graham was a baby. As she sang she moved around the room raising the shade, turning off the white noise machine, turning on a lamp, then finally, giving kisses and pulling back covers. She ended the song doing fake tap dancing with her arms spread out, reaching for the sky.

"I'm not a baby!" Paul complained. Faith smiled. He might not like the song anymore, but it did get him out of bed in the morning!

"Do you know what day it is today, boys?"

Graham sat up in bed and rubbed his eyes. "The worst day of my life?"

"Why would it be the worst day of your life, Grump Grouch?" Faith asked, hands on hips.

"Because I have to go to school," he grumbled.

"Well, then I know you'll love to hear that it's Friday. Also known as THE DAY BEFORE THE WEEKEND." She said with big eyes and a flourish.

"Yay!" Paul cried, "I'm going to stay in my pajamas all weekend and play Mario Cart Wii!" He turned to his brother. "And YOU can't stop me!"

"Well, I know you can't do that, but we will have a lot of play time. Now let's get dressed and see what Mrs. Lucie has for breakfast."

The two boys chattered away about pancakes and swimming with all of their clothes on while Faith and Chris dressed them, got their teeth brushed and combed their hair. Then all four of them went down to breakfast.

At breakfast, Paul changed his mind midway through his pancakes and demanded toast with cream cheese. "Paul," Faith said. "You chose the pancakes and we are not going to waste them. Eat the pancakes or excuse yourself from the table."

"Yeah," Graham chimed in. "Don't be so PD, baby pants."

"I am not a baby!" Paul was poised to blow a gasket.

"What is PD?" asked Mrs. Lucie, who was putting their lunch bags in their backpacks.

Graham explained, "Poopy Diaper. It means he's acting like a stink bomb."

Faith raised her eyebrows and acknowledged Graham's words as truth.

Chris laughed and said to Faith. "Did I tell you I used PD in a meeting at work? Totally confounded everyone."

"Time to go, boys," Faith chuckled, looking down at the clock. "Let's move out." She said goodbye to her husband, marched the boys down the hall to the bathroom, then out to the waiting minivan.

"Mom, when are we going home?" Paul asked as she strapped him into his car seat.

"Paul, your Dad and I have decided we're going to stay here."

"What about our toys? Our books?" Graham asked with concern.

"We'll bring them all here."

"But why can't we go home?" Graham asked.

Faith decided it would be too much for them to understand about security, so instead she said. "Your great-grandfather wanted you to have this home. You never met him, but he loved you very much. This house is where my father – your grandfather – lived when he was a boy. It's our home now."

"The video game room, too?" Graham had a mischievous look.

"Yes, honey, that too." Faith smiled.

"The big room where we do our running, too?" Paul asked.

"Yes, honey, that too."

"I think I can live with that," Graham said with a smile.
***

"Mrs. Warrior," Mrs. Abernathy said. "May I introduce you to Miriam Webber, your grandfather's corporate assistant. Ms. Webber has worked for your grandfather for ten years. Even after he stopped going to work regularly, she remained his eyes and ears and supported any of his informational requests."

It was mid-morning. Faith had been going through her grandfather's things in his home office when Mrs. Abernathy had mentioned Ms. Webber was there. She had come to pick up some documents. Mrs. Abernathy suggested it might be a good, impromptu chance for the two women to meet. Faith jumped at the chance and sat her down at the small conference table in her grandfather's office. Mrs. Abernathy rang Mrs.

Lucie for tea.

Ms. Webber was an athletic-looking blonde in her mid-forties with a wonderful smile that reached her eyes. The divorced mother of a six-year old girl, she was overqualified for the job of assistant by virtue of her Ivy League MBA and prior job experience. She explained that she had taken the job because Mr. Blithe offered flexibility. She worked from home two days a week, which allowed her to be more involved with her daughter's school and her extracurricular activities.

It was clear, through their discussion, that Fritz Blithe was well loved by those who worked for him. He saw value and opportunity where others saw inconvenience.

Faith asked Ms. Webber to give her a rundown of the occupants of Blithe Building and the characters she might meet at the Board Meeting.

"Blithe Building houses all of the parent company's staff." Ms. Webber said, as she made a rough sketch of an organizational chart. "This includes senior executives such as the CEO, CFO and COO, all centralized functions such as Human Resources, Accounting, Taxation, Government Relations, Information Technology, Sourcing, Advertising and Corporate Development. All of the department heads report up through the senior executives. So do the operating companies' CEOs, though each subsidiary company's CEO resides at each subsidiary's headquarters. The operating companies are spread out across the country."

"Tell me more about the CEO."

"Gregory Von Heiden. He's been with Blithe about fifteen years, I think. He came in through a large tobacco acquisition – he was CEO of the acquired company. He rose through the ranks. He shared many of your grandfather's interests. When your grandfather decided to step down as CEO a few years ago, Greg was promoted."

"What's he like to work with?"

Ms. Webber looked uncomfortable.

"Come on, give it to me straight," Faith said encouragingly.

"He's a very smart man but he can be prickly. People… tread carefully around him."

"That surprises me. What I mean is, what little I know of my grandfather suggests he'd value someone more evenly

107

keeled."

"Well," she said with a small smile, "he wasn't so prickly with your grandfather."

"Hmm." Faith nodded. "Okay, what about the Board of Directors?"

"It is comprised of people selected by Mr. Blithe. Though Mr. Blithe's financial ownership stake has been diluted over the past few decades by his decision to include ownership shares as part of employee compensation, he always retained voting control and controlled the Board."

"This is not to say that these people had no voice," Ms. Webber emphasized. "In fact, they had a very strong voice because Mr. Blithe handpicked them. Mr. Blithe stocked the Board with huge talent, from exceptional financial minds to visionaries. The Board held increasing sway as Mr. Blithe gradually stepped back from the company, but Mr. Blithe has always drawn the line. There were certain things he would never consider doing, despite suggestions by the Board."

"What sorts of suggestions did he reject?" Faith was eager to gain some insight into her grandfather.

"I don't know for certain. I wasn't privy to those meetings. However, I'd heard rumors that some Board members urged him to divest certain businesses and your grandfather refused."

The assistant pulled out her laptop and flipped it open. She navigated to a document, plugged it into the printer beside her grandfather's desk and printed something. She handed the paper to Faith. "Here is a list of Board members and their bios."

Faith looked at the twelve names on the list. In addition to her grandfather and the CEO of the company, she saw a retired general, retired CEOs of two of the largest Fortune 500 companies, well-regarded academics in the fields of finance, accounting and organizational behavior, a hugely successful technology visionary, a retired investment banker, and a leveraged buyout legend cum philanthropist. The last name on the list took her by surprise. The man, Geoff Michaels, was described as Trustee of her grandfather's foundation and president of a Washington-based environmental think tank.

"One second, please." Faith turned to the laptop on her grandfather's desk, woke it up and Googled the man. She scanned a few paragraphs, which was enough to learn that Mr.

Michaels was considered a guru in the green-living world, an authority on clean water, clean energy, organics and conservation. His think tank was funded by an endowment — an endowment created by Frederick Blithe.

Faith looked at Miriam Webber. "I'm puzzled. Blithe Industries is in a number of environmentally unfriendly businesses. Yet it's got Geoff Michaels on the Board. How did that all come to pass?"

"Yes, it seems strange, doesn't it?" Ms. Webber nodded. "Your grandfather had me contact Mr. Michaels right when I first started working for him -- about ten years ago. Your grandfather spoke with him extensively over the course of several months, and then worked with him to set up the endowment for the think tank. Simultaneously, he added him to the Board. From what I've heard, he's provided good advice. Interestingly, though, from the very beginning, he never suggested Mr. Blithe divest those environmentally damaging businesses."

Because he already knew my grandfather wouldn't divest. But he agreed to get involved because he knew my grandfather would help in other ways -- perhaps after he was dead?

Faith exhaled sharply, then turned to Ms. Webber.

"I'd like a meeting with Mr. Michaels. Given the funeral is tomorrow and the Board Meeting is Monday, perhaps Tuesday?"

"Yes, of course." The assistant looked carefully at Faith. She appeared to be bursting with questions but knew better than to ask them this early.

"Ms. Webber, while I work out this Rubik's Cube that has become my life, I'd like you to continue on as my corporate assistant, just as you were for my grandfather. You'll be my eyes and ears at the corporation, help me out with any informational and coordination needs. Is that agreeable to you?"

"Mrs. Warrior, I'd like that very much." The two women shook hands. "Would you like some help with this?" she offered, gesturing to the stacks of papers and books Faith was going through.

Faith sighed and smiled gratefully. "That would be wonderful."

***

Faith and her assistant powered through the office. Corporate documents that Ms. Webber recognized as unimportant or duplicates of documents also found at the office were placed in a corner for shredding. Books were sorted, with most designated for donation. Personal memorabilia was boxed and stacked in another corner.

Faith asked Ms. Webber to have a member of corporate IT come to the house to evaluate her grandfather's Internet security and was told that her grandfather had one individual designated as his IT contact. This man visited Blithe House once a month to do IT maintenance, explain new gadgetry to her grandfather, and assist the security detail with any of their systems needs. The assistant placed a call to the man and arranged for him to come one afternoon the following week so that her entire family might benefit -- including the children, who clamored to play with everything in the media room.

***

After a quick luncheon shared with Ms. Webber, Faith finally went to her grandfather's rooms. Within the family suite, Faith walked down the right hand hallway. She arrived at the first door on the left, which she expected was another guest room. As she opened the door, a musty smell greeted her. Though the spacious room appeared to be regularly cleaned, she recognized it to be the room of a young man – possibly a member of the Brady Bunch. She smiled to herself.

Sports trophies and old photos lined bookcases alongside old textbooks. The printed brown floral wallpaper looked vintage early 1970s. It matched the bedspread, curtains, pillow shams and a small couch in an astonishing sign of commitment to the pattern. *Groovy!* A mustard yellow shag carpet picked up some mustard in the wallpaper and matched some throw pillows. A peace sign hung above a well-used desk. A Green Peace poster hung alongside a framed announcement about the very first Earth Day.

Faith looked closer at the photos and saw her father's smiling, young, handsome face. Some were sports shots. Others were family photos with her grandparents and her uncle. They all looked exquisitely happy.

Once the shock of the décor wore off, new shock set in that her grandfather had preserved her father's room after he died. She gently closed the door and proceeded on to her grandfather's room.

Unlike her father's room, the master suite had clearly been updated over time. Once inside the main door, Faith found another hallway. The first door revealed a sitting room with a comfortable couch, a flat screen TV and a lovely mahogany secretary with matching chair. A bookcase held what she guessed were her grandfather's favorite books. A fine oil painting hung over the couch.

Faith looked at old photos that hung along the hallway, carefully matted and framed to match the décor. She spotted her grandparents' wedding photo. Her father had looked so much like her grandfather as a young man.

Further down the hall, Faith opened the door to the master bedroom itself. On the left side, Faith saw a door to the master bathroom. This sumptuous room had marble floors and counters, Jacuzzi tub and shower room, double sink and separate commode room. Sunlight spilled in through a window above the tub. A door in the bathroom led to a huge walk-in closet. The master bedroom itself was flooded with sunlight. Decorated in neutral tones with punches of cranberry red, it housed a beautiful, mahogany king-sized sleigh bed and matching bedside tables. The view from the corner windows was breathtaking – a vista of downtown Washington, and just below, the courtyard, office suite/garages and back garden. A flat panel TV hung on the wall opposite the bed. The room couldn't have been more comfortable.

Her cell phone rang as she gazed out the window. She looked at the number and saw it was Mrs. Abernathy.

"Hi Mrs. Abernathy."

"Mrs. Warrior, the movers confirmed that all of your belongings are packed and on the truck. As we discussed, the furniture will go into your Grandfather's storage facility but everything else will come to Blithe House. Would you like them to bring it all by today or should they come another day?"

Faith's head was spinning. She exhaled. She'd been through many moves and they'd all been a huge pain in the neck. "Can they bring it today and put it somewhere where I can go through it – maybe the ballroom?"

"Yes, ma'am, but they will also stay and unpack. All you need do is tell them where things should go and they'll take

care of it. Also, if there is something you would like to put in storage after all, they'll take care of moving it to storage."
Having someone else unpack from a move sounded heavenly.

"Thank you, that would be great."

"Very good. They'll be at Blithe house in thirty minutes." Mrs. Abernathy hung up.

Whoa! She needed to act quickly if she was going to surprise her family.

***

The moving van arrived and TEN tidily uniformed men began moving things into the house. One burly man stepped forward, announced himself as the foreman and went on to explain the procedure. They would bring everything in to the ballroom, and then things would be distributed from there.

The men moved quickly. As boxes were delivered to the ballroom, they were carefully grouped. Faith was astonished to see how the men had packed their things. Each room from her house had been packed up as a collection and was brought to the ballroom that way. This made the identification of what went where exceedingly easy.

Mrs. Abernathy arrived. "Mrs. Warrior, would you like to move into your grandfather's suite now?"

"I... don't know," she said, closing her eyes with a pained look on her face. "This is all happening so quickly."

"Do you plan to stay here in the house?"

"Yes, Chris and I decided we'll stay. It's just... my head is kind of spinning with all of this."

"I understand, ma'am. But... may I speak frankly?"

"Yes, of course." Faith nodded.

"I'm sure by now you've seen your grandfather's bedroom," the assistant said seriously. "I know he would have wanted you to make yourself at home in this house. All of it. And, you should not feel the need to arrange things the way your grandfather did. This is your house now, no one else's. You are not disrespecting him by moving in. You are doing what he would have wanted you to do."

Faith bit her lip and looked around.

"How about this. Why don't I ask the men to move your grandfather's things down here? That way you can properly move your family in upstairs and you will still be able to go through his things at your leisure."

"Okay, Mrs. Abernathy." Faith had mixed emotions but saw the logic in what Mrs. Abernathy said.

Mrs. Abernathy nodded and took three of the men to her grandfather's rooms. Within an hour, her grandfather's things, including his mattress and box spring, were in the corner of the ballroom and Faith's family's things were heading upstairs. It didn't feel entirely right to Faith to move into her grandfather's rooms, but she knew her children would adjust faster if their own bedrooms were set up right, and if they saw that their parents were settled in, too. It was the best decision for her kids.

Their kitchen items and linens were sent downstairs for Mrs. Lucie and Mrs. Loper to sort and put away.

Office things were sent to her grandfather's home office.

Toys were left in the ballroom for now. Faith agreed with Mrs. Abernathy's suggestion that her father's early 1970s bedroom be redecorated as a playroom/library for the boys. The assistant would handle that the next week with guidance from Faith. She'd only asked for Faith's thoughts on a color scheme (celadon green or pale yellow and white) and if she had a preference on prints (stripes, gingham, toile). Faith wanted it to be cheerful and crisp.

At 2:30pm, Faith left to pick up the children. When they returned at 3:30pm, the movers were gone. She left the boys with Mrs. Loper for snack and went upstairs to see what had happened in her absence.

Faith could not believe her eyes. The bedroom the boys had shared had been transformed into a space just for Paul. All of his artwork and photos were hanging on the walls, grouped in the same manner they had been at the Arlington house. Bookcases held his books, his clothes were neatly arranged in his closet and drawers. His toys were arranged in precisely the same way they were in the old house. *They must have taken pictures before they packed up!* One of the queen-sized beds had been removed and the desk put in its place. His toy chest was in the sitting area.

The room Faith and Chris had occupied was now Graham's room, with his things arranged similarly well. The attention to detail was astonishing. Her boys were going to love it!

She walked down the hall and found that her father's

room was empty of everything but the 1970s wallpaper. Her grandfather's room had been transformed into a space just for Chris and Faith. Fresh flowers were arranged on a glossy table in the bedroom. The bed was dressed in their linens.

Down in the ballroom, Faith saw her father's things carefully boxed and labeled. Beside them were her grandfather's things. Faith blinked away tears and went back down to see her boys.

***

"You did a great job, Faith." Chris looked around the boys' rooms. The boys were riding their bikes in the ballroom. Faith could hear them honking their bikes' squeezable, rubber horns.

"I didn't do anything. Mrs. Abernathy and the movers did. It's just astonishing, isn't it, that they could do it so well, so quickly." Faith shook her head slowly.

"Well, you directed things well." Chris pulled Faith into his arms and kissed her. "Anything else happen today?" It always amazed Faith how her pulse so easily quickened around her husband, even after so many years. She smiled and kissed him back.

"I learned a bit about the executives and the Board. I also came across something very interesting. The Trustee of the foundation that would have inherited everything is on the Board of Blithe Industries. He's a very green guy."

"But your grandfather wasn't really in the green space, was he?"

"Nope. I really want to talk to this guy, figure out what was going through my grandfather's head."

Faith's cell phone rang. She pulled it from her pocket and looked at the caller id. "It's Anne. Let me get this." Chris let her go and went down the hall to change out of his work clothes.

"Anne? How are you?" Faith was pleased to hear from her old friend.

"Forget how I am! How are *you*?" Faith closed her eyes and allowed herself to acknowledge the enormous stress and sadness the last few days had brought.

"I've been better," she said. "I'm glad to hear your voice. It's been absolutely nutty."

"I'm really sorry to hear about your grandfather. It must

feel surreal to have met him and lost him all in one day. I know how you'd always wanted to know your father's side of the family. I'm sending a hug through the phone line," Anne said supportively.

"Thanks, sweetie. The vigil is tonight and the funeral is tomorrow. Meanwhile, we had to move to his house because of the media attention. I'm amazed how well the kids are handling all of this."

"It's testament to how well you've raised them. They're happy, confident little guys, which makes them especially resilient."

"You're very nice to say that. So, what's up with you?" Faith changed the subject to get the conversation onto a more upbeat path.

"Well, I broke up with Jeremy," Anne said stoically.

"Really, truly broke up, or just taking a break? Your answer has bearing on what I may say next," Faith said wryly.

"Really and truly, I'm afraid," Anne said wistfully. "I realized I kept going back to him because I didn't have time to find anyone else. That's not a good reason to keep dating someone. I hope we can remain friends, but probably not."

"Wow, you just said exactly what I was going to say!" Faith exclaimed.

Anne laughed. "Well, it helps that I usually ask myself 'what would Faith do?' whenever I'm in tough situations. Only the last few times I asked the question, I wasn't really ready to hear the answer."

"Okay, so what are you going to do to change the situation -- i.e., the lack of opportunity to meet men?"

"I've got no idea." She sighed.

"Your main problem is that you're stuck in Podunk USA. You need to get back to a town where people don't typically marry their high school sweethearts. Really, any city with more than 200 people would be great."

"Very funny."

"Actually, I'm not kidding. You need to get out of there. Why not move home?"

"I'd say, 'where do I sign up'? But there aren't too many venture capital positions in the DC area."

"Hmm. Let me see what I can dig up," Faith said thoughtfully. "Any chance you're coming home for a visit sometime soon? Or maybe a long weekend?"

"Is this your way of asking me to come for the funeral? I never met the man, but you know I'll come to support you whenever you want."

"You're very sweet. No, I'll be okay. But I would like to see you. What about next weekend?" Faith asked hopefully.

"Yup, I could do that. I need to see my parents, anyway. So I'll call you when I get in on Saturday morning?"

"Sounds good. Mwah!"

"Mwah!" And they hung up.

Chris walked in. "What's your overachiever friend up to?"

Faith laughed. Anne was definitely that. "I got her to agree to come to town next weekend. It'll be good to see her. Plus, I've got something percolating in this mind of mine." She tapped her temple with a devious expression.

"Oh, and what, pray tell, is bubbling away in there?"

"Remember my telling you years ago that over the course of my life I've kept a mental list of people I'd like to have by my side - my 'perfect world' list? Hugely capable people who make life better, happier, more interesting, people whom I'd love to be around each day?" Faith started pacing.

"Mm-hmm." Chris sat down and propped his feet on the toy chest. "Prompted me to do the same. What about it?"

"Well, I now find myself in a position to actually deploy that list." Faith's eyes flashed with excitement. "And the first person I want to bring onboard is Anne."

Chris's smile grew wider. "Think there's room on that ship for a few of mine?"

"Absolutely." Faith grinned at her husband.

***

Faith's mother, Vivian, had been overjoyed to be asked to put the boys to bed so Faith and Chris could attend the vigil that evening. When she arrived at six o'clock, the boys had been bathed and fed, and were running around excitedly in their pajamas. Faith gave her mother a sad smile and stepped back to let her into the house. She clutched her daughter's shoulder as she stepped in, but didn't push for a hug. Faith was still upset, and her mother knew it.

She looked around and sighed. "It looks so much like it used to. I guess Fritz didn't change much after Mick died. Such a huge house – do you feel settled in yet?" She asked

Faith.

"It's been an adjustment, and I can't say that it feels like home yet, but we're getting there." She showed her around, reminded her mother of the kids' nighttime routine, then left them to play so she could get dressed.

At seven o'clock, the limousine pulled up in front of the funeral home. Faith and Chris joined a steady stream of people heading in.

George Hopewell stood just inside the door and directed her into the room where the vigil was held. It was crowded but quiet. People filed by the casket, whispering quiet prayers. Fritz was dressed in a formal, black robe emblazoned with a large, distinctive white cross. He rested atop a simple white cloth that also draped over the sides of the casket, concealing it. The effect was dramatic.

Faith and Chris joined the queue. As she approached her grandfather, she looked down at his peaceful face, his unruly, thick white hair, his hands. She saw his signet ring and remembered the talk they'd had. She absorbed the sight of his face.

A large number of people sat together. An elderly, well-dressed man led them in the rosary. She noticed most of them wore a particular pin on their lapel – a white cross on a red background. The cross was eight-pointed and had the form of four "V"-shaped elements joined together at their tips, so that each arm had two points. It was the same shape as the cross on her grandfather's robe. She quietly asked Mr. Hopewell about it.

"Those men and women are Knights and Dames of the Sovereign Order of Malta, and that is the Maltese Cross," he said. He glanced down at his pocket square and straightened it, revealing his own pin.

Faith seemed to remember hearing this name before but couldn't quite place it. Mr. Hopewell continued, "The Sovereign Order of Malta is a Catholic lay religious order your grandfather joined many decades ago. He encouraged me to join, too. It's the modern form of the Order of St. John of Jerusalem – the monastic community that ran the hospital for the pilgrims in the Holy Land starting back in about 1050. Their mission is defense of the faith and assistance to the suffering.

"Your grandfather was very involved in it. In fact, he poured his heart into it, volunteering his time and money. For as long as I've known him, he also took annual pilgrimages with the Order to Lourdes, in southern France, bringing critically ill people to the healing waters there."

Faith looked at the men and women with the pins, their heads bowed. She wondered if she would ever understand her grandfather's many facets, and felt a fresh wave of sorrow.

"Would you like to meet them?" he asked.

She swallowed hard and gripped Chris's hand. "I certainly would."

The funeral director entered the room at that moment, greeted Faith and Chris, and then went to the podium alongside the casket.

"Ladies and gentlemen. The microphone is now open for those who wish to say a few words." A young Dominican friar immediately stood, grasping a book. He moved to the front of the room.

He seemed shy and was clearly nervous to speak, but he admirably pushed past it. "Fritz Blithe greatly admired Pope John Paul II. When I graduated from seminary, he gave me this book. It's a collection of his quotations over the course of time. When I read it, I found he'd highlighted several passages. It was… a glimpse into Mr. Blithe's heart. I'd like to read a few of them to you tonight, that you may share that glimpse…."

For the next three hours, Faith listened to story after story of Fritz's thoughtfulness and generosity. He was clearly a contemplative man, as evidenced by several readings people made from a few of his other favorite authors. These people stepped forward, each holding a book Fritz had given them, each reading passages he'd highlighted.

The last speaker of the evening was George Hopewell. "Fritz Blithe and I did not often talk of our personal lives. He was, after all, my employer. But he knew I was also Catholic and therefore felt the freedom to talk about faith, and it was through his encouragement that I also joined the Knights of Malta. And when he learned that my wife's cancer was terminal, we prayed together. Right there in his office, we got down on our knees and prayed.

"After her passing, he gave me this book." He held up an old, worn book for the crowd to see. "It is *A Grief Observed*, by

N.W. Clerk. I later learned that N.W. Clerk was a pseudonym for C.S. Lewis. In it, I found several passages highlighted, and I'd like to read this one to you:

"You never know how much you really believe anything until its truth or falsehood becomes a matter of life and death to you. It is easy to say you believe a rope to be strong and sound as long as you are merely using it to cord a box. But suppose you had to hang by that rope over a precipice. Wouldn't you then first discover how much you really trusted it?...Only a real risk tests the reality of a belief."

"He hadn't pointed out the passage to me. He'd given me the book and told me it had helped him through the deaths in his family. Only later did I come to appreciate that he'd highlighted these passages for his own benefit. Not mine. This had actually been his copy from his own library, not one he purchased for me. And as our Dominican friend said earlier, it was a glimpse into his heart. I will always treasure this gift he gave to me."

Later, Chris and Faith sat quietly in the limousine, the street lights rhythmically illuminating their faces through the windows as they returned to Blithe House.

"He was an amazing man, Faith. All of those stories we heard, all of those tributes. You should be very proud."

"I am," she said, choking up, "I really am." She closed her eyes and a tear rolled down her cheek. "I hadn't realized what a spiritual man he was. It's amazing to me, given all he went through, that he emerged with such strong faith. He really was an astonishing example for the rest of us."

Chris pulled her close and put her head on his shoulder.

Chapter 6

The funeral was held at eleven o'clock in the morning.
Given the crowd expected, it was held in the Upper Church at
The Basilica of the National Shrine of the Immaculate
Conception, in northeast Washington, rather than at her
grandfather's home parish.

Faith knew that the National Shrine was the largest Roman
Catholic church in the United States and North America, and
one of the ten largest churches in the world, but she'd never
been there before. 'America's Catholic Church', as some called
it, was Byzantine-Romanesque in style and housed over 70
chapels and oratories. Everywhere Faith looked she saw
beautiful mosaics, arches, domes, marble work, stained glass. It
flooded her senses.

Faith and Chris accepted service programs from a priest
and walked up the center aisle clutching their boys' hands. It
was very quiet, save an occasional cough, the rustle of paper,
the movement of a kneeler.

Hundreds of people were already there. Clutches of clergy
were visible among the crowd: nuns from various orders,
including the Missionaries of Charity; monks from different
orders; priests; and a huge section of Knights and Dames of
the Order of Malta dressed elegantly in their long black robes
emblazoned with large, white crosses; Cardinals and Bishops.
Political figures mixed with socialites and captains of industry.
She felt self-conscious as she passed so many people looking
at her with sympathy and interest.

A massive profusion of yellow and pink frangipani
completely obscured the casket displayed at the top of the
aisle.

Paul tugged at his necktie as they stepped into the front

pew. An astonishingly lovely and elegantly attired blond-haired woman was already sitting there. She glanced up as they sat down.

"You must be Faith," she whispered and put out a delicate hand. She gave her a sorrowful look. "I'm Cassandra." Looking puzzled, Faith shook her hand, so Cassandra elaborated. "Your late uncle Thomas' wife."

Faith closed her eyes a moment, then opened them and nodded, "of course," she whispered, "I hadn't realized he'd been married. He was quite young when... It's very nice to meet you. I wish we'd met under better circumstances."

"So do I," she said. Just then, a small orchestra and choir began Mozart's 'Ave Verum Corpusa'. They sat down. The music swelled and lulled, drawing Faith's emotions along with it. She fought back her tears.

She heard the sound of people standing and reflexively stood in response. Faith turned to see the opening procession. It included four altar servers, the Reverend Monsignor who was Rector of the Basilica, five other priests in a variety of formal garb, and lastly, the retired Most Reverend John Cardinal Mayse. The Cardinal, listed in the program as an old friend of her grandfather's, sprinkled holy water on the guests as he walked the aisle to the altar. He sprinkled holy water on the casket, then handed the aspergillum to an alter boy and stood beside the Rector, who was principal celebrant and homilist for the Mass.

The Rector gave his greeting to the congregation, then stepped back to allow four pallbearers, all wearing the long, formal robes of the Knights of Malta, to remove the flowers from the casket.

There was an audible intake of breath at what was revealed beneath: a shockingly simple unfinished pine box. The only adornments were the handles on the sides, and a Maltese cross branded on the top.

Frederick McWallace Blithe, billionaire, would be laid to rest in the most humble of ways.

After the flowers were placed around the altar, the Reverend Monsignor blessed the body, then beckoned Faith to step forward and assist in draping the pall, a large white cloth, over the casket. The stark, white pall, Faith recalled, was symbolic of baptism. It also symbolizes equality. We all stand on equal footing before God's judgment. With shaking hands, Faith smoothed the fabric of wrinkles, and then sat down again.

A short, stout soprano with a shock of red hair stepped forward. Accompanied by the orchestra, she sang a heartbreaking rendition of 'Ave Maria', with a slight Irish lilt. Chris wrapped his arm around Faith's shoulders and handed her a tissue. Graham took her other hand. Paul drove a small car across the kneeler.

A white-haired old man with a rather large scar on his left cheek stepped forward to give the first reading, from the Old Testament, Wisdom 3:1-6,9. The program indicated his name was Richard Whitman. Beside his name was the simple word, 'friend'. His voice shook a bit. Whether from old age or from emotion, it affected Faith tremendously.

"The souls of the just are in the hand of God,
and no torment shall touch them.
They seemed, in the view of the foolish, to be dead;
and their passing away was thought an affliction
and their going forth from us, utter destruction.
But they are in peace.
For if in the eyes of men, indeed they be punished,
yet is their hope full of immortality;
Chastised a little, they shall be greatly blessed,
because God tried them
and found them worthy of himself.
As gold in the furnace, he proved them,
and as sacrificial offerings he took them to himself.
Those who trust in him shall understand truth,
and the faithful shall abide with him in love;
Because grace and mercy are with his holy ones,
and his care is with his elect.
The word of the Lord"

Faith hung her head and looked at her hand clasped in her husband's strong grip. She was reminded of something her own parish priest had once said – that funerals are not performed to comfort the living. They are opportunities to celebrate their loved one's life and pray for their recently departed soul. Comforting the living too much on their loss quickens the grieving process, depriving the dead of the prayers that could save their souls. We can only hope our loved one is in heaven. We can't know for certain, so we must pray for them.

Mr. Whitman finished and the Psalm Response was sung. *The Lord is my shepherd, nothing shall I want; in verdant pastures he gives me repose…*

As it came to an end, an old woman in an elegant black suit stepped forward to the podium. Faith glanced at the program and saw the name Tuppence Rivera. She had no idea who she was, so she looked at Cassandra expectantly. Cassandra mouthed *'friend of Elena's'* and Faith nodded in understanding.

The second reading, from the New Testament, was from the First Letter of St. Paul to the Corinthians (1 Corinthians 15: 20-28). The woman read the passage clearly and with care.

Faith watched her walk back to her seat and sit beside a very handsome elderly man. He lovingly took her hand in his. She saw the wedding ring and concluded this was Tuppence's husband.

Cardinal Mayse read the Gospel, John 12:23-28 – the story Jesus tells about the grain of wheat that falls to the ground and dies, only to produce much fruit. Then the Rector stepped forward to give a homily on that theme and did a wonderful job explaining the multiple lessons one could learn from that passage. Homilies were not always so relevant and compelling. Faith was impressed.

Mr. Hopewell stood and led the guests through General Intercessions, then the Cardinal assisted the Rector through the Liturgy of the Eucharist.

The soprano began to slowly sing 'Make Me A Channel of Your Peace', accompanied simply yet devastatingly by a single guitar. Chris, Faith and the boys stepped forward to accept the Eucharist. The boys crossed their arms on their chests and received a blessing from the Cardinal before all four returned to their seats, knelt and bowed their heads in prayer.

After the Mass was concluded, Cardinal Mayse once again took the podium, this time, to do the eulogy.

He gripped the podium and breathed deeply. "Ladies and gentlemen. We gather here today to pray for the soul of Frederick McWallace Blithe. Friend, colleague, advisor, benefactor," the Cardinal looked directly at Faith and continued, "grandfather. I have known this man most of my life. Over sixty years. I can tell you that this is simultaneously the easiest and the most difficult eulogy I've given, and I've given a few. It's the easiest because he lived an exemplary life. It isn't hard to highlight his good qualities. It's the most difficult because it is very hard to eulogize one's lifelong best friend."

The Cardinal took the crowd through Fritz's life, his milestones, achievements, his family, his faith. He touched on their friendship, explaining that he had met Faith's grandfather on a spiritual retreat shortly after his graduation from the Pontifical North America College in Rome. Fritz had himself just graduated, but from Harvard Law. The two became the best of friends. There were many funny anecdotes, many examples of his kindness.

"Fritz Blithe was a generous man. Generous with his time, with his money, with encouragement, and with kind words. He was also a very private man. He made clear to me that he did not want me to enumerate the instances of his generosity. He was far too humble for that, as evidenced by his choice to be laid to rest in a simple pine box built by Trappist monks. Of course, I couldn't enumerate them if I tried. There are simply too many. Many of you here today personally experienced or knew of the positive impact this man had on people's lives. In honor of his wishes, I will not elaborate. I will merely say that he made a difference, and that that is a vast understatement."

Faith looked for Mr. Hopewell and found him sitting two rows back on the opposite side of the aisle. She saw that he had bowed his head and was discretely wiping his eyes. Seated behind him, several Missionaries of Charity, draped in blue and white striped habits, more openly did the same.

"He had his struggles, as humans do. He struggled through terrible tragedy in his personal life – the loss of both sons and the wife he adored. He struggled with stubbornness, and with pride, and he suffered for that, too. But he did not give up. He tried to find meaning in life, meaning in death, and did his best to leave a positive mark on the world. He felt his beloved Elena would have wanted that, and he also saw it as his duty to God."

"Let's talk about his stubbornness." That got a relieved chuckle from the weeping crowd.

"Fritz was a proud, unyielding man at times. He was not

averse to change, as evidenced by his acumen for investing in up and coming things, but he did not like being told what to do. And believe me when I tell you that I tried." There was more laughter.

"He was always that way. He joked that while reverse psychology has been utilized since the dawn of time, no one used it more often – or more effectively -- than his own mother did when he was a child... until he got wise to it." Everyone laughed, and Faith laughed harder when Chris pointed at Paul, as if to say, 'we need to think about doing that with him!'

He went on, more seriously, "This stubbornness, which accounted for much of his success with Blithe Industries, also hurt him. It may have kept him from knowing his only grandchild." The crowd sobered and the Cardinal looked over at Faith.

"Mrs. Warrior, Fritz would have benefited greatly from knowing you and your family, and you would have benefited, too. He was a good man, and I'm very sorry for your loss. Very sorry." He paused, and then looked around at the audience, "Fritz Blithe believed in heaven, this I know. And I hope he's there now, with God, reunited with his beautiful wife and sons, and happier than he's ever been. Let us pray for his soul." He bowed his head.

"Incline Thine ear, O Lord, unto our prayers, wherein we humbly pray Thee to show Thy mercy upon the soul of Thy servant, Frederick McWallace Blithe, whom Thou hast commanded to pass out of this world, that Thou wouldst place him in the region of peace and light, and bid him be a partaker with Thy Saints. Through Christ our Lord. Amen."

"Amen," replied the crowd.

Faith struggled to hold back tears. She gave the Cardinal a watery smile and a nod as he stepped down from the podium. Her husband squeezed her hand.

The Cardinal looked at her discreetly to see if she was willing to speak. She took a deep breath, stood and stepped forth on shaky legs.

"Hello," she began quietly into the microphone. She looked at the main aisle rather than people's faces because her nerves were frayed, but pushed on. "My name is Faith Warrior, and I am Frederick Blithe's granddaughter. As most of you know, I didn't meet my grandfather until the day he died. It was a huge coincidence that we crossed paths that day. Perhaps it was more than that. My grandfather told me he thought it was a gift from God." She swallowed, then looked up with tears in her eyes, her throat painfully tight. She clutched the tissue.

She glanced at the Cardinal. "Your Eminence, I really appreciate your words. I may have only had two hours with him, but I've learned a tremendous amount about him in the past six days. He was kind, contemplative, passionate about many things, and he was open-minded. He took chances on people and on ventures, and in doing so, made some people's dreams come true. He was complicated and stubborn, too. ...I may have gotten that from him." She laughed a bit and the crowd joined in. "He was human. And I really wish I'd had more time with him.

"Thank you to all who have shared your stories with me. He has clearly had a positive impact on many lives. Despite his complexities – or maybe because of them -- he's been an inspiration to many people." She turned back to the Cardinal, "Your Eminence, I take comfort in my belief that my grandfather has joined my father in heaven, that they are both at peace. And I vow to honor their memory."

She turned back to the audience. "I hope you'll all say some prayers for my grandfather, my grandmother, my uncle and for my father. Thank you for coming today."

Faith stepped down from the podium and looked around. She saw some tears, some sympathetic smiles, some heads bowed.

As she returned to her seat, Paul impatiently and loudly said, "can we GO now?" Faith whispered to her husband, "we should be grateful he lasted this long without complaining, right?"

He smiled, put his arm around her shoulder and kissed her temple. "Right."

***

Following a police escort, the funeral procession moved slowly through sun-dappled streets to the historic Oak Hill Cemetery on R Street. Their limousine – one of many in the procession -- followed the hearse. Faith felt a crisp autumn breeze on her cheek as she stepped from the vehicle.

Her grandfather was laid to rest on a grassy knoll beside his wife and sons, amidst other ancestors.

Guests gathered around and the Monsignor gave her grandfather a final blessing before the casket was lowered into the rich, dark earth. Faith plucked a few stems of frangipani from an arrangement and handed them to her husband and her boys, then they each dropped one on the casket. Other guests did the same. She thanked the priest and then they quietly returned to the waiting limousine.

Guests were invited to a reception at the Army and Navy Club on Farragut Square. Though the boys had behaved very well through both services, they were clearly getting tired and irritable. Faith was glad she'd prearranged for Mrs. Loper to watch them during the reception. The housekeeper had planned a fun afternoon for them, with playtime, a movie and an early dinner. The boys were eager to get out of their jackets and ties. They'd gone home with Sawyer in the minivan.

The limousine pulled up the curved drive in front of the Club. Roberts opened their door, and then Chris exited and helped Faith from the car. Flash bulbs went off while they walked up the stairs to the front door. As they entered the building, Mr. Hopewell and Ms. Webber stepped forward and guided them to the 2nd floor, where the receiving line would form outside the main dining room.

"Mr. Hopewell, when did Fritz serve in the armed forces?" Chris asked.

"World War II was just ending when he became eligible to serve, but he felt it was his duty, and in 1944, he enlisted in the infantry. His father was livid. After all, Fritz was an only child. But, as the Cardinal pointed out, he was stubborn. He spent the last seven or so months of the war with the 106th Infantry Division, in France, Belgium and Germany, then came home. He had terrific respect for the military, and really enjoyed being a member of this club."

As each guest approached, Mr. Hopewell or Ms. Webber made the introduction. Faith met all of the company's senior officers and a few of the Board members. She thought the CEO, Gregory Von Heiden, looked impatient as he waited in line. He solemnly offered his condolences and moved on to speak with the Board members.

Tuppence Rivera, one of the readers from the Mass, came through the receiving line with her husband, Alexander, and gave her a hug. Later the other reader, Richard Whitman, did the same.

Politicians and corporate executives were there. She also met management teams from a few of the technology startups in which her grandfather had invested. Conspicuously absent was the one person Faith most wanted to meet: Geoff Michaels.

A sit-down lunch followed the receiving line. Seats were not assigned. She scanned the room. "Let's sit over there," she murmured to her husband, and pointed to a table by a tall window with a few empty seats. She wanted to talk with Tuppence Rivera.

When they approached the table, Alexander Rivera stood and extended his hand. "Mr. and Mrs. Warrior, won't you sit with us?" Tuppence stood also, and smiled at Faith.

"We'd love to," Faith said with a smile. "Please call me Faith. And this is my husband, Chris."

"I'm sorry for your loss, Faith. Fritz was a good man," said Tuppence.

"Thank you, Mrs. Rivera. So you were a good friend of my grandmother's?"

"Oh yes," she nodded, "Elena and I went to boarding school together at Le Rosey, and we both moved to Washington, DC. Our children were born around the same time. She was like a sister to me. I even insisted that Alexander buy a house in the neighborhood after we were married, so we could be closer to the Blithes." Her voice caught. "I still miss her."

Faith took her hand. "I'm so glad you came here today."

"We would not have missed it," Alexander said.

"It was such a beautiful ceremony." Tuppence said.

"Yes, it was. I was particularly struck by the profusion of beautiful flowers."

The old woman smiled and nodded. "It was a romantic touch."

"Romantic?"

"Oh yes. Frangipani were Elena's favorite flowers. She had them in her wedding bouquet and always had them in the house."

Faith's jaw dropped a bit. Frangipani were still in the house. They were in the greenhouse. They were everywhere.

"It sounds like my grandparents shared a great love. I mean, he never remarried…"

"Oh yes. Undoubtedly. The way they looked at each other, well, it almost felt like an intrusion to be standing beside them."

"How did they meet?"

Tuppence smiled, "they met the summer after we graduated from Le Rosey. Elena's father was working at the Embassy here in Washington, so she came here for vacation. She was invited to play doubles tennis with another young man – Richard Whitman." She pointed to another table. "He read at the Mass." Faith nodded her understanding. "Fritz was there with a date. But when Fritz and Elena saw each other… well, she said it felt like the earth stopped. They were married two months later." She laughed, "I remember it was exactly two months, because they married as soon as her dress was ready. It shocked everyone. But you know, she was from a good family, and she clearly made Fritz happy, so his parents were thrilled."

"And she was a Catholic?"

"Yes, she was, a Roman Catholic – not Greek Orthodox. It didn't matter to Fritz's parents. They weren't Catholic. But it mattered to Fritz."

"My grandfather was a convert? I had no idea."

"Oh, yes. In fact, Cardinal Mayse baptized him."

"But I thought they met on a religious retreat."

"They did. Fritz was in Rome on holiday after he graduated from law school. On a tour of the Vatican, he met some other students who told him about the retreat. He was intrigued, so he joined them. It had a profound impact on him. He converted the next year."

Over the next two hours, Faith heard countless stories from people who adored her grandfather. She found herself growing envious that they all knew him so well.

Finally, Chris murmured to her that it was time to leave. As he escorted her to the foyer of the club, Faith spotted Cassandra surrounded by several older gentlemen, including Richard Whitman. The older woman was clearly a charming conversationalist. Cassandra broke away from her admirers and walked over.

"Dear Faith, what a day you've had. The service was beautiful."

"It really was. Thank you for coming. I understand that my uncle died quite a while ago. It's nice that you stayed in touch with my grandfather."

"Thirty-five years ago. It was the worst day of my life," she said, getting misty eyed. "Your grandfather has been very supportive over the years. He was a wonderful man."

"How did it happen?" Faith asked compassionately.

"A scuba diving accident. Both Thomas and Elena died."

"And then my father a few months later. Just horrible."

"It was a very hard year."

"Did you remarry? Do you have any children?" Faith asked.

"No, I never married, but I have a son, Daniel. He's a wonderful boy, well, a man now. I had him two years after Thomas died. Daniel was very close to your grandfather, you know. Fritz treated him like a grandson." She smiled sadly. "You expressed surprise that we stayed in touch with Fritz all of those years. I'm not sure we would have, given Thomas was dead. But Daniel was so attached to Fritz..."

"And he isn't here today?"

"No, he's in Switzerland right now, working. It took him months to coordinate the trip, so he couldn't leave in the middle of it."

Chris tapped Faith on the back of her waist to signal it was time to go. "Well, I look forward to meeting him one day," Faith said.

"We'll set it up." Cassandra stepped in and hugged her.

"Excuse me, Mr. and Mrs. Warrior?" Richard Whitman spoke up from behind them. Cassandra wandered away.

They turned toward him. "Hello, Mr. Whitman," Faith said warmly. "I'm sorry for your loss. Thank you for doing the reading at the Mass."

"It was the least I could do for my old friend." He nodded seriously. The scar on his left cheek was gnarled and white. It stretched from the corner of his eye to just above his jaw, and it caught the light when his head stilled. Faith though it resembled a twisted, wet noodle.

"You knew my grandfather a long time. Longer than

anyone else here – is that right?"

"I think so, yes. We went to high school together – college, too. And when he was at Harvard Law, I was at Harvard Business School. We've been friends ever since."

"My goodness. I'd really love to talk with you more about him, when you have time. But now we have to get home to our children."

"I understand. Another time." He smiled at them, but the smile didn't quite reach his eyes because one cheek didn't move that way. Chris shook the old man's hand.

***

She groaned when Roberts shut the limousine door. "My feet. My feet." She slipped out of her heels and propped them up on the seat in front of her, then exhaled and closed her eyes. "Oh frickety frick!" She pulled at her slim-fitting black dress and snapped fabric into place.

"What in the world was that?" Chris asked, looking at her in alarm.

"Spanx," she looked at him sheepishly. "It's a beautiful but torturous device that helps me look all smooth. Goes from mid-thigh all the way up my rib cage. Basically, I've spent the afternoon inside a sausage casing." She paused. "Okay, here's where you say, 'oh honey, you don't need sausage casing - you're beautiful just the way you are.'"

Chris smiled, gently spun her to the side, pulled her feet onto his lap and began to rub them. "You and I both know you don't need that thing. But if it makes you feel more confident, go right ahead." He lifted her skirt a bit to see the edge of the Spanks and shuddered.

"Chris!"

He smiled and rubbed her feet. "It really was a lovely service. It's clear that everyone thought the world of him. That should bring you some comfort."

"It does. I only wish I'd had more time to get to know him. Maybe some of his good qualities would have rubbed off on me." She gave him a lopsided smile.

"And yours would have rubbed off on him. Even if you had to kick his butt to accomplish it." He smiled back and she elbowed him affectionately.

"So, we met Cassandra." Faith said.

"Yes, she's really lovely. Hard to believe she's in her mid-fifties. I spoke with her briefly a little earlier. She seemed genuinely sad about your grandfather. Apparently, he's treated her like a daughter all of these years."

***

The stress of the last few days finally got to Faith and she decided it was time to work it out. She changed into shorts and a sweatshirt and pulled on her running shoes.

"I don't know why I need to take him along," she said to Chris about the Sawyer. "I've taken self-defense. I know how to pop a guy's eyeballs out with my thumbs!" Faith stood indignantly in the foyer, ready to step out the front door. She was beginning to feel really stifled by the security.

"Faith, I don't get it. You let a bodyguard drive you to and from school with the kids. Why do you think it's safe to go out running alone, in the dark? Your own father was murdered just outside that very door."

She blanched. "It's six p.m. And my father was attacked by a crazy vet." Faith put her hands on her hips.

"But it will be dark by the time you get back."

Faith grumbled as Sawyer entered the foyer in a track suit and running shoes. "Ma'am," he nodded and stood at ease.

"Okay, okay," she said belligerently. "But you'd better not slow me down."

"No, ma'am."

Her husband snorted with laughter. She grumbled some more.

The bodyguard opened the door for her and she popped in her ear buds. She fired up her iPhone with some disco classics and stepped out onto the sidewalk. She'd decided to do a loop going north on Massachusetts Avenue to Wisconsin Avenue, then south to DuPont Circle, then back to the house. Mapquest.com indicated it would be roughly 4.25 miles. She explained the route to the bodyguard. He indicated they should stick directionally with traffic. So as they climbed Mass Ave, they ran on the north side of the street.

She started out at an aggressive pace up the hill. About half a mile into it, her lungs were burning. She looked back at the bodyguard and saw he was giving her some room. Five paces behind her, his face was perfectly placid, not a drop of sweat on his brow. *Mother f-er,* she thought, uncharitably.

The first leg was straight up hill, totally killer for someone who ran as infrequently as she did. But she kept on going. She reached Wisconsin Avenue and rested, stretching against a lamppost before crossing the street and running down Massachusetts Ave on the opposite side of the street. Downhill, she learned, can be just as hard a workout. Her legs felt rubbery after her Nike+ app read only 1.4 miles. While she ran, she thought about the events of the day.

She continued to be perplexed by the fact that Geoff Michaels hadn't shown. *What in the world could he be up to that was more important than being at my grandfather's funeral? My grandfather bankrolled his think tank, put him on his Board of Directors and appointed him Trustee of his foundation.*

In her anger, Faith neglected to see a car pulling out of a driveway and almost ran right in front of it. Her bodyguard lunged and grabbed her by the waist at the last second. "What the what?" She pushed him away and then saw why he'd done it. "Oh, I am so sorry," she said as she turned to him. She leaned forward and put her hands on her knees, catching her breath. "I don't know what to say. It's just been a really crappy day and you've been on the receiving end of it. I'm very sorry."

He looked sympathetically at her and said, "No worries, ma'am. Shall we press on, or would you like to return to the house?"

"I think I'd like to return to the house." Before she could finish the sentence, the bodyguard had raised his arm and the limousine pulled up in front of them.

"Well, I'll be," Faith said with eyebrows raised, and she slid into the back seat.

"The benefit of running with traffic, rather than against it, ma'am."

Chapter 7

After Mass on Sunday, Chris took the boys to the rear garden to play on the jungle gym while Faith did some research online. They'd skipped the Parish Picnic because she needed to prepare for the Board meeting on Monday. She also had to fire off a few emails to Mrs. Abernathy and Mr. Hopewell on a variety of topics.

She decided to create a "cheat sheet" for each business segment, so that she'd have critical details at her fingertips during the meeting. She took the information Ms. Webber had given her and started reading. In a fresh Word document, she wrote summaries of each business, including estimated growth rates, profitability levels, key drivers, biggest competitors, top customers and greatest threats. She left the summary for "strategy" blank – she would go back later, after speaking with segment management, and fill that in. She included the top executives' names and pasted photos of them, if she could find them.

Then she looked at each business and tried to find comparable companies. She wanted to get a sense of relative performance, and where there might be opportunities for improvement. She also assessed the economic sensitivity of each business.

Once she felt she had enough to make her comfortable during her first meeting with management, she printed it out and tucked it into her handbag.

She changed her focus to her ideas for the future. She'd established her objective of honoring her father and grandfather.

She pulled out a fresh piece of paper and wrote two headers. 'Granddad' on one side. 'Dad' on the other.

Beneath 'Granddad', she wrote the following:

1. Passionate about the company, its history.

2. Farsighted about employees – making investments in them.

3. Loved technology.

4. Unafraid to take a chance.

Beneath 'Dad', she wrote:

1. Passionate about environment.

2. Farsighted about the earth – preserving it for future generations.

3. Loved green technology.

4. Unafraid of authority, but loyal to family.

Faith sat looking at the list for some time. Her pulse quickened. For the first time in her life, she had the means to do exactly what her heart told her was right. She felt her mind open.

She began to write a list. Ever the stickler, she titled it 'Eutopia' rather than the homophone 'Utopia'.

Firstly, Faith decided that in order to make the company an embodiment of both men's visions, some businesses had to go and some needed to be added. She looked at the business segments as laid out on the sheet Mr. Hopewell had given her a few days before.

Blithe Defense - Blithe Rifle Company, two military weapons companies, and a fire and security business

Blithe Materials - four companies in the paper and chemicals industries, and a large engineering and construction company

Blithe Media and Technology - online media programming, advertising, electronic gaming and syndicated radio

Blithe Essentials - basic household products, personal care products, food processing and tobacco.

The most environmentally damaging businesses included the Materials segment (except the E&C business) and the tobacco business. She'd need to learn more about the Defense business to assess the dangers there. There might also be some problems within the other Essentials businesses. She didn't know yet. She knew that the businesses she wanted to add included technology and green venture capital.

Secondly, she wanted to make Blithe the best company to work for in America. No simple task, she was sure. She knew the key to engendering employee pride and loyalty was to demonstrate that the company values its employees.

She navigated to a few websites that offered comprehensive "best company" rankings and reviewed some key drivers: good healthcare; on-site childcare; flexible work where possible; unique, regular perks; teaming up to support special world causes such as the fight against illiteracy, infant mortality or hunger; feeling like employees are a valued part of a team; a sense of security in a work world where that is rarely encountered anymore.

Faith did not want to dampen corporate profitability in order to improve benefits. She suspected that there might be some low hanging fruit from an efficiency standpoint that would help offset additional costs in the near term. Organizations that haven't been shaken up in a while can have such opportunities. She also suspected that lower employee turnover and higher employee satisfaction could yield some margin. She'd need someone to do some research into it.

The doorbell rang. Shortly thereafter, her cell phone rang. It was her security detail.

"Mrs. Warrior, you have a visitor. Mr. Geoff Michaels."

"Thank you. I'll be down in a moment." Faith hung up and stared at her page. *Well, I'll be.*

Faith walked rapidly to the stairs and descended two flights to the main floor. She smoothed her hair back and regarded her outfit. A black mock turtleneck, slim black pants and black loafers. Maybe a little *Funny Face* in Paris, but it'll do. *At least I'm not in my running shorts and t-shirt.*

Faith walked into the room with her hand extended. "Mr. Michaels? I'm Faith Warrior."

Geoff Michaels was a lean, studious-looking man she guessed to be in his early 40s -- he had the rumpled hair and attire of an academic. His wavy, light-brown hair was on the long side, as if he'd been too busy to have it cut. "Mrs. Warrior. I am very sorry to intrude on a Sunday, but I just returned to the country and learned of your grandfather's death." His gray eyes were filled with grief. "I can't believe it. And I missed his funeral." He looked completely stricken, his mouth drawn tightly.

"It was very sudden, a shock to everyone who knew him." Faith regarded him carefully. The emotion he exuded seemed real. Her preconceived notions of him started to thaw. "Please, sit down Mr. Michaels." She looked around, wanting to offer him something to drink and spotted a bodyguard just outside of the room. She mouthed the word, "water." The man nodded and stepped into the butler's pantry in the center of the house.

"I understand you knew my grandfather for about ten years," Faith said.

He looked up, eyes clouded, as the bodyguard handed him a glass of water. "Oh, thank you," he murmured to the bodyguard. "Yes, your grandfather contacted me about ten years ago. I'd been an environmental lobbyist and was an adjunct professor at GW. He said he wanted to make a difference to the planet. That he needed help to do it. Shortly thereafter, he funded the think tank and put me on his Board." He laughed, ruefully, "I wish I knew what sort of epiphany he'd had that made him reach out to the green cause – there are a few other major corporations that could use the same experience."

Faith looked at him. "My father was interested in environmental causes. He passed away before I was born. Perhaps he had something to do with my grandfather's interest." She paused a moment. "Mr. Michaels, I know you were appointed Trustee of my grandfather's foundation. As you may now know, my grandfather changed his will before he died. There is no longer a foundation."

He nodded slowly, absorbing it. "Yes, I understand. Frankly, it's not something I was really focused on, given your grandfather was still very much alive a week ago. My attention has been on the think tank."

"Yes, well, I'm sure that a lot of people are wondering what will happen now that I've suddenly appeared on the horizon. I have to ask, why did you stay on the Board when my grandfather was clearly uninterested in making improvements to the environmental impact of the company?"

"I wouldn't say he was uninterested. The main reason Mr. Blithe wanted me on the Board was so I could be a voice of reason against further environmental missteps. And, in the damaging businesses, he wanted advice on remediation."

"Did you ever advise him to sell certain businesses?"

"Regularly, in private. Despite our differences, I respected your grandfather immensely. He was trying to do the right thing without compromising his ancestors' vision. He wouldn't have drastically changed the company until it needed to be liquidated to fund the foundation. In other words, not until after his death. He couldn't watch it happen to his family legacy. I understood that." He put up his hands in emphasis. "I'm not a rabid activist. I'm focused on making whatever steps are realistic and possible at any given time. He was making effort to lessen the environmental impact of existing operations. I understand that Blithe is a big ship to turn, and I'm patient. I imagine that's why he felt comfortable with me."

Faith let that sink in. She listened to the way he spoke, watched his body language, and began to feel more relaxed about him. Years of watching company management teams talk about their operations, gauging their sincerity and then monitoring to see if they followed through on promises helped inform her decision: Geoff Michaels seemed to be sincere.

"Mr. Michaels, I plan to honor my ancestors, too. But my ancestors include my own father, who was a diehard environmentalist."

"Your grandfather had mentioned that. He seemed to really admire Mick." He cocked his head to the side. "It sounds like you're planning some changes."

"I'm not prepared to discuss anything in particular now – we're in the early days here – but yes, I imagine there will be some changes." She paused, unsure whether to press on, then continued, "If so, may I conclude that you'd be supportive?"

"Most supportive, yes, and most interested" he quickly replied. "As I said, I encouraged your grandfather repeatedly over time to exit certain businesses and redeploy funds into areas that would benefit the world."

"Okay, thank you, Mr. Michaels." Faith stood. "So I'll see you at tomorrow's Board meeting?"

"Yes, indeed. Thank you for seeing me." He stopped as he reached the door, "and I'm very sorry for your loss."

"I'm sorry for your loss, too." Mr. Michaels nodded grimly and left.

    ***

Faith finished explaining to her husband her thoughts about divesting certain businesses, establishing an Environmental segment, doing some environmental venture capital and dabbling in green corporate philanthropy. After meeting with Geoff Michaels, she was considering asking him to head the new segment. She already had her grandfather's posthumous endorsement, given he'd originally selected him to run the foundation.

"So, I go out to play with the boys and suddenly you've established a new business segment and hired the executive to run it? No moss grows beneath your feet, that is for sure! Just wait until the CEO hears about all of this." Her husband chuckled and shook his head. "Not to mention the Board."

"Ok, firstly, this is a privately held company and I hold all of the voting shares and own the majority economic interest. Secondly, the Board stood behind my grandfather, and my grandfather stood behind me. If he hadn't, he wouldn't have left me in control. Thirdly, the CEO works for me now, just as he used to work for my grandfather."

"Good points."

Faith finished laying out lunch for the boys in the downstairs dining room. "Anyway, I haven't green lighted any specific ideas, I've just mentally lined up the talent – well, *some* of the talent." She smirked.

"What are you up to?" Her husband poked her in her side.

"Nothing that my friend Anne couldn't help me out with," she responded in a singsong way while looking innocently up at the ceiling.

"Are we talking work or love life here?" He asked her with suspicion. "You are NOT acting as matchmaker, are you?" Faith smiled. "Faith, Anne doesn't need any help – she just needs to get out of the backwoods and back to civilization."

"What are the backwoods?" Paul asked.

"It's a place that's near Podunk but not as far as Jerkwater," Chris said. Paul looked blankly at him and ate a grape.

"I know, I know, but I can't help but hope. They're smart, single, and attractive; one never knows…" she trailed off as she walked over to tickle the boys. Loud squeals ensued.

She returned to her husband, who was getting a cup of coffee on the sideboard. "But seriously, I need to talk to you, too."

He sat down at the table and bit a cookie. "Shoot."

"So, I reviewed the businesses and made a list of my priorities. One of those priorities is technology." He nodded, having heard this before. "The way I see it, and I want to get your thoughts on this, I've got three totally separate tech jobs. One is a corporate job, overseeing technology across the entire corporation. The second is heading up a new technology segment – I'm not even sure what we'd invest in. I only know that it was my grandfather's passion. The last job is managing all of our personal existing and future tech investments. That huge portfolio my grandfather left me - someone needs to manage it. Many of the investments are in private companies for which there is no secondary market. So we've got to stay on top of the investments. And interaction with these companies could lead to more interesting ventures."

Chris thought for a moment. "Well, I've done the corporate job before, though on a smaller scale. That would be no problem. I just need a good staff. If they don't already have the talent there, then cue my 'Perfect World' list. As for starting a new leg, I'm sure I could give input to ideas but this objective seems very vague to me. Tech is a very broad tapestry."

Faith rubbed her chin as she thought. "You know, we might get a better idea of where to look by examining what he's already invested in. I've never heard of half of the companies. Maybe there is some theme here that we haven't yet seen."

Chris nodded. "That's a good idea. A good starting point." He scrubbed his face with one hand, then exhaled. "Okay, listen. Here's what my heart is telling me. I don't want to closet myself away in your office over the garage. I like being around people. Frankly, I like what I do as CTO. So I'll take the corporate job and I'll oversee the evaluation of investment ideas. As for the personal portfolio, why don't we get Anne to handle that?"

Faith's eyes lit up. "Yes!"

"Okay, so who else is on your 'Perfect World' list?" Chris

took another sip of coffee and they compared notes on people they would love to have beside them every day. The light-hearted, happy people, the capable and reliable people, the smart and witty people, the people who make others feel good about themselves, the people who make others feel safe, the warm people.

"Am I on your 'Perfect World' list?" Paul said from across the table.

Graham chimed in, "yeah, am I on the list too?"

Faith smiled and ruffled their hair, "Absolutely! You two and Daddy are at the top of the list!"

***

The four of them took a swim and then Chris put on a movie for the boys in the tech room while Faith prepared dinner. As Faith left the tech room to make her way down to the kitchen, it occurred to her that there were a few places in the house she hadn't yet explored. One of these was the room across from the formal living room, just off the foyer. The door had been closed ever since they arrived the week before.

She turned the ornate bronze knob and opened one of the double doors. Heavy drapes covered the windows, so Faith fumbled for the light switch. The room was suddenly bathed in light. It was sumptuously appointed music room. The central focus was a glossy grand piano, but there was also a gilt harp. Clusters of elegant, plush seating were dotted through the room, and near the piano, four gilt caned chairs sat before music stands, as if ready to receive a string quartet. The floor was a massive, intricate inlaid wood medallion. Crystal wall sconces gave the whole room a soft glow.

As beautiful as the room was, it had the feel of sadness and neglect. She wondered why the door was always closed. She'd have to ask the housekeepers.

Faith had a mental map in her head of the house. As she descended to the kitchen, she realized that the only portions of the house she'd yet to explore were the guest rooms on the 3rd floor and whatever occupied the northeast portion of the basement. She decided that she'd get dinner in the oven and then explore that floor.

She dipped the boneless chicken breasts in beaten egg, then into seasoned flour, then again into the egg, then into panko break crumbs with parmesan, oregano and other spices.

They went into a 400-degree oven. Her trusty thermometer was tucked into her apron. 165 degrees and they would be done – nice and juicy. She scraped and sliced up some sweet potatoes, put them in a Pyrex dish and covered them with water. Those would go into the microwave in the last ten minutes. Salad was ready to go. She had spied a pumpkin pie in the refrigerator, too. It was a basic meal, but nutritious and tasty. Not exactly Chef standards, but it would do for a Sunday night.

Faith left the downstairs dining room and entered the hallway that ran from the front of the house to the back. She knew that if she went right, she'd head toward the bathroom, stairs, cleaning closet and elevator. There was a door straight ahead and she opened it.

As the door opened, she was struck by the odor of stale smoke. It wasn't the more nauseating smell of cigarette smoke, but rather, the sweeter smell of cigar and pipe smoke. She found the light switch and flipped it, revealing a small wood-paneled room with four leather club chairs and a marble coffee table that housed a big, brass ashtray and a stack of financial magazines. A flat screen TV hung on the wall. She heard the gentle whirring of an exhaust fan kick in. Impressive oil paintings dotted the walls. A fine, Oriental rug covered the floor. *Granddad had a smoking lounge.* She saw two doors along the far wall. One was glass and the other solid wood.

She stepped forward and opened the wood door, revealing a walk-in humidor. Dozens of boxes of cigars lined shelves that were tilted forward to better display them. *Blithe Tobacco, present and accounted for.* One shelf was dedicated to cigar accessories such as cutters, scissors, cases and lighters.

Faith saw a light switch on the outside of the glass door and flipped it. Through the door, she could see a large wine cellar. This was no ordinary wine cellar. It was a temple to wine. She opened the door and was bathed in cool air.

Lacquered mahogany shelves and racks lined the entire room. The racks of wine were carefully labeled -- grouped according to type and provenance. Subtle, recessed lighting highlighted key bottles and glimmered against the marble floor. One shelf housed a vast library of Wine Spectator magazines.

A rack of wine glasses of various shapes and sizes was

nestled amidst the bottles along with a basket of bottle openers and stoppers. The ceiling was slightly domed and delicately lit to highlight a lush mural of rolling vineyards. In the center of the room, a marble-topped table displayed a large, heavily used silver candelabra. Dried wax hung in an impressive formation from the arms, resembling an oyster-colored frozen river. It looked very romantic. Intricately carved wood chairs surrounded the table. *I guess granddad liked to linger in the ambience.*

She closed the door and looked around again. *'Man cave'*, was all she could think.

Traveling further along the hallway, she found a last door. Inside, Faith found a 1950s-style bowling alley. It was certainly not modern, but the lane was automated and decorated in the style of the 1950s. She spied some removable bumpers – handy with small kids.

A couple of retro bowling shirts were framed on the wall along with photos of groups of teenagers hanging out in the room. She saw her smiling, teenage father and uncle in a few of them.

A wet bar was tricked out like a 1950s popshop with red and white leather stools at the chrome counter. Against one wall stood a refrigerated ice cream case, and a huge jukebox alongside it. 1950s neon signs hung on the walls and red and white leather seating surrounded the top of the lane. The linoleum floor was checkered black and white.

While the room looked clean, it was certainly not used. It had the mildly stale smell of an antique store.

Faith looked at the song selection on the jukebox and pressed Marvin Gaye's *Mercy Mercy Me*.

She stood there, swaying to the music, remembering finding her mother singing along to it when she was a teenager. She was standing in their dark living room. She'd had her eyes closed and was singing, tears on her face. Faith had felt like an interloper. Only now did she realize her mother was probably thinking of her father that night, and the thought brought tears to her eyes.

She heard footsteps behind her and her husband put his arms around her, turned her toward him and tucked her face into his neck. He rubbed her back as she cried.

"Look honey," Faith snuffled and wiped her face with the

back of her hand. "We have a bowling alley!" She smiled through her tears, trying to be upbeat.

Chris kissed her.

"Mom, what's for dinner?" Faith heard Graham running down the hall toward the bowling room. "Mom, I'm hun…" Graham screeched to a halt and stopped midsentence to stare at the bowling alley. His mouth looked like a perfect 'o'. Paul crashed into him from behind.

"What the…?" Paul's face was scrunched up at his brother. "Graham!" Then he, too, looked at the bowling alley.

"Mom! I want to play! Mom, can I play?" Graham started hopping up and down. Paul joined him as he hopped, then they both ran over to select balls.

Faith chuckled and wiped her cheeks one last time. "I'll go check on dinner." She said to Chris as she walked toward the door. "You see if you can get the bowling alley working."

Chapter 8

The Board meeting was scheduled for nine a.m.

Faith got up early so she could shower and primp before the kids woke up. She dressed carefully in the dark suit she'd worn the day she met her grandfather. It was, after all, the only suit she owned. She'd donated her work wardrobe to Goodwill years before and had bought that new suit just for the interview with Bruce Holland.

She brushed her hair until it fell as a glossy curtain against her shoulders. Her makeup was painstakingly applied. She needed all of the confidence she could get this morning, and making sure her 'armor' was in perfect shape was essential.

After checking that she had her notes and laptop in her oversized handbag, she took one last look at herself and walked back to the bedroom to wake up Chris. It was his turn to suit up.

The kids were unhappy about getting up for school but they cooperated after she explained how important today was for her. Teeth brushed, uniforms on, they all trooped down to breakfast.

Mrs. Lucie had prepared the usual nice spread. Faith sat down and the housekeeper brought her a cup of coffee, prepared just the way she liked it – skim milk only. She placed Chris's coffee in front of him – half and half for him. The boys sipped their morning juice while Mrs. Lucie filled their plates. Everyone contentedly munched, sipped and read until it was time to leave.

Roberts stepped forward and opened the limousine door. "Mrs. Warrior, given the nature of today's schedule, I thought you might want to take the limousine?"

Chris looked at Faith and nodded. The kids started yelling

and jumped into the backseat. "Well, the cat'll be out of the bag at school today," Faith said ruefully.

"It was going to happen eventually," replied Chris, "and maybe a limousine ride will help you feel like you have a place at the table, so to speak." He paused, "you do, you know? I'm not just saying that because you have a legal right to it. You are capable and you are his granddaughter. You've got Blithe in your blood."

Faith took a deep breath and exhaled. She cupped her husband's cheek and kissed him. "Thank you, honey."

Faith answered a stream of questions from the kids about the various gadgets in the limousine and twice rejected their pleas to stand up through the sunroof during the ride.

Drop off went fairly smoothly since Faith requested that they be dropped in front of school so they could walk the children in. Only a few people saw them exit a limousine.

Back in the car, Faith pulled out her bag and reviewed her notes. Her cell phone rang.

"Mrs. Warrior?" Miriam Webber's competent voice cut through her thoughts. "Mr. Von Heiden just issued an updated agenda for the Board meeting. I'm faxing it through to you right now." The fax machine in the limousine's office space began to hum. "There's an item on there that you'll want to see."

Faith caught the paper as it exited the fax machine and took a look. "Well, I'll be," she whispered as she read. Chris looked at her and she handed him the fax, then pointed to the line item in question.

10:20 am   Presentation by Faith Warrior

"Thank you. I'll see you in a few minutes." Faith disconnected the call and looked at her husband with surprise.

"So he doesn't bother to call me to even introduce himself, let alone discuss the Board meeting, then puts me on the agenda at the last minute to make a Board presentation?" Faith started to laugh, the tension flowing out of her. "That's a passive aggressive, controlling move if I've ever seen one."

"Faith, it's not that surprising. He's feeling threatened and he made a stupid decision, but he might still be a good guy."

She thought about that. "Maybe, maybe not. If he were confident he would have contacted me himself or waited and offered me an opportunity to address the Board at my leisure.

A passive-aggressive leader is dangerous. I saw that time and again as an analyst. I'll give him a little room and see what happens." She smiled again. "Wow, that move of his just gave me a major advantage, and he doesn't even know it."

Chris started to smile. "And: there she is." He referred, of course, to the strategic thinker in her.

Miriam Webber met Faith and Chris in the lobby of Blithe Building.

As she led them to the elevator bank, she gave them the run down of who would be in the room. "Ten of the Board members will attend the meeting in person. This is actually a high number for us – as you saw on Saturday, several of them flew in for the funeral. Five more will be on video conference from various points around the world."

Faith nodded. The steel elevator door slid open and they stepped inside. Faith schooled her features and mentally reminded herself that she could do this.

The three exited the elevator on the 10th floor. The marble floor of the reception area gleamed. The burled wood of the furniture looked rich against cream-colored carpeting. Courier and Ives lithographs hung on the walls.

The receptionist smiled at Miriam Webber and said good morning to Faith and Chris as they walked through a door to another hallway. They passed cubicles, filing rooms, a pantry, restrooms and a copy room to reach a suite of offices. Ms. Webber walked purposely to a door to a corner office and opened it

"Here is your grandfather's office – your office."

Slowly, Faith walked inside and looked around. She looked around at the floor. She didn't know where exactly he had been found and inexplicably didn't want to step wherever he had been. Her assistant tentatively spoke, and gestured toward the carpet by the bookcase, looking uncomfortable. "You were wondering where... over there."

Faith shook her head quickly in assent and then took a deep breath. Two of the office's walls were largely glass, offering a superb view of downtown Washington. The furniture was all burled wood, like the lobby. More Courier and Ives prints hung on the walls. They all had a firefighting theme.

A small sofa sat by a window. It was upholstered with a

pale yellow silk embroidered with cream-colored bumblebees. In one corner, four burled armchairs upholstered to match the sofa surrounded a round conference table. A large built-in bookcase occupied most of one wall. She spotted a number of well-regarded financial texts from her CFA prep days. She raised the corner of her mouth.

Faith walked past what she guessed was a globe bar to the desk and put down her bag. She ran her hand along the top of the leather inlay of the desk, as if trying to feel the heat of her grandfather's hand.

Her assistant continued, "My desk is just outside your office. This is the executive suite. Mr. Von Heiden's office is just next-door. The CFO's is just beyond, and so on. If you need anything, please ring me. I'm my own button on your phone." She pointed it out. "The meeting begins in twenty minutes. Can I get you anything?"

"Where do I get coffee?" Faith knew better than to ask an assistant to get coffee. It's better to throw it out a different way and see what happens.

"I'm happy to get you some from the pantry down the hall. I'll be right back. Milk? Sugar? Cream?"

"Milk only. Thanks very much."

She ducked out and softly closed the door.

"Okay!" Chris spoke up. He looked at the view and whistled, then looked back at her. "Let the games begin!"

Faith raised and wiggled her eyebrows at her husband, then walked to the door.

"Bathroom," she said, lost in thought, and exited the room.

Ten minutes later, Faith sat at her grandfather's desk with her coffee, her legs crossed, thinking. She recalled all of the videoconferences she'd done as a portfolio manager. To break the ice with a particularly tough audience, she'd often arrived early and engaged in some small talk.

She abruptly stood and collected her things. "I want to be the first person to walk into that room. Come with me." She breezed to the door and down the hallway with Chris in her wake. As she passed a puzzled Ms. Webber, she said, "You've never been in a Board meeting? Here's your chance." She motioned for her to follow them. Miriam jumped up, grabbed a writing pad and pen and had to jog to catch up with them.

A breakfast spread with coffee sat on a sideboard. Glasses and carafes of water had been placed on the table. Pens and notepads with the company logo sat on each blotter around the table. *Just like the old days*, she thought, sinking into the familiarity, feeling herself relax.

An A/V tech was connecting the Board members who would attend by video. Faith sat down at the head of the table, in full view of the Board members who had just joined. They were on mute, and so was she.

Chris and Miriam got cups of coffee. Miriam gave a fresh one to Faith before she joined Chris in the seating along the side of the room.

Faith turned to the tech. "Please open up the sound. Thank you."

When the tech gave her the thumbs up sign, she spoke to the five board members on the screen. "Good morning, ladies and gentlemen. I am Faith Warrior and this is my husband, Christopher Warrior."

A chorus of greetings followed, and after expressions of condolences, an easy banter emerged among the group. On the monitor were a retired CEO of a major consumer products company, a technology guru, a renowned finance professor and a retired general.

The general spoke up during a lull, "Mrs. Warrior, I knew your grandfather for forty years. He was a good man. I also knew your father when he was young, another good man. I'm very happy Fritz connected with you before he died. This company needs a Blithe at the helm. Obviously, your grandfather recognized that." The others were quiet after he spoke but didn't look uncomfortable. She regarded him carefully, seriously.

The door abruptly opened. Mr. Von Heiden stopped and saw Faith at the table, then glanced at the monitor. "Well, I see the meeting started without me." His eyes flashed at Faith.

"Not at all, Mr. Von Heiden. We were just saying hello. Please," she motioned to a chair next to her. "Won't you have a seat?" she said pleasantly. She remembered something her mother had once told her about debate: if you lose your temper, you lose the argument.

He did a good job of hiding it but was clearly shaken by being forced into an inferior seat. Faith sat at the head of the table.

The eight other board members arrived over the next few minutes, including Geoff Michaels, who smiled warmly at Faith. The meeting was underway. The CEO stood and walked behind Faith's chair. He talked to the room while standing behind her. Rather than appear miffed, Faith swiveled in her chair and smiled at him.

Von Heiden updated the Board on strategic initiatives to grow a few of the segments. He talked about a few acquisitions and took them through the growth that would result. "What are the projected ROI's on these investments?" Faith asked when he was finished.

He looked at the CFO, Kevin MacGuire, who was sitting in a chair at the side of the room. The CFO's face was rigid. "Kevin has the figures." He said dismissively.

The CFO looked at her uncomfortably, then down at his binder and quoted the figures.

"Can you refresh our collective understanding of the targeted ROI hurdles?" She persisted.

Von Heiden cut in. "These are *strategic* acquisitions, meant to pave the way toward future profitability. Near term ROI will be diluted." He looked down at his notes and pressed on. "Now, let's turn to page thirty five."

"Mr. Von Heiden," Faith persisted. "My understanding was that my grandfather had a very strict policy of adhering to ROI hurdles. My *understanding*," she emphasized as she looked around at the other Board members, "was that this was non-negotiable. Am I under some misapprehension?"

"Your grandfather was not at the last Board meeting," Geoff Michaels explained. "These acquisitions were discussed at that Board meeting. *Our* understanding was that your grandfather had approved them." Other Board members murmured agreement.

"And who indicated that my grandfather had approved them?" Faith asked.

"Mr. Von Heiden did." Michaels responded.

Faith looked at the CEO. "Mr. Von Heiden, do you have written documentation of this approval?"

"I didn't need written approval," the CEO spat back. "Your grandfather put me in charge, and then completely stepped away from the business. Who are you to come in here and judge me? You knew him for two hours. I've worked for this company for fifteen years." He inhaled sharply, as if the words had uncontrollably popped out of his mouth and he instantly regretted them.

Chris partially stood up but Faith looked at him to stop. Her husband was furious. The room was quiet.

"Mr. Von Heiden, it is my great personal loss that I only knew my grandfather for two hours. However, the amount of time I knew him is irrelevant. Nor is the amount of time *you* knew him. My grandfather left his entire stake in this company to me. He was, in fact, so eager to do this that he changed his will within hours of meeting me. He trusted me to take care of this company, and I plan to do just that."

She paused to control her temper. "I will start by ensuring that his disciplined approach toward investment endures. What you've just told me conflicts directly with what I understand to have been his strictest policy. Unless you can produce written documentation that my grandfather approved this deviation, then you can consider yourself terminated."

Faith was shaking but controlled her face. Von Heiden looked confused and fearful at the rapid turn of events.

The general spoke up, "Mr. Von Heiden, you've just insulted the memory of a great man. You've also insulted your employer, in case you have not yet figured out that you work for Faith Warrior. Did you even look at Mrs. Warrior's resume? She's got a better education than you have and she's looked at a hell of a lot more companies than you have. I think you have some growing up to do, son."

Faith looked around the room and saw the shocked faces of the Board members looking at the CEO. She turned back to Von Heiden. "Do you have written documentation?"

"I can't give you written documentation. His approval was verbal." The challenge returned to the CEO's eyes. He was trying to call her bluff.

"Ladies and gentlemen of the Board, do you believe that my grandfather would ever intentionally deviate from his ROI discipline?" She looked at each of them.

The former LBO expert shook his head no. "Fritz Blithe was an absolute stickler on that. He must have repeated it at least once at every meeting I've ever attended." The rest murmured agreement with that statement.

She looked at Chris, who nodded, then turned to the CFO. "Mr. MacGuire, please call security to escort Mr. Von Heiden from the building, then call the General Counsel and have him meet me in my office at," she looked at her agenda, "12:15, please." When the CFO stood frozen, she added firmly, "Now, please." This set him in motion. He picked up a phone and punched the operator, then murmured instructions.

"You can't do this! Your grandfather put me in charge! I will sue you!" Von Heiden was seething.

Faith stood up and walked toward him. She stood inches from his face and enunciated slowly and carefully. "Corporate officers serve at the pleasure of this company's majority owner. That would now be me. I may terminate an officer at any time, subject only to any rights the officer might have under an employment agreement. Did you think I neglected to pull your file before I came in here? You don't have an employment agreement. You'll receive whatever standard compensation exists for our terminations. Don't bother collecting your things. You can leave a forwarding address with the guard."

She continued to stand there, nose-to-nose with a twitching Von Heiden, his fists clenching and unclenching, until two guards arrived seconds later to escort him out. She then stalked back to her seat, picked up the agenda, and asked the CFO to begin the next item.

When no one started speaking, she looked up at the group and raised her eyebrows. "Let's get on with it, shall we?"

"Heck yeah," said the technology visionary, who chuckled. The rest of them looked at her and smiled broadly. One of the academics raised his eyebrows and smiled in astonishment to another.

The CFO stood up and nodded to Faith. "Ma'am," he said, nodding to her. He then gave an update on segment performance and discussed the outcome of a few more recent acquisitions.

After that, one of the Board members gave a brief presentation on executive compensation. Suddenly, it was ten twenty, time for Faith's presentation.

Faith looked around the table, then turned to the CFO. "Thank you, Mr. MacGuire. You can go now." He mouthed a 'thank you,' packed up his papers and left the room.

She collected her thoughts for a moment. "When Mr. Von Heiden surprised me with this item on the agenda, I thought I didn't have much to share with you at such an early date. I had some trepidation about telling you my ideas for the company. I thought to myself, why in the world would you consider my thoughts at such an early point?" She widened her eyes. "How quickly things can change."

The Board murmured agreement.

The general spoke up. "Mrs. Warrior, we were always very frank with your grandfather, and he was very frank with us. Given your recent experience with Mr. Von Heiden, I can understand your reluctance to trust, but your grandfather did trust his Board." She looked around as they nodded. "Tell us your thoughts and we'll give you our opinions."

Faith nodded, opened her folder and pulled out her notes. "Very well."

She looked around at the Board members. "Something Mr. Michaels said to me the other day resonated with me. He said my grandfather wouldn't make major changes to the corporation because he wanted to honor his ancestors' memory. Well, I plan to do the same. The difference is that my ancestors include my father, a man who was very similar to, yet very different from, my grandfather.

"As some of you may know, my father was an environmentalist. Honoring him would mean some changes to Blithe Industries' portfolio of businesses. Exiting some of the more damaging ones."

Faith looked around at the Board members' faces. Some of them slowly nodded – an action that could have meant assent, but also could have meant they were absorbing something they thought was inconceivable. Not knowing this crowd, it was hard for Faith to gauge. Others looked expectantly at her for more information. Then she saw Geoff Michaels, who had a big grin on his face.

"At the very least, the paper, chemicals and tobacco companies will need to go, providing we can secure the right prices. Possibly more. In their place, I would like to build another leg to the business. I'd like to call it Blithe Earth. It will utilize the same capital discipline that my grandfather employed with respect to buying or building businesses. I expect us to gain exposure to green energy, green materials, green technology and organic foods. I also expect us to develop a portfolio of green venture capital investments."

Faith looked at Geoff Michaels, "I'd like Geoff to run this unit."

His smile faded and he looked shocked. She continued, "Geoff, my grandfather trusted you with the entire proceeds of his stake in Blithe Industries. He wanted that money to make a positive difference in the world and he handpicked you to be the one to do it. Now that I'm here, the situation has changed. Blithe will not be broken up and sold off. But I continue to believe in my grandfather's choice. With your help, I do believe that we can make a difference in the world, one profitable and forward-thinking investment at a time. What do you think?"

She looked intently at Michaels. He was staring at his hands. He cleared his throat and looked up at her, overcome with emotion. "I would be honored to do it." He nodded his head and wore a serious expression.

"Good stuff," Faith said. She turned her attention back to the other Board members.

"Now I'd like to introduce you to Blithe Industries' new Chief Technology Officer, my husband, Christopher Warrior." Chris smiled comfortably and waved his hand.

"Blithe doesn't currently have a CTO. Chris has held this position at several other companies and has a lot of ideas on how to improve efficiency and reporting across the entire organization. He will also consult on any tech investments Blithe might make. I mention this because technology was one of my grandfather's personal passions, though he hadn't brought that passion to Blithe. We plan to change that." She smiled fondly at her husband.

"Lastly, I have one other vision for Blithe, and it's not a small one. It doesn't involve building another leg to the business. It involves enhancing every part of the corporate body."

Faith paused and looked very seriously at everyone around the table. "You know that my grandfather cared about Blithe's employees. Some of you may have heard stories of how he took a long-term perspective on people. He was very open-minded, for instance, about the concept of flexible work. He felt that good talent should be utilized. Period. He viewed employees as the most important investment he could make in the business." The Board nodded and murmured their agreement.

"I'd like to take this sentiment further. I'd like to make Blithe Industries a role model for corporate America."

Eyebrows rose around the table. People sat forward in their chairs and looked at her.

"I know that this type of metamorphosis does not come for free. It will take investment. However, it is my objective to accomplish this while adhering to my grandfather's long-standing capital discipline. All enhancements will be brought to the Board for discussion. All of the numbers will need to work."

She continued, "I expect that whatever changes we ultimately make to benefits will serve to lower employee turnover and increase job satisfaction. This will translate into greater productivity. It is my hope that an improved corporate environment will also result in Blithe attracting the best and the brightest. Greater productivity and greater talent should bolster margins. But part of this endeavor is about changing attitudes in America, bringing back loyalty. Bringing back that sense of pride that comes from working for a company you admire, that openly values its employees. Blithe will set an example for America. And it will do it while demonstrating that valuing employees and maintaining good corporate profitability are not incompatible objectives."

Faith put up her hands. "All of this sounds very difficult to quantify, but as part of the financial analysis, we will investigate the margin impact experienced by other companies that have made such changes. Publicizing the research we do and the results we experience might actually help other companies make similar changes. We could be at the forefront of a sea change. And who knows? Maybe America will reward Blithe by choosing Blithe's products over other companies'. This would be icing on the cake."

The general spoke up, "I think I can comfortably say that none of us expected such sweeping change right out of the gate, Mrs. Warrior. But I like what I'm hearing. I look forward to hearing more about it. What do you folks think?" He looked at the other Board members.

One of the retired Fortune 500 CEOs laughed and then

said, "my company was number three on one of those 'best companies to work for in America,' lists when I was the CEO. Our conclusion at the time was that certain enhancements to benefits were financially justified. I'm happy to help in any way I can."

"And I'll take you up on that!" Faith smiled and laughed.

"The implications could be astounding," said a leading professor of organizational behavior. "I, too, would like to help in any way I can."

"Ladies and gentlemen, let me introduce our co-chairs for the 'Best Company' committee," Faith announced and gestured to the two gentlemen. She sat back and smiled at the Board for a moment.

"Okay, moving on," Faith said, and queued up the next topic on the agenda.

***

Faith and Chris left the meeting as the Board broke for lunch. A caterer had set up a spread in an adjacent conference room. The meeting would resume in an hour.

"Eventful morning," Chris said with extreme understatement. "Guess I need to call my employer and submit my resignation."

"Guess so," Faith glanced at him with a smile.

The couple hustled from the meeting down the corridor to her office. Faith pointed to the CEO's office, "feel free to use that for now. If you like it, keep it. If you don't, we'll find you a space you like better."

"Thanks, Boss!" Chris laughed and turned into the office – a huge space with a panoramic view. He turned back to her and smiled again – as he shut the door on her face.

"Goofball," Faith whispered to the closed door and smiled as she entered her own office next door.

She was just about to sit down at the desk when a tall, balding man entered the room, "Mrs. Warrior? I'm Jack Costello, your General Counsel."

He stepped forward and shook her hand.

"Good to meet you, Jack. One second," Faith picked up her phone and rang Miriam. "Send the Director of HR up in half an hour, please. Thanks."

She put the phone down. "Jack, thanks for meeting me." She exhaled. "It's been a big day," she said and raised her eyebrows.

"So I hear!" He responded.

"What do I need to know about what just went down in there?" Faith asked directly.

"As you already know, he had no employment contract. Given what you've alleged, he'll cooperate to avoid any press. To play nice, he'll receive what's customary when an employee is terminated."

"And that's it?"

"Yes, ma'am, that's it." He paused. "Should I expect to be handling more such situations?"

"If you mean to ask if I'll be cleaning house, the answer is 'not necessarily.' There will be a lot of changes around here. If folks don't get on board, they can leave or I'll ask them to leave. It's pretty simple." Faith looked at him level in the eye. "Look, I am a very reasonable person but I've got a lot to do. While I expect and welcome input and opinions, once I've made a decision, I won't tolerate anyone standing in my way."

"Understood," he said. He rose from the chair and shook her hand. "Welcome to Blithe." He smiled, inclined his head, then turned and left.

Faith swiveled her chair to look out of the window at downtown Washington, DC. She imagined that her grandfather had done the same thing countless times. She ran her hands down the armrests and gripped tightly, remembering an old Bette Davis movie quote, 'fasten your seatbelts, it's going to be a bumpy night.' "Bumpy year is more like it!" Faith muttered.

There was a knock at the door and the vice president of HR entered. Beth Baxter was an excruciatingly slim and well-dressed woman in her forties. "Good afternoon, Mrs. Warrior." She advanced into the room and shook Faith's hand as Faith rose from her chair. "It's a pleasure to meet you."

Faith gave a rueful laugh. "You might not think so after our discussion. Please, take a seat." Faith motioned to a chair in front of her desk.

"You've likely heard what came out of today's Board meeting."

Beth nodded. "Yes, ma'am. There's been a change of control." The woman sat angled slightly away from Faith, legs crossed away from Faith, fingers laced around one knee. *Bad body language*, Faith thought.

Faith looked at her carefully. "No," Faith said slowly. "There was a change of control over a week ago. Now there's been a change of management." She watched the woman's response. The woman's jaw clenched. "I need to arrange a webcast to all employees. I'd like to introduce myself."

Beth looked a bit flustered. "Of course, that's an excellent idea. I can set it up whenever you're ready." She made a few notes on her notepad.

"Also, you and I need to talk at length about changes I'd like to make at the corporation."

"Changes?" She frowned a bit.

"Yes, and many of them will impact your area."

The woman looked at her suspiciously. "Things have operated pretty well around here for a long time. What sort of changes are you talking about?"

"The ones that specifically fall into your area could include improving the healthcare package; greater compensation transparency; benchmarked pay; rectifying any discrepancies between what men and women earn for the same job; rewards for innovation and collaboration; 401k matching; tuition reimbursement for night school; tuition assistance for employees with college age children; more open consideration of talented people who need flexible positions; subsidized on-site daycare. We'll need to do a lot of analysis to determine the impact of these changes on profitability. But, in short, big changes, Beth."

Beth laughed.

Faith's eyes narrowed. "Do you find these ideas funny?"

"No, the ideas aren't funny. Well, they are a little. After all, this isn't Google. But I was laughing because Miriam Webber raised similar ideas last year. I rejected them. The cost associated with them would never have been approved."

"Did you do the analysis?" Faith asked.

"No, of course not. The ideas came from Mr. Blithe's *secretary*, for goodness sake. Mrs. Warrior, I run a cost center. There's no room in the budget for greater benefits. In fact, Mr. Von Heiden and I worked closely together last year on a project to streamline HR, to wring *more* out of the HR budget. I run a tight ship, Mrs. Warrior."

Faith cocked her head a bit. "Are you fundamentally

opposed to improving the benefits at Blithe?"

"We already reviewed the entire benefits package, and in my view, it's adequate. No enhancements are required. I do my job well, Mrs. Warrior." She sniffed and smoothed her skirt.

"How does Blithe compare to comparable companies with respect to healthcare?"

"Well, it's difficult to benchmark. Blithe is so unique."

"Beth, I'm sure this company utilizes a standard group of comparables, regardless of its uniqueness."

"Yes, well." Beth cleared her voice. "We are slightly below the mean with respect to healthcare."

"And you think this is adequate? What about the pay gap between men and women in the same jobs? Where are we with that?"

"We haven't actually done that analysis, but I'm sure we're being fair to women."

"But you don't really know because you don't have the data to back up your assertion. Beth, we have opportunities here to do better, and I'd like to do better in a profitable way. We won't know what we can do until we do some analysis." Faith stared at her while Beth stared back.

"You've made a mistake in firing Greg. He was very good at his job." *The implication being that I'll suck at the job*, Faith thought.

"Yes, well, people who don't follow directives from their employers often find themselves out of work," Faith said, looking pointedly at her. "Thank you for your time, Beth."

As soon as the VP of HR left her office, Faith picked up the phone. "I'll be calling you Miriam, now, if that's okay. And please call me Faith."

Miriam laughed, "Yes, that's okay."

"Miriam, can you ask Jack Costello to return to my office? Thanks."

Five minutes later, Jack Costello entered her office, eyebrows raised.

"As it turns out, you can expect to be doing more of 'that' for me." Faith said and gave him a sheepish smile.

"Who is it this time?" Jack asked

"Beth Baxter." Faith gazed out the window and slowly shook her head.

"Well, that's going to cost us. She has an employment

contract."

"She's been here for, what, fifteen years? Why would she have an employment contract?"

Jack coughed. "Von Heiden appreciated the work she did. He didn't want to lose her to another company. This is what he told me."

This just gets more and more fascinating, Faith thought. "So she was sleeping with Von Heiden?"

Jack looked a bit uncomfortable. "Well, one hears things sometimes. Things… such as that."

"Good grief. If this is what I find on day one, what will day two bring me? I'd better put you on speed dial!" Faith laughed.

"The good news is that she can't sue the CEO for sexual harassment anymore," he said in a deadpan voice.

Faith laughed out loud and ran a hand through her hair. "Thanks, Jack. Can you take care of ejecting her today?"

Jack looked at his watch. "It's almost one now. Let me go and review her file. But, I think I can get her out today."

"Good stuff." Faith picked up her phone as he turned to go. "Oh, and can you do some poking to see if she has any capable lieutenant who can take over for her?" She mouthed the word 'thanks.'

"Miriam, can you come in here?"

Miriam walked in and softly shut the door, then sat in a chair in front of Faith's desk, pen and pad in hand.

"Miriam, did you go to Beth last year and suggest improvements to benefits?"

Miriam nodded vigorously. "Yes. I thought they were consistent with your grandfather's posture, even though he'd never officially implemented such changes across the company. I was shot down."

Faith nodded and rubbed the back of her neck.

"How would you like to personally oversee making those enhancements?" Faith smiled at Miriam.

"Are you kidding? I'd love to do it. Do you mean working in conjunction with the Board members to determine what to do?"

"Yes, and then implementing whatever makes sense. I need a smart, capable, disciplined partner to make my dream for this company a reality. As VP of Corporate Development, you would oversee all of it. I've got a laundry list of things that will push this company to the top of the 'best companies in America' list, and I'll bet you've got other ideas I haven't even thought of. We need to do a lot of analysis to see which ones will clear our financial hurdles."

Miriam was silent and pensive.

"If you're concerned about the impact of more hours on your daughter, you needn't be. You can work from home some of the time. You're disciplined enough to get the job done, regardless of where you are."

Miriam was speechless. "I – I don't know what to say. It's a massive undertaking, but if I'm able to do some work from home... So, I'm no longer an assistant? I'm VP of Corporate Development?"

"As of tomorrow morning, yes. With commensurate compensation." Faith smiled.

Miriam shook her head and smiled. "Thank you," she said.

"No, thank *you*. I look forward to seeing what you come up with!"

"I need to find you my replacement."

"Yes, you do, but we might start by looking at Von Heiden's assistant. Is she any good?"

"Valerie Sims? She's very capable and certainly knows how to get things done. Shall I ask her to step into your office?"

"That would be great. And Miriam, find yourself some suitable office space," Faith said and Miriam walked from the room, wearing a huge smile.

Chris walked in and flopped down on the couch. "Why do I get the sense something major just happened?"

"Because you have 'the ESP,' as Paul likes to say." Faith stretched. "You're totally right. I fired someone else – the head of HR."

"Come on, Faith. How are you going to fire *more* people without the head of HR? Who's going to do the exit interviews?" Chris asked sarcastically, eyes twinkling.

"Oh, a WISE guy, eh?" Faith said in her best Three Stooges imitation. She started tidying her desk. "I feel like a whirling dervish. Or do I mean a Tasmanian Devil?"

"You're definitely not acting like a peace-loving dervish, Faith."

"I've got to slow down." Faith slumped in her chair.

"You've got to slow down."

"That's what I just said."

"You said it, but between the two of us, I'm the only one who meant it." Chris stood and walked back to the door. "Don't burn yourself out the first day. You're facing a marathon, not a 100-yard dash."

"I know, don't worry. I just can't help wanting to act quickly. When a surgeon finds disease, do you think he leaves it there if cutting it out will help the patient? These two people were bad for the health of the company. They had to go."

"Ok, first of all, you'd make a lousy surgeon. You can't even carve a turkey. But I believe you. I just want you to take a breath for a minute. For instance, don't immediately assume that the CFO needs to go just because he didn't speak up when the CEO made some acquisitions that violated Fritz's policy. You haven't yet asked him about the situation." Chris looked closer at Faith. "That's just what you were thinking, wasn't it? Well, hello nail head, let me introduce you to my hammer."

"I hear you. I know you're right. I'm going to give him a fair shake. But you need to know that I already have someone else in mind for the CFO slot. A friend from b-school." Chris looked unimpressed. She emphasized, "from my 'perfect world' list."

Chris closed his eyes a moment and nodded. "Okay. Just think about it carefully before you do anything. Think about what the Wall Street Journal will say about all of this change."

"I will, I will. But don't forget that every new CEO cleans house and brings in their own people. It's the way it goes."

Chris walked to the door. "Good point. Just pace yourself. Oh, and the meeting resumes in five minutes."

"Frick."

"I know, it's a bummer you can't fire anyone in five minutes." He smiled and walked out.

"Why I oughtta...." Faith waved her fist in mock menace at her husband just as Valerie Sims stepped into the doorway.

Faith picked up her phone, "Miriam, please ask the CFO to meet me in my office tomorrow at 9 a.m. Thanks!"

"Ms. Sims? I'm Faith Warrior," Faith stepped around the desk and shook her hand.

Valerie Sims, a round, bespectacled woman in her mid-thirties, looked at Faith with trepidation. "It's nice to meet you."

"Valerie – may I call you Valerie?" The woman nodded her assent. "I only have a few minutes before I head back into the Board meeting. I need an assistant. As Mr. Von Heiden is no longer with the company, how would you like to work for me?"

Valerie smiled with relief, "I'd like that, Mrs. Warrior."

"Call me Faith. Excellent. Well, Miriam Webber has a new job here starting tomorrow, so why don't you move over to her cubicle once she's settled in her new space? I need to get to this meeting now. I'll speak with you later?"

The woman nodded as Faith breezed past. "Thank you, Mrs. – er, Faith."

Faith gave her a warm smile and a wave as she walked down the corridor.

***

"Mom, where were you at lunch today? I thought you had lunch duty." Graham grouched at her from the back seat of the minivan.

Faith blanched. "Oh, frickezoids! I totally forgot!" This was bad, very bad. The lunch crew was notorious for being short-handed as it was. They could not afford to have someone forget. "How did it go?"

"Well, we had to wait in line for a long time to get lunch, so I had to eat really quickly. Jason's mom was handing out the trays and she had to keep running back to the kitchen to get more trays while the lunch lady put the food on them. She seemed sweaty and maybe a little mad."

Oh no. Meredith. She would never hear the end of it from Meredith. "I'll give Jason's mom a call and apologize. Thanks for reminding me, sweetie."

Things are already falling through the cracks, Faith thought to herself. *I'll have to merge my personal calendar with the office calendar so I can keep things straight.*

"Well, did you boys have a good day?" Faith asked.

Paul immediately started talking. "Matthew S. made 'splat' on my puzzle. I told him to stop but he didn't stop, so I made 'splat' on HIS puzzle."

"What's 'splat' and did you get in trouble for it?"

"'Splat' is when someone hits your puzzle with their hand

and the pieces go flying all around. It wasn't nice. I was almost finished with that puzzle, too."

"Did you get in trouble for 'splatting' back?"

"No, but Matthew S. did. He got a time out and couldn't go outside to play. He's a poo-poo head."

"Paul, we don't say 'poo-poo head'. Wow, that's a big punishment."

"Well, he 'splatted' a lot of kids, not just me."

"Ah, I see. Graham, how was your day?"

"The teacher made me 'special helper' today!"

"Hon, that's great! Good for you!"

The boys chatted on about their day as the minivan wended its way back to Blithe House. Faith thought to herself how happy she was that she didn't have to miss out on the daily post-school data dump.

When they arrived, Faith took the boys out to the backyard to play on the incredible playhouse her grandfather had had built. Faith inhaled deeply. She loved the fragrance of fall. The nip in the air and the faint smell of someone enjoying a fire in their fireplace. She walked around the garden to the cute little door embedded in the stone wall. It had a steel ring for a knob, but no lock was visible, nor could she see any hinges. She guessed it was decorative. Faith walked back around and sat on a stone bench to watch her children climbing.

"I'm a mermaid on a rock and you're on a ship. Go!" She called to them. She loved to play this imaginary game with her kids. She laid out a scenario and then they jumped in. Suddenly, the boys were sailors on a tall ship, yelling 'ahoy!' at one another. Paul decided he was a pirate and started hobbling around like he had a peg leg, growling 'argh!'

George Hopewell approached her moments later.

"I saw you from my office window," he said as he strode up to her. "I wanted to give you an update."

"Well, you've got good timing – fire away."

"We've made good progress on transferring your grandfather's assets into your name. I don't foresee any complications." He paused as Faith slowly nodded, then slowly started shaking her head.

"Why do I sense a 'but' coming?" Faith's brow furrowed.

"Cassandra Blithe," he said.

"What about her?"

"Well, it appears she's been the recipient of support from your grandfather for the past 35 years."

Faith frowned. "Why?"

"I'm not really sure. One could speculate that he took Cassandra under his wing after Thomas died and Mick left the family. Perhaps she seemed like the only family he and your grandmother had left. She never re-married. Anyway, with his support, she didn't have to. And of course, she had Daniel."

"Well, that makes some sense. My grandfather was a very wealthy man and Cassandra seems very nice. She never told the father? I notice that Daniel has the last name Blithe." Faith asked.

"I don't know if she ever told the father. We never knew who he was. Your grandfather spent a lot of time with Daniel, arranged for his entry into top schools. The boy is now in his early-thirties. I've met him. He seems like a nice man. He's certainly very smart. From what I could tell, there was genuine affection between Daniel and your grandfather."

"Where is he now?" Faith's curiosity was peaked.

"Daniel works in high technology out in California. I believe the company is called Xnard."

"Znard? What the heck is Znard?"

"X-N-A-R-D is how it's spelled. I've no idea what they do." And then it hit her. Xnard was on the list of her grandfather's high tech investments.

Faith mulled that. "So what do you suggest we do about Cassandra Blithe?"

"She's been remarkably litigious during her life, or so I've heard. Despite how pleasant she seems, I would not be surprised if she attempted to get some money from you. Her inheritance from your grandfather's estate was not big."

"What kind of argument could she possibly make to get money from me?" Faith said with surprise.

"Well, her attorney could argue that the support your grandfather regularly gave her over thirty-five years constituted an implied-in-fact contract."

"Which is?"

"The Supreme Court defines it as a 'meeting of minds', a 'tacit understanding', inferred by the parties' actions rather than through express contract. In other words, your grandfather, through his regular and consistent support of her, demonstrated an ongoing willingness to support her. It's a valid argument but it's hard to quantify."

"But surely, any contract is void upon one of the parties' death?"

"Typically, yes, but since he left such an enormous estate, she might still try."

"So what do you recommend I do?"

"Well, nothing, unless she makes an overture. Mrs. Abernathy showed me an accounting of everything your grandfather gave her. He wrote checks to her annually, if not more frequently than that. Mrs. Blithe is now 53 years old. If she received ongoing support until she's 65, the net present value of that sum could be estimated at this amount." He showed her a spreadsheet and pointed to a figure.

Faith's eyes widened, then narrowed. "Wait a minute. This doesn't make sense." She scanned the annual payments.

"Pardon?"

"The clothing and jewelry she wore when I met her would have cost half of what my grandfather gave her in an average year. Not to mention the amazing hair color and the plastic surgery." *Well, well, People Magazine might actually be worth the exorbitant subscription fee, after all.*

"She's had plastic surgery?" He looked surprised.

Faith laughed. "I don't care how well a woman maintains herself, there's no way she looks that good at her age without a tug here and an implant there."

Faith looked up at Hopewell. "Does she have a career or is she independently wealthy?"

"No on both counts. She inherited a bit when Thomas died – not enough to support her for the duration of her life. If he'd lived a few more years, she'd have gotten his trust, which was considerable." Hopewell said.

"Then someone else was helping her along. I'd like to find out whom. And why." She paused.

"The plot thickens." He said.

She laughed. "Like custard over heat, Mr. Hopewell."

He rose, waved to the kids and went back to the building. *Daniel Blithe, techie. Well, I'll be.*

***

Chris came home just as the doorbell rang. Mrs. Loper

found Faith in the lower dining room helping Graham finish his homework. Chris took over for her.

"Mr. Whitman, it's so nice to see you," Faith said as she reached him in the formal living room.

"Mrs. Warrior," he nodded. "I'm sorry for the intrusion. I've just… felt at a loss since Fritz died." He put up his hands, looking very tired. "I miss him. And you're the closest person to him now. So here I am." He smiled sadly.

"You're very welcome here, Mr. Whitman, and please call me Faith," she said warmly. She glimpsed Roberts in the hallway and nodded reassuringly at him. He raised an eyebrow, stepped back into the shadows and sat down in a hall chair. *What is that about?*

"Faith. That's a nice name. I remember meeting your mother once. At Thomas and Elena's funeral, I think. What an awful day."

"Tell me about it."

"Well, Fritz was an absolute mess," he said levelly. "Understandably. And Mick looked lost. The way he clutched your mother's hand, well, it's amazing they didn't stay together. Your mother told me about their plans to study environmental law. I encouraged Mick to follow that path, but, well, he just couldn't leave Fritz. A shame."

"I think the fact that he sacrificed that dream for his father was really admirable," Faith said.

"Well, yes, but maybe he wouldn't have been there a few weeks later, the night that crazy man appeared. Maybe he'd still be alive."

"I… hadn't thought of that." Faith looked at him seriously. *He has very dark eyes. The darkest brown I've ever seen.* "So you went to Harvard Business School. What did you do after that?"

He laughed. "Make money, of course."

She smiled. "Well, I should hope so, given how expensive that school is. One must make enough to pay for that investment."

"And I did. I ran a corporate buyout and turnaround firm. You know the type: buy slightly broken companies, fix them up, then sell them at a profit."

"It sounds challenging."

"It was, but I love a challenge." He smiled. "And I was

good at it."

"Did you specialize in any particular industry?"

"I did at first, but then I branched out as I got more comfortable with the turnaround process. I was able to advise Fritz on a number of deals – tobacco, chemicals, paper. Let me know if you ever need any help – I heard about the CEO shakeup today -- I don't do that work anymore, but I still own a slice of the company I launched and I try to keep current on things."

If I hear any more about tobacco, chemicals and paper, ugh… I certainly don't need any more acquisition advise in those areas… Faith mentally rolled her eyes. "Yes, it's been a momentous day. Thank you, Mr. Whitman. That's really generous of you."

"Well, you are Fritz Blithe's granddaughter. And there isn't anything I wouldn't do for his family."

They chatted a bit more, then Faith realized she needed to get the kids into the bath. "I really appreciate your visit, Mr. Whitman. I hope we can get together again soon."

"You can count on it, Faith," he said, and gave her a hug.

After the door shut, Roberts stood up. "You might want to watch that one, Mrs. Warrior."

"Mr. Whitman? Why?"

"Your grandfather didn't talk about it, but I'd noticed that he didn't see much of Mr. Whitman over the last few years. Not since a golf trip they took to Carmel. I just got a sense that they'd had a disagreement. What I mean to say is, they weren't as close as Mr. Whitman described. At least not recently."

   ***

The kids were asleep and Faith and Chris were relaxing with cups of green tea in their sitting room.

Faith absentmindedly pulled a Thin Mint from an open box of Girl Scout cookies on the table. She brushed the crumbs from her fingers and looked at the side of the box.

"They need to change the servings on the box to two. Sleeve one and sleeve two."

Chris smiled at her. "Bu-dum-tish." He mimed the vaudevillian punch line sound effect.

"Okay," she said, handing him the box. "Lock them up and throw away the key, before I polish off the whole box."

Without looking up from his papers, he shoved the box in

a drawer and mimed locking it.

"So. Xnard. The company's name is Xnard. Ever heard of it?" Faith asked as she Googled the word. Her search only yielded information about the city of Oxnard, just north of Malibu, California. "I've got zippo."

"Nope." He looked up. "And there's nothing on the web? That is really curious. Even a tiny startup would leave footprints on the web, particularly if it's tech." Her husband looked perplexed. "Where is that spreadsheet with your grandfather's holdings?"

Faith rummaged at her desk and pulled out the printout. Before she handed it to him, she looked again at the cost of the investment. "Ten million dollars. He sank ten million into it and I can't even find it on the web!" She handed it to him.

"The date of the investment was about a year ago. It should have a presence by now, even if it was just an idea a year ago. There's a phone number. Here, reverse lookup the number." He handed the spreadsheet back to her. She navigated to whitepages.com and typed in the phone number.

"Landline. San Jose, California." Faith looked up. "What does it mean?"

"Not much. Silicon Valley looks right, given the business we're talking about." He tossed her his cell phone. "Give it a jingle. All we want to know is who is on the other end, capice? Don't engage in a conversation, don't reveal who you are."

"Right, godfather. Because whoever answers couldn't reverse lookup your number, too."

"Well, of course they could. The point is not to give them any reason to try."

She punched the numbers. He stuffed napkins in his cheeks and gave her his best Marlon Brando look. Faith raised her eyebrow at her husband.

"Yakmak." A young man answered the phone.

Wait – what? "May I speak with – er, Mario Puzo, please?" Faith asked innocently. Chris rolled his eyes.

"One moment, please, " said the young man in American-accented English. Faith clapped a hand over her mouth to keep from laughing. "I'm sorry, there's no one here by that name."

"What number did I reach?" persisted Faith. He recited the number. "Oh, that is so strange. Is this a company?"

"Yes, ma'am. Yakmak." *Oh frick, I did hear that correctly!*
"Oh, okay, sorry – wrong number!" Faith hung up.

"Yakmak, Chris. The number is for Yakmak." Yakmak was one of the biggest, most successful companies in Silicon Valley. It was started by a legendary technology visionary Ptolemy Gunesdogdu – a brilliant man with, from her American perspective, a really unfortunate last name. She looked around, thinking. "Hmm. Maybe this is a Yakmak joint-venture of some sort."

Chris spat out the napkins. "Sounds like we need to have a little conversation with your – er, not-your-cousin."

"I'm thinking you're right. But first, I'll let our Green Berets have a crack at it. They seem to have a knack for this security and investigation business." Faith smiled, picked up a house phone and pushed a button.

"You just like saying you've got Green Berets working for you."

"Mr. Hopewell, this is Faith Warrior." She winked at her husband. "When you get in in the morning, can you please share with me whatever file you've got on the Xnard investment? Many thanks, and I hope you're enjoying your evening." She hung up the phone. "It's much easier this way."

Chris laughed. "Yes, Godfather, it is," he replied in a mysterious voice.

Chapter 9

At nine o'clock sharp, the CFO, Kevin MacGuire, knocked softly on her office door before poking his head in. "Mrs. Warrior, you wanted to see me?"

Looking up, Faith smiled at the CFO. Beyond him, she saw Miriam and Valerie talking as Miriam packed up her cubicle.

"Mr. MacGuire – may I call you Kevin?" Faith rose from her chair and stretched out her hand.

"Of course," he said and he shook her hand.

"Call me Faith. Please, have a seat. Yesterday was quite hectic and I never had a chance to circle back with you. Thanks for meeting me."

He smiled in bewilderment, clearly expecting a far less pleasant encounter, then sat in a chair in front of her desk.

"We need to clear the air about the ROI situation. I need to understand how it came to be that Von Heiden pushed through those acquisitions despite clear violation of my grandfather's investment principles."

The CFO nodded. "I can understand your concern. Frankly, I was similarly concerned when Greg approved them. Let me explain how acquisition targets are identified and then approved, then I'll explain what happened with these deals."

Kevin went on to explain the manner in which investment ideas bubbled-up from subsidiary companies to corporate, then the rigorous vetting process that the CFO's team utilized to weed out unacceptable targets.

He handed her a sheet that itemized the deals that had been discussed at, and closed after, the Board meeting three months before. A few of them had been the trigger for Von Heiden's dismissal. All of them were in the environmentally unfriendly business segment, *Blithe Materials* – the paper and chemicals businesses.

"Do you have a comprehensive list of acquisitions from the last year or two?" Faith asked.

"Yes," he responded and dug through a stack of papers. He handed her a list two pages long.

Faith scanned it. "It appears that most of the acquisitions were bolt-ons to existing businesses." She read further. "All were projected to add value almost instantly due to cost synergies." She looked up. "Has this proved to be the case?"

"Yes. The bolt-ons were in existing or adjacent businesses. We understood the businesses well and had an existing infrastructure to plug them into. This is a delicate way of saying we were able to lay off a good deal of redundant staff. But we also were able to plug them into existing sourcing arrangements that lowered the cost of inputs. These were value-added deals."

Faith nodded. "Ok, so what was the rationale for these latest acquisitions? They were in existing industries but from what I can tell, these companies did not have overlapping end markets or similar raw materials. What was the strategy?" Faith looked at the CFO.

The CFO was very serious. "Greg felt we could leverage our marketing and lobbying expertise. You see what industries they are in. We've had to develop political connections and influence to make the businesses successful, given the environmental concerns. His argument for making the acquisitions was that he could leverage those connections to reduce costs and enter new markets."

"What sort of lobbying expertise does Blithe have?"

"We've got a government relations department dedicated to supporting these businesses. In the past, we've not only been able to successfully lobby for our businesses, we've been able to successfully lobby against other companies. Including, it would seem, the very businesses we acquired this quarter."

Er, what? "Did Von Heiden's rationale make sense to you?" Faith asked.

"Yes, given the strength of our lobbyists. But I couldn't reliably quantify that benefit, and the ROI projections reflect it. This made Greg unhappy, but I was adamant about not changing them. My projections are what you spotted in the

Board meeting as being inconsistent with company policy."

Faith nodded. "So how did these deals get done? Von Heiden needed to have you on board, too."

"You're right. If I hadn't felt comfortable that your grandfather supported the deals, I would have spoken up at the Board meeting three months ago. I asked Greg very directly what your grandfather thought of the acquisitions and he said he approved of them. And since Greg had spoken to the Board about the deals, it wasn't my place to go over the CEO's head and ask your grandfather directly. I assumed they'd been approved. Clearly, I was wrong."

Faith was silent for a moment as she regarded him. "Tell me more about how Blithe lobbied against these companies we acquired."

"It's not an uncommon strategy to weaken a reluctant acquisition target so they acquiesce – and do so at an even more favorable price. Greg gave instructions to the government relations staff to do what they could to dampen their business."

Faith's eyes widened a bit. "That sounds predatory."

The CFO inclined his head. "Predatory, unsavory, pick your word; but not illegal. Your grandfather was very clear with the staff about that. Though they do tend to walk closely to the line. Frankly, I was surprised to hear that your grandfather was open to being even close to the line."

"And you never saw written documentation that he'd approved the deals?"

"No."

"Did you see this as unusual?"

"Yes. He was very careful about documentation."

"I'm still perplexed about the question of 'why'? Why did Von Heiden push through deals that hadn't been approved?" Faith shook her head. "What was worth the risk?"

The CFO looked left as he spoke. "Well, I think he had an axe to grind with someone involved with one of the companies. He took some delight in doing the deals."

Faith tried to remember the eye-movement rules she'd learned years before from an ex-CIA operative she'd once dated. If someone looks left while speaking, he's recalling something that actually happened. If someone looks right, he's imagining something. Looking up and to the left means he's recalling something he saw. Looking to the side means he's recalling something he heard. Looking down means he's recalling something he smelled, tasted or felt. Unless the CFO was deliberately using these rules to throw her off, he was probably telling the truth.

Faith thought for a moment. "Kevin, how long have you been with Blithe?"

"Twelve years. I started as Controller and was promoted to CFO three years ago." He looked to be bracing himself for bad news.

Faith nodded. "If you hadn't had the backbone to keep your ROI projections realistic, it would have taken me far longer to realize what Von Heiden was doing. I need people like you on the team."

The CFO's mouth dropped open.

"I can see you're surprised by my reaction. Look, I'm not happy that you didn't push back more against Von Heiden, but I understand how it all happened. It's time to move on. I know that in future you'll be a strong partner in maintaining fiscal discipline at Blithe. Correct?"

"Yes, absolutely." Kevin swallowed.

"Good stuff. Ok, as I said, moving on. I understand from Miriam that you've created a deck?"

The 'deck' was a comprehensive document that detailed budget, projections, segments, business units, economic drivers, acquisitions, corporate schedule, tax schedule, legal issues, the organizational chart – virtually all key information for the company, kept in one place for easy reference, constantly updated.

"Yes, I have one. In fact, there should be a copy of it in Greg's old office. Shall I look for it?"

Faith nodded. "Certainly. My husband now occupies that office but everything that had been in there was boxed up and is stacked by the door. Only his personal things were shipped to him."

"There are only two copies regularly updated. The CEO's and mine. My assistant manages the process and forwards updates to the CEO's assistant." He pointed to the door, "I'm guessing you'll have Valerie take over from Miriam?" Faith nodded. "When I find it, I'll make sure it's up to date before giving it to you. You'll have it by the end of the day."

"Thanks, Kevin. Tomorrow morning, I'd like to sit down with you again and discuss the changes I'm contemplating for Blithe. Say nine o'clock?" The CFO agreed and Faith exhaled as he closed the door. The meeting had gone better than she thought it would. She was relieved to feel that the CFO was worth keeping.

***

Hopewell called Faith later in the morning.

"Daniel Blithe is on Yakmak's payroll. The nature of Xnard's business appears to be quite secretive. I could not discover anything about it. I pulled the file from the investments drawer. The terms of the deal are curious. I hadn't been involved on this one."

"What are the terms?"

"Your grandfather is a 25% owner in Xnard. Yakmak's founder owns 40%. Mitchell Curzon owns another 25%. Daniel Blithe owns 10% and is running Xnard. We just don't know what Xnard actually is. The investment terms are very restrictive – you can't easily monetize it if you wanted to get out."

Faith's brow furrowed. "Ptolemy Gunesdogdu and Mitchell Curzon are investors? Good grief, those are big names."

Mitchell Curzon was a British entrepreneur who, like Ptolemy Gunesdogdu, had become fabulously wealthy at a very young age. But whereas Gunesdogdu had made his fortune in high tech, Curzon had snatched up majority stakes in Soviet businesses in the late 1980s thanks to Gorbachev's perestroika and his own personal connections. He expanded his toehold in the former Eastern Bloc countries in the early 1990s after the Iron Curtain fell. Glasnost and perestroika were very good for him.

Over time, Curzon had divested those interests and set about opportunistically investing in other volatile parts of the world. No one, it seems, knew better how to make money out of economic turmoil than he did.

Faith asked, "What do people out there know about Daniel?"

"He's brilliant, has a doctorate in physics. He's been involved with experiments that could render obsolete

Einstein's Theory of Relativity. Shocking for anyone to achieve, much less someone so young. His work involves something about particles called neutrinos. I won't pretend to understand any of it. I only know that some of his research has turned the scientific community on its head. Daniel Blithe is considered a genius in that neck of the woods. No one knows exactly what he's doing but everyone knows who he is."

"Well, that explains how he got people like Gunesdogdu and Curzon to invest. Thank you, Mr. Hopewell." Faith gazed out at the city below her office window, lost in thought.

"Would you like me to look into the other investments on the list?"

"Yes, I'd be most grateful for that." Faith thanked him and hung up.

She walked to her husband's office door and poked her head in. "Can I interrupt?"

"One second." He finished tapping away at his keyboard, and then looked up. "What's up?"

She filled him in on what the attorney had told her.

"Okay, then," Chris said. "Daniel is one of the big boys in all of this. Let's get him on the phone and find out what's going on." Faith closed the door and sat down in a chair by Chris's desk.

Chris checked the number they'd called the night before on his cell phone, then dialed it into his office phone and put it on speaker.

"Yakmak." A young woman answered this time, but with the same deadpan delivery. It almost sounded like a duck quacking.

"Christopher Warrior calling from Blithe Industries for Daniel Blithe."

"One moment, please."

"Mr. Warrior?" A young man asked.

"And Faith Warrior, yes. Is this Daniel Blithe?"

"It is. It's nice to speak with you. I was in Switzerland and couldn't get to the funeral."

"Daniel," Faith interjected. "The reason we're calling is, well, you were quite close to my grandfather. I'm very sorry for your loss."

"He was a very good man, certainly very good to me. He was like a grandfather to me, even though we weren't actually related. He didn't seem to care. He treated me like family."

Faith nodded as she looked at the phone. "Yes, I understand that. I didn't know him for long at all, but I've come to know him through the things so many people have told me about him. He seemed to have been a very good man."

"He was," Daniel said quietly.

Faith paused a moment, out of respect, before moving on. "Daniel, the other reason I'm calling is to find out about Xnard. My grandfather must have really believed in you to make such an investment. We'd like to know more about it."

He was silent for a moment. "I see. Well, I never imagined I'd have to tell anyone else about the investment. As you know by now, there are only four shareholders in this venture. Before I tell you about it, I want to make you aware of the two conditions that were built into the investment." Daniel said matter-of-factly.

"Go on," Faith encouraged.

"The first relates to the investment itself. If you ever wish to sell your stake, it must be sold to one or more of the original investors."

"Yes, I was aware of that. Highly unusual."

"It is a highly unusual term. Then again, the nature of the business is highly unusual, and this term helps to limit access to a trusted few. By Fritz' passing, the trusted four now become five." He said. "The second term involves confidentiality. Under no circumstances are any of the investors to discuss the investment with the outside world. Mr. Warrior, this includes you, as it does Mr. Gunesdogdu's spouse. If any evidence comes to light that an investor has talked, that investor forfeits his – or her – investment to the other stakeholders."

"Those are very strict conditions. I am very curious to know what three wealthy, intelligent investors thought was worth tens of millions of dollars, sight unseen, with hands tied."

"I'll be happy to fill you in, Faith, alone and in person."

Faith and Chris looked at each other and frowned. *'Curiouser and curiouser'*, thought Faith.

He continued. "The only thing I can tell you now is that Xnard was my concept. It relates to the particle physics research I'm doing." Daniel said. "So when are you coming to California?"

Faith frowned. "I have no plans to go to California." She thought for a moment before saying, "why don't you come here? I can have Mrs. Abernathy make the arrangements."

Silence. "Alright. I suppose a visit would pacify my mother. My phone has been ringing off the hook since Fritz died. I can come this weekend if that works for you."

Faith smiled, "good. I'll have Mrs. Abernathy call you. You're welcome to stay at Blithe House, if you wish."

"I'd like that. Thanks, Faith."

"It's my pleasure. I look forward to meeting you, Daniel."

"And I, you." Daniel hung up.

"What the heck was that?" Chris asked. "Who ever heard of such investment terms?"

"They are very strange. I don't like that I can't discuss the investment with you. I'll have to see if I can find a legal way to do it. I'll call Mr. Hopewell."

Faith's stomach rumbled loudly. Chris laughed. "Is Madame hungry?"

"Starving. Let's order in some lunch." Faith picked up the phone and punched Valerie's extension. "What places deliver here?"

Valerie gave them a few options, then called in their order for them.

While they ate, Chris updated Faith on his efforts to understand how technology was managed across the corporation. He described the corporate technology department and how it relates to each of the subsidiaries – what decisions were made centrally and what were made 'locally'. He'd already identified several changes that would improve productivity and lower costs, and was working with the finance department to quantify the impact of those changes.

Faith spent the next two hours working on her game plan for the corporation. She combed through Kevin's deck to solidify her understanding of the corporate structure and the different businesses. She began to assemble a list of changes she wanted to make – divestitures, mainly.

As her mind shifted to thoughts of investment, she lobbed a call into Geoff Michaels to discuss the timing of his joining the corporation. Faith was pleased to hear that he could begin part time the following week, while transitioning things at the think tank.

She also ascertained through Jack Costello that the second in command in the HR department, a man named Owen Lively, was a suitable replacement for Beth Baxter as VP of HR.

Faith called Lively to her office and promoted him on the spot. *No time like the present.* She asked him to assist Miriam and Geoff in finding appropriate office space and requested he contact Geoff to wrap up compensation negotiations. She also asked him to help her husband find an assistant. Finally, she confidentially let him know what Miriam was up to with respect to benefits and asked that he support her in any way he could.

At two o'clock, Faith popped into Chris's office. "Ok," she said. "So here's where we have to figure out the child situation."

Chris looked up at her. "Child situation?"

"Yes, dear." She sat down. "We've always said we wanted a parent home with them after school. Now that we both have jobs, I propose that we split the responsibility 50/50. Well, as close to that as possible given there are five work days in a week."

Faith was conflicted about this. She knew it would be wrenching to miss out on the daily 'data dump' from the kids each afternoon, but she couldn't do this job 8:30-2:30. The only thing that made this decision easier was knowing that Chris would be the one getting half of the afternoons. He wasn't mommy, and he didn't do things the way Faith did, and she'd still be jealous of those lost afternoons, but it was the best she could do. She just needed to keep telling herself that.

They decided that they would each go home early every other day to pick up the children. Chris offered to take the first afternoon. He tidied his desk, grabbed his coat and called Roberts on his mobile as he left the office. Roberts would meet him in front of the building and they would pick the children up from school.

Faith nodded to herself as she sat down at her desk. The kids were taken care of, things were perking along at work, and her best friend was coming into town this weekend… Her thoughts came to a screeching halt as she realized she'd scheduled two guests for the weekend – Anne O'Malley and Daniel Blithe. *Oh well*, she thought, *the more the merrier!*

She called Mrs. Abernathy to let her know about the guests and asked her to make their travel arrangements and coordinate with Mrs. Lucie to get their rooms ready. She told the assistant what their phone numbers were, then thanked her for taking care of the details and hung up.

Faith refocused her attention on her game plan and worked steadily on it until four o'clock when she began to write the script for her intranet webcast. She didn't plan to address her radical changes – only wanted to put a face with her name, express her condolences to all of the employees who personally knew her grandfather, and reassure them that someone was at the helm.

Once she'd drafted a script, she called Owen Lively to schedule filming for the next morning.

At five o'clock, she called Roberts, then organized herself for the morning and bid a surprised Valerie goodbye. She paused by the woman's desk and said, "Valerie, every other day, I'll be leaving work at two thirty in the afternoon so I can be with my kids. On other days, I'll leave work at five o'clock. It's all on my shared calendar on the system. I would like you to be here until five o'clock each day but I do not expect you to stay later unless there is some sort of emergency."

Valerie looked at her with wide eyes. "Oh. Mr. Von Heiden had me stay until seven o'clock most nights."

"I am definitely not Mr. Von Heiden. This is not to say I don't work hard, nor is it to say that I don't expect others to work hard. I simply value getting things done in the time allotted." She smiled at Valerie and then wished her a good evening.

***

As Roberts pulled through the gate, Faith saw there were a few trucks parked in the courtyard. "What's up?" Faith asked.

"The day your grandfather died, he had requested Mrs. Abernathy get a few things done. Most of those things were done today," he replied.

"Such as?"

"I believe Mrs. Abernathy will fill you in on it. Here she is now," he motioned to the side door and she saw the assistant approach the car.

Faith stepped out of the car. "What's going on, Mrs. A?"

The older woman exhaled and smiled. "Well, your grandfather had asked that the bowling alley be spruced up, so there are some workmen down there right now." The two women walked inside the house. "He also asked that the Music Room be reopened." Mrs. Abernathy motioned for Faith to accompany her there.

As they entered the foyer from the back of the house, she saw that the Music Room doors were open and sunlight streamed through. The musty smell was gone and Faith could see that the room gleamed. She spotted a young man at the piano, cleaning and tuning it.

"Your grandmother was an accomplished pianist. When she died, your grandfather asked that the door be kept closed. Other than basic cleaning, no one went in there."

"I'd wondered about that," murmured Faith.

Faith heard squealing from upstairs. Mrs. Abernathy smiled. "Ah yes, the other improvements. Let me show you."

As they ascended the staircase to the second floor, the assistant added, "The playroom in your private suite was finished today, too, and your toys and books were moved in there. I hope the boys like it." She smiled. "It's very cheerful."

"Mommy!" Graham and Paul ran to hug her as she walked into the Ballroom. She staggered back when the hurled their giggling selves into her arms. When she straightened up, she took in the scene.

"Fritz's special delivery arrived," Chris said as he sauntered over to her.

"Oh my gosh! This is amazing!" Faith stepped into the room and gazed around. Her grandfather had ordered a net-enclosed trampoline, a bounce house, a huge tee-pee and two battery-operated riding vehicles.

The boys started speaking a mile a minute about their new toys. Paul ran off to show her how high he could jump in the bounce house, while Graham showed her how well he could drive one of the vehicles.

"This is it, right Mrs. A? I'm not going to come home tomorrow and find a carousel set up in the living room? Or a helipad on the roof?"

The older woman laughed. "No, no, this is it."

Faith shook her head in wonder at the room. "Well, thank you so much for arranging it all. It's just wonderful. I can't imagine how you got it all done that very afternoon."

"I didn't. I called a playground superstore in Virginia, gave them the list of items and they handled it."

"Well, I'm impressed. Oh, did you make the arrangements for our guests?"

"Yes, they are all set. Mrs. Lucie has readied their rooms, too. The pilot will pick up Mr. Blithe in California first, then stop to pick up Ms. O'Malley. They will fly the last leg together and will dine aboard the airplane. As they'll arrive quite late on Friday, security will let them in and show them to their rooms."

"Terrific. Thank you, Mrs. Abernathy."

They bid each other goodbye and the assistant left for the day.

"So we'll have a full house this weekend?" asked Chris. "This is going to be fun!" he said. 'I'm thinking cookout," he said, rubbing his hands together.

"You're going to step on the chef's toes so early?" Faith pretended to look afraid.

"Oh, I'll throw him a bone and let him do all of the prep work. You know he's going to love having a night off." Chris responded, then added to himself, "I need to see if we've got a grill."

"We do. There's a large one next to the patio outside the pool house."

"Excellent," he said, in his best Mr. Burns voice. "And if you're inviting a friend, I get to invite one, too. If only I had a pseudo-cousin to add to the mix."

"Right-e-o. So who's it going to be? Norm?" Faith named Chris's high school friend. "Because he and Anne get along so swimmingly," she said sarcastically. The last time they'd all gotten together, Norm and Anne had spent the entire evening arguing about politics.

"Nope, I think I'll save us the agony. How about Jim?"

"Sure – that sounds like a good mix!"

"And now," Faith announced in her best British accent, "I shall partake of the bouncy house!" She kicked off her heels and raced down to join Paul in the bouncy house, where she dived in and started laughing and jumping with her four-year-old.

"Hey, what about me?" yelled Graham, and he ran down to join them.

Chris finally muttered, "oh what the heck," and kicked off his shoes, too.

    ***

After everyone had eaten and the kids were bathed and their teeth were brushed, the four of them sat in the newly decorated playroom next to Faith and Chris's suite and read. It felt good to finally get back to this routine.

Graham started off by reading aloud a chapter from a Frog and Toad book. Then Paul read aloud one Bob book, carefully sounding out each letter. Faith finished by reading them a few chapters from Beverly Cleary's book, *Henry and Beezus*. They were slowly making their way through the series of *Ramona* books, thoroughly enjoying each one.

Faith looked up from the book. "It is amazing what parents let kids do in the 1950s."

"Kids were free-range back then." Chris said matter-of-factly.

"It's amazing anyone survived," Faith chuckled. "Between the lack of seatbelts, lack of helmets and the overall lack of supervision…"

Chris cut in, "and don't forget the total lack of a sense of entitlement. Truly, it is amazing that anyone survived."

"What's entitlement?" Graham asked.

"It's when you grow up expecting you're going to get things without working for them," Chris said. "Don't let any of this pretty scenery make you forget that you need to work for a living when you grow up."

Faith nodded, and then whispered in aside to her husband, "Easier said than done – we need to formulate a game plan, mon amour."

"Yup," he agreed.

"Wait!" Faith's eyes flew open. "Did Graham do his homework?"

"As soon as we got home, before we even investigated the surprises," he smiled smugly.

"Smart man! I think I'll keep you!" Faith gave him a big smile.

"Okay, buddies, time for bed," Chris announced.

"No!!!"

"Boys, if you don't get to sleep now, "Faith announced, "You'll be grouch faces tomorrow because you'll be so tired. Now march." Faith pointed toward their rooms.

She herded them down the hall to their rooms. After a trip to the bathroom, she turned down the lights in both rooms, opened the connecting door and settled Graham into his bed. Faith pulled Paul onto her lap and led the boys through their bedtime prayers, then sang some songs. She kissed Graham goodnight, then carried Paul through the connecting door to his own room and tucked him in.

"Mom, you can only give him eight kisses and one hug, because that's what you gave me!" Shouted Graham from the other room.

"Don't worry, Graham, I'm counting the hugs and kisses!"

She gave Paul his hug and kisses and told them both she loved them, then said goodnight and left the room.

Faith padded back down the hallway to the master suite and changed into her PJs. After brushing her teeth and washing her face, she found Chris in bed watching prime time TV. "Tired?" she asked.

"Nope," he reached out his arm and she snuggled up to him, giving him a kiss. Faith silently repeated her own personal mantra that helped bring a relaxing sleep: *Happy Children. Warm Husband. Happy Children. Warm Husband.*

Chapter 10

Early the next morning, Faith surfaced to the strains of John Lennon's song, *Beautiful Boy*. She softly sang along to the lyrics 'life is what happens to you while you're busy making other plans,' and thought to herself that she wished she could always remember that. Savoring the moments made every day more meaningful. But, like working out or taking vitamins, it was just so easy to forget how much better that could make things.

She groaned when she realized she hadn't worked out in days.

Chris rolled over and pulled her into his arms. "Have I told you lately how beautiful you are?" He asked, eyes still closed.

Faith chuckled and hit the snooze bar.

Thirty minutes later, they finally got up to shower and prepare for the day. Chris whistled as he shaved.

Faith checked her look in the mirror and gave a nod. She was getting back into the swing of the work attire, but noted she would need to get more suits.

She glided down the hallway toward the boys' rooms only to see they were already up and playing in their playroom. "Good morning sweeties! Time to get dressed!"

After a bit of grumbling, they followed her into their rooms. Ten minutes later, they trooped downstairs for breakfast.

Mrs. Lucie bustled in with a platter of pancakes, bacon and fruit. After serving the boys, she popped their lunch and snack bags into their backpacks. She returned to the kitchen.

"Mom, when are we going to have a play date?" Graham asked before he took a big bite of bacon.

"Yeah, mom, when are we having a play date?" Paul chimed in.

"I don't know – who do you want to have over for a play date?" Faith asked.

"Nicholas, mom. He's my new friend. I asked him if he'd be my friend and he said sure. Does that mean he's my friend?" Graham said.

"Usually, 'sure' means yes. Hmm. So that's how it's done? You have to ask?" Faith asked curiously.

"I guess so. That's what Bruno did when we became friends last week, so I did it that way with Nicholas."

"Do you want a play date with Bruno, too?"

"Sure, Mom, that'd be swell."

Faith laughed. Graham was picking up the 1950s lingo from the Beezus books.

"I want to play, too." Paul said, with his lower lip thrust out.

Faith stuck her lower lip out, too. "Well, of course you will! You and Graham are best friends, so you'll all play together."

"Yes, but you have to play *our* games, Paul."

"I can play your games. I can run faster than you, anyway." Paul said indignantly.

"No you can't, Paul." Graham shook his head and smiled to himself.

"I can too, I ran past you the other day." Paul had his hands on his hips.

"I'd stopped running, Paul." He rolled his eyes.

"Ok, boys, that's enough. Paul, you are a very fast runner for a four year old. When you grow up, you'll be as fast as Graham is. Maybe even before you're grown up. So everyone just relax. Graham, I'll send an email to Bruno's and Nicholas' moms and see what we can do." Faith looked at the clock on the wall. "It's time to go."

They all got up from the table, thanked Mrs. Lucie for breakfast and made their way to the limousine.

***

By eight thirty, Faith and Chris were at Blithe Building, getting organized for the day.

A few minutes after Faith sat down at her desk, Chris came into her office. "Faith, who do I need to clear it with to hire a few people from my 'perfect world' list?"

"Ah, our first professional interaction! The CFO holds the reins on the budget, so you'll need to speak with him. Who are you thinking of hiring?"

"I want to hire Ron Caskie. Remember him?"

"I do, and I thoroughly approve. He seems like a reliable, smart and affable guy."

"And I need the help. I've reviewed the structure Blithe has in place and it could be dramatically improved if I had the right talent. I think I could realize almost immediate cost savings by making a few changes and Ron would be the guy to do it."

"Sounds good to me. Where are you in assessing the current talent?" Faith asked.

"Well, so far, I'm guessing I can do without the director of IT. As for the rest, I'm still feeling my way around. I think it could take a few weeks. The staff is kind of spread out."

Faith nodded. "Ok, well, Kevin MacGuire is the guy to speak to about additions to the budget. You'll also want to speak with Owen Lively, whether it's about new hires or layoffs. Owen is the new VP of HR I told you about."

"Got it," he smiled at her and left.

Faith picked up the phone and dialed Jack Costello's extension. His assistant picked up and immediately buzzed him.

"Oh no," he said when he got on the line.

"No, Jack, I'm not calling about another layoff."

He laughed. "Okay. What can I do for you?"

"I need you to look into the Government Relations department. I don't like what I've heard about them, particularly relating to the most recent acquisitions. It sounds as if they've been walking the legal line."

"I'm aware that they've been very active, but Von Heiden kept that department fairly well separated from everyone else. I'll make inquiries."

"Good. Let me know what you find out."

"Will do."

As Faith hung up, Kevin MacGuire walked into her office with his deck, a calculator, a pad of paper and a pen.

"Well, good morning," Faith said cheerfully. It felt good to be back at work.

For the next three hours, the two of them poured over the details of each business. Faith made copious notes and began to formulate a plan regarding certain divestitures. She peppered the CFO with questions as she worked through the segment projections and reviewed the underlying assumptions.

Faith worked through lunch. At one o'clock, she put down her segment analysis work and pulled up the webcast script she'd worked on the day before. Satisfied with its tone and contents, she emailed it to Owen Lively and Jack Costello for their opinions.

She then got to work on a memo she wanted to send out to the presidents of all of Blithe's subsidiaries. She would need to make plans to meet the executives in person and visit their operations, but decided to kick things off with a memo, and then reach out to each executive individually by phone. The memo would go out early Thursday morning and she'd make the phone calls Thursday and Friday.

Faith looked at the clock on her computer screen and realized it was time to get the kids from school. She lobbed a call to Roberts, then emailed the memo to Chris for his opinion, wrote a quick to-do list for the next day, checked the calendar for the next day, and tidied her desk. She picked up her copy of the deck and shook her head. *There has got to be a less paper-intensive – and labor intensive – way to do this*, she thought. *It should be on a secure area of a shared drive, accessible only by the CFO, CEO and their assistants.* She put the binder in a drawer in the desk and locked it.

She did a few stretches to ease her cramped muscles before picking up her bag and leaving the office.

"Would somebody please unblock Dropbox?" She overheard her husband in the next office and poked her head in.

Chris put the phone down. "Arrrrghh!" He looked up from his monitor and grimaced at her.

"That bad?" Faith asked sympathetically.

"No, just typical corporate stuff. I'm trying to use some tools I left in my Dropbox and can't get to them. Had to call the Help Desk."

"The irony of that is not lost on me." Faith smirked.

Chris threw a balled up piece of paper at her, which she easily dodged with a laugh. "What are you up to?" he asked.

"Off to get the kids," she said.

"Ok, see you at home."

Valerie smiled as Faith approached her cubicle. "See you tomorrow, Mrs. Warrior. I mean, Faith."

Faith smiled. "Call me on my cell if anything comes up. Have a good evening."

On her way to the elevator, she walked through a labyrinth of cubicles in the accounting department, past a dozen windowed offices. She looked at the people working there, smiled and nodded. They smiled and nodded back. *My employees*, she thought. *This just blows my mind.*

Roberts was waiting in front of the building. He opened the car door as she approached. She slid in and mentally tried to change gears to focus on her kids. The limousine headed down Pennsylvania Avenue while Faith gazed out of the window at the trees changing color. It was mid-October. "Costumes," Faith murmured, as she remembered the boys hadn't yet decided what they wanted to be for Halloween.

"Ma'am?" Roberts said from the front.

"Sorry, Roberts, I was just thinking that I need to take the kids shopping for Halloween costumes at some point. Better sooner than later, before they're sold out. Let's stop at Target after picking up the kids. There's one on Route 50."

"Yes, ma'am. I know the one."

Faith looked out the window again. As the sun hit the window, Faith caught a glimpse of her reflection in the glass. She realized she was wearing one of only two work outfits that were any good. She'd already had to interchange the jackets and skirts and was mixing them with different blouses, but she needed to get to a store soon or she'd be wearing jeans to work. "Roberts, tomorrow I'll need to go to a store to buy some more work clothes. Can you pick me up at 3 instead of 5?"

"Of course, ma'am. Where would you like to go?"

It had been so long since Faith had shopped that she had to think a moment. "I need a bit of this and a bit of that, so let's go to Nordstrom. There's one in Pentagon City."

She exhaled. It had been such a whirlwind the past week and a half, but she felt things were beginning to calm down. She took stock of her situation. Her family was settled into her grandfather's home and was adjusting well. The kids were happy. She felt like she was beginning to get a grip on the work situation. She liked the people with whom she was working. Her husband seemed happy. All in all, things were going all right.

"Ma'am, I sent you an email message with a link to a secure website where you can view images from the various security cameras around Blithe House. Today, I arranged for security cameras to be installed in the ballroom and the solarium so you can more easily monitor the children. Here is the password," he said and passed a sticky note back to her.

"That was very thoughtful of you, Roberts, thank you. I'll check it out."

Her cell phone rang as the limousine crossed the Potomac River into Arlington. Caller id indicated it was an unlisted number.

Faith answered on the second ring. "Hello?"

After a second, she heard music. *'I've got the moves like Jagger, I've got the moves like Jagger, I've got the moooooooooooves like Jagger.'*

Faith smiled. Only one person did this to her, in an effort to get a tune stuck in her head. Her friend and former business school project partner, Neal Lau. Over the years, they occasionally left each other voice messages with songs, purely to annoy one another. Neal was now a partner in a hedge fund.

"Well played, Mr. Lau, well played. I'll be humming that for the rest of the day." Faith said. In response, she heard laughing. The music stopped.

"Faith, it's been a while. I saw the news – are you okay?"

"Yeah, but man has it been a crazy few weeks. How's Jen? How are the kids?" Faith asked after his wife, who also went to business school with them. Neal and Jen had two small children.

"Everybody's sick with this year's 'welcome back to school' virus. I'm doing all I can to stay away from home until it runs its course." He chuckled ruefully.

"I hear you. I can't explain how we've been so lucky so far, but we've been pretty healthy."

"So, Faith, what does it feel like to be on the other side of the table now?"

"You mean on the corporate side? It's nice to get answers to questions for a change." She laughed. "Sarbanes-Oxley made analysts' jobs a lot harder."

"Tell me about it. I have to do twice as much work now to build a model than I did ten years ago."

"Hey, are the tools you use now for equity research basically the same as the ones from seven years ago? Bloomberg, Fact Set, Value Line, First Call?"

"I guess so. But mainly, I use Bloomberg and source broker research directly from the brokers – I don't use a research aggregator. Doing some research?"

"Yes – on my own company. I've got a whole slew of subsidiaries in different markets and I have to get up to speed on the industry dynamics."

"Ok – well, let me know if you need any help. Say, have you heard from Anne lately? I tried getting her on the horn last week and she didn't respond."

"Yes, and she's actually coming into town for a visit this weekend. I wouldn't take it personally – I think she's just been swamped with work."

"Well, tell her to call me, will 'ya? I've got some tech company questions for her. After the last sector dip, I'm thinking of putting a toe in the water."

"Ok, will do. I'll call her right now."

"Thanks. Take care, Faith. Say hi to Chris for me."

"I will. Talk with you soon."

Faith hung up and dialed Valerie. Her voice mail answered.

"Hi Valerie, can you please check to see if we have any licenses for the following online resources: Fact Set, Value Line and Bloomberg? We may very well. If we do, please have IT send me the links, userids and passwords. If we don't, please contact those services and get me access tomorrow. Within Fact Set, I specifically want access to broker research – but check if I can get that research through Bloomberg. If I can, then forget Fact Set. Also, make sure that Kevin MacGuire has access to the same tools. That would make a total of two seats for each license – in other words, if Von Heiden already had a seat, just have that transferred to me. Thanks."

She disconnected, and then dialed Anne.

Anne answered the call by immediately talking. "A private jet, Faith? This friendship thing is really working out for me." She laughed.

"Yes, well, I aim to please. Listen, Anne, give Neal Lau a call, will you? He needs some help with tech."

"Yeah, yeah. I'll call him. I've just been really busy. But I'll call him today."

"Thanks. Have you packed yet?"

Anne was so hyper-organized at all times that she typically packed for trips two days before leaving. "Very funny. But yes."

"Hee hee! I knew it. Ok, see you this weekend."

"Latah dahling," Anne drawled and hung up.

Faith's heart felt full. She smiled as the limousine pulled up in front of the school. As had become her habit, she had Roberts stay there while she walked around to the pickup area.

"Mommy!" Paul ran into her arms and Graham darted toward her. She squeezed them both tightly and gave them big, smacky kisses on their cheeks. "Mommy," Paul buried his face in her neck and wrapped his arms around her, patting her on the back. *This has to be what heaven feels like,* Faith thought.

"Did you two have a good day?" Faith smiled as she waved at their teachers and took the boys' hands. A few parents waved hello to her as she walked them around the corner of the building. She smiled and nodded at them.

"Mom! Wait, there's Bruno's mom. Can you ask her for a play date? Please?" Graham looked up at her with a pleading expression.

"Okay, sure honey." Faith steered the boys toward the other mother, who was busy loading her three kids into a minivan.

"Hi, are you Bruno's mom?" Faith asked.

The woman straightened from fastening one of the kids' seatbelts. She smiled. "Yes, I am. Oh, you're Graham's mom? Bruno just talks nonstop about Graham. I'm Mary," she said and put out her hand.

"I'm Faith," she said and shook Mary's hand. "Graham talks all of the time about Bruno, too. He was wondering if we might set up a play date. Do you think this weekend would work? If so, we'd love to host. I have to caution you that we live in DC now, though, so it's a bit of a hike."

"Oh, you moved to DC? That commute must be fun," she said with a grimace.

Faith laughed. "It's not great, no, but we love the school."

"We do, too. Yes, I think Sunday afternoon would work for us. I've never dropped Bruno at a play date before -- do you mind if I tag along until he feels comfortable?"

"By all means! You and I can have tea or coffee while the boys play. Great – so I'll email our address to you and we'll see you at 1pm?"

"Sounds great. We're in the school directory. See you then." Graham and Bruno bumped fists and Faith led her boys around the building to where Roberts waited.

Roberts opened the door for them and the boys dived in just as Chris called on her cell phone. He wanted to stay a little later at the office and wouldn't make it back for family dinner. Faith offered to eat with him later, then called the Chef to arrange it.

The boys chattered about the play date until it was clear Roberts was taking them to Target. The boys howled with delight. A trip to Target almost always led to a new toy.

"Costumes, boys, not toys. Halloween is coming!" The boys squealed with delight.

Roberts parked the car and escorted them into the store. The boys ran screaming down the aisle toward the massive Halloween area while Faith pushed a cart behind them.

Forty minutes later, the foursome left the store with several shopping bags of costumes and, of course, toys. Faith rolled her eyes at her weakness. The boys did NOT need more toys.

The boys ran off to the ballroom to play and Faith went upstairs to change and shoot off the promised emails before dinner at 5pm. She joined them in the lower dining room while they ate and they chatted about their day, Halloween, and plans for the play date. After the boys' dinner, Faith guided Graham through his homework and then took the boys downstairs to bowl until bath time.

Chris got home at six-thirty and went up to change, then gave the boys a bath. By seven-thirty, both boys were in bed and Faith and Chris had dinner by candlelight in the formal dining room. They tucked into chicken paillard with lemon caper sauce, whipped sweet potatoes and steamed broccolini.

"I'm looking forward to this weekend. Two house guests, a cookout on Saturday night and a play date on Sunday. Something for everyone!" Faith said with a smile.

"I called Jim – he'll be able to make it on Saturday night. He has his sister in town this weekend, so he'll bring her along."

"Great – what do you know about her?"

"Her name is Sarah. She's a pediatrician, I think. Jim says she's the brains in the family."

"That's saying a lot. Jim is a really smart guy."

"Yup. Skipped a grade in high school, graduated first in his college class."

The two men had met at Stanford. Jim was earning his MBA while Chris his Master's in Computer Science. Jim dated one of Chris's roommates. He later married her.

"Too bad about his marriage. Is he dating anyone now?"

"Not seriously."

"Hmm," Faith murmured.

"No. Stop that. Do not set him up." Chris looked sharply at her.

"Who me? No way would I meddle in anyone's life like that," she said with mock indignation.

"He's still pretty raw. Hilary really did a number on him. Just let him find his feet. I promise, by this time next year, it's open season on Jim again."

"Okay, okay. It's just a shame to miss this opportunity, given Anne is coming to town too." Faith clucked. But she understood. Jim had to be pretty destroyed by the way his ex-wife cheated on him. No one deserved to be treated like that, particularly not someone as nice as Jim.

They finished up dinner, thanked the chef and went downstairs to the media room, where they'd spotted some board games earlier. They picked out the game 'Chronology' and went up to their room.

"Now this feels like home," Chris commented as they lay on the bed and played a third round of the game. They smiled at each other.

"Feel like turning off the light?" Faith asked, wiggling her eyebrows suggestively.

"You win!" Chris scrambled to put the game away.

Chapter 11

Faith woke up before the alarm clock went off and stared into the darkness. A glance at the clock showed it was five-twenty. She lay there for a few minutes listening to the wind rustle leaves in the courtyard below the bedroom window.

Her husband's deep breathing sounded so peaceful and she turned toward him, examining his features. He hated his aquiline nose but she loved it. It added a human element to an otherwise too perfect face. She resisted the urge to tidy an errant lock of hair on his forehead and slowly got out of bed, her mind too wired to go back to sleep.

A shiver passed through her, so she pulled on a robe before padding down to the sitting room, where she clicked on a lamp and sat down at the laptop. She pulled up her schedule for the day and reviewed her to-do list:

- Finalize and email intro memo to executives.

- Finalize script and film webcast.

- Prioritize calls, and then begin calling executives.

- Check in with Mrs. Abernathy and Mr. Hopewell.

- Shop for clothes.

- Prep for weekend visitors.

Checking her email, she noticed her husband had given

feedback on the memo. She pulled up the attachment and reviewed his suggested changes. Liking them, she accepted the changes, saved the document, and then forwarded the revised document on to Jack Costello for a last glance.

Next, she reviewed the feedback she'd received from Owen Lively and Jack on her webcast script. Each suggested different changes. Owen wanted to soften the tone. Jack wanted to avoid a few potential landmines. Faith decided to mull the suggestions while showering.

She shot an email to Valerie and Kevin to suggest putting the deck onto a shared drive to facilitate updating and save a few trees, and then logged off.

Pen in hand, Faith began to make a list of the things she knew she would need to buy today at Nordstrom: a few suits, a few blouses, appropriate accessories, shoes, a briefcase, a dressy winter coat, hosiery and some fresh makeup. Given her time constraints, she thought she'd just cut to the chase and ask for a personal shopper to help her – someone who could run around the store pulling things she should consider. Faith thought she might try St. John Knits first. She'd always liked their timeless elegance, and she had to dress the part of a CEO.

Tucking the list into her handbag, she glanced at the clock. It was almost six o'clock. She went back to the bedroom and kissed her husband awake. "Hello sleepy head," she said affectionately, and then brushed the hair from his forehead.

"Hello, Wifey," he said sleepily. "Is it really time to get up now?" The alarm went off and she shut it off.

"I guess that answers the question." She laughed and walked into the bathroom.

Forty minutes later, Faith put the finishing touches on her attire. Since the webcast would be today, she took special care with her makeup. She wore exactly what she'd worn a few weeks ago to the interview on that fateful day. *Faith slowly shook her head in astonishment at what had transpired in just eleven days.*

At six-fifty, Faith woke up the children and got them dressed and ready. They all went down to breakfast together at 7 o'clock. The routine was now very familiar.

"Paul, are you looking forward to 'movie and popcorn day' at school today?" Faith asked as she sipped her coffee. She knew the Catholic school would show a movie about three different saints.

"No," he grouched. "It's a Holy Spirit movie. I hate Holy Spirit movies. Why can't we watch Max & Ruby?" He thrust his lower lip out and looked so cute that Faith had to restrain herself from scooping him up for a cuddle.

"Max & Ruby is a baby show," Graham said with disdain.

"It is not a baby show, Graham," Faith cautioned, "it is a pre-school show. Since Paul is in pre-school, that makes it the perfect show for him. He doesn't need to be watching SpongeBob or Power Rangers."

"Yeah, Graham," said Paul defensively.

"Did you see my suggestions for the memo?" Chris asked.

"Yes, I did. Great advice, as usual, Mr. Warrior." Faith smiled. He nodded with mock smugness.

"Boys," Faith said, "tomorrow is the weekend!" She threw her arms up in a big V above her head. They cheered.

"Yay! So we don't have to get up early!" Graham said.

"And we can play all day and stay in our pajamas if we want to!" Paul chimed in.

"Well, no, you'll need to get dressed. We have company coming. Mommy's friend Anne and another guest, a man named Daniel." Faith said to them.

"Anne's coming? Will she bring me Legos like last time?" Graham looked hopeful.

"Don't count on it – remember, it was your birthday last time she visited."

"Oh," he looked crestfallen, "right."

They finished breakfast, and then scooted out to the waiting car. At drop-off, the boys cheerfully joined their friends and trooped into school, excited it was the last day of the week.

At eight-thirty, Chris and Faith stepped into the elevator at Blithe Building.

"I forgot to ask - what did your company say about your resignation?" Faith asked.

"They were understanding but a little annoyed at the timing. I agreed to help with transitional issues while they start the search for a new CTO. So I'll be straddling both companies for a few weeks."

Faith nodded.

"How are you feeling about the webcast today?" Chris

asked.

"I don't know. I need to make a few final changes to the script. General consensus is that I need to tone it down a bit. Can't go scaring people that a lot of change is coming." She took his arm and stopped walking. "This is all happening so quickly, Chris," she whispered and frowned. "I'm feeling really overwhelmed."

Chris looked at her with care. "Let's talk in here," and he guided her ahead to his office.

She sat down on the couch and he sat next to her, taking her hand. "It's understandable that you're feeling overwhelmed. You went from a stay-at-home-mom for five years to CEO of a massive company in the span of a week. Remember how overwhelmed you felt when you first had Graham?"

She nodded and took a deep breath.

"Like a fish out of water. Your whole identity had been tied up in your work, in your education, in your paycheck. And then suddenly you were an at-home mom, a total neophyte at infant care, and we'd moved to a new city. It was overwhelming then, too. Understandably so. But that experience showed you something – and it showed me something, too. You're able to find yourself in any situation. It just takes a little time. So be patient with yourself. Take your time at things. Give yourself some slack. You'll get there."

"In the meantime, I've got to engender confidence, though. I can't go worrying all of these employees." Faith looked at him with concern.

"You won't. Just pace yourself. You've prioritized things correctly. You know you've got to reach out to the executives of the subsidiaries and reach out to the employees across the whole company. You're doing that. Just reassure them that you're here to stay, that you're taking time to go through the company and fully understand all of its parts. That, in the end, you might not do things exactly the way they were done before but that you are dedicated to honoring your family's values and doing what you feel is best for the long-term success of the company."

Faith nodded and looked into his eyes, and then she hugged him. "Thanks, honey. You always seem to know what to say to get me back on track."

He squeezed her, and then gave her a kiss. "We make a good team," he said and smiled. "Now get out of here so I can get some work done."

She laughed and stood up, took another deep breath and went next door to her office.

Faith sat down at her desk and reminded herself just to put her head down and work through her to-do list. She pulled up the webcast script and reworked it, incorporating some of the sentiment her husband had underscored. When she finished an hour later, she was satisfied that it was confident, optimistic and warm – this was the tone she wanted. She sent it out one last time to Owen and Jack.

Within the hour, she'd heard back from Jack on both the executive memo and the script, and he approved of both. Owen agreed that the script struck the right balance. He told her the conference room would be set up and ready to record the webcast just after lunch.

Faith forwarded the executive memo to Valerie and asked her to email it out to the top executives at each of the subsidiaries. She then looked at the clock. It was ten-thirty. She wanted to give the executives a chance to read it before placing any calls, so decided to spend the rest of the morning prioritizing those calls and following up on personal business with Mrs. Abernathy and Mr. Hopewell.

***

Faith brushed her hair and reapplied her lip-gloss, then lightly powdered her nose. She took one last look and exhaled loudly at the mirror.

In the conference room, Faith instructed one of the A/V crew to hold the script up by the camera so she could refer to it. She'd printed it in extra big font so she could read it from afar. "Okay," she said. "Let's do a few trial runs. We'll keep at it until I'm satisfied." The A/V techs nodded. She glanced at the chairs along the wall and her husband gave her a thumbs-up. Owen and Jack also sat watching.

She cleared her voice and then raised a finger to signal them to start filming.

"Good afternoon. I'm Faith Warrior, Frederick Blithe's granddaughter.

"It was quite a shock to me to discover just eleven days ago that I am a member of the Blithe family. It was even more of a shock to lose my grandfather just hours after I'd met him. I understand what a wonderful man he was and I share your grief at his loss.

"As his heir, his responsibility toward this company has become mine. It has been made clear to me that my grandfather wished the company to be run by family. I have therefore assumed the position of CEO. I'd like to thank Gregory Von Heiden for his fifteen years of service to the company. He was instrumental in moving the company forward over the past few years, and I wish him well in his future endeavors.

"While I have no prior operating company experience, I did spend years on Wall Street examining companies like Blithe as prospective investments. So, much of the work is familiar to me. It will take me some time to absorb the nuances of every business, so I hope you will be patient with my many questions.

"My priorities at Blithe are three-fold. Firstly, I strive to honor the values and memories of my grandfather and father. Secondly, I will work tirelessly toward the ongoing success of the entire company. And finally, I want Blithe to be one of the best companies to work for in America. This last priority is no small task. It will involve a lot of effort, effort on my part and effort on the part of everyone in this company.

"I'd like to close by reassuring you that I am here to stay. My expectation is that Blithe will continue to be a premier, privately owned company for generations to come.

"Thank you."

Faith stumbled a few times over the text but on the third try, she gave a very smooth delivery.

"Can you play it back, please?" She asked the A/V tech.

The executives watched the replay. When it was over, she looked expectantly at them.

"That was excellent," said Owen.

"Yes, just the right tone," concurred Jack.

"Nicely done," said her husband.

She nodded. "Right. Let's do that one more time," she called to the tech, confident she could do better. Her husband shook his head and grinned.

***

At two-thirty, the webcast link was emailed to all

employees and she pulled out her prioritized call list.

Her first call was to the largest subsidiary, *Blithe Engineering & Construction*. She introduced herself and had a congenial talk with the president, John Kreeger, who also had founded the company forty years before as Kreeger Engineering. Blithe had acquired the company in the mid-eighties and kept John Kreeger on as President. It had grown considerably over time and now operated globally in a handful of disparate end markets.

After about thirty minutes of discussion, she assured him that she would make a visit out to his headquarters sometime in the quarter and thanked him for his time. She felt good about her first interaction with a subsidiary and hoped her introductory phone calls next week would go as well.

She tidied her desk, grabbed her things and strode quickly to the elevator, hit speed dial on her cell phone and pressed it to her ear. "Hi, Mrs. Abernathy, it's Faith."

"Mrs. Warrior, hello. What can I do for you?"

"I need to buy some work clothes, and I imagine I'll be spending a bit." *Good thing my American Express doesn't have a limit*, she thought to herself.

"Not a problem. I've updated the addresses on your cards and the bills will come right to this office. I'll make sure they are paid. Get whatever you need."

"Thank you."

***

The parking garage at Pentagon City was sparsely filled near the door to Nordstrom. Roberts parked the limousine and opened the door for her, then moved to accompany her into the store. Faith put up her hand, "Roberts, I think I'll be safe in the store. Why don't I call you on your cell when I'm ready to leave and you can come and help me with the bags?"

Roberts reluctantly agreed and Faith entered the store through the cosmetics department. She took the escalator to the correct floor and located the St John department.

She figured she needed five work outfits. A few of them should be staples – navy and black – that she could mix and match. She approached an extremely elegant saleswoman.

"May I help you?" The woman said with a big smile.

"Yes, actually. I'm heading back to work after years as a stay at home mom and I need a fresh wardrobe. I pretty much have nothing, so I'll need suits, blouses, heels, accessories, makeup and some new undergarments. Also, a dressy winter coat."

The woman smiled. She looked across at the next department and snapped her finger. Another saleswoman hurried over.

"It's a work makeover," she informed the other woman who nodded and quietly waited.

"Ma'am, what sort of look are you going for?" The elegant saleswoman inquired.

"Classic, clean, elegant. I've admired St John in the past. I want to look polished but timeless. Above reproach," Faith said.

"Well, you've made a good start with what you're currently wearing – is this representative of your taste?" the woman inquired.

"Yes. I bought this recently."

"Alright, let's see what we can do to build on that." She guided her around the department asking her preferences and before Faith knew it, she was in the dressing room with the two women bringing her a huge variety of business apparel for her to try. Thirty minutes later, Faith had narrowed it down to exactly six suits – a bit more than she'd hoped. One navy, one black, one very pale blue, one beige, one red and one cream-colored. These were not old-fashioned power suits, not female versions of menswear. They were feminine, flattering and stylish, well-fitting but modest. In them, she truly did feel above reproach.

Another forty-five minutes and Faith had a variety of shells and blouses to wear beneath the suits, accessories and several pairs of elegant heels, plus new undergarments. It was astonishing how quickly things appeared in the changing room. The ladies even convinced her to try a sleek, navy blue evening gown and a deceptively simple black cocktail dress, both of which she loved. She paired these with some delicate silver high-heeled sandals and a matching evening bag.

A seamstress came and fitted the suits to her. Faith looked at her watch. "I have fifteen minutes to get out of here," she said. She handed her credit card to the saleswoman, who said she'd process it while Faith looked at makeup and perfume downstairs.

Sure enough, fifteen minutes later, Faith was finished with everything. She'd never spent so much money at one time before in her life, other than to buy a car, that is. She knew she needed to dress the part but was still a bit shell-shocked by the amount she'd spent.

Roberts came and collected the bags and the saleswoman told her the suits would be ready on Monday for pickup. Roberts took note of it and said he'd collect them.

By six o'clock, Faith was home. Mrs. Loper took the bags up to the room and unpacked them into her closet and bathroom. She also took the undergarments to the laundry. Faith kissed the boys and dropped into a chair in the media room where they were watching a cartoon. Chris handed her a glass of pinot grigio.

"You've had quite a day," he remarked. "Feels good, doesn't it." It wasn't a question. Chris knew Faith liked the fast pace, even if it was tiring.

"Did you and the boys have a fun afternoon?"

"Yes, despite the lice scare."

"The WHAT?" Faith sat forward in the chair.

"Relax. They don't have lice. But some other unfortunate child at school does."

"Good grief. Welcome back to school."

"So, the boys have been fed. You might want to check to make sure everything is as you'd like it for the weekend. Chef Massey is in the kitchen. He insists on helping with the cookout – even if he's not doing the grilling."

Faith laughed. "Well, that is his territory! What's he got in store for us?"

"He's got some New York strips, burgers and brats, plus he'll have some marinated vegetables to grille. Beyond that, I don't know. Said he'd have a bar and dining table set up for us in the garden. All I have to do is show up and grille."

"And you're complaining about this arrangement?"

"Good god, no. He's doing all the heavy lifting and leaving the fun part for me. I like this arrangement very much." He smiled. "Okay, boys, time for bath!"

Faith sighed and sank back in the chair. "Thanks, honey. Have I told you how handsome you are today?" She asked sweetly.

"No, and I think it's terrible of you. You'll have to make it up to me tonight." He gave her a slow smile and a wink.

She smiled and stood up, "I guess I'll go find myself a plate of leftovers."

"No need," Chris interjected. "I told the Chef I didn't think the family dinner thing was working, so he's going to start preparing two separate meals. One of us will always sit with the boys while they're eating, but we grown-ups can have our own meal later. Is that okay?"

"Yes, I think that's a good solution. Thanks, hon."

He herded the boys out as they yelled about which toy they would each bring into the bath that night.

Faith got to her feet and slowly walked through the house down to the kitchen. The smells wafting up the staircase were heavenly. She guessed lasagna or chicken parmesan. Comfort food!

Chef Massey was checking the oven when she entered the kitchen. "Hi, Chef!" She called.

He straightened and turned. "Hello, Mrs. Warrior. Dinner will be ready at seven-thirty. Is there something I can get you in the meantime?"

"Goodness, it smells good in here. I can't wait! But no, I just wanted to ask about tomorrow night."

"I've got the proteins and will have marinated vegetables ready for the grille, accompanied by buns and condiments as indicated. I'll also have a salad with walnuts and sliced pear, pumpkin ravioli in sage brown butter for any vegetarians, and a fresh strawberry shortcake for dessert. The produce will come from the garden. A full bar will be set up by the table. Mrs. Loper makes excellent cocktails if you need a bartender."

Faith was taken aback. "That sounds wonderful. I'm sure we'll all enjoy it immensely. But won't it be too cold to dine outdoors?"

"We have outdoor heaters and the table will be set up between the greenhouse and the solarium, so you'll be protected from any wind." he reassured her. "You and your guests should be quite comfortable."

"Thank you, Chef. See you at seven-thirty." Faith smiled and left the kitchen.

She passed Mrs. Loper in the stairwell.

"Mrs. Warrior, I took the liberty of asking Mrs. Lucie if she might watch the children tomorrow evening so I could help with the dinner. She is available if that is acceptable to you."

Once again, Faith was impressed with the thoughtfulness of the staff. "That would be wonderful. Chef said you're an excellent bartender."

Mrs. Loper looked pleased. "I do know a thing or two." She nodded and continued on her way to the kitchen.

Faith was really looking forward to her guests arriving later. She dialed security. "Hello – I just wanted to check that someone will pick up my guests at the airport later? Oh good, thank you." She should have known better. Mrs. Abernathy thought of everything.

She ducked into the guest suite before helping her husband get the kids to bed. Everything appeared to be in order.

As she entered the family suite, she heard splashing and laughing coming from the master bathroom. The boys loved to bathe in the huge whirlpool tub. She peeked in and saw bath toys and puddles everywhere and her husband sitting on the floor by the door reading Sports Illustrated. The boys were making beards from the bubbles and pretending to be Santa Claus, cracking each other up.

She cleared her voice and Chris jumped. "Oh, *heh*, hi honey!" He then said sternly to the boys, "now, boys, no splashing. And it's time to get out," and he bustled about tidying up the bathroom.

Faith smirked and went to the closet to change. *Busted.*

Chapter 12

Faith's head bobbed to the beat as she slowly surfaced. The clock radio was playing *Dancing Queen* by ABBA. *Now this is going to be a good day*, she thought. *No way could a bad day start like this*. She smiled and stretched, then slipped from the bed and danced across the floor lip-syncing into her hand.

She turned her head and looked out of the window. Rain was coming down in sheets. *Nope, don't care! ...You are the dancing queen, young and sweet, only seventeen!!* She spun around again and froze, facing the bed. Chris was sitting up, watching her with a big smile on his face. "Well, maybe not seventeen, but you're definitely the dancing queen," he said. Faith laughed and bowed deeply in response, then skipped to turn off the radio.

"Good morning," she said cheerily and kissed him.

He sighed and looked out of the window. "There's something about a dark, rainy day that just makes me want to go back to sleep."

Faith smiled. "Well, I for one am excited. I'm going to make a bunch of calls today, get more familiar with the company, then Anne is arriving tonight!" She danced a little jig. "I can't wait. This is going to be a fun weekend!"

"Well, you deserve a little fun. It's been a tough few weeks." He stretched, sighed and then flopped back against the pillow.

"I had a pretty freaky dream last night. Want to hear about it?" Faith asked.

"Sure," he said with his eyes closed.

"Well, for some reason I was a single parent, and I was being chased around the kids' school by a dweebie, oversexed single dad waving a box of condoms."

Chris opened his eyes. "What is with your subconscious mind? You need to stop telling me about your dreams." He got out of bed and headed for the shower with a grouchy face.

Faith called after him, laughing, "I had a metal pole -- it looked like a part of a clothing rack from a store -- and I brandished it as a weapon to get the guy to leave me alone."

"You can stop talking now!" Chris shouted over the noise of the shower.

"Mom?" Graham walked into the room slowly.

"Sweetie, you're up really early." Faith walked toward him to give him a hug.

"I'm not feeling so well," he said, looking practically green.

Faith knew what was coming and hustled him into the bathroom. Just as they crossed the threshold and were safely on the tile floor, he threw up.

"Okay, you're definitely not feeling so well." She sat him down in case he was sick again and cleaned up the floor.

Fifteen minutes and another episode later, Graham was cleaned up and in bed. The bed was lined with thick towels as a precaution, and a plastic waste paper basket sat beside his bed. She'd found a box of antibacterial wipes and had disinfected the bathroom floor.

Faith tuned the boys' iPad to Spider Man cartoons on Netflix and propped it on his nightstand, along with a sports bottle full of water. Graham looked up at her and said solemnly, "Most villains have this really funny laugh that ends with a cough."

She smiled and nodded at him. "Just relax. I'll be back in a second."

As Chris got ready for work, Faith quickly showered and dressed in jeans and a long-sleeved cotton top. She sat down at her laptop and sent an email to his teacher and the school nurse. No school today for Graham. Since Paul was only in Pre-K, he would stay home, too. Then she shot an email to Valerie to let her know she'd be working from home.

She picked up the phone and dialed Housekeeping. When Mrs. Lucie answered, she filled her in on the situation and Mrs. Lucie said she would bring breakfast upstairs for Faith and the kids. They could eat in the sitting room.

Paul awoke at seven o'clock, just as Chris was leaving to go downstairs. He was thrilled to learn that the weekend had started early and shouted a goodbye to Chris as he ran into the playroom.

    ***

Faith spent the morning tending to Graham, playing and reading with Paul, and making a few phone calls. She didn't accomplish nearly as much work as she had anticipated she would just hours earlier, but she still felt she'd made some progress.

Graham had only thrown up one additional time, though to be fair, she couldn't imagine there was anything left in his body. He'd done a grand imitation of a geyser. Though tired, he seemed to be feeling better. He didn't have a fever. She decided to keep him on the BRAT diet for the next twenty-four hours, a bland selection of bananas, rice, applesauce and toast that would give his stomach a rest. She also had Mrs. Lucie give his room, the bathrooms, the playroom and all of the doorknobs and light switches a good going-over with antibacterial wipes. She asked that the same be done one more time tomorrow to make sure her guests' visit to Blithe House didn't emulate some disastrous cruise.

Just after lunch, Valerie called Faith on her cell phone to say she had a call on hold at the office from Cardinal Mayse. Faith asked her to give the Cardinal her cell phone number, then waited for his call.

"Mrs. Warrior," he began, "thank you for taking my call."

"Of course, Your Eminence. And please, call me Faith. How can I help you?" Faith responded.

"Faith, I received a voice message from your grandfather. I should add that he left it the day he died. It's been sitting in the inbox of my private cell phone. The battery had died and I rarely use it so I didn't discover it until today," he said.

"I see. Was there something in the message that I should know about?"

"It was really very upsetting. He asked if Thomas was my son."

Faith frowned. "Why would he think Thomas was your son?"

"I've no idea. He was very upset. He sounded as if he really believed it was possible." The Cardinal sounded agonized.

"Was Thomas your son?" She had to ask.

"Of course not! The idea is ridiculous! And the worst part about this is that Fritz had this on his mind when he died. Can you imagine how tortured he must have felt? Elena and his children were *everything* to him. The notion that Elena betrayed him, that I, his best friend, betrayed him, it's just unbearable."

"Okay, I'm going to make a few calls to see if I can find out who might have told him such a thing. If you haven't already deleted the message, please don't delete it."

"No, I didn't delete it. It's the last time I heard his voice. I might never delete it, despite the awful nature of the call."

Faith swallowed hard. "Thank you," she said quietly. "Oh - when did he call, and what phone number did he use?"

"Just a second. Let me see if I can read that while I'm still on a call with you." He fumbled a bit and then she could hear him put her on speakerphone. "Okay, yes, he sent it at 6:17pm from a number that's not associated with his entry in my address book." He read the number out to her and she wrote it down.

"Thank you for the call, Your Eminence. I'll let you know if I find out anything."

"You're welcome, Faith. God bless." He hung up and Faith stared out the window.

Well, now I know it wasn't meeting me that killed him. Provided the Cardinal was telling the truth, someone had lied to her grandfather, and it had made him so upset that his heart gave out. Her rage was growing.

Faith dug Special Agent Maxwell's business card out of her handbag and dialed the number.

"Maxwell here."

"Special Agent Maxwell, this is Faith Warrior calling."

"Mrs. Warrior, what can I do for you?"

"Well, you mentioned I should call if you can help in any way. I'm not sure if this is important to the investigation, particularly since it's now closed, but I received a call just now from Cardinal Mayse. He was one of my grandfather's oldest friends and gave his funeral Mass. He said my grandfather left a voice message for him literally minutes before he died. He just retrieved it."

There was silence at the end of the line.

"Agent Maxwell?"

"Mrs. Warrior, we checked his phone records and there were no calls made to the Cardinal that day from his work line, his home office, his residence or his cell. I can say this with confidence because very few calls went in or out on those lines that day."

"Cardinal Mayse said he didn't recognize the number. Maybe he used someone else's phone." She read the number out to him, and then also gave him the Cardinal's number from her caller id. "Agent Maxwell, my grandfather asked him if he was Thomas's father -- Thomas was my uncle. The Cardinal said my grandfather sounded very upset."

"I see." He paused a moment. "I'll look into it and get back to you. And thank you for the call." He disconnected.

Faith picked up the house phone and dialed Security. She filled Roberts in on the information and asked him to see what he could find out about the circumstances surrounding Thomas' death.

She put down the phone and stared at it.

Faith slapped her hands onto her jeans and stood up. It was of no use to dwell further on it now. It was time to get Paul outside for some fresh air. She called Mrs. Lucie and asked her to come up and read to Graham for thirty minutes while she took Paul to the back yard. When Mrs. Lucie arrived, Paul was hopping up and down with excitement, all ready to go. Faith scooped up her cell phone and their fleece jackets and they trooped outside.

"Mama, can we get a baby cat?" Paul looked up at her hopefully as Faith zipped up his jacket.

"No, sorry, honey, I'm allergic to cats." Faith kissed his nose.

"Well, maybe you wouldn't have allergies to a *baby* cat."

Faith smiled. "Sweetie, a baby cat is still a cat – it's just a small cat. I'm allergic to cats no matter how big or small they are."

"That's not good. You should get that fixed."

"Maybe some day I will," Faith said and looked around. "Oh look, a black squirrel!" Faith pointed to the squirrel and a big smile appeared on Paul's face as he ran off to chase the squirrel. Faith chuckled at his cuteness and wondered how long distraction would remain a handy tool in her tool belt.

Thirty minutes later, Faith emptied their pockets of rocks and acorns and hung up their jackets. Mrs. Lucie said goodbye for the day. Mrs. Loper arrived and brought a tray of snacks up to the playroom. Faith gave Paul a plate of toast with cream cheese and some apple slices and put on an episode of Olivia. Then she brought the tray in to Graham's room.

"Here is some buttered toast and ginger-ale, honey. Would you like me to read to you?"

"Oh, Mom," Graham said excitedly, looking up from his Calvin and Hobbes book. "This one is really funny. There's this monster under Calvin's bed. First he offers Calvin a shiny toy if he'll go under the bed, but Calvin's too smart for that. Then he offers Hobbes salmon if he'll push Calvin over the side of the bed. So Hobbes says, 'is it fresh?' and the monster says, 'let me check... yeah, it's fresh'. And Calvin shouts 'Hobbes, don't listen to him!'" Graham rolled over on his back laughing. "I just love Hobbes! I wish I had a tiger just like him!"

Faith laughed too. She bent down and felt his forehead. It was cool. His color had improved and he was laughing. All good signs. She picked up the book and settled in next to him on the bed. As he sipped his drink and nibbled on the toast, Faith entered the world of a precocious little boy and his imaginary friend.

Chris arrived home around 5 o'clock just as Faith was getting the boys out of the bath. He kissed Faith and ruffled the boys' hair. "How was your day?" He asked.

"Quiet, which was a nice change, actually." Faith smiled and dried Paul's hair. "And yours?"

"Not bad. Just formulating my to-do list, figuring out the low-hanging fruit, and so on. Valerie told me Cardinal Mayse called."

Faith filled him in while the boys put on their PJs in their rooms. "Why would someone lie to my grandfather about that? I want to know who placed that call."

"Well, it's a good thing you've handed that news over to the Feds. They'll figure it out."

"I certainly hope so."

"Well, we've got guests coming this weekend. Are you excited?"

A big smile bloomed on Faith's face. "Yes, I am! I got a text from Anne earlier. She said she was picked up by a town car, not a limousine, and what was up with that?"

Chris chuckled. "Text her back and let her know that there

aren't any gold toilet seats onboard the jet, so she should brace
herself."

A knock sounded at the door to the suite. Chris strode
over and opened it to find Chef Massey there with a room
service cart. "A room service cart?"

"Yes, sir, Mr. Blithe sometimes requested dinner in his
room, so this convertible cart was ordered. I thought you
might prefer the children dine up here this evening, given
Graham's illness."

"That was very thoughtful of you, Chef," Faith said.

Chris followed the chef down the hallway to the sitting
room. "How is it convertible?"

"The sides fold out and make a table. The food and
tableware is stored in compartments below. See this here? It's
an insulated compartment for the hot food."

"I'm digging the cart," Faith said to Chris, who nodded.

Chris brought chairs from the children's rooms while the
chef laid out the meal. Clearly, Mrs. Lucie had conveyed to
him the request for food that would be gentle on Graham's
stomach. When dinner was ready, the boys were called to the
table.

"Your dinner will be in the formal dining room tonight at
7pm."

"Thank you, Chef, we will be there!" Faith smiled at Chris
and then helped the boys cut their food.

   ***

Faith's cell phone rumbled at around eleven o'clock,
signaling a text had arrived. She glanced at it. "They're on their
way from the airport!"

She checked her look in the mirror, then tiptoed quickly
down the hallway from their bedroom and made a beeline for
the guest suite. She turned on bedside lamps and made sure
everything looked perfect, then descended to the first floor
and waited by the back door peering through the adjacent
window. Chris joined her there.

"I wonder how they got along on the flight," Chris said.

"Anne probably relentlessly peppered him with
questions," she said. "And in response, he likely numbed
himself with alcohol." Chris laughed.

The limousine pulled up and Roberts got out to open the
door. A tall, slim, red-headed woman in a white, short-sleeved

v-neck t-shirt, long, low-slung, slightly flared black jeans, a black leather belt with an elegant silver buckle and black leather high-heeled boots stepped out, looking annoyed. Red hair tumbled in a riot of long curls around her shoulders when she glanced back into the car. Her pale, delicate features and green eyes gave her an ethereal look despite her considerable height. With her high heels, she was over six feet tall -- a very striking sight.

Roberts half climbed in and hauled out the other passenger. The young man wore jeans, an un-tucked pink striped oxford shirt and preppy loafers. He shook his head to get his thick blond hair away from his eyes and almost fell over. His cheeks were flushed. Faith saw the resemblance to Cassandra.

"No. Way." Chris regarded Faith with awe. "You totally called it."

Faith shook her head sadly. "It's not the first time it's happened with Anne." She opened the door and held her arms out. "Anne!"

"Faith!" Anne half jogged to her, curls bouncing, and wrapped her in her arms. "It's so good to see you!"

Faith hugged her back, then raised an eyebrow and inclined her head toward Daniel. He was propped against the side of the car while Roberts retrieved their baggage from the trunk. "What happened?"

"The better question is: why does every man I meet turn out to be a binge drinker? Ugh. Men! Oh, hello Christopher!"

"It's good to see you, Anne," Chris gave her with a smirk and ducked in for a quick hug.

Faith smiled and shook her head. "Chris, will you show Anne upstairs to her room? Anne, do you need anything to eat or drink?"

"No, your flight attendant gave us a great meal. I'm all set, thanks." Chris escorted Anne out of the room. Faith turned toward Roberts and Daniel.

"What happened?" She asked Roberts quietly.

"According to the flight attendant, young Mr. Blithe cannot hold his liquor. Or stop asking for it."

"I see. Let's take him up in the elevator. I'll hold it for you so you can bring the bags, too." Roberts inclined his head and headed toward the bags.

"Daniel?" Faith said as she approached Daniel. He had his eyes closed and was leaning unsteadily against the car.

"Faith? Iss nice to meet you." He put out his hand to shake hers, then bent over and vomited on his shoes.

Faith closed her eyes and murmured, "seriously? I've seen just about enough vomit for one day." She helped him out of his shoes and socks and then led him inside.

Once upstairs, Roberts took over, helping him into the guestroom's bathroom. The door clicked shut and Faith heard the shower start. Ten minutes later, Roberts brought him back out in a bathrobe and helped him into bed. Faith had him drink a tall glass of water and gave him some Motrin, then tucked him into bed. She left a full glass of water on his nightstand and shut off the light.

Roberts told her he'd take care of the shoes and socks and bid Faith a good night.

Faith went into Anne's room and found her completely unpacked and ready for bed.

"The room is gorgeous, Faith. Well, the whole house is gorgeous." Anne took Faith's hands and they sat down on the bed. "How are you holding up? It's certainly been a whirl wind for you."

Faith smiled and hung her head. "Whirl wind is an understatement. I'm doing okay. The kids are doing well, which has been my bigger concern. If they are okay, I'm okay. And Chris has been so great through it all."

Anne nodded at this. "He's a keeper."

"What happened to Daniel?" Faith asked.

Anne put her hands up in front of herself. "I swear I did not play twenty questions this time. I can't account for why he drank so much. I made some polite conversation with him, that's all. I asked what he did for a living on the West Coast, how he got to be out there rather than back east, that sort of thing."

Faith's brow furrowed. "That sounds benign enough."

"It was. But in the time it took me to finish my one glass of wine, he'd had three mixed drinks. Followed up with cognac. All of that plus the dehydrating effect of flying and he was totally smashed by landing."

Faith nodded. "Okay, my dear. I'll let you get some rest. We can catch up in the morning."

"Excellent. Pancakes and girl talk. And no mimosas at breakfast for Daniel." Anne wagged her finger.

"No mimosas," Faith confirmed with a chuckle. "I'm so glad you're here," she said and gave Anne a big hug. They exchanged a smile and Faith left.

Chapter 13

"Good morning!" Anne breezed in to the downstairs dining room. "Kids!"

The two boys raced around the table and threw themselves into her arms. Graham excitedly said to her, "I threw up yesterday!"

Paul furiously nodded his agreement. "He did, but I didn't." Paul said.

"Well, I see there's a lot of that going on around here," she said over their heads to Faith. She pulled two flat, wrapped items from her back pockets. "Let's see, who are these for?"

"Presents!!" Both boys squealed in unison and tore them open. "Invisible Ink books! Cool! Thanks!"

"Boys, get back to your seats now and finish your breakfast." They scrambled back and sat down while they chatted quietly about the books. She looked at Anne. "Thank you, Anne, you are very sweet and far too generous."

"It's just the way I roll," she said loftily, then laughed. "And your boys are so adorable I can't help myself." She walked to the sideboard and took a plate. "So, where's the adult vomiter?"

"Hasn't surfaced yet. I'll give him another half hour and then poke my head in and check on him. Try the yogurt. Chef makes it himself and it is incredible."

"What's that stuff floating in it?" She asked suspiciously.

"Toasted quinoa. Very good for you. Super grain and all that."

"I think I'll pass, thanks. Oo, bacon!"

"So, any men on the horizon?" Faith asked, trying not to watch Anne make a bacon sandwich with flapjacks and syrup. Faith had been trying to reform Anne's eating habits for years.

Though Anne was blessed with an extraordinary metabolism which kept her reed slim, she did not eat healthfully.

"I think I'm going to give the quest a rest for now. Jeremy kind of wore me out." She took another bite and chewed thoughtfully, then jumped up to get a cup of coffee. "So, what's on the agenda for today?"

"Nothing much. I do need to speak with Daniel for a bit, and we're having a cookout this evening with friends, but that's it. Is there anything you'd like to do?"

"Mom, when is Bruno coming over?"

Faith smacked the side of her head. "I almost forgot! That's tomorrow afternoon, honey. Thanks for reminding me. If you stay healthy today, no throwing up and no fever, then we'll do the play date tomorrow."

"I feel good, Mom," he said earnestly.

"That's good. Let's hope it stays that way, sweetie."

Paul started to pretend he was throwing up. "Knock it off, Paul. You stink!" Graham yelled.

"No, you stink!" Paul yelled back.

"Boys, you can leave the table now. And no clobbering each other." The two of them raced out to play in the ballroom.

Faith heard a floorboard creak and turned to see Daniel in the doorway. His hair was still wet from the shower and he wore fresh clothes. "Well, good morning, Daniel!" He visibly winced at her volume.

"Good morning, and please accept my apologies for last night. It's highly unusual for me to get drunk. I made a very poor first impression, I'm afraid."

"Don't feel badly." Faith got up and stepped forward to shake his hand.

"Thanks for saying that. Because I don't feel good enough yet to feel badly."

"How about some coffee?" she said sympathetically.

"That would be wonderful, thank you."

He sat down at the end of the table. "Good morning, Anne," he said.

"It is for me, at least," she said with a smile.

Faith placed coffee and some toast in front of Daniel and he sipped the coffee with a grateful expression.

"Anne and I were just discussing the day, Daniel. I know

you said you'd like to see your mother at some point, and you and I need to have that talk," Faith stopped talking when Daniel started coughing.

He looked embarrassed. "Sorry, went down the wrong pipe."

"Then we've got a friend coming over for a cookout tonight. It should be good fun."

Daniel nodded. "I spoke with my mother briefly yesterday. She'd like to get together this morning."

"Okay, so you and I can have that talk after lunch. Say one o'clock?"

"Certainly," he replied, then said no more.

The silence in the room was momentarily uncomfortable. "Okay, well, I'll let you enjoy your breakfast. I need to go and check on the boys. Anne, come and find me when you're done. I'll be in the ballroom."

"Of course, dahling. The ballroom it is," Anne said in deadpan.

Daniel called out to Faith as she was heading out the door. "That cookout sounds like fun. Do you mind if I invite a friend to join us?"

"Not at all!" She called back. "The more the merrier!"

Anne winked at Daniel and leaned in. "Do you want more coffee?" she said very loudly in his ear.

***

Faith was giving Anne a tour of the house when her cell phone rang. "Mrs. Warrior," Roberts said. "Special Agent Maxwell is here to see you. He is waiting in the formal living room."

"Thank you, Roberts." She turned to Anne. "Be back in a minute. Keep browsing – I'll find you."

Faith passed the ballroom where Chris was doing Nerf sword fighting with the boys. As Faith descended the main staircase, she saw two men standing in the living room. Both were dressed in dark suits.

"Mrs. Warrior, thank you for seeing me." Maxwell shook her hand. "I'd like to introduce you to another member of my team, Special Agent Tierney."

"How do you do?" Faith said as she shook Tierney's hand.

Maxwell continued. "Mrs. Warrior, we're here because we were looking into the matter of the phone call to Mr. Blithe and we had a few more questions."

"Of course. Please sit down." She motioned to the couch and the men sat.

"We've determined that the phone number Blithe used to call Cardinal Mayse was actually a Skype number that had recently been set up. The FBI had overlooked the possibility that such an old man would use Skype on an iPad. This was an inexcusable error. The iPad was sitting on Blithe's desk when he was found in his office and no one had paid much attention to the Skype icon. Plenty of people have the Skype app but don't use it. Particularly, as I said, older folks."

"I see. Well, you know my grandfather was quite a technophile. He enjoyed learning about new technologies, trying them out. And he invested in a lot of technology startups. I agree, it's unusual for older people to embrace new technologies, but apparently, he relished it."

"Mrs. Warrior," Tierney spoke up. "A call came in via Skype to Mr. Blithe just before he called Cardinal Mayse."

Faith sat up. "Really? Who called him?"

"We're not yet sure. Our team is looking into it." Maxwell said.

"But the real reason we're here," Tierney continued, "is that the only other calls to go in or out of that account were made from or to Daniel Blithe."

Faith frowned. "So you need to speak with him. He's our guest for the weekend."

"Yes, we know." Tierney said.

Faith stood up to go and get Daniel and then remembered that he'd left to meet up with his mother. "He's meeting with Cassandra, his mother, right now but is expected back by one o'clock. Would you like to come back then?"

The two men rose. "Yes, ma'am. We'll be back just before one o'clock. Thank you for your time."

Faith's frown deepened as she ascended the staircase. She explained the conversation to Anne. She also explained the meeting she was going to have with Daniel at one o'clock and how uneasy she was about not being able to talk about the investment with any non-investors.

"Well," said Anne, "why don't you do that? Talk to the other investors, I mean? Gunesdogdu..." She doubled over laughing. "I'm sorry, I can't say it without laughing,"

"Yeah, yeah. What about Gunesdogdu?" Faith was becoming impatient with all of the question marks surrounding the investment.

"Sorry." She pulled herself together. "Well, Ptolemy understands technology. He might be able to explain things to you in terms you'll understand."

"Good point." Faith picked up her cell phone and asked Security to see if they could find a private number for the tech guru. She asked them to check with Mrs. Abernathy and Mr. Hopewell, and if that failed, to try to find a number through their own means.

When they struck out, she Googled Yakmak and reached the main switchboard.

"Good morning. My name is Faith Warrior and I'd like to be connected with Ptolemy Gunesdogdu's office, please."

"Ma'am, there is no one in his office today. It's Saturday."

"Can you find someone who can contact him and have him call me back?"

"Ma'am, I'm sure you can appreciate how many people would like to speak with Mr. Gunesdogdu. We don't connect the vast majority of the calls, and particularly don't do it on the weekends. Anyone who knows him knows how to reach him. But I'll transfer you into his assistant's voice mail."

"Ok, thank you," Faith said with a sigh.

She left the message and put her phone in her pocket. "That went well, I think," she said flatly.

"You'd think rich people would all have access to each other's phone numbers. Through some secret directory or something." Anne sniffed. "Like dub dub dub dot we're all rich so let's hang out dot com."

Faith gave her a sideways glance and the two burst out laughing.

***

Lunch was over and it was approaching one o'clock when the front doorbell rang. As Faith descended the front staircase, Mrs. Loper let Daniel in. She had almost closed the door when Special Agent Maxwell knocked on it. Mrs. Loper recognized the men and stood back for them to enter. Maxwell nodded to Faith and directed his gaze at Daniel.

"Mr. Blithe? I'm Special Agent Maxwell, with the FBI. This is Special Agent Tierney. May we have a word with you?"

Daniel looked surprised. "Of course. What's this about?" The three men went into the living room and sat down. Faith asked Mrs. Loper to bring a tray of coffee for the four of them and then entered the living room, too.

"Mr. Blithe," Maxwell began. "We understand you and Frederick Blithe made and received calls through Skype on his iPad. Is this so?"

"Yes, we did. Fritz wanted to try it out, so I set it up for him, including a Skype number. In fact, I'm the one who sent him the iPad. I loaded a few apps onto it before I sent it, including Skype. I guided him through the process of setting up his account. Why?"

"Who else knew his Skype phone number?" Tierney asked.

"No one that I know of. Why?"

"Did he request to use Skype?" Tierney persisted.

"Fritz enjoyed trying out new technology. I often sent him the latest and greatest for him to tinker with. Sometimes, I'd even get my hands on prototypes for him to look at. Folks in Silicon Valley knew Fritz invested in tech and were eager to have him take a look. Again I ask: why?"

Maxwell and Tierney exchanged a look before Maxwell spoke. "He received a Skype call just minutes before he died."

"Have you figured out where it came from?" Faith asked.

"Yes. It was from a business number, an exclusive health club here in DC. We've been through the staff and guest logs and haven't identified anyone who might have known Mr. Blithe well enough to call him, much less call him on a number no one but you seemed to know about."

"I see." Daniel looked at Faith and the two men. "I wish I could be of more help, but I don't know of anyone who would have called him on that number."

Maxwell looked at him for a moment, then stood up and extended his hand. "Thank you for your time. Here is my card. If you think of anything later, please call me."

"I'll do that, Special Agent." Daniel turned and watched the two men leave.

"Daniel, after my grandfather received that Skype call, he placed a call to Cardinal Mayse and left a message for him." Daniel turned and looked at her. "My grandfather asked the Cardinal if he was Thomas's father."

Daniel's eyes grew large. "His father?"

"Yes. Someone must have said something to my grandfather that night that led him to believe it was really true. And that news may have gotten him so upset that it triggered a heart attack."

Daniel's eyes narrowed. "That would be despicable."

Faith nodded. "And if it were true, I fail to understand why someone would wait so long to say something about Thomas."

Daniel inhaled and exhaled sharply. "Well, it's good the FBI is on it. Certainly there are DNA tests that could be done to determine the truth of Thomas's paternity."

"Good point. If they can find some DNA to test. Thomas has been dead for thirty-five years."

They sat in silence for a few moments pondering the situation until Daniel spoke up. "Well, there's nothing we can do about it now. Would you like to discuss Xnard?"

"I would, indeed." Mrs. Loper walked in with the coffee. "Oh, I'm sorry, Mrs. Loper. The Special Agents just left. But I'm sure Daniel and I would enjoy a cup."

"We should talk somewhere more private." Daniel said, so Faith showed him into the media room.

Faith sipped her coffee and relaxed into the armchair. "So what is this uber-secret business you're running?" she said with a smile.

Daniel smiled back at her as he sat down. "You might have heard the term 'molecular nanotechnology.' It's a term that's been in use for a few decades, now. In layman's terms, it's about building things smaller and smaller. It has implications for computer chips, for instance. Chip companies are always trying to load more and more power and stability onto smaller and smaller chips. Well, nanomedicine uses nanotechnology for medical applications. In general, nanomedicine presents the possibility for major enhancements in human health and happiness. It will enable earlier testing for illness, better cancer treatments, repairs in the human body that were previously inconceivable...."

Daniel looked a little vacant, as if lost in thought. Just as Faith was about to interject, he suddenly continued speaking.

"So, about the concept. I mentioned happiness. Well, a few years ago, I was working in Europe, spending long nighttime hours doing experiments with a nuclear particle accelerator. Night was the only time I could secure with the machine, since demand for its use is so great. It's scheduled twenty-four hours a day.

"Anyway, on one particularly long night, my mind wandered a bit. I got to thinking about Fritz." He gazed out the window. "He suffered so much. He was nearing the end of his life and I thought, what if I can give him – or anyone – some peace from painful memories? Physically erase or suppress them? It sounds a little sci-fi, messing with a person's memories. But on EEGs, your brain lights up in certain spots when you laugh, when you remember a traumatic or tragic experience – any extreme emotion.

"I married this idea of reaching and treating memories with some research I'd read coming out of the Czech Republic, relating to the way parasites attack the brain. Again, yes, I know it sounds horrific. But parasites have proven to have very reliable agendas with respect to brain infiltration. Take the rabies parasite, for instance.

"My idea was to find a way to attach nanotechnology to a parasite to reach and treat specific parts of the brain in a non-invasive manner. Swallow a serum containing the modified parasite, the parasite makes its way to its predetermined destination and it is programed to disintegrate upon arrival, a la pesticides and certain insects. So the technology would be delivered without the detrimental, ongoing presence of the parasite. Much the way a rocket booster falls away as a satellite launches into space.

"The tricky part was learning how to modify the parasite's innate directions. But it turns out that top scientists in several key labs in the UK and Eastern Europe have done a lot of studies on this, with applications at the ready.

"Anyway." He shook his head as if to clear it, "I got a job offer out of the blue from Yakmak the following year. I was brought on to apply new advances in molecular nanotechnology to its nascent chip business. When I got there, I met with Ptolemy Gunesdogdu. He took a genuine interest in my work, so I told him about my nanomedicine idea. It went like wildfire from there. As Ptolemy helped me realize, the business really has huge possibilities, beyond what I'd envisioned as a solution for your grandfather. For instance, people suffering from post-traumatic stress disorder could be pulled back from the brink of losing their families and lives by sending in Xnard's nanomedicine to search out and neutralize damaging memories. That, and related areas, give the technology a rather astonishingly large end market.

"Ptolemy and I went through the idea carefully. Since he's not in the medical field, he brought Mitchell on board. Mitchell has some interests in that area and connected me with scientists who are helping to bring the vision to fruition. And since Fritz was so keen on technology and he was my inspiration, I brought him on board." He took a sip of coffee. "And that's how it all came to be. At the point of Fritz's funeral, I was in Europe doing some tests on an accelerator there."

"It sounds fascinating, Daniel. Yes, a bit gruesome in that it brings to mind lobotomy, but if successful, the opportunity to enhance people's lives with it is tremendous."

Daniel grimaced. "Let's not use the word lobotomy. Not only am I not proposing its use for psychosurgery, but I'm also focused on it being a completely voluntary procedure."

"I understand. Sorry for the reference."

"So, I'm about a year into full time focus on it and we're making progress. I might have something ready for testing in another twelve months."

"How involved is Ptolemy with the project at this point?" Faith asked.

"I update him monthly. I'd been updating everyone monthly, so now I'll give you those updates, too."

"That's great. I'm curious about the name of the company, Xnard. Where did that come from?" Faith asked.

"Oh," he laughed, as if the very word was funny. "When I first arrived in California, I took a drive up the Pacific Coast Highway. I passed a sign for Oxnard that was missing the letter O. It visually jumped out at me and I pondered it for a while as I drove.

"When I was a small boy, I had a favorite stuffed animal. I took it everywhere with me. But on a trip I took with my mother, I lost it. I'd been sure I put it in a certain drawer when I went out to swim, but I couldn't find it later. After I lost that stuffed animal, I was never the same. I can't describe the devastation. Well, I was a lonely child, so you can imagine how much the stuffed animal meant to me. I grew up overnight – I was unrecognizable to myself after losing that thing.

"And not that I'm equating the devastation of losing one's entire family to losing a beloved toy, but Fritz once told me that he became a stranger to himself after his family died. Just like Oxnard is unrecognizable without the letter O. You see, Xnard was the perfect name for the business."

"Wow, it really is," Faith said. "I have to say, Daniel, and I hope you're not offended by it, but for someone your age you are so impressive. Not only incredibly smart and talented, but also very sensitive. That is such a rare combination. I'm sure my grandfather was extremely proud of you."

Daniel stared at Faith and his eyes watered. He dropped his head and started to weep. Faith sat down next to him and gave him a long hug.

***

Faith sent Daniel off for a late lunch and got the kids a snack. Then, Chris, Faith, Anne, Daniel and the boys spent the remainder of the afternoon splashing in the pool. At five o'clock, Faith took the boys up for a bath while the others sat watching a football game on the TV in the gym area. At the kids' request, Chef Massey brought their dinner to the sitting room again. While the kids ate, Faith and Chris took turns showering and getting ready for the cookout.

At six o'clock, Mrs. Loper joined the kids in the playroom for a movie while Faith and Chris went down to prepare for the cookout. Chef Massey had made it all exceptionally easy.

The food was laid out in the kitchen, ready to be brought out. Hamburgers were ready for the grille and every conceivable accompaniment was ready to go, including fresh baked buns, sautéed onions, thinly sliced raw onions, tomatoes and avocados, crisp bacon, sliced cheddar and monterey jack cheese, and crisp romaine lettuce. He'd prepared a lovely salad of chopped kale and sliced brussels sprouts, slivered almonds, dried cranberries and wild rice in a light dijon lemon vinaigrette. A vegan acorn squash soup was ready to be poured into hollowed acorn squashes, one for each guest. He'd also enhanced their idea of a simple cookout by adding lightly marinated petite steak and shrimp kabobs interspersed with onions, peppers and tomatoes. He admitted taking a page from Martha Stewart by using rosemary stalks instead of metal or wood skewers. To accompany the kabobs, a chafing dish held spiced jasmine rice. For dessert, the chef had made cinnamon gelato with fresh apple tart, accompanied by small ramekins of fresh fruit. It all looked divine.

Venturing out to the backyard, Chris and Faith found patio heaters warming the dining area. A small bar was set up next to a serving table. Upon the bar sat a large covered tray, inside of which were oysters on the half shell resting on ice and a dish of cocktail sauce with a small spoon alongside them. The impressive gas grille was warming up. The dining table itself was beautifully laid out with linens and flowers in autumn colors. Hurricane candle vases provided warm, protected lighting at the bar and table. The ambiance was completed by the music flowing from the outdoor speakers, Etta James' 'Sunday Kind of Love'.

"May I have this dance?"

Faith turned to Chris with a slow, deep smile. "Why yes, sir, that would be delightful." He took her in his arms and they swayed to the music. She wrapped her arms around his neck.

Chris pulled her close and inhaled her fragrance. "You look beautiful, you know." He looked at her and his eyes traveled down her body, admiring the way the wrap dress hugged her figure, his gaze lingering on her décolletage. "You haven't dressed up in a while. Evening clothes suit you."

Faith nuzzled his ear. "Thank you for noticing." Chris pulled back a bit and kissed her.

"Should we interrupt?" Faith heard Daniel say softly.

"No," Anne replied loudly with a smile in her voice. "That would be rude."

Neither Chris nor Faith looked at them. "Can't we just ignore them? Particularly the loud woman?" Chris asked Faith.

Faith laughed and kissed him, then stepped back. "Welcome to our cookout, mes amis."

At that moment, the door from the pool opened and Chris's lanky friend Jim stepped out with a small, slim woman who had the same sandy blonde hair and brown eyes as Jim.

"Jim!" Chris walked to him and they did the handshake/one-armed 'bro' hug.

"Good to see you, Chris. Here's my baby sister, Sarah."

Sarah gave Chris a warm smile and a firm handshake. "Thanks. I wonder how old I have to be for him to stop calling me his baby sister."

"Well, I still call Faith my bride and we've been married almost eleven years. I think you've got a ways to go with that moniker."

"Great," she said sarcastically, smiling.

Chris introduced Jim and Sarah to the group and then began serving drinks from the bar. A few moments later, the pool door opened again and a late-twenties African American man in preppy attire stepped out.

"Nick has joined us! The festivities may now begin!" Daniel proclaimed and went over to him, clapping him on the back. "Folks, Nick and I were classmates at Gonzaga."

"I didn't know you went to Gonzaga," Faith exclaimed. "I went to Visitation!"

"Another excellent Catholic school," Nick said with a smile.

The group chatted amiably over their drinks and oysters, jazz music playing softly in the background. Chef Massey arrived with the food cart and began setting up the serving table.

Dusk darkened to evening and Chef lit tall, gas torches around the patio. He then whispered to Chris that it was time to begin grilling. Chris finally conceded that it might be a good idea for Chef Massey to do the grilling, since he was already there and hovering.

Fifteen minutes later, the seven of them sat down and dinner was served.

The guests commented repeatedly that the food was the best they'd had in ages, which visibly pleased Chef Massey. Over dessert and coffee, Chef asked Chris if he would like cigars brought out. Chris raised his eyebrows and looked around. "Anyone?"

Jim, Daniel and Nick said they'd love to try one, so Chef went off to retrieve them from the cigar closet. When he returned, he had a decanter of cognac and seven small glasses, as well.

Faith declined the cognac and cigar and contented herself with her coffee. At that moment, one of the security detail arrived and whispered in Faith's ear that Cassandra Blithe had arrived. Would she like her to join them? Faith, though surprised at the visit at such a late hour, nodded her head and the man disappeared.

Moments later, the pool door opened and Cassandra stepped out. She looked stunning and wore a mink coat. "It's far warmer out here than I expected. Nice touch having those warming lamps." She smiled at the group. "Hello, I'm Faith's Aunt Cassandra."

Jim stood to shake her hand and Faith made introductions all around.

Cassandra looked at Nick and shot up her hand. "Holla!"

Everyone looked at each other in surprise at her use of urban slang.

Nick smiled graciously at her and nodded his head. "Mrs. Blithe, it's a pleasure to see you again. You look lovely this evening."

"Oh thank you, dear boy." She turned to the group. "We've known Nick for ages and ages." Cassandra gave Faith a warm look but did not explain her presence.

Faith wasn't about to embarrass her by asking in front of all of her guests.

"What can I get you to drink, Cassandra?" Chris stepped forward and pulled a chair out for her.

"Oh, well, I can't stay long," she said as she sat down. "I just wanted to stop by and see my son one more time before he left for the west coast. I didn't expect to find a party." She narrowed her eyes at Daniel, who shrank a bit in his seat. Turning to Chris, she gave him an adoring look, "A vodka tonic would be lovely, thank you Christopher."

Conversation resumed around the table. Nick leaned close to Faith's ear and murmured. "She is a walking meme. The woman thinks she needs to talk ghetto to me whenever she sees me." Faith stifled a laugh. "Look at Daniel. He's so embarrassed, poor guy. That's why I don't say anything to him about her."

"Well," Faith whispered back, "you're a better person than I am. I don't think I'd be so polite about it. So you've been friends with Daniel since high school. Anne and I have been friends since high school, too. It's nice to have that consistency in life, isn't it? People who've known 'you' through all of the different 'yous' there have been."

"I know exactly what you mean," Nick said. "Each time I moved on to a new phase in life – college, grad school, moving to a new city -- I made a concerted effort to change the elements that I didn't like about myself. It's much easier to do that when you're in a fresh, new environment with a lot of people who don't know you. But it's also nice to have friends from way back, who've known you throughout. These are the people who really know you to your core. Jack's like that."

"Jack?" Faith asked.

"Oh, sorry. Yes, Daniel's pseudonym is 'Jack.' Specifically, Jack Kelly."

"He's got a pseudonym? Wow, suddenly I feel very boring." Faith smiled wryly.

"Don't. There's a kind of sad story behind it. When Daniel was young, he imagined that there was a boy out there named Jack Kelly who had a big, loving family and was hugely confident and popular. Jack Kelly became his nickname over time, because he used it when making reservations or going to bars. He never used the name Daniel Blithe for that sort of thing. So people eventually started calling him Jack. It just kind of stuck. Most people think it's a middle name or something."

"I didn't know he was so unhappy growing up." Faith said.

"Well, he didn't have a father and his mother is pretty self absorbed. Your grandfather was probably the best part of his life. And he wasn't even related to him."

Faith looked at Daniel across the table. He was laughing at something Sarah said. Faith glanced to the end of the table where Cassandra was leaning in to talk to Jim. Her fur coat was resting on the back of her chair and the cocktail dress she wore left little to the imagination. She was blatantly flirting with Jim.

"Do me a favor," Nick said. "Don't tell him I told you that. I think it would only make him feel badly about himself. I should have thought of that before I told you."

"I won't say anything. You have my word."

***

At eleven o'clock, Jim, Sarah and Nick left. Anne went up to her room. Chef Massey had cleared all of the food and dishes after dinner, so there were just a few glasses and the tablecloth left to bring inside. Faith went to the kitchen to get a tray while Chris went upstairs to check on the boys. As Faith approached the pool door, she heard arguing from the patio.

"No, really, mother, what did you say?" Daniel said angrily.

She couldn't hear Cassandra's response but knew she was talking aggressively.

As she reached the door, she understood why she couldn't hear her properly. Cassandra was standing with her back to the door, while Daniel was facing it.

"That's not an answer." Daniel fumed. He brushed past her and stalked toward the door just as Faith opened it.

"Excuse me," he said quietly to Faith and went through the pool area to the stairs.

"Everything okay, Cassandra?" Faith asked.

Cassandra turned, a bright smile on her face. "Oh yes, dear. Thank you, again for allowing me to join your party. I'll show myself out." She put on her coat and went into the house. Faith frowned and stared after her, then cleared the glasses from the table, folded up the tablecloth, turned off the heaters and gas torches, and double-checked that the grille was turned off. She locked the pool door on her way in.

After dropping the tray and tablecloth in the kitchen, Faith turned off lights in the house as she ascended from floor to floor. When she went to check the front door, she passed one of the security detail.

"Mrs. Blithe just left. Shall I activate the alarm now?" He asked.

"That would be great. Thank you, have a good night." He nodded to her and she ascended the front stairs to the second floor. She decided to check in on Anne before she joined Chris. She could tell by looking at the crack beneath Anne's door that light was off, so she closed the door to the guest suite and went across to the family suite.

The boys were making sweet sleeping noises when she checked on them, which brought a smile to her lips. She went down the hallway, turning out lights as she went, then joined Chris in the master bedroom. He was watching Saturday Night Live. She quickly washed up, got her pajamas on and joined him in the king sized bed.

"That was fun," Chris remarked.

"It was, wasn't it? I think everyone else enjoyed themselves, too. The food was so good."

"What was the deal with Cassandra showing up?" Chris asked.

"No idea. I never had a chance to ask Daniel. Oh, by the

way, I overheard Daniel arguing with Cassandra right before she left."

"What about?"

"I don't know. I couldn't hear that well. But he was really steamed with her." She filled him in on what Chris had said about Daniel's childhood.

"Sounds like Cassandra has been a less than ideal mother to him, as pleasant as she might seem to us."

"Single parents' relationships with their kids can be tough. It's not easy doing it singlehandedly. It's sometimes hard raising kids even with *two* parents," Faith laughed.

Cuddled up together, Chris and Faith watched Alec Baldwin host SNL for what must have been his fiftieth time. And she knew she'd laugh just as hard when he hosted for the fifty-first time.

Chapter 14

Sunday dawned crisp and sunny. Faith woke up to the sound of Super Mario Brothers wii echoing down the hallway from the boys' playroom. She smiled sleepily and turned to see Chris propped up in bed with the newspaper and a cup of coffee.

"How did you get all set up with this without waking me?" She asked with surprise.

"Very carefully," he said with a smile. "There's a tray with coffee and milk on the table if you'd like a cup."

Faith smiled and kissed him, then slipped out of bed. "Did you get the boys something to drink?"

"Yes, ma'am."

She sat back down on the bed with her coffee and flipped through to the front page of the Washington Post, then to the business section, checking to see if there was any shocking news.

"All clear," Chris said while looking at his paper. Faith nodded.

"So, what's on your agenda today?" He asked.

"Not much. Mass. Anne and Daniel leave for the airport at noon. Play date with Bruno at one o'clock. Other than that, it's a quiet day. What's on your agenda?"

"I really need to work out. And get a haircut." He ran a hand through his hair.

"Okay. Well, Mass is at nine. It's seven-thirty now, so we should leave in an hour. I'll let Anne and Daniel know, in case they want to join us."

Faith put on her robe and went down the hallway. "Hi boys!" She called as she passed the playroom. "Hi Mom!" She heard in a chorus.

Faith crossed the central hall that separated the private bedroom suite from the guest suite and entered the guest suite's sitting room. She knocked softly on Anne's door, "Anne? Are you up?"

The door swung open. "Of course!" Anne was already showered and dressed. Her bag on the luggage rack was almost packed. She looked casually elegant in winter white jeans, a chocolate brown cashmere cable knit sweater over a crisp, white oxford shirt, and chocolate brown riding boots. The light scent of jasmine and citrus floated by, fresh and clean.

"I should have known you'd make us all feel lazy. What time did you get up this morning?" Faith asked with mock disgust.

Anne raised her nose at Faith and then laughed. "Seven. That's late for me, but I have to give myself some slack for dealing with the time difference."

"But on a Sunday?"

She turned and went back to her packing. "My system gets all whacked out by Monday morning if I don't stick to an early wakeup during the weekend."

"Okay, I guess I can understand that." Faith acknowledged. "But it's still nuts, as far as I'm concerned."

"Don't be crude."

"Crude. You've got the sense of humor of a thirteen year old boy."

"I'll take that as a compliment." Faith started to laugh and Anne joined in. "Yeah, you know you love me. Well, I love you, too."

Faith gave her a hug. "I do love you. And you are crazy."

"Yes, I know."

"So let's get you some coffee. There's a minibar right out here in the sitting room. If you're interested in going to Mass with us, we leave in an hour." Faith walked out to the sitting room and got the coffee machine started. "There are little boxes of cereal, sugar, apples and bananas up here." She ducked down to the mini-fridge and said, "and down here you've got some pastries, OJ, bagels, milk cream cheese, butter, and nonfat yogurt." She stood up again. "Help yourself and show Daniel what's there, too, while I jump in the shower. We'll have brunch when we get back."

While Anne investigated the mini-fridge, Faith tapped at Daniel's door. "Come in!" he called.

Faith poked her head in and saw Daniel standing by the window in his PJs. He was gazing out at the backyard. "Daniel, good morning." Faith said.

"Hi, Faith." He turned. "Thanks again for the cookout last night. It was very fun to see Nick and meet your friends."

"You're welcome. We're heading to Mass in an hour if you want to join us. And Anne can tell you about coffee and some breakfast out there in the sitting room. We can have a more formal breakfast when we return."

"Thanks, I think I'll join you." He smiled but the smile didn't reach his eyes.

"Is something wrong, Daniel? I don't mean to pry, but I heard you raise your voice to your mother last night."

"I'm sorry. I didn't mean for you to hear that. What did you hear?"

"Just you asking your mother what she said. That's it. I didn't hear her response."

He nodded and kept nodding while he stared at her, as if he were thinking about what to say. He took a deep breath and exhaled sharply.

"It's nothing. We just haven't always had a smooth relationship."

"I understand," Faith said sympathetically.

"I miss your grandfather."

Faith nodded, not knowing what to say.

He sat down on the bed and ran a hand through his hair. "Your grandfather was a good man. He was a solid presence in my life. I don't think I always recognized or valued it properly."

"It's hard to understand the significance of relationships when you're young. Often, we don't see it until we're older, or until it's too late. While that is sad, it's understandable. I hope you aren't giving yourself a hard time about it."

He looked up at her with sadness in his eyes. "It's hard not to."

"He wouldn't want you to feel badly, I'm sure of it."

He nodded his assent. "I'm still really curious about who called him the evening he died. I feel like I could help figure it out if I could just see the list of people who were there at the health club. Maybe there's someone on that list whom I would recognize."

"Well, we can call the FBI and have them bring it by. It's worth a shot. Might not happen today, though, given it's a Sunday."

He ran a hand through his hair. "I could stay for a few more days, if you don't mind it."

"No, I don't mind. Ok, so I'll see you downstairs at eight-thirty." She smiled at him and ducked out.

Faith assembled two plates of food and brought them to the boys to hold them over until after Mass, then got in the shower. Chris was already out of the shower. He said he'd get the boys dressed.

At eight-thirty, the six of them were in the limousine headed to church in Arlington.

"Anne, Daniel's going to stay a few more days to work on something. You're welcome to stay, too, or go back today as planned." Faith said as they glided down Massachusetts Avenue.

Anne pondered this. "Well, I could stay on for a few days. There are a few tech companies here that I could visit. But I don't have any work clothes with me."

"That's not a problem. You can forage through my closet. Oh! And my new work wardrobe should be ready tomorrow. Dude. St. John Knits." Faith said with eyes narrowed.

"Sweet!" Anne replied, rubbing her palms together.

The car slid up in front of the church and they trooped up the stairs to the main door. Inside, the Faith walked into a comfortingly familiar wall of 'church scent', that potpourri of stale incense, Communion wafers and missal paper. Faith took Paul's hand and led everyone through the foyer to the second set of doors. Organ music had begun playing and the church was very full. The canister lights far overhead cast regularly spaced pools of light throughout the pews. Virtually every illuminated spot included a small child. It was, after all, the Family Mass.

Faith, Chris and the boys found seats in the second row. Daniel and Anne found separate seats toward the back. As Faith sat, she exhaled deeply. Church was her time to quiet her thoughts and relax. Paul unfolded the kneeler and plopped himself down. His tiny elephant 'stuffie' was soon on a new adventure climbing in and out of the pew bookrack, as he softly whispered narration to himself. Graham nestled himself against Faith and leaned into her. Chris opened a missal and followed along. A peaceful feeling crept over them.

After Mass, the group returned to Blithe House. The kids changed into shorts and t-shirts and went to the ballroom to play while the grownups had coffee and relaxed with the newspapers in the dining room across the house.

Faith went upstairs to the sitting room and called Special Agent Maxwell to ask him if Daniel could take a look at the list from the health club. He agreed to bring it by her office on Monday morning.

At noon, Faith and Anne laid out a lunch spread in the downstairs dining room. In the walk-in refrigerator, Chef had left a platter of sandwiches, a large serving bowl of salad, bowls of fresh strawberries and grapes, and a pasta salad with mozzarella balls, chopped basil and sliced cherry tomatoes. There was a variety of sandwiches, including chicken with pesto and tomato on ciabatta bread, chicken Caesar salad with grated parmesan wrapped in lavash, rice and bean burritos ready to reheat, turkey with avocado and tomato on wheat, and ham and swiss cheese on rye. Faith added a pitcher of lemonade and a few bottles of chilled sparkling water. They all ate heartily.

The doorbell rang at one o'clock. Faith dashed to answer it, with the kids yelling "Bruno!" in the background. Bruno's mother was wide-eyed when Faith answered the door.

"Faith, I had no idea you lived in such a huge house. Good grief!" Mary ushered Bruno inside. "Is my minivan okay parked there?" She gestured to the shallow, curved driveway in front of the house.

"Of course, no problem. Please come in!" Faith closed the door behind them and looked at Bruno. "Hi, Bruno! Graham, do you want to show Bruno upstairs to the ballroom?"

The kids ran screaming up the stairs as Graham excitedly told Bruno about what they would find there. Paul scrambled to keep up. Mary turned to Faith. "Ballroom?"

Faith smiled and nodded sheepishly. "I inherited this house from my grandfather. Yes, it's," she paused and gesticulated around her, "overwhelming, to say the least. Let me show you where the boys are, then we can go have some tea or something." She led Bruno's mother up the grand staircase as the woman looked around, bewildered.

As they entered the ballroom, Bruno yelled, "Mom, look mom! They've got a trampoline inside their house!" He was bouncing as high as he could and was nowhere near the cherubs on the ceiling.

"Good God," Mary said flatly.

"Graham, Paul and Bruno, only one at a time on the trampoline. Yes, ma'am?"

"Yes, ma'am," they replied in chorus.

"They should be okay up here unattended for a few minutes. Here," Faith said as she passed Mary her iPhone while they walked down to the kitchen. "You can watch them on this while we get our tea. It's what I do whenever I'm not in the room – just to see that they're following the safety rules. A camera was added in that room last week and the feed is hooked up to a private web service. It allows us to watch the streaming video from anywhere, right on the iPod or iPhone. There are cameras in the backyard, around the perimeter of the house and at the pool, too."

"That is amazing!"

Faith nodded. "It definitely helps when we live in such a rambling place."

"Wait, did you say pool?"

"Yes, there's an indoor pool, too. But the boys are never allowed there unless an adult is present. The door is kept bolted with a passcode keypad."

Mary nodded. She touched the display and the image changed to the pool. "Oh, oops. Wait, people are swimming." She passed the iPhone back to Faith.

"That's my husband, my sort-of cousin and my childhood friend. We've got visitors this weekend."

They reached the bottom of the back stairwell and entered the kitchen. Mary whistled at its size and the commercial appliances. "This is big enough to feed an army."

"My grandfather liked to entertain."

"May I?" Mary pulled out her own mobile phone to take a photo of the walk-in refrigerator. "This needs to be on my Pinterest 'Dream Kitchen' board."

Faith laughed. "Be my guest."

Faith prepared two cups of tea and filled three sports

bottles with a 50/50 blend of water and apple juice. She gave Mary a quick tour as they made their way back to the ballroom. They settled themselves into a window seat there and chatted away until the play date was over at three o'clock.

The boys did not want to say goodbye to Bruno, but they all promised to have another play date soon. When the door closed, Faith sighed deeply. First play dates were like first dates in the way parents download their life stories to each other. Now that her life story had taken such a big twist, telling it had become exhausting. She wondered how long it would take to feel comfortable owning such a home, being in this new situation.

She took a glance at the iPhone and flipped through the cameras until she spotted Chris, Daniel and Anne out on the patio behind the garage, enjoying a beer in the afternoon sun. Faith herded the boys to the kitchen to get snacks and then out to the play set in the backyard. Daniel jumped up and joined the kids on the zip line.

"Was the play date fun?" Anne asked as Faith sat down on a chaise lounge.

"The boys had a great time. I did, too. Mary's nice." She leaned back and closed her eyes. "Ahh, that's the ticket. Wake me for dinner."

"Roberts found a cell phone number for Mitchell Curzon. I texted it to you," Chris said.

"Really? I didn't get a text." She frowned and looked at her iPhone. "Oh, there it is. Didn't hear it come in. It was pretty loud in the ballroom." She looked up at him. "I'll give him a call later. Any idea what time zone he's in?"

"Nope."

Anne shielded her eyes to watch the kids on the jungle gym. "I'd love to be a fly on the wall during that phone call. I wonder what he's like."

"I'd love for you to be on the call, too, especially given the topic, but that is verboten."

"Look at you with the high school German," Anne teased Faith.

"Oh, please. I know a ton of German. Wiener schnitzel. Bitte schön. Haltet den Dieb!"

Anne doubled over with laughter. "And don't forget the phrase all the cool kids in high school knew 'hast du eine

Zigarette für mich?'"

"Definitely an 80s phrase." Faith chuckled. "Gosh, that brings back memories."

Chris raised an eyebrow. "From your club-hopping days?"

"I told you I got a marriage proposal when I was sixteen."

"Oh, here it is again," Anne said. "Dude, he was some green-card seeker at Café Med in Georgetown."

Faith looked at her with mock disdain. "It still counts. I was in demand, even back then."

Anne and Chris rolled their eyes and they all laughed.

"Ugh," Anne said. "Suddenly I can remember the taste of a Fuzzy Navel."

"Oh man," Faith blurted, "you got so sick drinking those things. And lemon drops!"

"That's disgusting," said Chris. "When I was in college, the cool kids drank flaming Sambuca. With a few coffee beans in the bottom."

"You were so Euro. I would have been all over you if I'd known you then." Faith said, giving him a dreamy look.

He smiled back at her and reiterated her phrase. "I was in demand, even back then."

"The first, the last, my everything," Anne sang out in her best Barry White.

Faith took over, "and the answer to… all my dreams. You're my sun, my moon, my guiding star, my kind of wonderful…"

They both jumped up and sang out "that's what you are!" and started doing disco moves as they sang along.

Chris sat back laughed.

***

Sunday night called for an early bedtime for the boys, which wasn't hard for them to accept, given how tired they were from the activities of the day. By seven-thirty, they were asleep.

Faith went to the sitting room and closed the door. She picked up her mobile phone and found the text with Mitchell Curzon's number and clicked on it. The call connected and began to ring.

"Yes?" said a deep, clipped voice.

"Mr. Curzon, my name is Faith Warrior. I am Fritz Blithe's granddaughter. I don't mean to disturb you, but I wonder if I can I have a moment of your time?"

"Fritz Blithe's granddaughter? Yes, I have a moment." His English accent was crisp.

"It's regarding Xnard."

"Xnard." He said, and stopped.

"Yes, I know non-investors are not to talk about it, but as my grandfather's sole heir, it's now my investment and I'm permitted to discuss it with you."

"Ms. Warrior, I am not in a position to discuss business matters right now. May I give you a ring back at another time?"

"Of course. I'm in Washington, DC. Perhaps sometime tomorrow at a mutually convenient time?"

"As it happens, I, too, am in Washington, DC right now. Would you care to meet for lunch tomorrow?"

"Yes, that would work."

"Is this a cell phone you're calling from?"

"Yes."

"I'll text you in the morning. Does one o'clock suit?"

"Yes, that's fine."

"Until then." She heard the line disconnect.

Faith's brow furrowed. What a curious man. She shrugged. She was pleased, though, that she'd connected with another investor. She looked forward to lunch.

***

At one-fifteen in the morning, she heard Paul crying. Faith threw back the covers and ran to her son's room. Paul was sitting up in bed, facing the headboard, obviously still half asleep. Faith knew that most of the time, when he woke in the middle of the night, it was only because he needed to use the bathroom. So, she scooped him up, carried him through to the night-light lit bathroom and sat him down. He was so sleepy that she had to hold him in place so he wouldn't fall off. When he was done, she cleaned him up and put him back in bed. He immediately settled in and fell back to deep sleep.

Faith stretched as she walked out of his room and decided she could use a few crackers. She couldn't sleep on an empty stomach. So she padded across the hallway that separated the guest suite from the residential suite and approached the staircase. She paused when she heard a voice. It sounded like Daniel. Though she was half-ashamed to do it, she crept closer to the guest suite and listened.

"What did you do?" He sounded exasperated. "You know what? I actually don't care anymore. I'm inclined to tell her myself." He was silent as he listened to the other end of the call. "We're done here." She heard him mutter an oath and his door opened, the shaft of light from his room piercing the darkness.

Faith flattened herself against the wall in the shadowy hallway, praying he wouldn't venture out and see her. He didn't make a sound. For a moment, she wondered if he was even there. A minute later, she heard the door close softly and the shaft of light was gone. The faint sound of his footsteps on the carpet told her he returned to his bed. Then, silence.

She exhaled quietly and quickly tiptoed to the staircase, wondering what the call was all about and tremendously grateful he hadn't known she was there. As she descended to the kitchen, a shiver ran down her spine that she should feel this way in her own home.

Chapter 15

They had woken up early and it was still dark outside. Chris had gotten up when he heard the shower running. With luck, Faith hoped she'd be fully dressed before the kids got up so she could quickly check her email before getting them ready.

"My eyebrows are a mess." Faith muttered to herself as she gazed into the bathroom mirror and twisted her hair into a chignon. She pinned it into place and gave it a quick blast of hairspray, then sat at the vanity to apply her makeup. She peered into a magnifying mirror. "How long has it been since my last lip wax? I'm turning into a man."

"I heard that," said Chris as he toweled off from his shower. "You are not supposed to talk about those things in front of me. You know that. Ruins the mystery."

"We've been married for ten years. Is there still any mystery left?" Faith asked.

"Of course there is." He walked over and kissed her on the nape. "And your eyebrows look perfect to me." She met his eyes in the mirror and they smiled at each other. He looked at her lip. "I wonder if you could make that into a handlebar shape…" Faith threw a hand towel at him and they both laughed.

She dressed quickly, then dashed into the sitting room and wrote sticky notes to Daniel and Anne. She instructed Daniel to have Roberts take him to Blithe Building for a ten o'clock meeting with Special Agent Maxwell. Then she wrote a note to Anne telling her to rummage in her closet for clothes and use her home office at will. She drew a little map to let her know where it was. Faith tiptoed over to their doors and stuck them on them, then went to wake up the boys.

The boys were sleepy but compliant about getting dressed and brushing teeth. She grabbed their backpacks and they joined Chris downstairs in the casual dining room for breakfast. When she saw Mrs. Lucie, she let her know that their guests were still there and would stay on for a few days. She asked Mrs. Lucie to wake up Daniel at eight o'clock.

On the way to drop off the children at school, Faith let Roberts know he'd need to get Daniel to Blithe Building by ten o'clock and he reminded her that he'd pick up her clothes from Nordstrom in the afternoon. She emailed Mrs. Abernathy to let her know she might be seeing Anne, and also emailed Mr. Hopewell to ask him to share the details of the tech portfolio with Anne, excluding Xnard, of course.

By eight-thirty, Faith was at her desk, sipping a second cup of coffee and going over the considerable corporate correspondence from the weekend. She reviewed her agenda for the day and discussed minor changes with Valerie, including her lunch and her ten o'clock meeting. Then, she set to work calling the next subsidiary president on her list. She was slowly making her way through the organization.

She had a brief meeting at nine o'clock with the CFO to discuss corporate tax issues and set up an afternoon appointment with her General Counsel to discuss what he'd learned about the Government Relations Department.

At nine-thirty, Geoff Michaels knocked on her door to let her know he was meeting with HR to finalize his employment, find an office, etc. He looked happy and she found that contagious. She felt good about her choice of bringing him on board.

At ten o'clock, Valerie buzzed her office to let her know that Agent Maxwell had arrived. Daniel had not yet shown up. A few minutes later, Valerie ushered him in, coffee in hand.

"Your assistant is very thorough. She had security downstairs ask me how I like my coffee and handed it to me when I got off the elevator." He looked back at Valerie through the door and she gave him a shy smile. He smiled back.

"She's very efficient." Faith agreed. "Please, sit down. Daniel hasn't yet arrived."

"I'm curious as to why he wanted to see the list." The

Agent asked pointedly as he sat down.

"Well, Daniel was very close to my grandfather. He thinks he might know who my grandfather's acquaintances were better than many would. If he thinks he can help, he should help, right?"

"Certainly," Maxwell inclined his head.

"Good morning, all," Daniel said as he breezed in to Faith's office. His blond hair looked windblown and he wore the casual clothes of a preppy college student.

"Good morning, Daniel." Faith said cheerfully. "Well, shall we take a look at that list?" Faith looked expectantly at Maxwell.

Maxwell pulled out four sheets of paper and laid them on Faith's desk, then stepped back to let Daniel and Faith look at them. There were three pages of a computer-generated report that showed the exact moment that member cards were swiped upon entrance and exit, the member names and any classes they took during their visit. The fourth page was a photocopy of the hand-written guest log from that day.

Daniel slowly ran his fingertip down the column of names. He moved carefully from page to page. When he finished looking at the guest log, he straightened up and sighed.

"Did you recognize anyone?" Maxwell asked.

"No, no one. I mean, I recognize some society names, but none whom my grandfather knew well. I'm afraid I've got nothing to add here," he said dejectedly.

Maxwell regarded him carefully. "Well, thank you for taking the time and making the effort. If anything occurs to you later, please call me." He packed up the papers into his briefcase.

"I will. Thank you, Special Agent."

Maxwell inclined his head toward Daniel and then turned to Faith. "Ma'am," he said. Then he turned and left. Valerie smiled at him shyly from her desk and said goodbye as he walked out. He thanked her for the coffee as he passed her desk and she blushed deeply.

Faith watched Daniel watch Maxwell leave. "That's disappointing," Faith said.

"Yes, very," Daniel agreed and nodded his head as he turned to her. "Thanks for setting it up, though, Faith."

"You bet. So, when do you want to go back to

California?"

"There was one more thing I was thinking of doing while I'm here. Do you mind if I return the day after tomorrow?"

"No, I don't mind at all. I'll have Mrs. Abernathy arrange for a Wednesday flight for you and Anne." She picked up the phone and called Mrs. Abernathy, who answered right away. "Good morning, Mrs. Abernathy. Can you please make return flight arrangements for Daniel and Anne on Wednesday morning?"

"Certainly," Mrs. Abernathy responded cheerfully.

"Thanks very much." She put the phone down and looked up at Daniel. "Is Roberts waiting for you downstairs?"

"Yes. Thanks, Faith." He stood a moment, as if to say something more, then smiled, turned and walked out.

Faith watched him leave, puzzled by his pause. She sighed heavily and sat down, feeling tired from the drama of the past few weeks. With considerable effort, she successfully turned her attention back to work and continued making calls to subsidiaries throughout the morning.

By noon, Faith felt she'd truly accomplished something. She was gaining a solid understanding of the company and its various moving parts, and felt welcomed by the senior executives, all of which boded well for the future. At twelve-fifteen, she received a text from Mitchell asking her to go to the Georgetown Harbor. She should look for a boat named *Natalia* at the dock in front of Sequoia restaurant. Faith rolled her eyes knowing how easily she became motion sick.

She got up and picked up her jacket and purse. Valerie glanced up from her desk. "You're going somewhere, Mrs. Warrior?"

"Yes, I've got a lunch meeting at the Georgetown Harbor. I shouldn't be more than an hour and a half or so."

As she walked past Valerie's desk, Valerie stood up. "Ma'am, wait. I'll have one of the security team go with you."

Faith looked at her with surprise. "I'm just going to grab a cab."

"Ma'am, there is always a car waiting for you out front. Your security detail goes where you go. I'll just call down so they know you're coming." Valerie picked up the phone and made the call. Faith's surprise was hard to hide. It hadn't occurred to her that they stayed around.

Faith turned and walked to her husband's office. He was crouched over his computer keyboard, a perplexed look on his face. He glanced up when he saw her movement by the doorway.

"So now I can't take a cab anywhere alone," she said with exasperation.

"Walk, run, cab, whatever. No, not alone anymore." He said matter-of-factly. "Neither can I."

"Right. I'm going to lunch with Mitchell Curzon. Be back soon." She pivoted on her heel and was walking down the corridor toward the ladies room when Chris poked his head out of his door.

"Can't I come? I'm dying to meet that guy."

"Nope, discussing Xnard. Next time, absolutely." She smiled at him and kept walking.

Faith exited the lobby through a revolving door and walked to the limousine at the curb, her heels clicking loudly on the sidewalk. One of her security detail held the car door for her while another waited in the driver's seat. The air had a snap to it – fall was definitely on the way, her favorite season.

"Ma'am, I understand you're going to the Washington Harbor but don't know the official destination."

"A boat named *Natalia*, at the dock behind Sequoia."

"Very good, ma'am." Her door clicked closed and he climbed into the front passenger seat. The limousine pulled smoothly into traffic.

At the harbor, her bodyguard opened her door for her and motioned for her to precede him down the steps to the dock along the Potomac River. She immediately saw a small, elegant wooden launch with the name *Natalia* painted on the end of it. Faith looked around in wonder. It was a beautiful boat, classically appointed with highly polished wood uppers, brass detailing, gorgeous blue and white striped awning and cushions. A British flag snapped in the wind at the stern. While it was impressive, she wondered how this could be her destination. As she neared the boat, the uniformed driver stepped forward. "Mrs. Warrior?"

Her bodyguard nodded and helped her into the boat. She sank back on the cushions while her bodyguard stood next to the driver. The engine came to life and the boat pulled away from the dock. The driver called back, "ma'am, it will just be a few minutes."

The wind whipped her hair as the boat turned away from the dock and began its journey in the direction of Key Bridge. Faith enjoyed the view of Roosevelt Island on the left and Georgetown on the right. It picked up speed as it settled into the middle of the river and powered under the bridge.

The launch zipped past Jack's Boathouse and abruptly slowed, which prompted Faith to turn her head toward the driver. And there, straight ahead of them, sat a beautiful yacht. A *huge* yacht, Faith thought, probably 150 feet long. three decks high, it was painted white and had smoked glass windows. Modern furniture was stylishly arranged on the exposed decks.

The launch slowed and gently reached a landing at the stern of the ship. There, above what appeared to be a garage for the launch, the name *Lyudmilla* was painted in script beside a full-length portrait of a scantily-clad, overly-painted woman Faith could only guess was Lyudmilla herself.

The driver threw a rope to a uniformed deck hand who quickly secured the launch, then Faith's bodyguard helped her step out onto the landing. "This way, please, Mrs. Warrior," said the deck hand with a British accent. He turned and ascended a narrow staircase beside the garage. The staircase led to what appeared to be the main deck. Here there was a swimming pool and spa surrounded by chaises, as well as a covered porch with a dining table and ten chairs. To one side was a fully equipped outdoor kitchen with a grill that would make a Texan jealous. The deck hand led her through a sliding glass door into a large art deco parlor with several grouped seating areas and a large bar on one side. Beyond this room was a spiral staircase, and beyond the staircase, separated by frosted glass pocket doors, was a formal dining room. Every detail was deco. It was breathtakingly beautiful.

"Please have a seat, Mrs. Warrior. Mr. Curzon will be with you momentarily. May I serve you a drink?"

"No, thank you," Faith responded with a smile. The man nodded and disappeared down the spiral staircase.

Faith glanced toward the sliding door and noticed her bodyguard standing just outside.

A moment later, Faith heard footsteps from the spiral staircase and a tall, elegant man emerged and walked toward her. He was tanned and his dark brown hair was graying at the temples. Faith guessed he might be in his mid-forties. He reminded her of James Bond in his exquisite suit and crisp white shirt, open at the collar. If she didn't know what a shrewd investor he was, she'd have thought him some sort of a playboy. Well, she supposed he could be both.

She stood as he stretched out a hand. A gold signet ring glinted. His polite smile was brilliantly white. "Mrs. Warrior, it's a pleasure to meet you," he said as he firmly grasped her hand and shook it. "May I express my condolences on the loss of your grandfather. He was a good man. I didn't know him well, but our paths crossed several times at functions, and we dined together in Moscow and London. We had mutual friends, and he struck me as a particularly intelligent and thoughtful man."

"Thank you, Mr. Curzon, many people seem to have had that impression of him."

"Please, call me Mitchell."

"And call me Faith," she said and smiled back at him. "You have a beautiful boat."

"Thank you. I just got it from a former Russian business partner who couldn't pay his debt."

"Ah," Faith nodded. "That explains Lyudmilla?"

He closed his eyes and groaned, "yes, indeed. She was Viktor's muse. She'll be gone very soon." And he laughed and looked around. "It carries the distinction of being the greenest luxury yacht ever made. Every efficiency has been addressed, from power to waste." He laughed again, "Viktor made his fortune through some of the most environmentally devastating businesses. And yet he took huge pride in this vessel, as if it vindicated him." He shook his head. "Natalia is his wife, by the way. He's a prince of a man, that one."

"Goodness. Well, I do appreciate your making the time for me."

"Of course. Shall we have some lunch? I think it's ready to be served." He motioned her into the formal dining room and she saw that two places had been set. He held a chair out for her and she slid into it. He smelled very good. *Good grief, I need to get Chris some of that cologne! Would it be rude if I rubbed my face on his neck?*

A uniformed staff member emerged from a swinging door

and placed bowls of steaming, fragrant soup in front of them. Another staff member poured sparkling water and placed plates of warm rolls and curls of butter beside the bowls.

"So, you mentioned you wanted to discuss Xnard?" He asked as he dipped into his soup.

"Yes. As my grandfather's sole heir, I've been going through his investments, trying to get to know each one of them. I've spoken to Daniel Blithe about it but thought I'd also speak with another investor to flesh out my still-cursory understanding of it."

She tasted the soup and found it to be delicious.

He nodded. "What has he already told you?"

Faith described what Daniel had told her about the concept and its potential applications. "He said he might have something to test in about a year."

"That's what he told me, too. I've had a few conversations with the people I've put on the job with him, and they seem to believe the idea has promise."

"Enough for you to invest so heavily?"

He silently studied her for a moment. "Even if the venture fails, the data it will provide will yield opportunities for me in other areas."

"Other areas?"

"Yes. I have considerable pharmaceutical interests." He raised his arm and a Caesar salad with warm, sliced chicken was placed before them. "What we learn from Daniel's work could help my company's efforts and prove lucrative for me regardless of his success."

"Daniel mentioned that Ptolemy brought you in."

"He did. I've known Ptolemy for a long time. He is a friend. Still, I'm not in the habit of exerting myself solely as a favor to friends. The venture had to have a favorable risk-reward profile. And, for me, it does."

"I see."

"Never fear," he said with a wink, "it's written into the deal agreement that anything I do with this endeavor's findings will be subject to a licensing arrangement. In other words, the other owners will benefit. That's something Ptolemy insisted upon. He knows me pretty well." He chuckled and speared a tomato. "So, how have you adjusted to such dramatic change?"

She took a sip of sparkling water. "It's been a tough few weeks. For all of us."

"You have a family." He nodded and glanced at her wedding ring.

"Yes. Married with two small boys. We're finally getting settled. Thankfully, the boys are doing alright."

He gave her a serious look. "They are your first priority."

"Of course."

He looked at her curiously. "Fritz talked of his children that way, too."

"That's really good to hear." She looked at her hands. "I've often felt at a loss talking to people who knew my grandfather. Everyone seems to think so highly of him. It's a terrible thing that I didn't have more time with him. That sounds very selfish of me, I know."

"No, quite the contrary."

They continued talking about business throughout the luncheon. As they parted, they shook hands and Mitchell offered his advice or help whenever she needed it.

"I'll be sure to call. If the risk-reward makes sense," she added with a chiding smile.

He laughed and returned her smile. "Oh, I think you'll do just fine, Faith. But do call if I can be of service."

The launch pulled away and quickly accelerated. Mitchell waved to Faith, then turned and stalked back into the salon. He picked up the phone. "Get me Ptolemy."

As the launch pulled into Georgetown Harbor, Faith's cell phone rang. It was a California number that she didn't recognize. "Hello?" she asked.

"Faith Warrior? Ptolemy Gunesdogdu here."

"Well, news travels fast," she said.

"I'm sorry, I don't know what you're referring to. I'm responding to a message you left for me over the weekend."

Faith closed here eyes and dropped her head back. "Right. Sorry. I just left Mitchell Curzon and assumed... never mind. Ptolemy, I do need to talk to you. About Xnard. Does this ring a bell?"

"Yes, of course," he said quietly. The launch touched the dock and Faith's bodyguard helped her out. She began walking up the steps toward K Street. "Faith, do you mind if I speak with you in person about this?"

"No, not at all. When?"

"Tomorrow night. In DC."

"Ok. Call me and let me know where."

"I will come to your home. And Faith?"

"Yes?"

"Please don't talk to Daniel about it until you and I have spoken."

"Why?"

"It's… complicated. Just trust me, okay?"

"Alright, but it won't be easy. He's staying with me until Wednesday morning."

"I know," he said quietly. "I won't come in. I'll come by in a car and collect you. We can drive and talk. Is eight o'clock too late?"

"No, it's alright."

Faith ended the call and dropped her cell phone back into her pocket. She shook her head as she continued up the stairs. "What the frick is going on?" she muttered to herself.

***

"Faith," Valerie said, "Jack asked to see you this afternoon. Your calendar would accommodate him at three p.m., but I'd like to clear that with you."

Faith looked up from her spreadsheets. "Yes, that's fine. Thanks, Valerie." She glanced at the clock. It was 2:45pm and she'd engrossed herself with segment reports for the past hour. Chris had just left to pick up the kids. She stretched and took a sip of water, then leaned back and looked out the window. She pulled out her cell phone and dialed Anne.

"Dude, tell me something funny," she said when Anne picked up.

"Knock knock."

Faith smiled. "Who's there?"

"Mask."

"Mask who?"

"Behind this mask is an ordinary banana."

"I don't get it."

"Neither do I. Take it up with your four-year-old – he told me the joke yesterday. He laughed like a hyena, too."

"That sounds like Paul."

"Mmm-hmm. What's going on?"

"Just a stupid, confusing day."

"I've had those. Did yours include carnies?"

"Did *yours*?"

"Yes. Well, one of my stupid, confusing days did. Not today, though."

"I changed my mind. I don't want to live vicariously through you."

"I could have told you that."

"Want to work out when I get home?"

"That's not some sort of euphemism, is it?"

"ANNE!"

"Okay, okay, bad day. I get it. Yes, let's work out when you get home."

"THANK YOU."

"You're welcome. Where are your workout clothes? Because I didn't bring any."

"Middle left drawer of my dresser."

"Okey dokey. See you later."

"Yup."

Faith looked up as the door opened and Jack stuck his head in. "Safe to enter?"

"Yes, Jack, no firings today." She said with a wry smile.

"Good, good." He closed the door and sat down in the club chair in front of her desk. "So, I've got an update on the Government Relations Department."

"I'm all ears," she said with raised brows.

"I took the circuitous route in my brief investigation and interviewed people who interact with the department, both inside and outside of the company. I did not speak with anyone actually in the department. It appears that GR has been walking a fine legal line in what they've been doing. Von Heiden had a take-no-prisoners attitude and used the department to put the screws on people. Let's just say that they've got a thick file of important people's weaknesses."

"They've been blackmailing people to advance the company's interests?"

"Not precisely – at least, as far as I can tell -- but they've been very close to that."

"Anyone specifically?"

"Well, one particular Senator's name was mentioned in confidence."

"Which one." Faith said firmly. It wasn't a question. It was a demand.

"Senator Messier."

Faith sat back in her chair and looked out of the window. Messier had been at her grandfather's funeral. "Thank you, Jack. Let's take this investigation to the next level. I want to know who did what, who's calling the shots, and if anyone broke the law. Tread quietly."

"Yes, ma'am, I'll put more resources on it." He turned and left, shutting the door softly behind himself.

Edward Messier was a seasoned, sixty-something Senator who held sway with the Defense Department. Successfully blackmailing him would serve to advance Blithe Defense, without a doubt. Faith exhaled and picked up the phone. When Chris answered, she said, "looks like the Government Relations department may have been exerting pressure on a Senator."

"Really?" Chris asked with surprise. "That doesn't sound like Fritz's style."

"I don't think it was. But it might have been Von Heiden's."

"What do you want to do about it?"

"I'm torn between telling Agent Maxwell and going to Messier myself to ask him. What do you think I should do?"

"Well, it seems potentially inflammatory for the company to bring the FBI in on a hunch. That said, I can't imagine Messier admitting to anything. What would be the upside for him unless you agreed to remain silent?"

"So, wait and dig some more."

"That's what I'm thinking."

"Hmmph." She switched gears. "I'm working out with Anne tonight before dinner, in the house gym. Is that okay?"

"Sure. See you at dinner, then."

Faith hung up and gazed out the window. She hadn't imagined her work would be easy, but neither had she imagined it would be so hard. A scandal could hurt the company and the employees, as well as tarnish her grandfather's memory, but she was already in process of cleaning house and wasn't about to shove a landmine under the carpet.

Von Heiden. Who the hell was this guy? She picked up the phone. "Owen," she said to the new head of HR. "Tell me, what company did Greg Von Heiden come in through? A tobacco company, right?"

"Yes. Albemarle Tobacco. About fifteen years ago."

"Okay, thanks." She hung up and dialed Jack's extension.

"Hey. Any idea who advised on the Albemarle tobacco deal – the one that brought Von Heiden in -- and was the company owned by another company, or was it privately held?"

"One sec." She heard a file drawer open, then the rustle of papers. "Okay. Uh, here it is. Albemarle was owned by a private equity firm, Lorraine Capital. No advisers. Looks like the deal was done directly between Fritz and the PE firm."

"Thanks." She disconnected and Googled Lorraine Capital. She didn't recognize the CEO's name, or any of the firm's officers. Then she clicked on the link to the Board and she sat back in her chair and saw one name she recognized. Richard Whitman was Lorraine Capital's founder.

Clearly, I need to have another chat with Mr. Whitman.
***

The rest of the day was spent on matters that needed to be settled before the company closed its books for the quarter. The process was fascinating from her perspective, given she'd never before seen everything that went into it from the corporate side. It was reassuring to see how capable Kevin McGuire seemed to be.

At five o'clock, she finished typing notes to herself on the day's developments. She'd resurrected her old habit of jotting notes to help her keep a record of events and her observations, decisions and conclusions, and tucking into the notes clippings from things she'd read or seen. Though these days, she eschewed an actual notebook for a tech version, Evernote, and the clippings were electronic attachments of photos and documents rather than actual papers she stapled into her notebook. Faith would never be called a Luddite.

The kids had finished dinner by the time she got home. Walking down the hallway to the lower dining room, she heard Chis.

"Boys, as soon as you finish dessert, we're going to do homework."

The boys had their backs to her as she crept up to kiss their necks. Paul whispered to Graham, "Brother, if I never finish my ice cream, then we'll never have to do our homework!"

"You don't have homework, Paul," Graham said crossly.

"Yes, I do!" Paul protested. "I've got a pumpkin coloring page I've got to color. That's hard work!"

"You don't know what hard work is, Paul. I've got to do a page of math and a page of word study, and then I've got to look at my word flash cards. THAT is hard work." He snorted in disgust.

Faith laughed and smacked kisses on their necks.

"Mo-om," Paul tattled in sing-song, "Graham said I don't do hard wo-ork!"

"Ok, ok, that's enough, boys. Both of you do hard work, you're just in different grades. Now, no more talk. Eat that dessert and get that homework done." She moved to Chris' chair and gave him a kiss.

"Good day, hon?" He asked.

"Busy, for sure. I'm going to scamper upstairs and change my clothes. I'll be done and showered in time to read the boys stories, okay?"

"No problem."

***

"... and then," Anne said, breathing heavily as she ran on the treadmill, "he gave me a copy of a self-help book on relationships." The treadmill buzzed and slowed down for the cool-down period after her 30 minute session.

"You're kidding me," Faith said from the elliptical machine. "But you broke up with *him*."

"Right. He couldn't fathom why I'd break up with him, given his perfection as a human, so he decided there was something wrong with me. Something that this awesome book would fix." She tightened her ponytail.

"Good grief," Faith groaned, "what a jerk! Wait – I can say that, right? You're really *really* not going to get back together with him, are you?" She asked suspiciously."

"No, I'm really and truly done. You may speak freely. But you have to admit he was a really good looking jerk."

"That only goes so far."

"Agreed." The treadmill beeped the conclusion of the program and Anne stepped off the belt. She sat down on a mat and stretched her legs.

"Well, there's always Matthew," Faith said in mock helpfulness.

"God, Matthew. I'd almost forgotten. Thanks much. Yes, we had a pact. If neither of us was married by 30, we'd marry each other. But he went and found a beautiful bride." Anne shook her head and added seriously, "he's a great guy, but it was for the best. Honestly, if I didn't have passion for him, it wasn't meant to be. Would have been awful for both of us, eventually."

"If you could just find a man that was half Matthew and half Jeremy."

Anne leaned forward and touched her forehead to her knees, stretching her hamstrings. "Right."

"You are one flexible chick. Maybe you should put that on a Match.com profile. I'll bet you'd get lots of attention."

"I don't need that kind of attention, thank you very much."

Faith finished her session on the elliptical and joined Anne on the mat, trying valiantly to do as deep a stretch as her friend, and failing. "You suck," she said enviously, and they both chuckled. "So, did you meet with any interesting companies today?"

Anne got up and walked to the free weights. "There's a biotech company in Reston I'd been researching. I was able to slip in for a half hour meeting with the CFO today, which was great. And he sent me with the VP of IR on a tour of the facility. The CFO is always traveling – setting up a meeting with him from afar was proving challenging, so this extended stay with you was serendipitous." She explained what she'd learned as she picked up a bar and two ten-pound plates and fastened them together. Then, she sank down into squats with the bar resting on her shoulders.

"That's terrific! You are welcome for an extended stay any time," Faith said with a smile. "Did your boss give you any trouble for not coming in today?" She grasped two eight-pound hand weights and reclined on a weight lifting bench to do some flies.

"He wasn't pleased. We had a client conference call set up for this morning. But I dialed in and did a good job answering some very pointed questions, so we're okay. And the meeting I had today generated a lead on yet another company – one of their suppliers. So I'll meet with that company tomorrow, and spend a good chunk of the day working on financial models."

"Sounds good." Faith glanced at the clock. "Oh – got to go shower for dinner."

"Okay, I'll just finish these last few reps. See you at seven. Say – where's Daniel?"

"No idea!" Faith waved cheerily as she jogged to the door.

On her way up the stairs, she popped her head into the office and saw Mrs. Abernathy still at her desk.

"Mrs. A., I was wondering if you could arrange something for me?"

"Of course, Mrs. Warrior. I was just leaving – is it urgent?"

"Oh, no. It's something that you could arrange tomorrow. I noticed that my grandfather has a hair station there in the spa area. Did he have someone come here to give him haircuts?"

"Yes, ma'am. A stylist and manicurist from Elizabeth Arden came here once every three weeks. Would you like me to set up a similar schedule for you?"

"That would be wonderful – thank you!"

"Will tomorrow afternoon work? That's an early day, isn't it?"

"Perfect."

"You, your husband, the boys – and would your friend, Anne, like one, too?"

"I'm not sure – why don't we just say yes for now. But Chris just got a haircut this weekend, so he should be all set."

***

Faith looked at the clock. It was after one in the morning. Something had woken her. A noise of some sort. She looked at Chris and saw him peacefully sleeping. The room was slightly chilly – just the way she liked it for sleeping, but not great for tiptoeing around in the middle of the night. A shiver ran through her as she pulled on her bathrobe and stepped into her slippers.

She crept down the hallway and checked on the boys, then opened the door to the main hallway. She saw the light on in the guest suite sitting room, so she went to investigate.

Daniel sat in an armchair looking at the gas fire, a tumbler of amber liquid in his hand.

"Daniel?" She said quietly. "Are you okay?"

He turned his head to her and gave her a weary look. "Yes,

I'm okay, thanks. Just wanted to unwind before bed."

Faith nodded and stepped closer, then slid into the opposite chair. "Tough day?"

He closed his eyes and exhaled. "You could say that."

"Want to talk about it?" She asked earnestly.

He gave her a pained look. "I would really like to, but I shouldn't."

"Why not?"

"We don't know each other very well."

She smiled. "You're right. But you're the closest I'll get to my father's family. Maybe we could think of each other as actual cousins."

"You know, I think you really are what you seem to be."

"I don't know what you mean."

"You seem to be a sincerely nice person."

"Oh," Faith smiled, flattered. "Well, I try to be. And thank you for saying that."

"You're welcome," he said with a smile.

"So, what is troubling you?"

"Do you remember a moment when you first heard a clock tick?"

She cocked her head to the side, in question.

"I mean, that moment when you're not actually focusing on the clock and yet the sound reaches you? It's a moment of awakening, of awareness of yourself alone in the world. For me, that moment was when I first realized my mother didn't love me. I was five."

"Oh," Faith said, her face blooming with sadness.

He glanced at her and waved his hand, as if to tell her he didn't want her sympathy. His gaze returned to the fire. "I was fifteen when I realized she might be completely incapable of loving anyone but herself. You'd think that would have made me feel better, but it actually just scared me. I mean, it was scary to admit I was raised by a sociopath -- or a narcissist – I'm not sure which. What does that say about me? Will I be one, too?" He shook his head. "Well, I'm not," he said quietly in answer to himself, "but I feared it for a long time."

Faith swallowed, not sure what to say. So, she just waited.

"I don't know what you know about my mother, or what you think about her, *if* you think about her. Just know that there is more to her than meets the eye."

"What happened today that brought you to this?"

He closed his eyes briefly, then looked at her. "I'm not ready to talk about it yet. And I'm sorry to dump that on you — that tidbit about my mother. But forewarned is forearmed."

"Okay, Daniel." She stood up. "Well, get some rest. And let me know if and when you want to talk more. I'm here."

"Thanks," he nodded and gave her a sad smile. "Cousin," he added very quietly.

Chapter 16

It took Faith a long time to fall back to sleep after her talk with Daniel. She awoke bleary eyed and lay staring at the ceiling after turning off the alarm.

"Something wrong?" Chris asked sleepily. "You're usually bright eyed and bushy tailed in the morning."

"You know how there's that message on the side view mirrors of cars, 'things are closer than they seem?' Well, replace that with the message 'things are actually worse than they seem.'"

He propped up his head with one hand. "What's going on?"

"Just a growing sense of unease. I hate it when my first impressions of people are wrong." She explained her conversation with Daniel.

"Good grief. That poor guy. Well, it's rare for someone to simultaneously be so awful and so talented at hiding it from others. But he's an extremely bright guy, so it makes sense his mother is bright, too. Sometimes really bright people have a screw loose – as if they took two trips through the brains line and skipped the sensitivity line altogether. Add to that self-absorption and cunning, and you're got a truly bad combination that's easy to miss."

She nodded. "Well, let's both pay close attention to Cassandra and Daniel. In case we *still* don't have the real story." She looked at him and raised an eyebrow.

"Ugh. Thanks for bringing me ashore to your island of unease."

She grabbed his hand and slapped his palm.

"Ouch! What'd you do that for?"

"Stamping your passport," she giggled.

He rolled over, pinned her to the bed and kissed her.

"What was that for?" Faith asked with a smile.

"Paying my duties." He smiled and kissed her again. "Wait, no, showing you my contraband," he said deviously.

She raised both eyebrows and gave him a dubious look. "I think I know where this is going, sir, and it's not going to result in a cavity search at this hour. We've got to shake a leg."

He shook his leg.

"Goofball," she muttered affectionately and slid out of bed.

"Tonight?" Her husband asked hopefully.

"It's a date."

Chris flopped back onto his pillow with a dejected sigh.
***

The morning sped by for Faith, as she worked her way through a quarter-end prep meeting with the finance department, a conference call with management from one of the Blithe Essentials companies regarding a prospective acquisition, and a meeting with her General Counsel and CFO regarding D&O insurance.

Just before lunch, Valerie buzzed her to say that Agent Maxwell was on the line.

"Agent Maxwell, how are you?"

"Just fine, Mrs. Warrior, thank you. I'm calling to let you know some news. Firstly, Cardinal Mayse offered to take a DNA test."

"That's reassuring."

"Indeed. The problem then became where we would find your uncle's DNA to test it against."

"Maybe in his things? Cassandra might have a snippet of hair from his baby book or something?"

"No, it seems she disposed of all of his things long ago."

"She... really? Well, it has been thirty-five years. But still. And she never married. I just..."

"I had a similar reaction. But this didn't stop us. We contacted the police department in Massachusetts that handled the scuba accident in 1972, just in case they had anything. It turns out that the chief in charge of the case is still alive. He's retired now, but he remembered the case. And he remembered that there was some DNA evidence. Skin cells scraped from beneath your grandmother's fingernails. He'd suspected they came from Thomas given scratch marks on his face. So we tracked them down and tested them. The Cardinal was not this person's father."

"Oh, well, that's very good."

"Well, you'd think so. Except that this person was not Elena's child, either. Nor Fritz's. The skin cells beneath Elena's fingernails came from someone entirely different."

Faith almost dropped the phone. "Someone else was down there?"

"That appears to be the case, yes."

"Who?"

"We don't know yet. We're tracking down everyone who worked on the yacht on that trip."

"Cassandra?"

"No. It was a male."

"Okay, thank you, Special Agent. Keep me informed?"

"Yes, ma'am. And thank you for telling us about the call to Cardinal Mayse. Let me know if you come across anything else."

"I will."

She hung up the phone and stared out the window. Someone lied to her grandfather the day he died. Why? Someone else was down there the day her uncle and grandmother died. Again, why? *What the hell is going on?*

She thought about her father's murder and immediately picked up the phone again.

"Maxwell," he answered.

"It's Faith again. Have you talked to my father's murderer?"

He was quiet for a moment. "You're thinking they're all connected."

"I'm beginning to worry that they are. I mean, someone was lurking around three of my family's deaths -- maybe the same was true for my father's murder."

"Nestor Carson was found not guilty by reason of insanity, and he's spent the last thirty-five years in Saint Elizabeth's hospital, here in Washington. I'll look into getting a meeting with him and I'll keep you posted."

She tried calling Chris but it rolled over to voice mail. A text arrived a few seconds later: "In a meeting. Urgent?"

She texted back: "nope. Tell u later." Concentration was

hard to come by, but she managed to complete a few critical tasks before her iPhone calendar chirped with a reminder about picking up the kids.

***

Increasingly, she found herself fielding texts, calls and emails during her time with the kids, so she finally put it on mute and tucked it in her pocket. She spent the afternoon playing with the boys, reading to them, having snack, and helping with homework.

At four-thirty, the hair stylist and manicurist from Elizabeth Arden arrived to give the three of them haircuts. She did the boys' first while Faith had a manicure. Then Mrs. Loper took the boys down for dinner and Faith and Anne finished up their treatments, including some much-needed waxing.

As they walked out, Faith mused to Anne that she was surprised the manicurist had brought wax.

"Mrs. Abernathy specifically asked for it," the manicurist offered helpfully.

Anne turned to Faith, who had blushed a deep crimson. "You need to give that woman a raise."

***

Chris got home at six o'clock and elected to work out while Faith bathed the kids and got them to bed. She hoped that this would become a weekday pattern for them, trading off workouts and childcare. It felt like they were a real team, with everyone's needs being met.

By seven-thirty, Anne, Chris and Faith sat around the table in the formal dining room enjoying pork chops stuffed with cornbread and chestnut stuffing. No one had seen Daniel.

"So, you head back tomorrow. Have you missed the backwoods?" Chris asked Anne.

"Is that even a question?" She had a twinkle in her eyes. "Seriously, this trip has shown me how urgently I need to address my living situation. I need to get back to civilization. Plus, I truly despise my boss."

"Well, I've been thinking…" Faith looked at Chris, who nodded to her in agreement. "How would you like to come and work for me?"

"For you? In what capacity?" She looked intrigued.

"Managing Fritz's personal tech portfolio. It's got a couple billion in it.”

“A couple billion. Are you kidding? I’d love it!”

Faith exhaled a big lungful of relief. “Great! That’s just so great! Let me get with Mr. Hopewell to figure out the best way to structure it. We can talk with him tomorrow morning, before you leave for home.”

“Oh my gosh, I am so excited. So excited! Thank you!”

The doorbell rang, alerting Faith to the time. It was eight o’clock, which meant that Ptolemy Gunesdogdu was outside. She quickly explained to Chris and Anne, and both walked down with her to the door. Ptolemy was in a limousine, his driver at the door.

Faith stepped out and the window slid down, revealing a handsome, mid-fifties, fair-haired man with blue eyes. She smiled and looked around the inside of the limousine.

“It’s a common misconception that all Turks have dark coloring,” he said with a smile.

“Actually, I did recognize you. Hard not to, given the numerous magazine covers,” she smirked. “I was just checking to see if anyone else was in the limousine.”

“Oh good. My ego was almost wounded.” The man had a charming smile, but she knew from those accompanying magazine articles that the man was ruthless. “Is it safe?”

“Yes, it’s safe. Daniel’s not in. I’m not sure where he is. This is my husband, Chris, and my good friend, Anne.”

“It’s a pleasure to meet you both.” As he reached for the door handle, Daniel’s rental car pulled up in front of the electronic gate and it swung open.

Daniel gave Faith a warm smile as his window slid down. “Hey, Faith. You all going out?”

Ptolemy’s window slid shut and Faith’s heart raced. “Oh, hi, Daniel! No, I’m just popping out for a bit. Be back soon.” She flashed him a smile and quickly climbed into the limo. Chris shut the door behind her.

“That was close,” Ptolemy remarked with relief. He wearily rubbed the back of his neck.

“Yes,” she sighed. “Frankly, I’ve had just about enough intrigue for a while.” She shifted in her seat to face him. “So, what is it you wanted to explain about Daniel and Xnard?”

“One moment,” he said to her, then spoke to the driver, “take us down around the mall, then back to Blithe House, please." The driver uttered his assent, then the partition slid up, leaving them to discuss matters in private.

"What I have to say needs to stay between us for now. I haven't quite yet figured out what my next steps will be."

"Alright."

He wore a pained expression as he began. "First, let me explain about Daniel."

Faith sat patiently, despite her burning interest to understand what was going on. It was an exercise in self control.

"As you might know, I went to school with Thomas and Mick. I was in Thomas's class at Harvard. We were good friends. Let's just say that we partied a bit -- or a lot. But in the spring of 1972, I dropped out of school to work full time on my venture. My partner in that start-up was my wife, Marisa. She and I married shortly after Thomas and Cassandra did. I suppose I felt that if a man like Thomas could settle down, so could I.

"The four of us – Thomas, Cassandra, my wife and I, socialized a lot together. And then Thomas died. Cassandra was distraught, adrift. She leaned heavily on your grandfather.

"Well, a few years later, I was in DC on business and met Cassandra for dinner. Honestly, I'm still at a loss as to how it happened. We both drank heavily that night. I never meant for it to happen. I loved my wife -- I still love my wife, and I respect her immensely. I can't entirely blame Cassandra. After all, it takes two to tango. My business was booming and Marisa and I were apart a lot, traveling. I suppose I was lonely. She was very forward that night and I was weak. Sounds like a big pile of excuses, I know. The bottom line is: I cheated on my wife. Me. No one else. I own it.

"Well, a few months later, Cassandra called to say she was pregnant. At first, I didn't believe it. But Cassandra didn't have a loose reputation and the math worked. When Daniel was born, I knew immediately he was mine. You see, we both have an unusual trait: webbed feet, just between two toes on both feet.

"I couldn't tell Marisa. It would have devastated her. Cassandra understood that, or seemed to at the time. She knew I didn't love her and was okay with it. I offered to help financially, and she took me up on it. In return, she kept quiet about the baby's paternity. The only other person who knows about Daniel is Mitchell. Daniel has no idea."

"And you kept it from him to protect your wife."

"Yes. Cassandra used that, and the huge success of our company, as leverage to increase her demands over time. I've given her a small fortune to keep the secret."

Anger was building inside of Faith. "Did you know Daniel was a miserable child?"

"No, I...."

"That she was completely self-absorbed? I don't know this firsthand, I only know what he's told me. He told me he knew at a very young age that his own mother didn't love him. Can you *imagine?*"

He looked stricken. "No, I didn't know that. I... didn't have much contact with him when he was little. We only came to know each other when I hired him at Yakmak."

"Which you did because he's your son?"

"No, I hired him because he's brilliant. The fact that he is my only child is why I'm grooming him to take over one day."

"He's your only child?" She asked with surprise.

"Yes. Marisa and I tried for years without success. She had an ectopic pregnancy that almost killed her, then a series of miscarriages. It was a devastating chapter in our lives, and it made it even harder for me to imagine telling her that I already had a child."

"Ptolemy, I'm really sorry to hear of her struggles. And I don't mean to be harsh with you, but you need to recognize that you sacrificed your son to protect your wife from disappointing news. To hear him tell it, Daniel was emotionally neglected his entire childhood. And she still has him in her clutches."

The man swallowed hard and tears pooled in his eyes. "I never meant for that to happen. I swear it."

"I'm sure you didn't. But now that you know what he's dealt with, I hope you'll seriously consider telling him and being the father – the parent – he never had."

He stared at her, then looked out the window, nodding and wiped his eyes. They glided past the Lincoln Memorial.

"What did you want to say about Xnard?" Faith shifted gears.

He swallowed hard. "Right. Well, when Daniel started

working for me, we chatted about this concept he had. I had no idea whether it would bear fruit, but I was eager to support his interests. Daniel doesn't know that I'm the only one who put money into the venture. I needed Mitchell's help, so I gifted a stake to him in exchange for that help.

"Daniel really wanted your grandfather to be a part of it. He loved your grandfather. So I gifted the stake and asked your grandfather not to tell Daniel about it. Fritz asked me point blank if Daniel was my son. I couldn't hide the truth on my face. He was furious that I had kept it from Daniel and made me promise to tell him soon. I agreed, and I've been working myself up to it.

"Anyway, I had no idea whether Daniel's idea would bear fruit, but I believe in him and want to support him. You don't need to worry about whether or not Xnard is profitable."

"Well, now I understand why you're risking telling me."

"Yes. It won't be a secret any longer. I promised Fritz. And now, knowing what you've told me, I know it's time for me to act."

They sat quietly for a few moments.

"I'm puzzled about why his attorney didn't tell me the investment was gifted," she murmured thoughtfully.

Ptolemy heard her. "That would have been a matter for the accountants. Maybe he doesn't know."

"Hmm. You might be right," she acknowledged. "So, what are you going to do?" She asked bluntly.

He straightened up and nodded, as if steeling himself. "My wife deserved better than me. But I've spent the last thirty-three years trying to compensate for that one night. And now I know what a price Daniel paid for that. It's time to tell them, to get it all out in the open."

Faith knew this would not be easy, for any of them. "Will you warn Cassandra?"

"She doesn't deserve any warning."

They sat in silence as the limousine sped down Rock Creek Parkway and up to Massachusetts Avenue.

"Tonight?"

"No. Tomorrow."

"Daniel and Anne are headed back to their homes tomorrow." His head whipped toward her.

"Can you change those plans?"

"I suppose so. Maybe engine maintenance? When should I reschedule for?"

"Don't bother rescheduling your jet. We'll take mine, the morning after tomorrow."

"Okay, but it'll be two stops including Anne."

"No problem. Good thing, anyway. Weather forecast is unfavorable tomorrow." He smiled. "Thank you, Faith, for everything."

"You're welcome. Just take good care of Daniel. We've decided we're cousins." She smiled out the window and realized that the tension that had built up in her chest was beginning to dissipate.

Chapter 17

"Another day? Good grief, my boss is not going to be happy." Anne stirred her coffee and shook her head.

"Good thing he won't be your boss for much longer," Chris added.

She looked up with wide eyes and a huge smile, "Ah yes, the sweet smell of an impending resignation!"

"Good morning, all!" Faith breezed in with the boys and Mrs. Lucie bustled about getting their breakfasts.

"You are particularly chipper this morning," observed her friend.

"I am, yes indeedlie doo," she inclined her head. "What is on the agenda for you this morning?" She asked Anne, glancing up at the muted TV on the wall. "Wait, what the?" She grabbed the remote and raised the volume.

The weather report displayed a map with a giant, swirling mass hanging over the mid-Atlantic seaboard. The weather forecaster explained, *"...this category 1 hurricane, which was expected to only affect the easternmost points along North Carolina and Virginia, merged overnight with another storm system and is now forecasted to develop into a so-called super storm, with possibly devastating results as far north as Massachusetts, and as far west as eastern Ohio. High winds and significant flooding are expected as early as late afternoon..."*

"Wow, Mom! Maybe we'll have a blackout! Paul, we need to find our flashlights." Graham said excitedly. Paul furiously nodded, his mouth full of blueberry waffle.

"No, you won't have a blackout, Graham," said Mrs. Lucie, who was tidying up. "You have a backup generator here. No need to worry."

"Awww," the two boys dejectedly said in concert. "Jinx!" They pointed to each other and smiled.

"Well, that's a relief," commented Anne. "I remember visiting friends in New Jersey during a blackout that lasted four days. That absolutely sucked."

"I can imagine," agreed Faith. She sipped her coffee and felt her cell phone vibrate on her hip. Pulling it out, she glanced at the callerid and answered. "Good morning, Special Agent Maxwell."

"Good morning, Mrs. Warrior. I have news. How would you like to take a field trip to St. Elizabeth's hospital with me this morning?"

"You were able to get an appointment?" She asked, eyes wide.

"Yes. Actually, Nestor Carson has made significant improvement with his treatment. His schizophrenia is stabilized through medication and he is able to have visitors."

"What time?"

"Ten o'clock. I'll meet you at your office at nine-thirty?"

"I'll be ready. Thank you." She disconnected.

"What's up?" Chris asked with interest.

"I'm meeting with Nestor Carson today. Maybe he can shed some light on things."

"Your father's..." Chris began with alarm, before Faith silenced him with finger in the air and a nod at the kids.

"Yes, *that* man," she confirmed.

"Shed light on what?" Chris pressed.

"Just... I don't really know. It simply seems to me that if A. someone lied to my grandfather and B. someone else was down there when my uncle and grandmother died, that C. there might be a connection to my father's death."

"That's good thinking," Anne said. "Just don't wear your good bag with your cheap shoes."

"He's not Hannibal Lechter, Anne."

"Really? He used a machete, didn't he? That's pretty 'slice and dice'."

Faith swallowed, suddenly sweating a little bit.

Her cell phone rang again. It was Valerie. "Hi, good morning. I'm just on my way," she said as she motioned the kids to hurry up.

"No rush, Faith. I was just calling to let you know that a Mrs. Tuppence Rivera is on the other line. She would like to know if you are free for lunch today."

"Oh, Tuppence? Sure. Why don't you ask her to come to the office whenever I've got a free hour. Ask her what she'd like to eat, then make arrangements to have it sent in." She glanced at Chris, "and order enough for Chris, too, whether or not he joins us."

Chris nodded and mouthed 'thanks' as he closed his newspaper.

"Will do." Faith clicked the phone off and dropped it in her bag.

"Time to go, kids!"

***

The limousine carrying Special Agent Maxwell and Faith turned into the drive at 1100 Alabama Avenue in Southeast DC. Contrary to Faith's ignorant expectation, St Elizabeth's campus was not surrounded by barbed wire, and it was incredibly spacious and picturesque.

The compound, which overlooked the juncture of the Potomac and Anacostia rivers, had been designated a U.S. National Historic Landmark. Glancing at the buildings, it wasn't hard to imagine why – the architecture was striking.

She'd heard that much of the campus had fallen into disrepair over decades. The west campus was abandoned and slated for refurbishment and redevelopment. Faith was glad to avoid seeing any run-down, boarded up mental hospital buildings – fodder for nightmares. The east campus was still functional and boasted a new, state of the art, facility that was good to see.

Wide, quiet lanes named Dogwood, Cherry and Oak Streets were all visible from the entrance. Tall, old trees and lots of green space were latticed with empty sidewalks. It all seemed a tad bit overgrown and sad.

"What do you know about St. Elizabeth's?" Maxwell asked Faith.

"I only know what I saw in a documentary a while back. An actress, who is also a lawyer, if I recall, made it. Hines? Haynes? Yes. Haynes. Joy Haynes. She bought a piece of patient artwork and was inspired to interview patients. The interviews were hard to watch, not just because of the crimes the men in the film committed, but because of the treatment they received over decades inside these buildings."

At the main building, a receptionist took their names and

IDs. A short while later, a doctor appeared in the waiting area. "I understand you wish to speak with Nestor."

"Yes, sir. I am Special Agent Maxwell, with the FBI. This is Faith Warrior."

The doctor looked at her carefully. "I read the newspapers, Mrs. Warrior. I know you are his victim's daughter."

"Yes, I am his daughter. I simply have some questions about the incident. I certainly do not mean Mr. Carson any discomfort, I assure you. I understand he was not himself when it happened."

"No, indeed, he was not. He's made great strides since then," replied the doctor.

"We are glad to hear it," replied Maxwell. "We simply wish to ask him some questions that he might not have been able to clearly answer back then."

"Questions that might help his case?"

"We don't know. We only know we've got to ask them."

"Alright, Special Agent. But I insist on being present during the interview."

"Of course."

The doctor shepherded them past a heavily locked door and into a hallway. There they faced another layer of security. They were buzzed through another door. Beyond, it was cheerful, with plenty of light from floor to ceiling windows that looked out on an enclosed courtyard. Faith noted that the glass appeared to be extremely thick.

He paused outside a door that had a small window in it. He looked in, then nodded at a closed-circuit dome camera attached to the ceiling. The lock opened and he pushed into the room.

"Nestor? You've got visitors."

Faith gingerly stepped forth behind Maxwell. The room was not large and did not have an external window. It was, in effect, a cell. Nestor Carson had his back to the door. *Who does that in a room without windows?* wondered Faith.

He was sitting backwards on his chair, so he stood up to reposition himself facing her. The man wasn't very tall, and he was quite bald. One shirtsleeve lay empty against his side. He had icy blue eyes with dark shadows beneath them.

"I don't get many visitors," he said suspiciously with a deep southern drawl.

"Sir, I'm Special Agent Maxwell, with the FBI. I'm here to ask you some questions, in an unofficial capacity."

"Unofficial capacity? Sounds like you got no good reason for being here."

Maxwell ignored the barb. "On the contrary. We'd like to ask you some questions about the incident in 1972. We realize it was a long time ago, but perhaps you can help us out."

"Special Agent, I was convicted of the crime. I am serving my time. Oh, isn't that a fun rhyme?" His smiled meanly. "What could you possibly offer me that'd make me want to talk about it? 'Cause you'd have to offer something."

"Why aren't you a free man yet, Mr. Carson? Why aren't you enjoying some of the freedom that even John Hinckley currently enjoys?"

"That S.O.B.? God knows." He snorted. "There's no saving me. There's no way out."

"Why do you think that?" Faith asked.

"Okay, lady, who are you? And secondly, are you kiddin' me?"

Faith steeled herself. "I'm Faith Warrior." She saw his blank reaction. "I'm his *daughter*." She stuck her chin out to emphasize the word daughter, and he knew.

"His… he had a child?" He looked wildly to the doctor, who pushed off of the wall he was leaning against. The doctor gave him a level gaze, his body alert.

"We didn't know until recently, Nestor," said the doctor. "No one did."

Nestor looked at his hands.

"I'd like to ask again," she said respectfully, "why do you think there's no way out?"

He looked at her remorsefully. "I been blocked so many times. I ain't got it in me to try no more."

Maxwell spoke up, "Mr. Carson, we're specifically interested in why you did what you did. To be clear: we're not trying to open old wounds. We have reasons for asking questions."

"Alright," Carson straightened. "But I been in here a long time and I know when I've got leverage. What do I get for my answers?"

"I'm not in a position to say at this time," Faith replied. "But I can assure you that at your next hearing, whenever that is, if you're helpful, I'll be willing to testify to that fact. That could only help *you*. So. Help *me* help *you*."

"Alright, I get that. What you want to know?"

Faith looked at Maxwell. He spoke up, "Mr. Carson, why did you kill Mick Blithe?"

Carson shook his head, disgusted with the question he'd been asked hundreds of times in dozens of years. "I was messed up from 'Nam. I thought he was a draft dodger and a woman beater. I eliminated him."

"Why did you think he was a draft dodger?" Faith asked.

"Casper told me." He said, rolling his eyes.

"Casper? Who was that?"

"Just a guy I knew. Used to make the rounds with me."

"He told you to kill Mick?"

"Nah. He told me about how this young fella liked to beat up women. You know, they're the fairer sex. My daddy always said you got to treat a woman right."

"Yes, indeed," Maxwell said. "What did Casper look like?"

"Pale, mid-40s, *really* blond hair, albino-like. Not a big guy. Looked like a 'vet in the way he dressed. But he was real clean."

"Clean?" Faith asked.

"Yeah. Some 'vets are really grimy, like they still livin' in the trench. I see that a lot here. To be honest, I was like that, 'specially when I was livin' off the land and before I got the meds. But others, they get real clean. Like, too clean. Like they never feel clean enough, so they keep scrubbin'. That was Casper, but his fingers didn't bleed like some do."

"What was Casper's last name?" Maxwell asked.

"No idea. Didn't even know his first name. I made it up, 'cause of how he looked. He was pale as a ghost. And you know that cartoon character, Casper... I never knew his real name. Wasn't important, know? He talked to me, man. No one else did. I believed him."

"Have you told anyone else about Casper?" asked Faith.

Nestor shook his head. "Yeah, sure, but they say no one found him. Anyway, what would be the point? I killed the guy, no one else, right? I got no one to blame but myself."

"But he gave you the wrong information, and he knew you were... not very healthy," Faith said diplomatically. "I would think he was partly responsible for what happened."

He looked down at his lap and shook his head. "Nah, I wasn't healthy. But I'm better now. Ain't I, doc?" He looked at the doctor leaning against the wall.

"Yes, Nestor, you are."

***

Faith's heels clicked loudly on the sidewalk as she hurriedly walked to the limo. "Someone else was involved with my father's death!" She said breathlessly. "Oh God, there's more here." When she got to the limo, she leaned over and almost vomited. "My grandmother, my uncle, my father, my grandfather... someone knows something about all of it. And I wonder now if it stops there?"

"Yes. It appears there is more going on here than anyone expected. I'll ruminate on this with my colleagues and get back to you." He ran a hand through his short hair. "Will you be alright?" He looked at Roberts, who nodded that he'd take care of Faith.

"Yes, yes, I'll be fine. Just... find out what's going on. Please," she said urgently.

There was a cab idling nearby. Maxwell flagged it and got in, leaving Faith to travel back to work alone in the limousine.

Streets, leaves, rivers, bridges – it all passed in a blur as she thought about the situation. Her heart raced. She called Chris and filled him in, then sat back.

***

Maxwell arrived back at his office and reported in to his Special Agent in Charge. The information he'd gathered finally warranted pulling in his Division Chief.

In a conference room, Maxwell wrote it all out on the white board. "Right. So we've got four deaths that we know of. All of Fritz Blithe's family has been decimated, with the exception of Faith Warrior. Fritz Blithe himself died the day he met her."

The Division Chief, a burly man in his late 60s, tapped his fingers on the table. "If there was a connection between Fritz meeting Faith and Fritz's death, that would make the action against Fritz the fastest work so far. Perhaps our perpetrator is losing control."

"That thought occurred to me, too," responded Maxwell.

"It would be a good idea to place extra protection on Faith Warrior for now," the DC said.

"She's guarded by a team of former Special Ops," the SAC countered.

Maxwell raised an eyebrow. "So was Fritz Blithe."

The DA continued. "Take care of it, Maxwell. And let's look into the Casper fellow. Any hits on the DNA sample from Elena Blythe's fingernails?"

"Nothing. The perp isn't in the system. We're still tracking down the crew that was aboard The Elena, and we're requesting DNA samples from everyone who was not on the bridge during their dive. The list includes nine crew members. We've ruled out four so far. Whoever resists among the last five is a target for further investigation."

"Good. What else? Oh yes, what about the phone call placed to Fritz Blithe just before he died?"

"We've figured out the point of origin but are having a hard time connecting it with a caller. It was someone visiting the health club, but we're stumped so far. We're still looking, though."

***

At one o'clock, Tuppence arrived for lunch. Faith was very distracted, but she pushed herself to focus on the older woman during lunch.

"Thank you for meeting with me, Faith," she said, as she made a plate for herself from the spread in the conference room. She was dressed in an orange silk suit with a mandarin collar. Simple pearl earrings matched the double strand around her neck. Her lipstick matched the suit and her white hair was perfectly coiffed.

"I'm so sorry if I seem distracted, Tuppence. It's been quite a morning."

The older woman sat at the table and crossed her ankles demurely beneath her chair. "No worries, Faith. I'm sorry I sprung this on you. I just wanted to reach out. I've missed Elena terribly." She smiled sheepishly at her. "I glommed onto the idea of connecting with her granddaughter. I guess that sounds a little sad."

"No, I understand. You were very close to Elena. I'm glad you reached out. Truly. I've got a few questions, though, if you wouldn't mind answering them. It seems a lot happened around the time my grandmother passed away. I can't think of anyone better to answer those questions than you."

"I'd love to help. What do you want to know?" the woman asked.

"Well, can you think of anyone who might have wanted to do her harm? Or Thomas?"

The woman looked concerned. "I thought it was an accident."

"That's what everyone thought, but now we think there was more to it than that."

Tuppence put a hand over her heart. "Oh my goodness!"

"Exactly. So. Was anyone particularly jealous of her? Angry with her? Anything?"

"No, no," the old woman said reassuringly, "everyone loved Elena. Everyone wanted to be around her. She was like a beautiful flower. People hovered around her like butterflies. Especially the men," she said with a smile.

"Men?"

"Oh, not in a bad way. Elena was completely in love with Fritz. But Elena was truly an astonishing beauty, and she was a very happy person. Being in her presence was like a breath of fresh air. People gravitated toward her."

"Anyone in particular?"

Tuppence sat thinking about that. "No one whom I would ever suspect of hurting her," she shook her head. "I mean, even old boyfriends still wanted to be around her – even though she was completely committed to and blissfully happy with Fritz. And as for Thomas? Well, he was a handsome man. The world was at his feet. And newly married, too. What a shame."

The two of them chatted on until Faith was called into her next meeting.

"Thank you so much for calling, Tuppence. I hope we can do this again soon." She gave Tuppence a hug and saw tears in the old woman's eyes.

"Your grandmother would have been so proud of you." She held her hands at arm's length and regarded her. "And look at you – so stylish, just like Elena."

A lump formed in Faith's throat. "Thank you."

Tuppence smiled and winked at her, then she squeezed Faith's hands and walked out to the lobby.

***

The rest of the afternoon flew by. Chris left at two-thirty

to pick up the boys from school. Human Resources gave her periodic updates on the weather during the afternoon. By three-thirty, Faith gave the green light for all staff to go home early. The coastal areas had already seen significant storm surge. The wind was picking up and flooding was expected. People needed to get home before the Metro was shut down.

At four o'clock, Faith packed up and headed out. She didn't bother with an umbrella as she exited the building. The rain was flying sideways. She looked around her on the street and didn't see Roberts, so she stepped back into the narrow shelter of the awning and waited.

The revolving door deposited another person onto the street, beside her. "Faith?"

"Mr. Whitman!" She said with surprise. "What are you doing here?"

"I was visiting an old friend who works in one of your departments."

"Oh, who?" Just then, a pedestrian lost his umbrella in the wind and chased it down the block in front of them, distracting her from her question. "Terrible weather today!"

"Indeed!" He had to shout over the sound of the wind and traffic. "Is your car here?"

"No. It'll come soon, though. Must have had to circle."

"No sense in getting wet. Why not ride with me? I'm headed up Mass Ave anyway. You can call your driver from my car to let him know you have a ride."

"Alright, thanks very much." She ducked into the waiting town car and pulled out her cell phone.

"I'm sorry, Mrs. Warrior. A police officer made me move from my spot in front of the building. I'll be around in a moment."

"It's alright, Roberts. Mr. Whitman is giving me a lift back to the house. I should be home soon."

"Black town car?"

"Yes."

"I'm right behind you. And in future, please wait for me inside the lobby."

"Certainly. See you at the house."
***

Maxwell sat at his desk looking at the white board. His phone rang while he was writing a note on it.

"Maxwell."

"Taymore here. We've found the identity of the man involved in the scuba deaths. A deck hand named Morris Wallers. Unfortunately, he died in late 1972 of a drug overdose."

"How did you learn his identity?"

"We located his mother, who is still alive. She had a lock of his hair in a scrapbook. It was a positive ID. The mother said she couldn't understand it. He'd been clean for nine months. Coroner's report confirmed that other than the marks from the injections that killed him, the track marks were long healed. And, he had scratch marks on his forearms."

"So the question is: why did he overdose? What did his mother say about it?"

"She said his life was actually taking a positive turn. He was pulling it together. She couldn't imagine how it could happen."

"Find out who his friends were and see if any of them will talk."

"Already did."

"And?"

"His best friend from back then said he'd seen him with, and I quote, 'some creepy pale guy with white blond hair'."

"Oh hell."

"My sentiments exactly."

"Alright. See if you can get a sketch. I realize it's a long shot given it was thirty-five years ago."

"And the perp is thirty-five years older."

"Just do it."

***

"Thank you for the ride, Mr. Whitman. Your timing was amazing. Who did you say you met with at Blythe Building?"

"I didn't say." He smiled, then winked. "I met with the head of your Government Relations Department. He had some questions about the tobacco lobby. I've got a bit of experience with that."

I'll bet.

"You know, I just found out today that you sold Albemarle to Blythe. That's how Von Heiden came to be here."

"Indeed." He raised his eyebrows. "Who knew he'd be so

successful? I might have been better off keeping Albemarle."

"But Lorraine Capital is not an operating company."

"Not all."

"Did you keep in touch with Von Heiden?"

"Why do you ask?" His eyes glinted.

"Just curious. It seems like you have lots of contacts within Blithe."

"I do. Don't forget I advised Fritz on many matters over the years. Yes, Von Heiden was one of my contacts. But he didn't share corporate secrets with me."

"I would never suggest he did. So, how is he doing?"

Whitman looked out the window at the rain. "I wouldn't know. But I imagine he's feeling no pain. He's made of stern stuff."

"Do you golf, Mr. Whitman?"

"I do, regularly." He ran a hand down his left cheek, over his scar.

"I understand my grandfather did, too. Did you golf with him?"

"Yes, sports were a shared interest. Hunting, golfing, skiing, scuba diving."

She nodded. "It sounds like you had a great friendship. It's nice to meet my grandfather's friends. Makes me feel closer to him. In fact, I had lunch today with Tuppence Rivera, if you remember her."

"Oh, yes," said the elderly man. "Tuppence. What a lovely woman." He looked out the window.

"Well, here we are. Would you like to come in?"

"No, thank you, though. I should head home. This storm is expected to intensify."

"That's what I heard. Well, have a nice evening." Faith opened the car door and it was practically ripped from her hands. After managing to get it closed again without dropping her handbag and briefcase, she was soaked by the time she stepped up to the front door and put her key in the lock. The downpour was deafening. When the door opened, she turned to wave to Mr. Whitman and found the driveway empty. She saw Roberts pulling through the gate.

"Mrs. Warrior, goodness! Come in!" Mrs. Loper rushed toward her. "Oh, your poor suit!" Faith looked down at what had been a gorgeous red knit jacket and slacks, now soggy and drooping. "If you change right away, I can try to save it."

"Ugh – thank you Mrs. Loper." She jogged upstairs with Mrs. Loper at her heels. "Hi kids!" Faith called after hearing their giggles from the ballroom.

"Hi Mommy!"

***

The wind had really picked up by the time the kids went to bed.

"Hon, I hope you don't mind, but I told Chef to go home. Mrs. Loper and Mrs. Lucie left a while ago, too."

"No, of course not. We can poke around in the kitchen and whip something up."

"Not necessary," Faith said. "Chef left dinner warming for us."

Anne was already in the dining room. "Daniel is MIA again."

"I have an idea of where he is," said Faith.

"And that would be…?"

Faith shrugged. "With Ptolemy. I think he planned to meet with him today – or tonight."

"Dude, that's your tell. What do you know that you're not telling us?"

Faith flashed her a look. "It's not for me to say." She got up and walked to the sideboard where their dinner was in electric chafing dishes. Suddenly, the lights went out.

"Oh boy," Anne said in the dark. "Anyone know where the flashlights are?"

"Hell if I know," responded Chris.

Faith stood up. "I'll go check on the kids. Chris and Anne, do you want to go down to the pantry and see if you can find a stash of either flashlights or candles? And maybe the fuse box?"

"The gang is somewhere creepier… the gang is somewhere creepier," Anne said in her best Shaggy voice as she followed Chris toward the back staircase.

The house was dark. Very dark. Faith had to remember the map in her head in order to keep from banging her shins or walking into walls. She glanced outside and saw that the street lights were still lit, which seemed odd.

Her cell phone rang just after she closed Graham's door. "Daniel?" She whispered when she saw the number.

"Hi Faith. Some storm, huh."

"Yes. We lost power. Where are you?"

"With Ptolemy. He told me that he already told you the news."

"Yes. How do you feel about it?"

"Simultaneously angry and thrilled, if that makes any sense."

"It does. Absolutely."

"Well, I just wanted to let you know I'll bunk here at his hotel tonight. Too dangerous on the roads."

"Okay. Get some rest."

"Faith?"

"Yes?"

"There's something else you should know."

"What's that?"

"I'm pretty sure my mother called your grandfather the evening he died."

Faith sat down in the dark, frowning. "She had his number?"

He took a deep breath, then blew it out. "I set both your grandfather and my mother up on new iPads while visiting a few months ago. I sat them down together to give them an orientation. During the orientation, I used my iPad to Skype Fritz, both to his Skype address and to his mobile phone, to demonstrate how flexible Skype is. Fritz recited his mobile number to me so I could type it into my iPad. She listened to the whole thing."

"Why didn't you tell the FBI when they asked if you knew anyone who might have his cell phone number?"

"Because I didn't explicitly give it to her, and I had no idea she'd remember a number she'd heard only once. I mean, how many times have you overheard a phone number? Do you ever remember them?"

"Ok, so let's say she remembered the number. How do you know she called him the day he died?"

"The FBI said the call came from a health club, but they'd reviewed all of the records and determined no one he was in regular contact with was there at that time."

"But maybe it was someone your mother is in contact with?"

"Right. My mother is not a member there and was not

logged in as a guest, but a friend of hers is a member, and that friend was there that day. I called her friend and she confirmed that my mother was there at that time. I can't explain why she wasn't signed in as a guest. She must simply have not signed in, or maybe pretended to sign in and no one caught it."

"Okay. I'll call Maxwell and let him know."

"Thanks. And please apologize to him about not telling him sooner. I wanted to check with her friend to confirm my suspicions, first."

"Got it. What's her friend's name?"

She called Maxwell as soon as she hung up and his cell number rolled over to voice mail. So, she left a detailed message explaining everything and left him Daniel's cell phone number.

Sitting there in the dark, she had a growing sense of horror. Her cell phone rang, startling her.

"Mrs. Warrior?" Maxwell asked.

"Yes," she whispered. "did you get my message?"

"I did. I want to talk to Cassandra Blithe in person but can't send anyone out in this weather. It's going to have to wait until first thing tomorrow. Let me know if you learn anything more."

"I wi --" She stopped talking as she heard footsteps coming up the stairs and saw the outline of a well built man approach.

"Mrs. Warrior?" Relief swept through her when she heard Roberts' voice. "We're investigating why the backup generator failed. In the meantime, I've asked Mr. Warrior and Ms. O'Malley to stay up here with you so you're all grouped together for security's sake. They'll be up momentarily."

"Alright. Thank you, Roberts."

"Is everything alright?" Maxwell asked.

"I think so. My nerves are just frayed. Talk to you in the morning."

Chapter 18

The power came back on at around six a.m. It was still dark outside, but Faith got up anyway. After checking on the boys, she padded down to the kitchen and found it empty. The storm still raged outdoors. Roberts walked in a few minutes later.

"Roberts, have you slept at all?" She asked with concern and motioning toward the coffee maker that had finished brewing.

He stepped to it and helped himself to a cup. "Sawyer and I took shifts. Mrs. Warrior, we've got a puzzling situation here."

"What's that?" She asked as she sipped her coffee and muted Morning Joe.

"The backup generator failed because someone messed with the circuits."

She frowned. "Messed with them?"

"Yes. The pool pump was hooked up to the backup generator. The circuit load was already maxed out on the backup generator. So, when the system tried to flip over to backup, it failed."

"Okay, so the generator installation firm needs to come in and sort it out."

"That change was not made by the generator installation firm. And it wasn't there a year ago when the last maintenance was performed on the backup generator."

Faith's heart rate accelerated.

"There's something else."

"What. Else?" She gritted her teeth, holding onto to her emotions by a thread.

"When we determined what was going on with the

generator, we did an exhaustive review of other security parameters and found that an unapproved IP address has accessed the camera system in the house."

"Which was just installed recently."

"No, but cameras were added recently to certain rooms. We think we know who this person might be. The same IP address was on the premises on one other occasion, and that coincided with a visit from this man."

"Don't keep me dangling."

"Your father's IT consultant – the man he brought in each month."

"This is the Blithe Industries IT guy, right?"

"Yes. But he's not really part of the main IT department. He's attached to the Government Relations Department."

"The Gov--." She shook her head and ground her teeth. "Mother f-er."

"Sorry – is that information relevant?"

"Let's just say that that department looks to be an ethical black hole." She closed her eyes and let off a mental string of expletives. "Block the IP address – no, shut the whole online thing down. Can we shift back to closed circuit?"

"It'll take a day or two to reconnect it, ma'am."

She nodded. "I've got some calls to make."

He turned on his heel and stalked out. She hit redial, "Maxwell, rise and shine."

"Already up, ma'am." He sounded tired.

"I've got more." She explained everything she knew about the Government Relations Department, what her security detail had discovered about the breech there at the house, and left him to do his thing.

Then she called her General Counsel on his cell number. "Jack, why do you think my grandfather had an IT specialist from the Government Relations Department service his house?"

"I wasn't aware he did." He paused. "That department is really beginning to stink, isn't it?"

"To high heavens. Give me the name and phone number of the individual who runs it. I'm done tiptoeing around."
***

Maxwell looked up at the ceiling and stretched. He was tired, very tired. He sat up and looked out the window at the dark morning. The wind was howling. A quick shower and a cup of coffee later and he was ready to go. Screw the weather. As he made his way to the underground garage in his apartment complex, he dialed the desk at work. A member of his team picked up.

"I need you to take another look at the iPad. See if anyone meddled with it."

"You suspect someone in particular?"

"Could be a corporate thing – an inside job. Just check it out."

"Will do."

"Don't forget to get that sketch from the deck hand's friend."

"Already have someone on it out of the Memphis office. They'll fax it when they have it – hopefully sometime early afternoon."

"Good. I'm heading over to talk to Cassandra Blithe. I've received information that suggests she made the call to Fritz Blithe just before he died – the call from the health club."

"Okay. Be careful out there."

The drive from Maxwell's Alexandria apartment to Cassandra Blithe's home in Kalorama took a lot longer than it should have due to detours he had to take around downed trees and power lines. By the time he arrived, his GPS had "recalculated" at least ten times. He shut off the motor and looked up at the house on Bancroft Place, listening to the rain pound on the roof of the car.

Cassandra's Georgian brick townhome was very handsome, set back a bit from the street. Not bothering with an umbrella due to the intense wind, he turned up the collar on his rain coat and pulled on a baseball hat that was sitting in the backseat. It was about nine-thirty in the morning, in a bad storm, and Cassandra did not work. He thought it highly likely she would be at home. Lights were on in the living room. He could see them through the front window. There was no answer at the door. He pushed the doorbell again and waited, grateful for the covered entrance.

He pulled his cell phone out of the inside pocket of his raincoat and looked up an email his team had circulated with cell phone numbers pertinent to the case. When he spotted hers, he selected it and waited for the call to connect. As he waited, his eye caught a reflection against the brass fireplace gate and he stepped closer, cantilevering his body out over a hedge to peer through the window. Yes, it was a reflection, and it abruptly ended at the same time his call to Cassandra's cell phone rolled over to voice mail. He called the number again to be sure, and again, the reflection appeared.

Maxwell slipped his phone back in his pocket, gripped one of the front shutters and stepped up onto the brick windowsill of the living room window. Taking small steps, he shuffled out into the center of the window and peered in. There, on the floor, was Cassandra's cell phone. He carefully scanned the rest of the room and saw the tip of a woman's pedicured foot behind an armchair. He blew out a breath and quickly shuffled back to the front stoop.

***

"Looks like blunt force trauma to the head," the detective on the scene said. With his crumpled raincoat and stained necktie, the older man looked out of place in Cassandra's refined living room but far from uncomfortable. He was too well-seasoned for that. "Looks like the weapon was the large crystal frame we found broken on the floor." He gestured to the frame a crime scene investigator was bagging.

"Can I see that a second?" Maxwell asked. The tech brought it over. It was a family portrait of Fritz, Elena, Mick, Thomas and Cassandra. "Thanks." He turned to the detective with a grave expression. "Someone needs to tell her next of kin. Mind if I tag along?"

"Sure. We haven't had a chance to identify or locate them, but we'll give you a call when we do."

"No need. I know who her next of kin was. Her son, Daniel. And I know where he's staying."

"Tell me again what brought you here this morning. Something about her father-in-law?"

"Yes. Her father-in-law was Fritz Blithe. We have reason to believe she called him with some alarming news just before he died. Could have triggered his fatal attack. We're trying to find out what was said and why."

"And she's murdered before you can question her. That's curious," he said in deadpan.

***

Daniel was back by the time Maxwell and the Detective

arrived at Blithe House. Roberts answered the door and let Faith know who was there before he went to get Daniel.

Faith appeared at the top of the stairs and turned her back to the foyer to look at her little boy. "I said no climbing, Paul. Yes, I'm talking to you. She took two fingers and pointed at her eyes, then straight out. "I've got my eyes on you, mister." She turned back toward the stairs with a smirk and descended.

A few steps from the bottom she shook her head at Maxwell and smiled. "Four year olds."

"Seems like he's good at it."

"That he is. So, what brings you here? Any news?"

"Yes, unfortunately, we do have news. Well, I'll let Detective Frey handle it, as it's his case."

"His case? Has my grandfather's case been reopened?" She asked.

"Ma'am, this is a new case and it concerns Daniel Blithe."

Daniel appeared in the foyer and looked confused. "Special Agent Maxwell. How are you?"

"I'm fine, thank you. This is Detective Frey," he gestured to Frey and stepped back to let the man take charge.

"Mr. Blithe, I regret to inform you that your mother was found dead at her home this morning."

"What?" Daniel's eyes grew large as Faith gasped. "Found dead? What happened?"

Faith put a hand on his arm and guided him to a chair.

"Yes, sir. I'm very sorry to share this news. And I'm sorry to have to ask you where you were last night."

"I was at the Four Seasons Hotel on M Street. Why? Am I some sort of a suspect?"

"This is routine questioning of close friends and family, sir. We have no reason to suspect you, no."

Maxwell spoke up. "Why were you there, Daniel? I thought you were staying with Mrs. Warrior."

"I was. Until I received some rather shocking news last night while I was at the Four Seasons. News that required lots of talking out. And with the storm raging, well, I just stayed on."

"Who were you with, Mr. Blithe?" The detective asked.

"Ptolemy Gunesdogdu," he answered

"Of Yakmak?"

"Yes."

"What was the nature of the news you received?" Maxwell asked.

"Well, I can't imagine why it's anyone's business but mine, but he confessed to me last night that he is my father."

"You had not known up until that point?" asked the detective.

"No."

"Was your father with you the entire night?"

"I think so. We talked most of the night. I crashed at about four o'clock, I think."

"Where is he now?"

"Still at the hotel, I'd imagine, doing work. We plan to fly back to California together once the weather breaks. Of course now…"

"Thank you for your time, sir, and again, I'm sorry about the news. I'll be in touch."

Maxwell walked Frey to the door. "I'm going to stay a moment and speak with Mrs. Warrior." The detective nodded. "What did your people estimate to be time of death?" he asked quietly.

"Sometime around midnight. If this story checks out, then we can rule out both the son and his father. I'll let you know." He opened the front door and stepped into the curtain of rain.

"Was there something else?" Faith asked as she approached Maxwell.

"I'm curious about how Cassandra Blithe kept the news to herself all of these years."

"Oh, that's easy," Faith responded. "Ptolemy paid her."

"She blackmailed him?"

"Well, he didn't explain it to me in precisely those words, but I did get the sense that she got a little greedy as time went on. He didn't want his wife to find out. I guess that's all changed now."

"Changed last night."

"Or yesterday, at least, yes."

"Thank you, Mrs. Warrior. By the way, a team has been assigned to watch the house for the time being. You may not have noticed them yet." He opened the door and she saw the black sedan parked in the lower curve of the drive."

"So we're not crazy to be worried."

"I think you'd be crazy not to be. But try to relax. You've

got your security team here in the house, plus the two in the sedan."

"I think I'd better go speak to my husband."

"Ma'am." He said and shut the door behind him when he left.

Chapter 19

Faith went back to the living room, found it empty and guessed that Daniel wanted some time alone. She pulled out her cell phone and dialed Ptolemy to let him know what was going on in his son's life.

Upstairs, Faith found the boys in their playroom reading stories with Chris. The three of them were cuddled under a blanket, a floor lamp casting a gentle glow around them. She sighed deeply. "Boys, I need to have a word with Daddy. Graham, can you read a small book to Paul?"

"Um, I guess so."

"Captain Underpants!" Shouted Paul and Faith led Chris to the master bedroom.

She took her time explaining things.

"Good grief, Faith. It's oozing in from every direction," her husband said in exasperation.

"I agree. It's everywhere. Every rock Maxwell turns over reveals some more. Honestly, I'm sick to my stomach."

The doorbell rang.

"Oh for God's sake!" Chris shouted as Faith jogged out of the room.

When she opened the front door, she found the elderly Richard Whitman flanked by two FBI agents. "Ma'am," one of them said. "Do you know this man?"

"Oh, yes, he's an old friend of my grandfather's. But thank you for checking," she said to the Agent with a stiff smile. "Please, come in Mr. Whitman." Between the connection to Von Heiden, the visit to the company and what Roberts told her about her grandfather distancing himself from Whitman, she wasn't overly happy to see him.

He shuffled forward. "I can't say that I've ever had such a

reception," he said good-naturedly. He pulled off his rain hat. "I'm sorry to be any trouble, but I've got no power and I had hoped I could just sit here a while, maybe in the music room? I live nearby and didn't want to drive very far. There are things flying about out there."

"Oh, I'm sorry to hear it. Of course, Mr. Whitman. Make yourself at home. Would you like something to drink?" she asked politely.

"Some coffee would be quite fine, thank you, Faith." He gave her a tired smile and she took his coat and hat to put in the hall coat closet.

Anne was in the lower dining room on her laptop when she went through to get the coffee. "Sweetie, I love your home and I love DC, but for the love of Mike, when is this rain going to stop?"

"I hear ya, sistah," she said and bustled through to the swinging door. "And when it rains, it pours."

Anne followed her, her head tilted questioningly. "Sounds like you're speaking metaphorically. Oo, making coffee? I'll take some."

"Yes, my grandfather's friend is without power, so he dropped by for a bit. And yes, I'm speaking metaphorically." She put the coffee on to brew and explained about Cassandra. She left out the business about the backup generator. No need to alarm her friend until they knew more.

Faith found a tray next to the coffee maker that already had a small vessel of sugar on it. She added a cup, saucer and spoon, a small pot that would hold about two cups of coffee, a little pitcher of milk, and a few cookies on a plate.

As she made her way up the stairs with the tray, she heard the piano. It was the first time she'd ever heard it played, and Mr. Whitman was very good at it. But every few moments, she heard an off note and she realized that the piano must not have been tuned properly. She'd need to tell Mrs. Abernathy about that.

Her mouth curved into a smile as she entered the room and he stopped playing. "You look…", he looked somewhat bewildered, "very much like your grandmother in this light."

"Oh, I don't think I was ever as pretty as she was," she said, glancing at the portrait in the other room. "But I do seem to have her hair." She smiled again. "Here is your coffee."

"Thank you, Faith." He got up from the piano and walked over to the table upon which she'd set the tray. "Do you play the piano?"

"No, I'm afraid I never had the inclination. Much to my mother's disappointment."

"A pity. The piano is so soothing. Elena was an excellent pianist. Like you, Fritz didn't have any interest in it." His tone was light, but held something else... she wasn't sure what.

"Well, if it's any comfort, I regret it now. To listen to how beautifully you play, well, I'm envious."

He looked up at her from his coffee cup and smiled. "Thank you. Though it would sound better if the lid were propped up."

Faith glanced at the very large floral arrangement sitting atop it. "It would take some effort," she laughed. "I think lifting that's a two man job."

He seemed lost in thought. "Have you any children, Mr. Whitman?"

"No, I'm a lifelong bachelor. But I lived vicariously through friends. Never found the right woman. Well, not one who was available." He smiled. Faith wondered if this kind old man could have been one of her grandmother's many admirers. He did, after all, introduce her grandfather to her grandmother.

***

Maxwell sat across the table from his Division Chief.

"Nestor Carson thinks it's the same man?" His boss asked.

"He thinks it's very possible, yes." Maxwell answered.

"Who else could take a look at it?"

Maxwell stuck out his chin in thought. "Someone else who was around at that time, who knew friends, staff, executives? There were a few such people at the funeral. I've got the guest list."

"Good. See what comes of that. You might start with Pall Bearers and readers since they might have been closest." Maxwell nodded.

One of the team popped his head in. "You're going to want to hear this," he said excitedly.

Maxwell and the Division Chief followed the man down the hallway into another room where an IT specialist was examining Fritz's iPad. He looked up. "Seems there's some spyware on the iPad. Well, it might have been directly installed rather than sent as a virus. I'd have to take a closer look to see."

"Spyware?"

"Yes. A program that forwarded every keystroke, every email, every text, and a copy of every Skype or FaceTime call to a web server."

"Location of the web server?" Maxwell asked.

"Blithe Building. Right here in Washington, DC." The tech responded.

"Were you able to access it? Locate the Skype call?" Maxwell leaned forward.

"Yes, sir. Take a listen."

The audio was crystal clear. Cassandra told Fritz that she had just learned that Thomas was Cardinal Mayse's son, that the Cardinal had been having an affair with Elena over the entire course of their marriage, and that Thomas had discovered the truth. Thomas had been so upset that he had taken his life and probably killed his mother, too.

She was very convincing. Maxwell had to give her that. It wasn't surprising that Fritz became upset, and it was difficult to hear it knowing Fritz would soon be dead on the floor because of it.

The next call they heard was the one that Fritz made to the Cardinal. It matched the voice mail the Cardinal had shared with them previously.

"Find out who called Cassandra Blithe at any time in the two hours before Fritz's death. Cell phone, land line, whatever." Maxwell instructed the group. He turned to another agent on the team. "I want to see the man Faith Warrior's security team thinks tampered with the backup generator and accessed the camera system."

***

Richard Whitman looked out the window. "The rain has slowed considerably."

She took a glance. "Yes, it has, and the sky is getting brighter. Finally!" She looked back at him. "Oh, I didn't mean, you know, *finally*," she waved her hands in the air, "because I want you to go. Or. Anything. I just..." She sighed and blushed a deep crimson at her social ineptitude. "Sorry. I'm a little tired." *And I'd really like to get some work done.*

"Faith?" Chris walked into the foyer and saw Faith sitting with Mr. Whitman. "Oh, I didn't realize you had company. Hi Mr. Whitman." He looked puzzled at the expression on her face but walked to the old man and shook his hand.

"Chris, Mr. Whitman's power went out, so he's relaxing here for a bit." She sat back, behind Whitman's eyeshot and widened her eyes a bit. It was code for 'that's right – yet another curve ball today.'

He frowned for a fraction of a second in acknowledgement. "Oh, you must be on a different grid. Where do you live?"

"Not far, my boy." He laughed and shrugged. "I don't know anything about the grids around here. Faith and I were just discussing the piano. Do you play?"

***

"Ptolemy Gunesdogdu's alibi holds. So does Daniel Blythe's."

Maxwell nodded to Tierney. His phone rang. "Maxwell."

"We've checked with the Pall Bearers. None of them recognize the sketch. Can't reach Richard Whitman, and we're just faxing it through to Tuppence Rivera."

"Ok. Thanks."

His door opened. "Agent Maxwell," one of his team said. "May I introduce Beau Meuller, an IT specialist at Blithe Industries' Government Relations Department."

Meuller was a tall, overweight man with dark, straight hair that fell limply on his forehead. His worn, brown belt was pulled tightly beneath his considerable belly, barely keeping his khakis from sliding down his flat behind.

"Please, sit down Mr. Meuller." Maxwell stood up and moved around the table. "Can I get you something to drink?"

"No. What's this about?" He bit out.

Maxwell looked at him for a moment longer than most people would find comfortable. "Let's go with fear, Mr. Meuller."

The man wiped his upper lip. "Excuse me?"

"I'm referring to the feeling that should be spreading through your chest right now. It should be fear, not annoyance." He leveled a look at him, then down at his open folder. "Infiltrating a private security system. Tampering with a building's electrical system. Planting spyware..." He looked up at another Agent on his team. "How many counts is that?"

"Let's see. Unlawful Access to Stored Communications. Wire Fraud. Intercepting A Communication. Wiretapping. And I think we could push for attempted murder."

Meuller stood up, his chair falling over in the process. "What? And attempted murder? I was just following orders! I work for Blithe Industries – I was doing work for Fritz Blithe!"

"Sit down Mr. Meuller." Maxwell commanded and the man complied. "So Fritz Blithe asked you to do all of this for him?"

"No. My boss did. On Fritz' behalf."

"How do you explain the work on the backup generator?"

"Well, I thought that was a little wacky, but I understand how electronics work and figured Fritz Blithe was just one of those super rich cheap guys. I figured I could take care of it."

"You overloaded the circuits and could have caused a fire."

"I – I did? I was told there was ample room on the system. I swear I didn't do it on purpose."

Maxwell exhaled and looked at him. "It would have been pretty easy to figure out if you'd bothered checking. Or were in any way familiar with that sort of work. Who told you there was ample room?"

"My boss."

Maxwell shot a look at the Agent standing by the door and he nodded before exiting the room.

***

"No, I don't play the piano. I never learned. But I admire anyone who does. Do you play, Mr. Whitman?"

"Yes, I do." He stood and walked over to the grand piano, running his hand across the glossy top.

"Did you play here often?" Faith asked the old man.

"Every chance I got. This is a particularly fine piano. Did you know it belonged to Elena before they married?"

"No, I didn't. Thank you for telling me. It certainly is lovely."

"Faith," Chris spoke to her, "I was going to take the boys out to the backyard for some puddle splashing now that the rain has basically stopped." He looked at her with a silent question and darted a look at Whitman, as if asking if he should leave her alone with him.

"Good idea," she agreed with a smile, nodding. "Maybe make some boats out of leaves and twigs, too." She glanced at Mr. Whitman, "I used to love doing that when I was a kid."

"Okay. Well, nice to see you, Mr. Whitman," he smiled and gave a wave as he walked out.

"You, too, Chris," the old man responded as he sat down again at the piano.

"Shall I call the power company to see if your power has been restored?" Faith asked.

"Oh, no, no. I've got a neighbor who will call me on my cell phone when she sees my porch light come on."

"Okay, well, I'm just going to check my email and I'll be back. Can I get you anything?"

"No, thank you, I'm fine. I'll just sit here reminiscing." He said and picked out a few notes.

Faith didn't want to leave him alone, but she had to get some things done. She went upstairs to the sitting room and sat down at her laptop to sift through correspondence that continued to pour in from subsidiaries not affected by the storm.

***

Maxwell downed the last of his fourth cup of coffee. "So a call came in to Cassandra at roughly five-thirty pm from a coffee shop in Adams Morgan. Get security footage from the coffee shop. Let's see who it was."

"No luck at the coffee shop, but the bodega next door has a camera trained on the sidewalk fruit stand. The door to the coffee shop is in plain view."

"And?"

"We're reviewing the footage now."

***

Thirty minutes later, Faith had waded through the bulk of the emails when her cell phone rang.

"Mr. Hopewell. What are you doing at work?"

"It's stopped raining, Mrs. Warrior. I figured it was safe to come out of my house."

She laughed. "Well, most people would have taken the rest of the day off if given the opportunity. But I suppose you're not most people."

"I'll take that as a compliment. I have a few things for you to sign whenever you have time."

"Sure. I'll be right down."

***

"The head of the Government Relations department pointed the finger at the former CEO, Von Heiden."

"Detain them all," Maxwell growled with exasperation. "And now get Von Heiden in here."

***

Faith breezed into the office suite and down the hall toward Hopewell's office. She could hear her kids' laughter in the backyard and her heart felt full.

"Mr. Hopewell, hello – oh, no, what happened?" She regarded his heavily bandaged hand.

He sighed and sat back in his chair. "A tree branch landed on my car and I cut myself moving it. Then, on my way to the emergency room to get stitches, both ends of my street were blocked by downed trees. Took me two hours to get there, only to wait hours more for the stitches. A real bother," he said, wrinkling his nose. "And now I can look forward to dealing with auto body work." He exhaled sharply. "Sorry, it's not been the best time."

"I'm even more impressed that you're here right now. *Why* are you here right now? Surely none of this is an emergency."

"I may as well be here and be productive than sit home in the dark. And I don't live far from here, so it wasn't a big trip."

"We're fortunate to have power."

"The backup generator didn't kick in?"

"It failed last night. Long story." She waved her hand at him and stepped toward his desk. "Well, after I sign these, I'd like you to go home and get some rest."

***

The Special Agents on the team stood in the tech lab and watched the video on one of many monitors on the wall.

Tierney spoke up, "Right there. Stop the tape. Isn't that George Hopewell? Her attorney?"

Maxwell's eyes darkened. "Find him."

A moment later, "his home number doesn't answer."

***

Faith walked back across the breezeway. Suddenly, she heard a crash from the front of the house. She ran toward the sound and found Mr. Whitman lifting the piano top. The massive vase lay shattered on the Persian carpet, the water turning the pink pattern red.

"Mr. Whitman? What happened? Are you alright?" She asked, winded from the adrenaline rush.

He pulled his head and arm out and stuffed a paper into his pocket. "Nothing, Faith. Just a terrible accident. I'll pay for the cleaning and for the vase."

Her cell phone rang. "Special Agent," she said into the phone to Maxwell as she and Whitman stared at each other.

"Do you know where George Hopewell is?" The volume on the cell phone was so high that his voice could be heard across the acoustically enhanced music room.

"Mr. Hopewell? He's here, in his office. Why?"

"I'm on my way. I'll explain everything shortly. Just don't go near him." The call disconnected as the doorbell rang.

Whitman darted a glance at the front door. As Faith turned to answer it, George Hopewell walked into the foyer. "Mrs. Warrior, I forgot one document," he called out to her. "Oh, hello Richard, what are you doing here?"

"You two know one another?"

"Yes," Hopewell said with a smile. "We've been friends for years."

She looked from one man to the other, her heart beating quickly. There was more banging on the front door. She slowly backed up toward the door and put her hand on the knob.

"Here, let me get that for you," Hopewell advanced toward her and she backed away just as a shard of the broken vase hurtled by her. It struck the attorney in the side of the head with a sickening thud and the man dropped to the ground.

She screamed when blood splattered on her face and her head whipped around. She saw Mr. Whitman breathing heavily, his eyes wide. "Why did you do that?" She yelled as she knelt down next to Hopewell and tried to put pressure on the wound. There was a lot of blood. More than she thought was possible.

"I overheard the call. He was clearly a danger," Whitman answered quietly.

The front door burst open, wood splintering, revealing the two FBI agents who had been waiting outside in the car. "We need an ambulance," she said with a shaky voice, tears pricking her eyes.

"What's going on in here?" Roberts came rushing in from the back of the house, followed by Chris and the boys. "Mrs. Warrior, are you alright?"

She nodded weakly as Roberts took over tending to Hopewell. One of the FBI agents was on his cell calling for backup and an ambulance. The other was questioning Whitman.

Chris gathered Faith in his arms. "What happened?"

"Mr. Whitman threw part of that broken vase at Mr. Hopewell. He said he thought he was a threat, but Mr. Hopewell really didn't look like a threat." She looked at Roberts and Hopewell. "He really just looked helpful. Like his usual self."

"What happened to Mr. Hopewell?" Asked Graham. "Is he going to be okay?"

She pulled Graham into a group hug with Chris. "I don't know, honey."

Paul clung to Chris's pant leg, his lower lip trembling at the sight of the blood on the floor.

"Chris, can you take the kids upstairs? They shouldn't see this."

"You okay?"

"Yeah, I'm okay" She nodded shakily.

He touched her cheek and then hustled the kids away.

***

After the ambulance left with the attorney, the police took Richard Whitman down to headquarters to get a statement. He looked very old sitting in the back of the police car.

"So Mr. Hopewell made the call?" Faith asked Maxwell as they watched the car drive away.

"It appears so."

They walked back inside and Faith walked him back toward the parking lot where he'd left his car.

"I can't believe it. He was so nice, so helpful. Why would he do that to my grandfather? I can't figure it out."

"He's lost a lot of blood. He's unconscious and in critical condition, so we may never know," the Special Agent responded.

The doorbell rang and Roberts answered it. "Mrs.

Warrior," he called down the hallway to them. "Mrs. Rivera is here to see you."

Faith walked back to the foyer as the older woman walked in, looking crisp in a lavender-colored twinset and black trousers.

Tuppence looked past Faith and saw Maxwell.

"Oh, I did intend to speak with both of you, so this is a happy surprise that you're here, Special Agent. I understand you've been trying to reach me. My cell phone service was down during the storm. But I got your message a little while ago and I meant to call you after seeing Faith."

"Thanks for coming, Tuppence," Faith gave her a quick hug.

"So, you wanted to know about that sketch?"

"Yes, ma'am."

"Well, it looks like Richard as a young man," the elderly woman said.

"Richard Whitman?" Faith asked.

"Oh yes. Well, Richard had dark hair, but he was very pale. I'd almost forgotten. Anyway, put a blond wig on Richard at that age and that's him."

"But Whitman's scar?" Maxwell asked.

"He didn't get that until a few years ago. Some sort of accident, I think. Fritz was with him when it happened. Carmel? Someplace like that."

Maxwell pulled out his cell phone and dialed his contact at police headquarters.

"Is Whitman still there? Detain him on suspicion of several counts of murder. How many? Four that we know of, from thirty-five years ago."

"Good grief. So Whitman killed my uncle, my father, my grandmother and the deck hand, and Hopewell killed Cassandra and my grandfather? What a pair of friends! I just can't figure out why, for either one."

Tuppence spoke up. "Mr. Hopewell was involved in this, too? That is truly shocking. He seems like such a nice man, and a Knight of Malta, isn't he?"

"I agree," Faith nodded, "It's hard to believe about Mr. Hopewell. But you don't seem surprised about Mr. Whitman."

"Well, you remember I told you that Elena had many admirers. Richard was probably the most fervent of them."

"You think he was in love with her?"

"Yes, I think so. Or at least deeply infatuated. She and Richard met at a Christmas party when she was home from school that winter break. They played a few piano duets. She told me about him when she returned to Switzerland. And then he introduced her to Fritz that summer."

"The tennis," Faith said.

"Yes. He was very upset when Fritz announced they were engaged. Elena told me he yelled at her. I suppose he was under the impression that she would marry *him*. But he must have gotten over it. They all remained friends…"

"And he never married," Faith added. "He told me he never found the right woman, or at least, never found one who was available."

"Sounds like he was referring to your grandmother," Maxwell said.

Chapter 20

Mrs. Lucie had outdone herself with breakfast, so it was fitting she served it in the formal dining room. It was Daniel and Anne's last meal with them, and Ptolemy had joined them before their flight.

The kids were carrying on about the storm and grousing about having to return to school that morning.

"Are you alright, Daniel?" Faith asked him quietly as he sat beside her, while conversation went on around them.

"I think so, Faith," he said.

Ptolemy, who was sitting on Daniel's other side, took his son's hand. "He'll be alright, Faith, I'll be sure of it." He nodded at Daniel.

The doorbell rang as they were finishing up. Mrs. Lucie let Maxwell in just as Faith came to the staircase and looked down.

He looked up at her. "Good morning, Mrs. Warrior. I'm sorry to disturb you so early."

"No problem, we get up early." She started down the staircase, followed by the entire group. "Is there any news on Mr. Hopewell?"

"Yes," he said, his face grim. "He's out of the woods, but he's in a medically induced coma while the swelling subsides in his brain. The doctors think he'll be alright."

Faith didn't know how to feel about that. She'd liked Mr. Hopewell and was grateful to him for the support he provided in the weeks following her grandfather's death. But if he was instrumental in her grandfather's death...

"I've got more news. Mr. Whitman's attorney intends to seek bail this morning. He's arguing that the sketches are not enough to hold him."

The air seemed to flow out of the room. "So. We've got nothing," Faith said.

"Not exactly nothing. We've still got some leads to track down. Mr. Von Heiden, for instance. Perhaps he can shed some light, if we can find him."

"He's gone missing?" Chris asked.

"It appears so, yes. But we're tracking his credit cards, his passport. If he leaves a footprint anywhere, we'll find him."

"Amazing." Ptolemy said, shaking his head.

"So, Richard Whitman is not going to go to jail," Faith whispered, horrified.

Maxwell squared his shoulders. "Don't lose hope. Perhaps when Hopewell regains consciousness, he can tell us something."

"And in the meantime," Chris interjected, taking Faith's hand, "we have to get on with the business of living."

"We'll keep a detail on the front of the house for the next few days at least. Beyond that, if we don't find more evidence, I don't think the FBI will continue the protection. Please let Roberts know."

"We will," Chris confirmed. "Thanks."
***

At seven-thirty, everyone was ready to go. Standing by their respective limousines out by the garage, Chris shook hands with Daniel and Ptolemy. "Don't be a stranger," he said to Daniel, who smiled warmly in return. "Ptolemy, good luck with everything."

"You, too, Chris. Thanks for being there for Daniel."

Faith hugged the two men, then turned to Anne. "Call me tomorrow so we can talk about your plans."

"I will. I can't wait to see the look on my boss's face when I submit my resignation." She smiled and hugged Faith. "Hey, rugrats!" Anne called to the boys who waited in the car, "be good for your mom and dad!"

As the turned west on Massachusetts Avenue to drop the boys at school, Faith relaxed into her seat. "Gosh, I'm tired." She closed her eyes and gripped Chris's hand.

"I still can't believe that after all of this, we don't have the satisfaction of finding someone guilty. I mean, it's clear as day that someone was behind all of this." He shook his head in disgust.

Missing Letters

***

The two of them threw themselves into work, barely grabbing a bite at lunch. Chris headed out at two-thirty to get the kids from school. Looking at the clock, Faith thought that there was a good chance that Richard Whitman was once again a free man. She felt sick to her stomach.

Because so much had happened during the day she was out, Faith stayed at work until six o'clock, then headed home. She looked forward to climbing into bed early, and by nine-thirty, Faith and Chris lay in bed watching TV together.

***

She awoke with a start at two o'clock in the morning, the TV still on. Chris was asleep on top of the covers, his magazine lying open on his chest. Faith hunted for the remote and clicked it off, drenching the room in darkness. Yawning, she stretched and padded down the hallway to check on the boys, then thought she'd go downstairs for a few crackers to calm her growling stomach.

Passing by the guest suite, she felt a pang of sadness that it was empty, and proceeded on, tiptoeing through the shadows out of habit rather than necessity. The concrete floor of the kitchen was cold beneath her bare feet and she shivered as she closed up the box of crackers. Popping one in her mouth as she walked, she wished she'd thought to wear her robe. It was really chilly.

As she retraced her steps up the rear staircase, she felt a draft. *Old houses*, she thought, and took another step. She watched her feet to make sure she didn't trip in the dark and saw the hem of her long nightgown billow in a breeze. *That's not just a draft*, she thought with alarm and looked around at the nearby windows. They were closed, so she ventured further toward the door to the parking area behind the main house. It stood ajar.

At first, she was frozen in panic. She wanted to shout for Roberts, or Sawyer, or *someone*, but didn't know who could be lurking nearby in the shadows. So she flattened herself against the wall and crept forward, avoiding the more heavily worn floorboards that she now knew tended to creak. Standing still to listen more carefully, she felt confident that no one was in the media room, so she slowly continued toward the front of the house.

At the head of the corridor, she could see that no one was in the foyer. The formal living room was also empty. She glanced up the curving staircase and her heart accelerated, thinking whoever it was might be upstairs with her precious boys.

But then she heard it. A footfall on a thick carpet. The scrape of something on the carpet. Faith stood stock still, her eyes involuntarily darting left and right in the darkness, trying to figure out where the sound came from. Then she heard it again and knew -- the music room!

Next to the coat closet to her left, at the fringe of the foyer, stood a large, ceramic umbrella stand that housed her grandfather's collection of walking sticks. She grabbed one with a heavy, brass handle in the shape of a swan and held it like a baseball bat, then stepped closer.

As she peeked into the room, she saw someone on their hands and knees in the dark, behind the couch. With her heart in her throat, she flicked on the sconce lights and saw it was a man. His body momentarily startled, then he slowly stood up and turned around. Richard Whitman.

"What the hell are you doing in my house?" She quietly demanded.

"Good evening, Faith. You're not happy to see me?" He advanced toward her. "I suppose you hoped I'd still be in jail. Preferably with the key thrown away."

She gripped the walking stick more tightly. "The thought had crossed my mind. Again, I ask, why are you here? You want to kill me, too? Oh wait, you get *other* people to do your dirty work. So, where's your helper?"

He smiled. "You have something of mine, and I mean to get it."

"And you can go to hell." She pivoted on her heel in order to run toward the garage.

"Stop right there, Faith," he said with a level voice. She heard a click and froze, then turned toward him. He had a gun in his gloved hand, trained directly on her chest. "Where. Is. It."

"Where is what, you psycho?"

"Name calling won't get you anywhere, you know. The paper, Faith. The one you saw me remove from the piano. Where is it?" He demanded.

"I have no idea. You stuffed it in your pocket. Maybe you dropped it in the street outside the house." She gestured toward the door. "Why don't we go look?"

"Nice try."

"I didn't see it."

"Why don't you and I just go on upstairs and wake up your precious sons and your husband? Maybe one of them will know where it is." Her face dropped and she began to sweat.

He closed his eyes momentarily. "I'm growing weary of all of this. I hadn't intended to harm you or your little family, but you leave me little choice. In fact, I now have no choice at all."

"Consider this," Faith said after thinking frantically, "if you do anything to us here, the FBI and police will be crawling all over the place. There are two agents just outside the door! They're sure to find that paper." She gestured toward the front of the house.

The old man squinted at her. "You don't seem to understand, Faith. I'm going to kill you all one by one to get what I want. You think I don't know how to do it without getting caught? There won't be any evidence to implicate me."

She noticed he wore gloves. Oh my God, he's going to kill me, then the kids. Chris. He's really going to do it. He's not just threatening me... Where the HELL are the FBI? Where is Roberts?

"But I'll make a deal with you. I'll leave your boys alone if you give me what I want. You do want them to wake up tomorrow, don't you?" He smiled coldly at her.

She swallowed. *No way in hell I'd trust you.* "Why are you doing this? What did this family ever do to you?"

He seemed to consider her question. "You may as well know." He raised a hand and shook his head, his face impassive, as if nothing mattered anymore. "Fritz Blithe's father destroyed my father's business. Crushed him as if he were little more than an unwanted ant in a kitchen. My father killed himself when I was a small boy. Couldn't take the pressure and humiliation. My mother sunk into alcoholism and let my baby sister drown in the bathtub. Then she killed herself, too. I was shipped off to an uncle who had no use for a broken boy.

"My schooling was assured through a trust my father set up when I was born, but I was destitute beyond that. I met your grandfather at boarding school. I knew who he was, what he was, and I vowed to take from him everything his family had taken from me."

Veins protruded from his neck as he emphasized, "I have spent my life building a fortune and a network with which to destroy Frederick McWallace Blithe and everything he ever cared about. I suppose it's only fitting that I dispose of you, too, even though he'll never know."

"So none of this had anything to do with Elena?"

He snorted. "The seeds of hate were sowed much earlier than that. It was just icing on the cake to obliterate the happiness of a man who also stole a woman I wanted."

"And my grandfather? Did you have something to do with his death?"

He rolled his eyes. "The man just kept *bouncing back*. Like an idiot boxer who wouldn't stay down. He just kept getting up and taking another beating. When you showed up, I just didn't have the energy to keep at it." His lip curled, causing the scar to wrinkle grotesquely. "It was time for him to go."

"How did you do it?"

"I didn't. Cassandra did. But then, she'd do anything to keep her little secret. She still thought she'd be able to land a big fish. Another stupid man to pay her way."

"You said stupid!" Paul gasped from the doorway. "He's a bad man, Mommy!"

Faith whipped around to see her little boy standing there pointing at Whitman, his little toes peeking from beneath his airplane pajamas. "No, Paul!" She dropped the walking stick and moved to stand in front of him.

"Too late, Faith. I can't leave behind witnesses. You'd best both be quiet or there will be more for me to do here tonight."

"I'll help you look!" She whispered desperately and got down on her hands and knees, looking beneath the furniture.

"Paul, why don't you go sit on the couch?" Mr. Whitman asked him.

"You've got scary baby eyes."

"What?" He gritted his teeth.

"Scary baby eyes. You know, like in those scary movies. Mommy told us about them. She won't let us watch them, though. Daddy calls them 'dolls eyes'. Something about a shark movie."

Whitman frowned at the little boy.

"Why does he have a gun?" asked Paul.

Faith glanced up at him nervously.

"Can I see the gun? It looks really good. My guns don't look that good. Can I get one like that, Mom?"

She looked fearfully at Mr. Whitman. "Um, we'll have to put it on your Christmas list." Faith tried not to cry. She moved faster, pulling back chairs, looking behind drapes.

"Whatcha looking for, Mommy?"

"A piece of paper, honey."

"I got lots of paper in the playroom." He looked at the old man. "Do you know how to make paper airplanes? Mommy only makes one kind, but they fly really good."

Whitman gestured at Paul with his gun. "Tell him to shut up," he said to Faith.

"He's a litterbug," Paul said to Faith, his lower lip stuck out. He looked at Whitman with a frown. "You know, if you litter, you make the earth sick."

Whitman cocked his head, his curiosity piqued, then bent and looked closely at Paul. "Why do you say I'm a litterbug?"

"You dropped a crumpled up piece of paper on the floor after Mr. Hopewell got hurt, and left it there. You're supposed to put that in the trash. So I did it for you, because I'm not a litterbug."

Faith moved quickly and knelt down in front of Paul. "Sweetie, what trash bin did you put it in?"

"The one with the ducks and dogs and stuff," he pointed at the decorative waste bin by the desk in the living room.

Whitman rushed to the bin and looked in. He reached in and lifted out the balled paper, then unfolded it to make sure it was his. At the same time, Faith scooped up her son and ran for the hallway. She ran smack into Roberts, and they all fell to the ground. Roberts' gun slid across the floor, out of reach.

She immediately examined Paul and found him okay, then looked at Roberts, who was looking past her, up at Whitman. As Faith turned, she saw Whitman's gun trained on Roberts' forehead. "Oh, dear god."

"So. The security team finally moves into action. You're just the tops, aren't you?" Whitman dead panned. "Honestly, a monkey could do a better job. So much for the special forces." He cocked his head to the side. "I speak from the experience of gaining entry to pretty much every corner of this property."

"How did you get on the property?" The bodyguard asked.

"Me or the rest of the people I sent in at various points? Figure it out."

"He came in the door off the parking area," Faith whispered.

Roberts nodded. "I saw that as I made my rounds."

Paul started to cry.

"Shut him up," the old man said coldly.

He cried harder and buried his face in Faith's shirt.

"Shut him up or I'll do it for you!" Whitman shouted.

The fury within Faith that had been banked by fear started to take hold, the fear dissolving as her heart pumped harder.

She glanced meaningfully at Roberts and looked down at Paul just before she shoved him at the bodyguard, stood to block the two of them and dived at Whitman. The gun discharged before she fell into him, knocking it from his hand. A searing pain pierced her side, but she gripped his throat, teeth clenched, eyes wide, and squeezed with everything she had -- until she passed out.

***

She came to as Paul called to her. "Mommy! Mommy, please wake up!"

The police were there. She was so tired...

She saw Chris was holding her hand, tears streaking his cheeks. His eyes were closed and he was mouthing words. Paul and Graham crowded around the gurney looking at her, telling her they loved her and that she should wake up. EMS technicians were tending to her. She felt a prick on her arm. She tried her best to smile and speak but nothing came out.

Roberts was talking to the police. She faded out again.

***

She felt someone holding her hand. When her eyes fluttered open, she saw Chris, his head resting on the side of her bed. She put her hand in his hair, felt the pull of the tape holding in her IV drip. He picked his head up and looked at her, his eyes quickly focusing. "Faith!"

She smiled at him, "goofball," she said. "I love you."

"I love you more," he said.

"Not possible." It was a routine they did, and it made her smile widen.

"Whitman's in custody."

"Permanently, I hope," she responded.

"I hope so, too," he answered.

"I'm really tired."

"Relax. Your mom is with the boys. The security system is hooked up at the house, monitors are back online, all of the passcodes changed. The men are standing guard. Rest." He kissed her forehead and she drifted off.

***

"The garden door was real? I looked decorative to me," Faith said the next morning as she rested in her hospital bed. Maxwell was leaning against a wall and Chris was seated beside her bed.

Roberts nodded. "It was decorative at one point. Whitman admitted to the police that he'd converted it to a functional door when Fritz was last on vacation. He was very proud of that maneuver – said he'd designed the hinge system himself and had the door replicated down to the last detail so they could fix the masonry and install the new door at the same time. He had to pay the workers triple to do the work after business hours so that Hopewell and Abernathy wouldn't see. It worked. No one guessed."

"Wow. I even pulled on the ring and it didn't move."

"It didn't open in to the garden. It opened out toward the back."

Faith raised her eyebrows. "Impressive attention to detail. But then I'd expect nothing less from a psychopath."

Roberts took a deep breath and let it out. "I'm very sorry, ma'am, for what happened to you. I'll understand if you want my resignation."

"That's not necessary," she said reassuringly. "It was the perfect storm. We'd shut down the IP cameras and the closed-circuit hadn't yet been reconnected. You were making rounds but you couldn't be everywhere at once. And who could have known about the garden door?"

"The door was permanently sealed today. The space it used to occupy will look like any other part of the wall."

"Thanks, Roberts," Faith smiled tiredly at him. "Don't even think of resigning."

Roberts nodded to her. "Very well. I'll let you rest." He quietly left the room.

"Well, would you like to see it?" Maxwell, stepped forward

with a paper in his hand. He held it out to her. It was crumpled but had creases and tape stuck to it, as if it had been folded and taped inside the piano.

"The paper he was looking for?" She took it and peered closely, then handed it back to him. "My eyes are exhausted. Will you read it to me?"

He nodded. "It's a letter addressed to you – from Cassandra. It reads: Dear Faith, if you're reading this letter, it will be either because your cleaning ladies are overzealous, or because you've read my will and knew to look for it. In the latter case, you should track down Richard Whitman. Richard, you see, is not the harmless old man he appears to be. But I'm getting ahead of myself. It all began in 1971, so I'll start there.

"I was a very bright girl. Exceptionally bright. Top of my class, despite what I had to deal with at home. I was also very beautiful. I knew the combination would take me places. Take me away from that.

"But I was poor, white trash. My mother was an abusive addict. I never knew my father. I got the hell out of California as soon as I could, courtesy of a scholarship to Radcliffe. I actually graduated from high school a year early, deferred my acceptance for a year in order to earn money for clothes and living expenses. No way could I go to Radcliffe looking like I came from a trailer park. I meant to land myself a rich husband, and you know the saying. You have to spend money to make money.

"Despite working full time from June to January, I arrived in Cambridge in the spring of 1971 with very little money. I needed a better paying job, so I started working as a "performer" in a particular type of club that catered to men who had specific interests. But let's call it what it was: a dom-sub brothel. It paid exceptionally well. That's where I met Thomas. He became obsessed with me, which suited me just fine. He was gorgeous and would soon be extremely rich. So I played it up as if I really enjoyed that lifestyle. When school started in the fall, he couldn't bear the thought of me meeting other young men, so he married me. I quit school and our lives revolved around each other.

"It was not an easy life, despite the beautiful place we lived and the fabulous clothes. Thomas had a great need to inflict pain. In fact, he was a monster of sorts. I figured I only had to

312

put up with it until he inherited, then I could divorce him, get a settlement and move on with my life. But then I met Richard. Richard knew about Thomas' predilections, and soon, he knew about me. Where I came from, what I'd done. He also tracked down my mother. He threatened to tell Fritz about all of it. You see, Thomas had lied to Fritz about me. He'd said I was from a good but poor family. Fritz had no idea I had a sordid past. That my mother was a junkie whore. That I was a bastard. Richard held it over my head and threatened me.

"The summer of 1972, when we were on that yacht cruise, Richard told me to seduce a particular deck hand by any means possible, and convince him to kill Mick during that dive. I don't know why he targeted Mick, but I do know that Richard loathed the Blithe family. You'd never know it from the way in which he ingratiated himself with all of them, but he truly did.

"When Mick didn't go on the dive, the idiot deck hand figured the man down there was Mick, not Thomas, and he killed him. Elena saw what was happening down there and he killed her, too. It was all a big mistake. Richard was livid. I was distraught. I'd lost everything.

"Richard used the evidence he had from <u>that</u> botched attempt to get me to help with Mick's murder weeks later. He had me dress up in a red wig and makeup, pick a fight with Mick on the front stoop, step back and stumble so that he'd grab me. Then I was to peel away in the car. I did as he asked. I had no idea what was coming. When I heard Mick's initial scream, I forced myself not to look in the rear view mirror. I found out about what happened to him when everyone else did, in the newspapers the next morning.

"I want to tell you that I'm sorry. I really do. But you have to understand that I was fighting for my life. I'd been fighting for my life since the day I was born. Did I have remorse at that point? No. I was in survival mode. I'd given up Radcliffe for marriage. My new husband was dead before he'd inherited, so I didn't get much money. I had to ingratiate myself with Fritz to support myself. I had to survive Richard's threats. I had to survive.

"A few years later, I had Daniel. I may as well declare it to the world now: Ptolemy Gunesdogdu is Daniel's father. Go ahead and tell Daniel. He's been asking the question ever since he could talk.

"Fritz was very kind to Daniel. Loved him like a real grandson, I think, which was good. Fritz helped us financially. So did Ptolemy, after I prodded him.

"Fast forward to September of this year when Fritz met you. That very day, I got a call from Richard demanding that I call Fritz and tell him that Thomas was Cardinal Mayse's son. I am no idiot. I did as he asked, but I did my best to cover my tracks. No way did I want to be connected to it. So I called from the health club to his Skype number. It looks like it worked. No one has figured it out by now.

"I am actually sorry about Fritz. Yes, he was an old man, but I didn't like having to tell him the lie. He was really upset and I don't enjoy confrontation.

"But now that everyone is dead, I wonder what else Richard has in store for me. Perhaps manipulating me to kill you and your family. Who knows? But now I have enough evidence against him to put him away. You see, I recorded the phone conversation we had the day Fritz died. We didn't just talk about Fritz. You'll find a memory card taped to the inside of the piano, too.

"I hope he left my face intact. I'd like an open casket. Cassandra. PS – Tell Ptolemy he was lousy in bed."

Chris whistled at the last line. "What a piece of work!"

"So this paper is why he was here and was so preoccupied with the piano. Cassandra must have told him where it was right before he killed her." Faith speculated.

"And Mr. Hopewell wasn't involved with this after all. It was Mr. Whitman the entire time." Chris said.

"That is such a relief. That poor man," she said, sadly shaking her head. "But there's something I don't understand. Whitman had left Fritz to suffer his family's deaths all these years. Why kill him now?"

"Good question," Chris nodded.

"Well," Maxwell postulated, "think of the timing. Mr. Blithe died literally hours after meeting you, Mrs. Warrior. Somehow, Whitman found out about you. Probably by meeting up with Hopewell, given where the call came from -- we'll take another look at the tape from the café. Maybe Whitman was there, too, arriving and departing separately.

It seems that you, Mrs. Warrior, were the metaphorical

straw that broke the camel's back. As much as he'd tried to destroy Fritz, beat down his spirit, your grandfather kept bouncing back. His faith, and then, you."

"Two faiths," Chris said.

Tears pricked Faith's eyes. "You couldn't have known, honey," Chris said, taking her hand.

Her husband sat on the bed. "And I think we can all guess who manipulated Von Heiden, wherever he is." He added, looking at Maxwell.

Faith took a ragged breath. "Can you imagine anyone hating another human so much that he would destroy everything that person ever loved?"

"And you and Paul were going to be next." He leaned into Faith, gingerly hugging her to his chest, and offered up a silent prayer.

The End.

www.ingramcontent.com/pod-product-compliance
Lightning Source LLC
Chambersburg PA
CBHW030243030726
47493CB00023B/574